About the author

Janet A Leigh is a London born West African journalist. After graduating from Kingston University with a Master's degree in Magazine Journalism, she worked for the *Daily Express* before joining Hearst UK as a food journalist for the UK's number one women's' magazine, *Good Housekeeping*, and is also a freelance film and TV journalist. Fiction writing has always been a lifelong passion for her. She's been writing stories since the age of nine, when her family first got a computer, and hasn't stopped since. *Gothic Angel* is her debut novel.

GOTHIC ANGEL

Janet A Leigh

GOTHIC ANGEL

Vanguard Press

VANGUARD PAPERBACK

© Copyright 2021
Janet A Leigh

The right of Janet A Leigh to be identified as author of
this work has been asserted by her in accordance with the
Copyright, Designs and Patents Act 1988.

A CIP catalogue record for this title is
available from the British Library.

ISBN 978 1 784658 37 3

*Vanguard Press is an imprint of
Pegasus Elliot MacKenzie Publishers Ltd.*
www.pegasuspublishers.com

First Published in 2021

**Vanguard Press
Sheraton House Castle Park
Cambridge England**

Printed & Bound in Great Britain

Dedication

I thank God for the gift of storytelling and for the people he has placed into my life.

To my daughter, Nayana, who helped channel my creativity, and my mama, whose stubborn belief helped get me to where I am. I thank you. A thousand times over, I thank you.

Prologue
Tuesday, 12th January

Light flooded in as they burst through the living room door, turning the small crack into a gaping hole. I don't remember screaming, but I was. Screaming so loud my throat burnt. PC Grayson had his arms around me. They were tight. I wanted him to stop touching me, to get away from me. But he wouldn't. I wasn't sure if he was trying to comfort me or to stop my violent shaking.

'It's okay,' he whispered. 'It's okay.'

It wasn't okay.

'S-h-he wasn't supposed to be there.' I heard my dad stutter. 'That's not how I wanted her to find out.'

But I had found out. I wished that I hadn't. I wished I had waited until morning. That I'd had one more normal night.

'She's just a kid. She's thirteen for Chrissakes. I didn't want her to know like this.'

That's all he could say. All he could focus on. He repeated it over and over again.

'She's just a kid. They're just kids.' My sister and I.

I reckon it's because he couldn't stand the pain. That the truth was just impossible to face; but it was there. The truth. In his eyes, in my screams. It was there. His wife, my mother, was dead.

'Mum,' I croaked, the dryness of my throat scratching at the word. 'Mum.'

My heart was thudding, burning. I could hear it in my ears, could feel it in my chest as it lifted and crashed heavily.

'MUM!'

My eyes ripped open, my hands flying to the knocking in my chest. I stared for a while, sweat trickling down my brow, strands of hair sticking to my face. I let my head drop backwards and waited for the terrible gasping to ease off. A dream. Just a dream. I listened for the sound of movement around the house. Nothing. I hadn't woken a soul. I tapped at my phone on the desk, searching the brightly lit screen for the time. It was early. 7:23, to be precise. My hands fumbled as I unwound the tangle of covers from my body. I planted my feet on the floor and stood for a moment, breathing in a steady breath while I tried to remember what I had been dreaming about, what had gotten me so worked up. *She's just a kid. They're just kids.*

'Mum.'

I tore out of my bedroom, making my footsteps as light as possible. I opened doors with great stealth in spite of my shakiness. Her side of the bed was cold-looking, the bathroom empty. I flew down the stairs, landing gently, careful to avoid the creaky step. I headed straight for the living room, grateful that the floor was carpeted because I could not stop running. She wasn't there. I didn't stop. There was a light on in the kitchen ahead.

'Mum?'

I made for it, dodging the glass coffee table. My toe caught something and I stumbled through the kitchen door.

'Crap,' I cursed on the way down.

An angry, searing pain spread along my toe and I turned to face what had caused it. The ironing board.

'Dad.' It was more of a growl than a word. 'How hard is it to put things away?'

I peeled myself from ground and stood gingerly on the injured foot.

'Maybe I should recite his lecture on energy bills too, while I'm at it,' I grumbled as my hand reached to turn off the light that *he'd* left on... again. My hand froze. I stood there in the doorway, my semi-dreamlike state gone. Just the cold, merciless morning left.

'Mum,' I sighed, the burning in my chest returning. I remembered the first time I'd had that dream, and the second and the third. I remember how confused I'd been relearning what had happened. That she was gone. Nearly five years on and the confusion had only grown stronger.

I flicked the switch and watched the blackness take the room. The house was still, the living room darker without the warmth from the kitchen light streaming in. I dragged my throbbing foot over where I guessed the leg of the ironing board to be. It landed safely on the other side. My mother's words echoed in my head from years ago. 'Back to bed my sleepy head.' They made me ache. I shook my head as if to shake away the hurt and continued back to my bedroom. Something tugged at me.

'Uh, gimme a break,' I groaned, realising that my other foot was now tangled in the cord of the iron. I jiggled my foot around and felt its bind loosen until I was free. I began to walk again, feeling the grogginess of the early morning returning, but my insides, they burned with grief. Hearing her words, remembering *that* day. It was too late when I realised, I wasn't free. I was already on my way down. I felt the air rushing beneath me as I fell. The sharp, heavy blow as the corner on the coffee table pierced my temple. For a while there was throbbing and wheezing, my breath. Only for a while.

Chapter 1
Thursday, 28th January

A hand beat heavily against my bedroom door. It was the third time this morning.

'For heaven sakes Luke, it's twenty past eight. Turn it down!'

She was using her angry tone this time; it made me get up faster. I almost tripped on the boot lying on the ground as I hurried over to my laptop. I dragged my finger along the screen, turning up the volume. Music blared from my speakers.

'Good morning to you too, Mae,' I smiled, scooping up the boot on the way back to my bed. I shoved it on my foot and yanked it up, despising what that meant.

'Almost ready,' I smiled again, a mocking smile.

I hauled myself over to the mirror, gripping the desk above where it hung. I winced as I assessed today's look: ink-black eyeliner smeared below dirt-green eyes and lips two shades darker than tar. I winced again. My head. A knocking was forming in my head. Stirring, I breathed in deeply to fight back the headache I knew was coming.

A growl slipped through the closed door.

'Your mother told you to turn the music down.'

Nick's breath was angry and gruff and I could sense his glare through the wood. He grunted before walking away. I glanced at my reflection; it was a mess of tense lines and scowls beneath my wayward jet-black hair. I turned away from it.

The angry baseline wrenched to a halt as I slammed the laptop shut. The speakers silenced.

Better. I'd rather have it off than catch myself listening to either one of them.

Downstairs, the house felt busy. Mae was flitting around like some airy-fairy child, her thick dark hair bobbing about her shoulders.

'Lost my keys,' she panted, brushing past me in the hallway. 'I don't suppose you've seen them?'

I thought about answering her, about saying, *yeah, hanging right out of your coat pocket.*

But I didn't. She didn't deserve to know. Instead, I picked up my bag and my sketchbook just as Nick's footsteps pounded the stairs. My coat slid off the rack with a tug, and I was out of the door before I had to see him.

The latch on the door clicked, but not soon enough. Mae's droning voice escaped, reminding me about my appointment this afternoon. As if I could forget.

Outside the air was thick with the clean smell of sleet. The ground damp and patchy. I slipped my arms into my trench coat, pleased that I had grabbed the jacket with the hood because, let's face it, it would've been too late to go back now. I was already outside the house, and outside meant free. Until I stepped foot on to college grounds, that was. Maybe I should have been tense about this. Normally I would've been, but not today. Today I all I could think of was yesterday evening; today, among my usual depression, I was busy feeling intrigued.

28ᵗʰ January

Dear Journal,

Someone noticed me... Someone noticed ME. That's all I can think about right now. It's all I have been thinking about since it happened. Someone noticed me. My first thought was that I'd snapped. That it was some strange side effect brought on by my crap-of-a-life. I stood there, and for half a second, I thought, I'm hallucinating or imagining things because I didn't actually see anyone. I just... knew they were there. It doesn't really make sense. Not a lot of it does though, so I thought I'd start with the facts. Work myself through what I do know until I hopefully figure out what I don't. Here it goes.

Fact 1: It was late when I left college. Way past the rush out of the building/I'm free hours. Avoiding Mac and his brainless disciples (as usual). They had been up to something; I could tell by the way they'd eyed me all throughout World Cinema Class (no doubt thinking up new ways to humiliate me). I hung back. Asked Miss Rubenstein questions I didn't need answering, and when that was played out, I headed to the library.

Fact 2: It was raining when I left. I just remembered. Which proves my point about me snapping thanks to my crappy existence. It was raining and, on top of everything else, (home, college) that was just one more piece of bad luck. I was listening to Untitled Grief by Sabishii again (such a killer underground band). It was supposed to make me feel... something, I guess. Maybe better. I mean, it's powerful. The words, the music... they become a part of me every time I hear them. It's like the strings of guitar are in sync with my life. My pain. My burning hatred for the world and everything in it.

Anyway, it kind of worked. Not a lot, because I was soaked and pissed off about it, but enough so that my head wasn't exploding in pain because of my mood (in other words, no headache).

I walked by that skanky park (the one that even tramps avoid) and that's when it happened. It was instant. It was magnetic. It was blood stirring, heart thumping, body filling with... with... I don't know, something I can't explain. It was pure, like wholeness... only that's the wrong word. All I can say is the hollowness — the one that's been living in my chest for the past few weeks, the one making me feel out of sync in my own body — it was filling. Only slightly, but I ached to top it up some more.

It was peaceful...

That's weird. I should be committed for the things I'm writing, it's so weird. Maybe Mae was right to call in the shrink patrol. (Funny shrink voice) Dr. Evans the 'psychiatrist specialising in teenage angst' and a bunch of other made-up theories that I don't really give a crap about (or so his card says). But it felt so real.

It pulled me closer and I followed. I felt like I had to. How do you ignore something that fixes the part of you that felt splintered, numbed? Something... or someone? Because that's the other thing. The main thing that makes this whole episode seem insane. I keep saying something, but what I really mean is someone.

A presence that made me feel normal again. One that silenced the feeling that never leaves me. The feeling that deep down inside of me something isn't right...

Fact 3: It was over behind the tall oak tree, next to the almost broken swing set. That's where it called to me from. I didn't see anyone, not even a shadow, but I was almost certain someone was there. Almost.

God, what is going on with me? I feel like I'm cracking up, but it had to be real because of the feeling. The one you get when someone's eyes sink into the back of your skull. When the hairs on the back of your neck rise and your skin prickles nervously. I felt it. Someone was watching me. A girl. Or at least I think it was a girl. It felt 'femalesque,' which means there had to have been someone there, right? Otherwise gender becomes irrelevant. And there was definitely a girl-like presence... I think.

Fact 4: I took out my earphones to concentrate. For me to have been concentrating on something, there has to have been something to concentrate on (a weak theory, I know, but my sanity is on the line so it passes).

I tried looking into the park. I was there for about 10 minutes but it was too dark. I would've walked in, but it was wet and cold and I wanted to get... well, not home, but where else was I going to go? So I left, and now a part of me wishes that I hadn't.

The hollowness is back now. It's deep and gripping and back. Worst of all, I'm no closer to figuring any of this out.

Did I really 'feel' a girl? Is that even possible? I don't know. Maybe I just wanted to be noticed for once. It would be kind of nice.

'Mr Andrews?'

I looked up from my journal and stared directly into the baleful eyes of my English teacher. I had no idea how long I'd been writing, but the violent shade of his flushed face suggested I'd ignored him for longer than I could get away with.

'Mr Andrews?' he snarled at my lack of response. I swallowed hard, feeling my Adam's apple stick in my throat.

'*Mr Andrews?*' he whispered menacingly, and I figured now would be a good time to speak.

'Yes, Mr T-t-t-taylor.'

Great. I was aiming for defiant but underneath all the glares and sniggers all I could manage was stuttering idiot.

'I'm sorry to disrupt your important daydream session with my insignificant, futile lesson, but could you tell me what the definition of pathetic fallacy is?'

'Um... um,' I let my hair fall over my face and clenched my teeth. I could feel my cheeks burning red and prayed that the dark strands would cover most of it.

'Well... ah, well... it,' I panicked and my teeth clamped shut, further sealing off any chance of me voicing the answer I already knew.

'Pathetic fallacy is when you attribute human emotions to an inanimate object,' said that high-pitched, squeak of a voice that pierced through my brain.

My eyes became slits of fury. Mr Taylor smiled, running a bony hand through his thinning peppery hair.

'Well done, Miss Neesman,' he crooned as if it pleased him greatly to say her name, and she giggled in that irritating way.

'Mr Andrews?' he called, his voice sleek and smarmy.

'Yes sir?' He was walking down my aisle now, pen and clipboard in hand like an OFSTED inspector.

Sweat beads lurked beneath my skin as a sickening thought entered my head, *please don't notice my journal, please don't take my journal.*

I shoved it underneath my English book and prayed for some good luck, but his eyes bulged gleefully. An oily smile played on his lips.

'Fat chance,' I mumbled to myself.

Mr Taylor placed his hands on my desk and leaned in, he was so close his rancid breath warmed my skin.

'Maybe you could spend *less* time scribbling down your *thoughts and feelings,*' he sneered, retrieving the black leather-bound book with his awkward fingers and tapping it with his pen, 'and more time paying attention to my lesson.'

The whole class erupted in laughter. Lucile Armstrong hid her beautiful lips with one hand, and I could feel the warmth underneath my cheeks spread along every cell, darkening my whole body with its ruddy glow. In that moment I was certain that death would've been a sweet release.

'Yes sir,' I murmured, my heart hammering wildly as I silently prayed for him to return my journal. Mr Taylor hesitated, his eyes lingering on what his hands possessed, my heart preparing to lunge. He released his grip, letting the book land with a dull thud. He looked directly at me and held my gaze a few seconds longer than necessary, then rolled his eyes and strutted back to his desk, not even bothering to conceal the smug look on his face. I clenched my fist and glared after him. At least he didn't take my journal, I reminded myself, cringing at the image of him actually reading it, a cup of tea in one hand and a tear of laughter rolling down his cheek.

'Miss Neesman,' he turned to Missy, a nasty smirk tugging at the corners of his cracked lips.

'Yes Mr Taylor, sir.'

'I wonder, could you give the class an example of pathetic fallacy for the benefit of those who *don't appear to have a clue*?'

Though his eyes never left her face, his tone was undeniably reserved for me. Missy smiled with her eyes and flicked her long blonde hair away from her delicate shoulders.

'Of course, sir.' She cleared her throat — meaning she was about to recite an essay — and a low groan from the class rippled through the room.

'I was reading the book *Fruit of My Loin* by Nicholi Raymous, and found that my favourite passage actually contained PF — that's pathetic fallacy,' she giggled again. 'May I?' she asked, flicking her perfectly manicured hands through the pages of the book she had all too readily dug out of her bag.

Mr Taylor nodded encouragingly.

'The sun embers raged at the street bel...'

And... zone... out, I thought. I wasn't about to stick around and listen to that pretentious puppet drone on when I already knew the answer, well, not stick around mentally anyway.

I leaned my head against the cool glass window and began scribbling circles on my notebook. My fingers itched to fill my journal some more, but I didn't dare take the chance.

I sighed inwardly, thinking about the moment Mac and co. would find out about it. I could just imagine them pulling out the entries, page by page, and gluing them to the back table in our form class where I sit… alone. Maybe they'd cover every desk in the room. Nah, that'd be far too original for those brainless gits. They'd probably just serenade me with a few extracts for the rest of the week. Or maybe, if they were really on form, they'd jam the pages down my throat just to see how much I would chuck up later. Violence wasn't really their style. They preferred the more subtle art of heartless humiliation. But their fists made an appearance from time to time, so who knows?

It was a case of survival of the fittest, and I — the loner goth with the jet-black hair and the clothes to match — was definitely on the losing side. I may have been tall but I was lanky, and though my body had a certain athletic quality to it I lacked brawn. No friends, was also an issue. I guess my sullen mood and personal style played a part in that, caused people to shy away? Naturally I was an easy target. Most of the time I didn't really care about all that stuff, but I guess today wasn't one of those times.

Dr Clueless Evans once asked me to sum up college in one word. I didn't. I chose to snarl and hiss instead, but if I had, if I'd spoken, I would have said 'lonely'.

I looked outside and groaned. The sleet that had started falling this morning had now turned into snow. Snow that was now settling on the ground, covering it like a thick woollen sheet. Translation: Mac's football practice would be cancelled, increasing my chances of a rendezvous later.

'Great.' I mumbled. 'This day is gonna suck royally.'

***

The rest of the day pretty much passed in that slow and torturous way that makes ice picks in the eyes seem like fun. No one really spoke to me, except to say unoriginal stuff like, 'hey freak where's the diary?' and 'do you sometimes cry at night, too?' I let them, not saying a word back. It was easier that way. Plus, I was busy. I had a decision to make. Face Mac and his cretins at the end of the day or hang around here again until they got bored and pissed off home. I weighed out my options. I considered the fact that I'd be too late to make my four o'clock with 'Dr-tell-me-how-that-makes-you-feel'. Turns out the decision was easier to make than I'd thought. No amount of money could make me want to spend time with Dr Evans. Especially not after today's events, which he would almost definitely drag out of me with *the look,* and I'd tell him, just so I didn't have to deal with the uncomfortable silence. Usually I was all right with his dumb routine, in fact I enjoyed it. Even under his annoyingly piercing stare I found peace in the quiet, found pleasure in the way my persistent speechlessness made sweat beads erupt on him in the most peculiar places, like above his top lip. He'd sit twitching and fiddling, waiting for me to open up, giving me *the space and time* to come to him first. I never did. It was a rule of mine, but not today. I just couldn't. My head was pounding hard against my skull, spreading the pain everywhere, and the deep sting beneath my hair felt rotten. The cocktail of pain was excruciating, and if Dr Evans was to fix his loathsome eyes on me today the sight of his pathetic, quivering state was bound to irritate me to the point of disgust. In other words, there was a good chance I'd slip up, say something I'd regret later.

I worked my fingers into my hair and brushed them lightly against the scalp. I winced. Three weeks on and it still felt tender, supple. My head began to tingle — the onset of a dizzy spell. I leant my shoulder against the nearest wall, sucked steadily on the air and waited for both the pain and the light-headedness to subside. Lessons had ended ten minutes ago, but still the hallway was packed. Bodies moved all around me, brushing me, knocking me slightly off balance, I counted, one Mississippi, two Mississippi, three Mississippi, until Mississippi no longer sounded like a word. I waited and waited for the crowd to thin, for the room to stop spinning, then peeled myself from the bricks and skulked off to the library, my decision clearly made.

Just to piss me off, the small stuffy room was swarming with people. I sighed bitterly and went straight to the back, sliding my body into my favourite chair. I rummaged around in my pocket for my earphones, a light smile playing over my lips once I'd found them. I plugged them in and set the volume to max, not caring that the sound aggravated my head. All I wanted was to drown out the voices, to cut myself off from this whole place until enough time had passed so that I could leave.

I let myself imagine. Sinking deeper into my thoughts the way I'd sunk deeply into the chair. I was in my room; those four familiar walls, my music pounding through the bricks, loud and eerie. And a girl, Lucile Armstrong. Her pretty, dark bouncy locks. Her rich brown eyes and her silky skin two shades darker. Yeah right, never in a million years would Lucile be in my room, but it was my fantasy, so screw it. She was standing there, in *my* room, studying the art that covers my walls, noticing the blood-red rug on the steel-grey carpet, telling me she thought it was *cool*. She might even brush aside the coal-black curtains and tell me she thinks it's hot the way I sneak in and out late at night. She might.

That fantasy sustained me for a while. Then another, then another. Before I knew it, a familiar leathery hand brushed against my cheek, the creased fingers forcibly removing my earphones. The music slowly slipped away from me, puncturing a hole in my perfect delusional world where it was just me… and Lucile… maybe.

'All right honey,' said Mrs Crawley, the ancient librarian, 'It's late. Library is closing dear,' her sweet motherly tone shook with age.

'Mmmm,' I grunted back. Late, but was it late enough? I checked the time. It was.

'Shouldn't a good-looking boy like you have a girlfriend to walk home?'

I chanced a small smirk.

'You know you're the only woman in my life, Mrs Crawley.'

She smiled back and nudged me out of my seat, ushering me along with a wrinkly hand.

She was nice, Mrs Crawley. Smelt like peppermint, butterscotch and brandy all rolled into one.

'Goodnight Mrs Crawley,' I said stuffing my earphones back into my ears before she had a chance to respond.

As I stepped outside, a sharp breeze whipped against my cheeks. I pulled the hood of my trench coat deeper over my head and pulled my phone out from the nick in the inner pocket. *1 New Message* flashed on the screen. I opened it.

Where are you? It's 4:20 and Dr Evans is waiting! Please don't do this to me. Show up! Mum.

I shrugged my shoulders and returned my phone to the deep hole in my pocket.

My phone buzzed again at some point on my short walk home. I didn't answer it. It was only ever going to be Mae and it was only ever grief she was going to give, so what was the point? What was the point in anything, I wondered? A deep ache seizing my chest. My heart beat erratically. It thrust itself against the surrounding muscles. My lungs searched for air, but shallow breaths were all I could drag in. What was wrong with me? I looked up from the pavement, searching for someone, for help. I needed help. I gawped, both understanding and not. I hadn't even realised I was there again, at that park, the same park I've walked past, dull day in and dull day out, for nearly two years. Any other day I would have just walked by without a second thought, but I felt it. I felt *her…*

Chapter 2

Breath, heart, blood. Skin, touch, feel. See. I can see... frosted grass, cracked pavements, slender limbs scaling walls. It's him. Those limbs belong to him. Now nothing. I see nothing. But always I feel.

28ᵗʰ January
Dear Journal,
I'm a freaking weirdo. A nut job. Criminally insane. What the hell is this? She was there again. This girl. Not just at the park but all the way home this time. I wanted her to go, just get the hell away from me, but at the same time I wanted her to stay. God, I wanted her to stay. She made me feel... complete. Whole. Like I'd felt before the hollowness, only better. Safer. It was like she was... a friend. Sort of. Like she, like we, were alike. Like we shared something. The same mind. The same mind? That's because it is your mind you crazy, crazy freak.
  I need help!

I shoved my journal into the drawer of my bedside table and slammed it shut. It was supposed to release my tension; an involuntary reaction, one that I wished I'd suppressed. Mae had the hearing of a bat, and the last thing I needed was her marching up here, busting through the door to launch into the very lecture I'd been trying to avoid. I'd gone to the effort of climbing through the window, the least I could do now was not blow my cover.

I climbed on to my bed and jammed the pillow over my face.

'Arrgh,' I growled into layers of fabric.

'I don't want to be a psycho,' I grumbled. As if my life wasn't painful enough dealing with the stigma of just being me, now I have to be the crazy guy who senses people who aren't there? What is with me? Am I so alone that I've made up an imaginary friend? What am I, five? I was sure even they had more emotional growth than me. I pounded my fist into the bed in frustration. In that moment the door flew open, crashing against the wall.

'Lucas James you little *shit*... oh... I'm sorry,' Mae mumbled regretfully, though her hands were balled up into fists at her side.

'Dr Evans said I shouldn't use those negative terms with you but... damn it, Luke, you little *shit*!'

I could tell she was really trying hard to suppress her anger from the several unnecessary breaths she took. Her deep blue eyes glinted beneath her glasses.

'Do you have any idea how much those sessions cost?' she breathed; her breath a little too measured. 'How much money we are paying to get a specialist psychiatrist, just to make you normal? This is all for your benefit, you know. To help you make friends.'

She was pacing up and down the room now, her knuckles starkly white.

'I just want you to have a life outside of these four walls and yet you throw it away like a spoilt little *shit*... brat, I mean brat. Damn it.'

She drew in a long deep breath, trying to steady her nerves.

'I don't suppose you have a good reason for not showing up.'

I shook my head, not really having an answer for her and not caring to think one up. Mae's face was composed. She was doing a good job at keeping her anger at bay, but here's the thing about my mum: no matter how calm her voice was, her eyes always betrayed her.

'Poor Dr Evans,' she droned on. 'What must he think of you, Luke? Luckily, I managed to convince him you weren't feeling well. Tummy troubles,' she whispered.

'Mae,' I growled.

'Well what did you want me to do Luke? Have him think you just don't care?'

'That's a good idea, and here's another one: stay out of my business.' I spat out the words through gritted teeth. 'What were you even doing there at *my* session? Spying on me?'

'That's exactly what I was doing, because I knew you'd pull something like this again. What does that make it now, Luke? Four missed sessions in a row?'

'I don't know. I lost count.'

My tone was ice cold but the anger bubbling inside of me was not. It blazed a fiery red. and I clenched my fist till the knuckles were drained of colour.

'Oh Luke,' she said in her exasperated tone. She slumped down on the bed next to me. 'I'm just trying to help you to move on. To be happy.'

You want me to be happy? I thought, *then shut the door on your way out.*

'Sorry,' I mumbled instead.

Mae sighed heavily, taking my hand in hers and stroking it in that uncomfortable way that made me cringe. I hated my mother's touch. It made me feel bad to think like that, but I did.

'You used to be so happy. You used to talk non-stop and popular.' She laughed like the vague memory was a joke. 'But it's like when Dean...'

'I don't want to talk about Dean,' I all but snarled.

The tension in the room thickened but she probed on.

'You won't talk to me. You won't talk to Dr Evans. You won't even talk to Nick; I just don't know what to do.'

Was she for real? Nick?

'Why the hell would I talk to *him*?'

'A... a father figure.'

I was so angry I could taste it on my tongue.

'Mae, Nick's a git. You could do so much better than to slum it with a prick like him.'

'That's what you want to talk about? My relationship with Nick? Well fine,' she said throwing down my hand in a huff. 'You can have that conversation with yourself.'

She stormed out of the room, slamming the door so hard it rattled. I knew it had been the wrong thing to say. She'd probably go and tell Nick all about this one, but right now I didn't care. It was worth it. How dare she bring up my brother Dean? As if I wanted to sit here and talk about him. What were we going to do? Take a stroll down memory lane together? What did she think would happen when we came skipping across the part where the motorcycle slammed right into him? Or when they sealed his body in that casket and dropped him into the earth? No. I wasn't going there with *her;* I wasn't going there with anyone. It was enough to push my mental stability over the edge. I already had one foot in crazyville, what with this figment of my imagination popping up unannounced, and I had no plans to encourage the other.

I looked at the clock hanging above my bed. It was pretty early but bed seemed so appealing that I stripped out of my clothes and put on fresh pyjamas bottoms, not bothering with a shower. I lay in between the sheets, willing sleep to find me but, as always, waiting for the inevitable.

Chapter 3

A blow to the ribs and the chest. A single tear down the cheek and the clenching of a jaw. Pain. All kinds of pain. One that crunches to the bone. One that rips open emotions, oozing despair. His pain, my pain, ours.

Chapter 4

28th January

Dear Journal,

My ribs are sore. Very sore but not broken, that's good. My jaw feels tight from tensing, but that'll go away by morning. Not the pain in my chest though. It's throbbing; that's a guaranteed black and blue right there. I think it's swelling a bit, but not too much. Never too much, just enough to teach me a lesson.

Chapter 5
Friday, 29th January

The rain poured down heavily the next day clearing away the snow. Its ice cool droplets beat hard against my window like pellets. Condensation spread over the glass, obscuring the world. I tossed and turned in my bed, groaning at the tenderness of my ribs. What time was it? I wondered. I glanced up at the skull clock hanging on the wall over my bedhead. The neon green light glowing in the subdued dark told me it was 5am.

'Mmmmm.' This time my groan was one of relief; five o'clock meant three more hours until I had to be up.

A loud thud came from the kitchen downstairs and my face twisted angrily. Nick was up, his drunken self, banging about. Probably searching for more booze, I guessed. It was the last Friday of the month and I was glad. He'd be off on his construction job all day, and when he came back, he'd scoff down a quick dinner before heading off for his guys weekend. I didn't know what he did, and I didn't care. Just as long as he was gone. If I was lucky and I stayed out late enough, I might not have to see him again before he left. The thought made me smile gratefully and, in spite of the bruises on my chest, I rolled over on to my stomach to catch what little sleep I had left.

***

I was lying down. The surface beneath me was solid and cold. My eyes were closed, and I had no idea where I was, but the smell of earth was all around me. My hands lay by my side and I gripped what was tickling my palms. Grass? Where was I? I tried to open my eyes but it was a struggle. I only half managed it before they clamped shut again. But I caught enough of a glimpse to know I was in the park. *That* park. The crooked red swings and the rusting iron slide had been a dead giveaway. I tried to open my eyes again to see more, but it was even harder than the first time, so I gave up.

Everything was pitch black. I relied on my senses. Sound, touch, they felt heightened. A strange bleeping echoed somewhere in the distance. I concentrated on what I could feel. No pain, for one. No welts, no burning chest or aching ribs… nothing. I released the grass, letting the ripped blades fall where they would, and stroked my torso. Clean and bruise free. It felt nice. I rocked my head from side to side, listening to the on-going bleep, not caring where I was, just enjoying the peaceful bliss that rushed over my body. Something tender brushed against my right side. It touched me without really touching me. A warm energy settled next to me and, if possible, I instantly felt calmer. My heart began to speed up in excitement. My body tingled as though an electric current ran through my veins. All of a sudden, I was struggling to control my accelerating heart. It thumped harder and harder as exhilaration shot through me. I started to feel uncomfortable, life-threateningly uncomfortable. I twisted and turned, but even moving was becoming difficult. I was panicking. I knew I was, but I couldn't stop. I was being swallowed up by my own dismay. Then it moved, the energy. It began loosely working itself over my hand, massaging the palms rhythmically, with purpose, yet still without really touching. It spread through my blood, settling its flow, and my heartbeat returned to normal pace. I felt the muscles in my cheek raise themselves to form a smile. I mouthed a 'thank you' as the distant bleeping sound rapidly closed in on me.

***

I jumped up with a start, wrenching the covers off my sweaty body. My heart was beating recklessly (though with not quite the same mania as it had in my dream). I was slightly disoriented. Still dazed. My hand closed around my phone and I threw it across the room, silencing the alarm, though not before catching the time.

'Half past nine, what the hell?' How could I have slept in that late? I scrambled to my feet and bolted to the bathroom, snarling as I tripped over a tiny section of upturned carpet, cursing Mae as I did.

'Oh sure, she bust my nuts whenever I miss a psych appointment, but when my education's at stake it's no big deal.'

If I was honest, missing a lesson or two didn't really bother me — it meant time away from the hellhole — what really worried me was *whose* lesson I'd be late for.

I turned the shower to full blast, medium heat, stripped off my clothes and climbed in. Warm water stung my tender skin. I looked down at my torso; the deep red areas were beginning to darken in places.

My shower lasted less than a minute before I tumbled out and threw on the first set of semi-clean clothes, I could get my hands on. My charcoal-grey top smelled a bit so I dowsed in body spray and pulled my black T-shirt over it, hoping to conceal the thrice-worn smell. I smudged some black on my face and was almost out the door when hunger ripped at my insides. Crap. Last night, no dinner. A rumbling stomach would only draw more attention my way in class, so I ran back to the kitchen and helped myself to a slice of dry bread. I winced as it went down. Damn Nick, I thought as I forced down another mouthful. I guzzled some water from the tap and legged it out of the door, coat in hand.

College was only twenty minutes away; if I kept pushing, I could catch some of the second half of English. Mr Taylor would still be completely narked, but I knew from experience, late was better than not showing up at all.

It had stopped raining, though water glistened on everything. I sprinted around the corner, feeling the sopping mud squish underneath the soles of my boots. As soon as my feet found the pavement, I pounded it hard, and almost knocked into the black bins, manoeuvring out of the way just in time to avoid the bin men wheeling them. I focused on my destination, making automatic turns. My mind was set on one thing, one place: college. I came to a sudden halt. I had no idea why, until I looked up and the park was staring me in the face. I hadn't even realised I was there, but my body knew. It was like I was being called. My heart drummed loudly in my chest and my skin prickled with excitement, but it made no sense. I had no connection with this place. I'd never even set foot inside, but the pull that I felt was real, unexplainable.

Raindrops made the grass sparkle invitingly, and for a brief moment I contemplated going in. My feet urged me to walk in, but my body trembled as I resisted. It was so hard to resist, it physically made me weak. I took a deep breath, chest burning as I did, and forced my feet to continue walking, running, sprinting. As I took off, I felt it: a warm energy just like the one in my dream — identical, but it wasn't possible. It was only a dream, right? It had to be. I looked back; I didn't know why. The park was now out of sight, but still…

I was so distracted that I didn't even notice I'd reached college until I turned around and slammed my face into the cool iron bars of the gate. There was an eruption of laughter and I felt my skin flush.

'Idiot can't even run right.'

I didn't turn around to see who had spoken. Putting faces to the words only made things worse. Instead I pressed the round silver buzzer, identified myself and walked in, head down with my hood drawn over it.

I was extremely late for English, but I didn't have any more run left in me, so I walked down the corridors, my hastiness flagging. When I entered the room, Mr Taylor had his back to the class. My breath was ragged, but I slid as silently as I could into my usual seat and prayed he hadn't picked up on my absence.

'Glad you could join us Mr Andrews,' he drawled, dashing my hope.

I kept quiet. It was always better to stay silent in these kinds of circumstances. I shrugged out of my coat and took out my books, even though it was far too late to catch up. Thanks to my new obsession with the park, I was later than I'd anticipated, so instead I spent what little time I had left studying Lucile from the corner of my eye. My gaze drifted from her deep brown eyes to her beautiful physique. She had one leg crossed casually over the other, and I watched as she tapped a foot. She was curvy in a way that sparked envy in even the most attractive girls, and the way she rolled her soft, full lips between her fingers made me lose focus on everything else but her. Before I knew it, time was up.

Maybe I could ask her to help me catch up on what I missed? I thought about it some more as she packed up her things. She seemed like a nice person, maybe she'd talk to me? I considered the possibility of her laughing in my face and decided against it.

With one sweep I shoved all my things into my bag, and was about to leave the class last when a firm hand gripped my shoulder and pulled me back.

'Do you consider yourself to be smart, Mr Andrews?'

Mr Taylor's question threw me off guard and I shrugged.

'Well you *must,* considering you think it is appropriate to miss *an hour and twenty minutes* of my class and then spend the remaining time gawping at Miss Armstrong.'

Crap. Had I been *that* obvious? I paused, wondering what the best thing to say would be.

'Well do you?'

'Do I what, sir?' I said as I searched my thoughts for a response that was both redeeming and surly.

He inhaled and slapped his foot hard against the ground.

'Do you think that your intelligence surpasses mine so greatly that you no longer need to pay attention to my lesson like everybody else does?'

'No sir. Not at all, sir.' I made my voice sound just as dull and boring as he was.

It was just the two of us now and my embarrassment was waning.

'Well then, if that's not the case, am I of disinterest to you?'

His tiny nostrils flared in his sharp nose, and though he was irritated by my lateness I could tell he was enjoying this moment by the way he chewed happily on his pen, staining his lip with the ink. I ground my teeth against each other before answering.

'No sir. You're a delight, sir.'

His cold blue-grey eyes studied my face.

'Well then, I *suggest* that next time you arrive in good time for my class and that you make a special effort to direct your *passion* to that which is related to *literature.*'

I blushed fiercely now, my humiliation making a slight return.

'Yes. Sir. May I go now?'

He twisted his mouth and eyed me with great disdain.

'Mmmm,' was all the response I got before he released his grip.

The rest of the day crawled by. I spent my free period in the library trying to catch up on Mr Taylor's literature lesson but my head was somewhere else. At some point in the day, I ran into Mac and his cling-on cretins. They added to the bruises Nick had given me and I left them with a bit of my blood, so I guess it was a fair trade.

Last period of the day saw me limping into the library with the rest of my Art class for some research project. As we entered, I broke away from the herd and found a computer some place quiet. I switched on the monitor and settled my things underneath the desk. There were her legs, long, slender but still curvy. I followed them up to her face, feeling ribbons of air being drawn from my lungs in snatches. Lucile. She was sitting at the computer next to me. I pulled my hair out of my face and gripped it nervously. Now was my chance. There was no one else around, so if she shot me down it wouldn't immediately get around college. I bit my lip, catching my piercing, then ran my tongue against the back of my teeth. I clenched and unclenched my fist, trying to steady my nerves, and breathed an airy 'hey.' There was a long pause; I hadn't looked at her as I'd said it and I could barely look at her now. My pulse rate sped up as I gave her a few quick sideward glances. Had she even heard me? I scratched the back of my neck, preparing to give it another shot, but as I worked up the nerve to say that three-letter word she vanished. The computer had been logged out and all her things had gone.

'Crap,' I slammed my fist on to the table. Stifled sniggers trickled from the other side of the bookshelf behind me. I glanced up and saw a group of girls from English suddenly busy themselves with the stack of books in front of them.

Among them was Missy Neesman.

'Did *it* actually try to talk to Lucile?' She whispered, a laugh caught somewhere in her chest.

'Loser, she just completely shut him down.'

'Leave him alone, Missy. He probably feels real bad.'

I recognised that voice, it was Naila Markson. She sat behind Missy in class.

'Besides, who knows if Lucile even heard him. She never hears anything with those earphones in.'

'Whatever, he's a freak. I'd say freaks should stick to their own kind, but he's so much of freak that even normal freaks won't hang with him.'

An embarrassed ache spread through my chest.

'Shut up Missy, he might hear you.'

'So what if he does.' She raised her voice in a mock whisper. 'You know I've actually heard the other goths say that they don't think he's normal. Can you imagine that? Even your own species won't accept you. It's kind of like when animals eat their young because they look weird.'

A collection of sniggers bubbled up.

'That's not why they eat their young, idiot. Why am I even friends with you?'

Missy shrugged.

'It's his own fault anyway,' said another voice I couldn't identify. 'I mean what does he expect? He's the one who won't speak to anyone, and then he sits there, face all *tortured soul* and that. He's the ultimate mood killer.'

That was about all I could take. I plugged in my earphones to drown out their voices and let the afternoon fade away into nothingness.

***

The rain had started up again by the time I was ready to go home. I stepped out into the coldness and breathed slowly with irritation. A strong wind whipped angrily against my face. I pulled my hood deeper over my head and trudged through the inescapably deep puddles. I walked slowly, giving the rainwater time to seep into my boots, soaking my socks and leaving my toes clammy. I hated that feeling, but it was that or a chance run in with Nick at home. I picked the rain. The long walk gave me a chance to think about the day. Not something I wanted, but not something I could escape either. Every minute detail dragged to the surface a pain that I was trying to hide from. It riled up inside of me, vicious and serpent-like, twisting and writhing, making me clench my fists. I kicked the puddles now, not caring about my damp socks or that the water was soaking my jeans. I just needed to do something, anything. I wanted to feel... better. I didn't feel better. In fact, I felt worse. My head began to throb deeply. I lifted my hands to massage my temples, but before I could place my fingers on the pulsing flesh a soothing warmth rushed over me. I stopped confused. The pain in my head lessened and lessened until it had disappeared. I looked up through the sheet of rain that was pouring down in front of my face and there, staring at me, was the park. In that moment, something clicked into place. The warmth, the comfort. The dream… was that… was that… the girl? Impossible, unthinkable but… maybe… true?

I stared into the park through the rain. A part of me wanted to go in, *needed* to go in. I just wanted to feel like someone understood me, even if it were just for five minutes. But this was crazy. She couldn't be real. Could she? I took a few small steps forward and placed my hand on to the wet rusty bars of the gate. Cracked flakes of old paint peeled off into the palms of my hand, pricking me gently, reminding me of what was real. I didn't let go. The lock was busted, and the gate stood ajar. It would be easy to slip inside, but I hesitated. It was a bad idea, stupid. A mistake to be here for even a second longer. But then that warmth… It brushed up against my cheek. Warmth so welcome in the mist of the cold evening that was approaching. I inhaled, deeply aware of the strange sensation washing through me. A mixture of emotions that ran through my veins, stirring my blood, replacing the poisonous anger that had caused my head to hurt in the first place. It felt… I felt… whole again yet, at the same time something about the warmth, its stroke, felt… longing. As if touching my loneliness somehow reawakened its own. I wanted to reach out and comfort this soul. To find pleasure and understanding in its warmth. To console and be consoled in a way I had never known.

I drew the gate further back, my body itching to slip inside, my heart squeezing with excitement at the thought. I lifted my foot, feeling my toes flex awkwardly, wondering what I would find, when a hole opened up in my mind. Words from this afternoon darted through the gap, striking me like lightning.

'Freak'. 'Loser.'

I planted my foot back on to the sopping ground. This is why they think you're insane, this is the reason you have no friends, because of things like this. I shook the chains on the gate angrily and slammed them down, smashing my frustration against the bars. How can you seek comfort from what you can't see? In what you can't feel?

'This is crap!' I shouted. 'What do you want from me?'

The air around remained un-responsive.

'This is nuts,' I yelled, wrenching my hands from the gate. 'Completely nuts!'

I swung around and stomped off down the street, my angry strides causing waves of puddles to crash back on me. The rain continued to pour hitting me heavily, making the exposed parts of my skin sting. The resulting chill made me shiver, but still I felt internally, emotionally, warm. She was following me. I was sure. I thought that once I'd left the park, I'd feel normal again, that this psychotic episode would end, but I was wrong. She was still here, with me. Unnerved, I punched the palm of my hand repeatedly, my frustrations rising. What was I thinking? She? *It! It* was still here. *It* was still following me. I wasn't going to dignify this insanity by giving this *energy*, my psychotic feelings, human qualities. I bounded down the street, desperate to get home. Desperate to shake off this unnatural, abnormal, *thing* that seemed to bring me comfort. I tried to force it from my mind, but it clung to my every fibre like static energy binding us.

When I reached my door, I couldn't bring myself to unlock it. I stood in front of it, staring, looking at the peeling yellow paint without really seeing it. I was afraid to go inside. I knew if I walked in with this girl, this *thing,* still here, I would never be able to get rid of it. It was an irrational thought, but what wasn't irrational at this point? I just somehow felt that if I let it into my house, if I continued to let it give me comfort in a place where I sometimes needed it the most, I might not be able to let it go. Might not *want* to let it to go.

I took a deep breath and turned around to face her, it. Floods of rain blurred my view, but it was clear enough for me to see that there was no one there.

'Leave me alone.' I whispered icily. 'Do you hear me? Whoever you are, whatever you are. If you're a figment of my imagination or whatever just… leave me the hell alone.'

In that small, sane part of my brain I knew that no one was with me, but somehow it only felt right to say the words aloud, as though my crazy mind needed the audio version.

'I don't need or want you.' I continued. 'I just want to be NORMAL.'

I belted the last word out like it would free me. I hoped to God that it did. I really didn't need to add more fuel to the freak fire that was my life.

Chapter 6

Quiet. Heartbreakingly silent. 'I don't want you,' that's what he'd said, 'normal' is what he'd screamed, and now everything's quiet. Now it's just me and the swirl. I can't find my way back. He said 'I don't need you,' and now I can't find my way back to him: but he lied. I know he lied because I feel him. From the inside of his heart to the outside of his skin, I feel him. Always. So, I know it was a lie. Now I wait for him to know it too.

Chapter 7
Thursday, 18th February

Over the next few weeks, the weather wouldn't let up. It rained so hard I thought roofs would cave in. That was fine with me though; it was in sync with my mood. I didn't feel the *girl* anymore. Except when I walked past the park on my way to college, and then I just cranked up the music and kept on moving. I told myself I was fine. That this thing, this presence, was brought on by a bout of depression, and now that I had a handle on my emotions, I was all right without it. But in truth, I somehow felt lonelier than ever. Sometimes I almost wished for the weakness to go back to her. I craved her, but then sense would fight its way in and convince me that loneliness was no excuse to encourage psychotic behaviour, so I started going back to see Dr-Piss-me-off. It was an experiment of mine. I figured if I could occupy my mind with some of his shrink crap, then maybe something he said, might actually help stop the delusions of this girl.

It seemed to be working. I hadn't had an 'episode,' as he would put it, since I started seeing him again. Proof that this *girl*, this comfort, was all in my head: no place else. Somehow Dr Evans was actually helping me. Maybe everything he said wasn't total crap. I guess it couldn't be if it helped to get rid of my stalker, imaginary friend. Not that I told him about her. I didn't trust him enough for that. He may have been helping on some sort of level, but he was still the enemy. I had to be careful what I said to him. I didn't want to give him any ammunition, any cause to cart me off to crazy jail. I knew that's what he was waiting for. Him and everyone else. Just watching and waiting for me to slip up. To say something or *do something* not normal and then, boom: white-jacket city for me. I can feel it, and if I'm not careful it won't be long until they see what I see, that it's true. That I'm not right. That I'm too much of a loner, too much of a freak to be a part of society, and that's where I'll end up. A padded cell... but that's stupid. Even if I am right, even if there was something different about me that meant I didn't belong with normal people, Dr Evans would never suss that out. He was usually way off the mark about everything, and I hated him. I hated him even more at this very moment, because it was yet another Thursday afternoon, which meant we had a session. Like an obedient lap dog, I was there, on time, and although I wasn't thrilled about it, it kept me away from Mae and Nick for a while, so what the heck.

I sat outside his office, sketchbook in hand, letting the pencil work freely over the page. I couldn't really think of what to draw. I'd had no inspiration for months, no urge to even consider continuing with my comic *The Adventures of Goth Kid*. I smiled at the thought of it. Even the title sounded lame. I allowed my wrist to carry out looping motions, and relaxed circles snaked across the page. I was just about to commit my thoughts to some place other than here when I heard my name being called.

'Mr Andrews, Dr Evans is ready for you.'

The secretary behind the desk put down the phone and smiled up at me, her bright white teeth sparkling in her round chubby face. She brushed back her brown curls and extended that grin. I half smiled back at her and pushed open the door to Dr Evans' office.

'Luke,' he beamed from his usual spot beside the window. 'Take a seat?'

His voice was that thick wheezy drawl that bugged me. I threw my things down next to the wooden chair and slumped into it. Immediately I set to work on my usual task — picking at the chipped wood on the arm of the chair while prepping to sort of listen.

The room was silent for a while. I didn't question why; I was too busy enjoying the bliss to care. Until he ruined it by opening his fat gob and allowing that wheezing voice to escape.

'I take it you're not a fan of my couch?'

He was going somewhere with this, but I wasn't biting, so I kept quiet.

'I always thought it was rather comfortable, myself. It's one of the reasons I kept the shabby-looking thing when I moved in. But you seem to disagree.'

I eyed him impatiently and shrugged.

'Well I only assume so. You've been coming here for over two months now and not once have you ever sat in it. It's very soft and you can't be opposed to comfort,' he chuckled stupidly. My responsive snarl went ignored.

'So curiously I ask, why don't you sit in it?'

I screwed up my face and shrugged again. It was a *very* stupid question.

'Verbal communication, Luke,' he prompted.

My face became even more twisted, and the idiot cleared his throat.

'I don't know,' I eventually said in my most fed-up voice: But that was a lie. I did know. The truth was I hated the thing. It made me sick. It fed into the whole stereotype of shrinks and mental patients. Even its presence in the room made me feel like I was being observed. I hated it and everything it represented. I hated it for making this whole place feel real when I spent most of my time here pretending, visualising that I was somewhere else.

'Luke,' Dr Evans wheezed.

I must have spent too much time in my head because he wore the expression of a person who had been ignored.

'Mmmm.'

'Verbal commu—'

'*Yes*,' I interrupted before he could finish his predictable request.

'You seem to have something on your mind. Would you like to talk about it?'

I ran my tongue over my teeth as I thought up a suitable response.

'Nothing in particular today. Sorry.'

'Well then.' He paused, allowing his eyes to scan my neglected things. 'What's new with you? I notice you're sketching again,' he said, gesturing to my sketchbook laying open on the floor.

I kicked it shut, but he wasn't dissuaded.

'How's that going? Drawn anything new?'

I cracked my knuckles, 'No.'

The moment of silence that followed was awkward. Him sitting there expecting me to say more, me wishing he would implode on the spot. Needless to say, we, were both sorely disappointed. He gave a great sigh when he realised this was all he was going to get out of me on that subject, then scribbled down something on a pad and folded his hands together.

'Luke.'

I looked up.

'This isn't going to work if you don't talk.'

I said nothing. He sighed again.

'Over these past few sessions, you've said little, as usual, and you've refused to submit your journal. It is difficult, therefore, to know what you are going through and, more importantly, how I can help.'

More silence. He squirmed uncomfortably in his chair and I grinned inside.

'However, I have noticed that you do seem more on edge than usual. Am I correct?'

I paused before speaking, wondering how safe it was to answer the question.

'I guess so,' I said. It couldn't hurt.

'Would you like to talk about it?'

'Not really.'

Another sigh from his never-ending bank of breathy exhales.

'In which case, I would like to set you a task,' he said pulling out wads of tissue from the box on the table and jamming them to his nose.

He was trying to block the leak bubbling at the rim of his nostrils. I cringed. He always had some kind of disgusting nasal issue, but today's, was something else.

'I would like to set you another writing exercise to do alongside jotting in your journal.'

'Right?' I was hesitant.

'I would like you to write an account of your day.'

I gave him a questioning look and he smiled at me.

'No emotions. No explanations, no "I felt", "this made me angry", "this happened because", "I'm so annoyed." None of that. Just a simple account. Things like "I woke up," "I took a shower," "I had bran flakes for breakfast." Do you get the gist of it?'

'Pretty much.'

'Is that something you think you could do for me?'

I deepened the hole in the chair with my nail while I thought it over. It seemed like a simple request so I agreed, a nagging feeling twisting in my stomach the moment I did. One that told me this was going to come back and bite me in the arse, hard.

'I would *still* like to see your journal though, Luke,' he was saying as he attempted to catch the fluttering tissues that had somehow managed to escape his pasty hands.

'Cool,' was the only non-committal thing I could think of to say.

Dr Evans spent the remaining forty-five minutes of the session trying to engage me in conversation, while I spent the time exercising my linguistic skills. It was like a mental workout trying to limit my responses to a maximum of three words.

When I stepped out into the fresh rain, I felt free. Being in his room, well, it was like I was suffocating, and now that I was outside, I could finally breathe again.

The cold rain flicked on to my face. Sharp and icy. It made my skin sting, but I welcomed it. It was refreshing after an hour spent trapped in Evans' stuffy office. It was all worth it, though, not to feel like I was going insane. I didn't feel crazy now that *she* was mostly gone, but I felt far from normal. Maybe I wasn't supposed to be, though. Maybe I never would. Maybe this was just me; I wasn't made to fit in and I would just have to accept it.

The journey home felt quick. Quicker than I wanted it to be. I kicked open the gate and resentfully made my way to the front door. I was greeted by the scent of fried chicken as I walked in. Mae was making my favourite? The smell made my taste buds ooze saliva. An uncharacteristic smile crept over my face and my stomach grumbled with pleasure.

'Mae?'

'In here.'

Her voice was coming from the living room, where the television blared. I slid off my backpack and slumped out of my jacket, letting it fall to the floor. I made my way to the where she was.

'Is that...?'

'Your favourite,' she said eyes beaming once they'd found mine. 'I thought, since you've been so open-minded about Dr Evans these days, you deserved a little treat,' she paused. 'I'm proud of you,' she said, then smiled warmly and for a moment I remembered why I used to love my mother.

'It's cool,' I said casually, my mouth threatening to twitch into a slightly broader smile.

I'd almost lowered myself into the couch when a hand clutched my shoulder in a vice-like grip.

'Yeah, Lukey boy,' Nick mocked, 'we're just soooo proud of you.'

He rolled his dark eyes and stumbled passed me, reeking of rum and sweat. I lost my appetite. I should have known he was home. Re-runs of *Only Fools and Horses* booming through the place was a dead giveaway. I was mad. Mad at him for being here, mad at her for not telling me, mad at myself for allowing the smallest gesture from her to alter my emotions.

My hands went red under the strain of my balled-up fists. I headed straight for the stairs.

'Oh no Luke, don't. What about your dinner?'

'I'm not hungry anymore,' but my stomach gurgled loudly.

Nick laughed and Mae whipped him with the back of her hand.

'Oh honey, please, there's some homemade chips too, just the way you like them.'

She was really trying, and I guess I felt a little bad, but the thought of digesting food across from that sweaty pig already made me want to bring up my last meal.

'I'll see you in the morning,' I mumbled and turned my back on them.

Nick's loathsome voice followed me out of the room and up the steps.

'Leave him Mae, he's a spoilt, attention-seeking brat. He loves this right now. Loves all the trouble he's causing.'

I lingered on the steps waiting for her response. Waiting to see who she'd defend, him… or me, but she said nothing.

'So how 'bout that grub then Mae? I'm starving.'

She sighed, heavily shifting her feet, and I slipped out of sight before she could see me.

I wrenched open the door to my room and slammed it shut. How dare he? I thought, flinging my things to one side. How dare she? Not once had she ever put me before that selfish arse. My blood was boiling. I threw myself on to my bed feeling incredibly riled up. I lay on my back and stared up at the ceiling, random thoughts filling my head. Dean was one of them. If he were still here, that prick Nick wouldn't have lasted a month. He would've thought of some way to get rid of him. He was good at that. Itching powder, boxers and one of Mae's exes sprung to mind, and I laughed so hard I almost didn't hear the tapping at my door.

Mae entered my room with a plate full of food and a curious smile on her face.

'Can I sit?' she asked.

'I guess,' I answered trying to sound moody but failing miserably.

The image of the ex, furiously scratching his arse and cursing about us little demon shits kept replaying in my head.

'What's so funny?' she asked.

'Do you remember Matt?'

A puzzled look appeared briefly on her face before the memory dawned on her, then she laughed too.

'You boys were so cruel to him.'

I grinned, still replaying the image.

'Especially Dean, he was such a little monster.'

The moment she said his name it stopped being funny.

'What do you want, Mae?' I snapped.

She shrugged as if to give up.

'Your dinner, she nodded towards the steaming plate in her hand. 'I thought I'd bring it to you before Nick has the chance to scoff the lot.'

'He's welcome to it.'

'Luke…'

'I said I wasn't hungry, and I meant it,' my stomach betrayed me again.

Mae's smirk was smug.

'You seem pretty hungry to me,' she teased, tilting the plate in my direction.

I said nothing.

'Just take the food,' she insisted, tugging on my overgrown fringe.

I hesitated before reaching for the plate. The anger had subsided a little thanks to Dean, and my appetite was creeping back, making it so much harder to ignore the hunger pangs. I tucked in, enjoying all the warm flavours as they mingled in mouth.

'Is it good?' she asked watching me hoover it in. 'It's good, right?'

'It's good,' I said through hearty mouthfuls.

There was a long pause, and all I could hear was the gnawing of her nails as she sunk her teeth into them, ripping them off in shreds. She wanted to say something, but she sighed loudly for a few more moments before working up the nerve.

'He does care, you know? In his own way, he genuinely does.'

My jaw locked, making it difficult to swallow.

'He just wants what's best for you,' she went on. 'I can see it in his eyes.'

'Yeah, because spoilt, attention-seeking brat is just another way of saying *I love you.*'

'He didn't mean that, he just wants you not to be so… so…'

'So *what?*'

'So angry all the time. If you could just try a little, I know the two of you would get on.'

'So what? You think it's all *my* fault?' I yelled angrily, anger ripping through me. 'Mae he's an egotistical git who doesn't give a crap about me.'

'That's not true. Just… come downstairs and eat with us. I know he wants that just as much as I do.'

Just then his voice thundered up the stairs, betraying her even more than my stomach had me.

'Mae, you'd better not be up there. Let him hide away in his hole of a room if that's what he wants. He's not spoiling my night with his whining, that's for damn sure.'

I stared at Mae, she looked back at me.

'Still think he cares?'

There was silence.

'You should go.'

She looked up at me as though she were torn. As though she was being forced to choose between the two of us and had no clue where her loyalties should lie. I laughed briefly, bleakly. She was *pathetic*.

'Don't worry Mae,' I spat, 'if you go it couldn't possibly make me hate you any more than I already do for actually sticking with that tool.'

She stared at me, eyes filled with hurt. I looked away before the guilt could creep in and when I turned back, she was gone.

Chapter 8

I run. Alongside him I run. Listening to the sound of his breathing. Heavy, strained. I run on effortlessly. His face is fixed in anger but his eyes, they're full of pain. Pain that I feel, strong, desperately ripping through him. Pain that, behind the rage, forces its way to the surface. Any other time I wouldn't be able to see this. On a normal day I wouldn't have access to his feelings, to his world, but here we are entirely connected. Our bond completely untouched. In this place, at this moment, he does not reject me. He cannot reject me. His subconscious mind wants me even if his conscious mind does not. It draws me near to him for comfort and willingly I follow.

His chest heaves, but instead of slowing down he pushes on. Thrusting one limb in front of the other. I wonder where he is running to or who he's running from. This dark space has no real direction, no path; it's not really even a place but rather a swirl of deep dark greys and dusty blacks. The ground below feels hard like concrete. A pavement? It's hard to tell; partly because I can't see through the thick, grey haze, mostly because I don't care enough to figure it out. I am with him. That's all that matters. My loneliness has been numbed; my pain sedated. But not for long. I know it, I can tell, when it's time to leave.

Pangs of loneliness well up inside of me, rushing through me till they fill my essence. Pixels emerge like before — then shatter, taking with them my sight. I see nothing. I am shut out from his world. He shuts me out and I go back to the black. Frustration again. I would scream if I could. If I had a voice, but there would be no one here to hear me. So I wait, patiently, enduring the painful day, longing for night when we will be together in his dreams.

Chapter 9
Friday, 19th February

Hunger pulled at my stomach muscles. It was only 6am, but the lurching woke me up. Sweat trickled down my face as I went over the dream in my head. I was running; that's all I could really remember, but there was enough leftover rage in me to know I'd been pissed off. I dragged my fingers through my hair and gripped it tight as I fought hard to remember more. I was angry and upset, but not alone. I never, not even for a moment, felt lonely. A sinking dread eclipsed me.

Was it *her*? I couldn't remember. Maybe I didn't want to remember. If it were true it would mean she was coming back.

'No,' I sat upright in my bed. '*She* doesn't come back unless you make it happen. I rubbed my face and flicked on my lamp. The dim light brightened my tabletop. I looked at my half-eaten dinner lying on the side — cold, unappealing. Reaching out my hand, I grabbed a piece of chicken, bit off a chunk and chewed. Congealed fat wriggled down my throat, sticking on its way down. I felt my abdomen fill slowly and sighed. At least my stomach would be settled. Something in me had to be.

***

The lights were low. Voices hummed all around me. A film of Othello was playing in the background, but no one was watching. No one really cared, least of all Mr Taylor who was doing his best to conceal the fact that he was sleeping by propping his limp body up on his hand while facing towards the computer screen. Everyone was excited about the reality of a lazy college afternoon. Everyone but me. I hadn't gone back to sleep after the dream and now my head was pounding, hard. I massaged my temples and breathed deeply through the wooziness. My skin felt warm beneath my fingertips; all signs that a migraine was coming on. That, along with the trademark spots that were clogging up my vision. I was blacking out. I could sense it, the dots closing in on me as my body began to shut down.

'No,' my voice was thin as the edges of everything began to take on a darker hue. 'Not here, not now,' I'd never live it down.

I pressed my eyes shut tightly and tried to focus my mind on something else, anything else. I needed a distraction, something that would anchor me to this world, to this present time. I opened my eyes and the answer was sitting some distance in front of me, twirling her hair between her fingers. My breathing was shallow, my heart raced so that I could feel it in my throat, but my head seemed to ache a little less and I was grateful for that.

Lucile parted her fingers and I watched as the thick frizzy strands slipped between the gaps. I studied her then. Drinking in every expression on her stunning face. My heart took a dip when I noticed the troubled lines that aggravated her brow. She was all but surrounded by her friends. Hushed gossip drifted from their mouths, but she sat barely listening. Hardly bothering to smile and nod at the right times. Her eyes were sad and, though the room was dark, I could tell that she'd been crying. I was desperate to know what was wrong. In fact, I envisioned myself walking up to the table, sitting next to her in the empty seat on her left-hand side. I'd ask her what the matter was, and she'd lean her head on my shoulder and talk. Her thick hair brushing against my lips. Maybe she'd even cry so that I'd have to hug her. The thought thrilled me. I played scenario after scenario in my head as she turned and fidgeted restlessly in her seat.

Time passed quickly and before I knew it, before I was ready, Othello had come to the end. The level of noise began to rise, but Mr Taylor didn't move.

'Oi! Taylor,' shouted a voice from the back. It was Ricky Hanisu. Fit Rick the girls called him, but to me he was just best friend to the prick of a guy dating Lucile.

'Taaaaaylorrrrr! He purred, 'movie's over, mate.'

A few of the girls from Missy's group giggled. Mr Taylor jerked and grunted a little, but that was it. Ricky sighed loudly before beginning the chant.

'Taylor, Taylor, Taylor.'

Like mindless halfwits, the rest of class joined him, but the most Mr Taylor did was twist in his chair. Then the booing and throwing began.

'Original, very original,' I mumbled, annoyed that my fantasies had been disrupted.

A balled-up piece of something flew past me and landed at the back of Mr Taylor's head. His hand slipped, letting his body fall. He knocked his chin against the table and cursed loudly. The class erupted in laughter, the kind that pulsates through the room.

Mr Taylor pulled himself together, and stumbling to his feet shouted, 'Which one of you idiots threw this?'

The class went silent, all except a few sniggers.

'I said who threw this?' he growled.

The undercurrent of laughter bubbled dangerously. Mr Taylor muttered something to himself just as the bell rang. He let a few empty threats slip from his tongue and then dismissed the class, heading for the door himself.

It was break-time and the school council were selling cakes and stuff to raise money for charity. These morons had been drooling all morning, so naturally there was a stampede in that direction. I expected to be the only one left in the classroom, but I wasn't. Lucile was still there. Lucile and a few of her friends huddled in discussion, their voices low. I hung back too. I had to know what was bothering her. It killed me to see her so upset.

Ricky pushed his way between the closely-knit bodies — making a few quiver — and spoke, not bothering with the secrecy (I was grateful for that).

''Sup Nay,' he smirked, his eyes roaming all over Naila's body.

'Hanisu,' she replied all cool and dismissive.

His smirk grew.

'So Luce,' he began peeling his gaze away from Naila. 'You got an answer or what?' Lucile shrugged.

'Leave her alone,' Missy squawked. 'Can't you see she's been crying?'

Lucile cut her a look.

'Hey, don't off load your oestrogenic rage on me. All I came to do is pass on a message.'

'And what's that?' asked Lucile, attempting to sound confident though her voice wobbled a little.

'Shane said, and I'mma pass this on word for word so I don't mess this up, he said, and I quote: "When you see Luce tell her I'm not gonna wait around for ever, either she wants to work things out tonight or you can tell her we're through," end quote.'

Missy sniggered at his impression of Lucile's boyfriend and Ricky winked in her direction, making her cackle some more. Lucile swallowed hard and looked Ricky dead in the eyes.

'You can tell Shane to grow up, man up, and come and talk to me face to face. I don't deal with go-betweens.'

Ricky smirked. 'Cool,' he said, clapping his hands together. 'Now that my job's done, it's cake t-i-i-ime,' he sang, already halfway down the hall.

Missy giggled, brushing back her silky hair. Naila rolled her eyes and turned her attentions towards Lucile.

'Are you okay Luce?' she asked, but that shrill voice cut her off.

'Can you believe that?' Missy shrieked. 'Can you believe *him*?' The girls fell back into their gossipy huddle, all except Naila and Lucile.

It always baffled me what someone like Lucile ever saw in a prick like Shane. Even the idea of Ricky being his friend threw me. They were decent people, but Shane, he was nothing more than a cocky, know-it-all git. She shouldn't have been crying over him. Not when she deserved so much more. Not when there was someone willing to give her so much more.

My eyes flickered up to the time. Class ended 10 minutes ago and I hadn't moved from my table. I had no reason to be there anymore. I'd packed and repacked all my stuff ages ago, and the 'searching for something in my bag' bit was beginning to look suspicious. I bit my lip and nervously ruffled the back of my hair. My heart called out to her. I wanted to make sure she was all right before I left. I wanted to talk to her, I *was* going to talk to her. It was now or never. I swung my book bag over my shoulder and marched on with determination, trying desperately not to think about what I was about to do. I stood in front of her, refusing to let the slickness of my palms and sudden dryness of my throat stop me from speaking. Her head was hung low and I tilted mine, trying to meet her gaze, ignoring the inquisitive stares around me, the ones that made my skin tingle with warmth.

'Are… are you…? You look… sad,' I mumbled quietly. 'Do you… need anything?'

Lucile looked up at me, forehead crinkled in confusion, and although it probably only lasted half a second the silence that followed seemed to be never-ending. My nervous heart swelled. She smiled at me briefly — a sweet, shy smile cut short by a hostile voice that was not her own.

'Go. Away. Freak.' Missy pushed herself forward from the centre of the herd and flung her arm around Lucile's shoulder.

'She doesn't need anything from *you*,' she spat, her eyes little more than vindictive slits. 'Unlike *you*, Lucile has friends,' she continued in a tone that matched her icy glare. 'Real friends who are there for her.'

Lucile shrugged away Missy's arm and resumed the action of packing her bag. My skin flushed. Rage made me ball up my fists, made me want to say something nasty and unforgivable to *her*, Missy Neesman, but embarrassment had me heading for the door. I pushed it open, letting it slam shut and sealing their sniggers inside the room. I was furious, blazing, white-hot mad. My head pounded viciously again, the black dots returning. I needed air; I stormed outside, the breeze thwacking me like a thick brick wall thrown on to the entire surface of my body. I staggered, grasping whatever I could to break my fall, stepping on something solid as I did.

'Hey,' sneered the last voice I wanted to hear. 'You touched me.' Mac flung me forward and I swayed a little, pinching the bridge of my nose. I inhaled deeply, feeling slight strength return to my legs, and spoke.

'Your point?' I was still angry and my voice reeked of bitterness, but for once I didn't care. He could smash my face till I was a bloody mess for all he wanted. I was done with this place and done with him. I kept on walking.

'Hold up, what did you say to me you little pansy freak?'

His words prodded me, shoving me back towards him.

'Do one, you shit.'

A cloud of spots began to eclipse Mac's face but I could still make out its contortions. Hard and bulky like the rest of him. He stepped closer, breaking through the personal space barrier, and loomed over me, his breath as harsh as the cutting wind.

'I'm giving you one chance to think about what you just said to me and the impact it's about to have on your *face* if you don't apologise.'
A deep smile smeared its way across my face. I leaned in closer, our faces now inches apart, and whispered: 'Sorry...'

Mac nodded, the closeness of our bodies making him uncomfortable.

'Better,' he said, stepping away.

'Wait,' I grasped his wrist and gripped, both the anger and pain causing me to do things I'd later regret.

'I'm not finished. I'm sorry you're so pathetic,' I went on, pushing him hard on his solid chest.

'I'm sorry you're such a pathetic loser and I'm even more sorry that you always will be. I can't stand you,' I laughed. 'With your stupid snarl and your arse of a face and that voice, *"I'm only giving you one chance,"'* I mocked, 'Shut up. Shut. Up. Don't you ever *just s*hut. *The hell. Up?'*

For a few moments all that followed was purest silence. The pain in my head was blinding, and the spots clouded my vision so badly now that I didn't even realised Mac's cronies had arrived at his side until they spoke.

'Woah,' one of them said, his shock undiluted.

'You're gonna mess him up, right?' asked the other with as much surprise.
I couldn't see Mac's face properly, couldn't read his expression, but I heard his laugh; menacing. This was going to hurt... badly. I braced myself. A powerful blow landed in my gut and I winced, drawing in a short breath. It was all I could manage until I lost my balance and fell, losing consciousness on the way down.

***

'Luke. Luke? Luke can you hear me?'

The ringing in my ears made the sound of my name buzz uncomfortably in my head.

'Luke! Lucas Andrews, can you hear me?'

'Mmm,' I groaned.

My brain pounded. It throbbed so hard I thought it would burst. But despite the relentless pulsing, the pain in my stomach ripped its way up to catch my attention.

'Oww,' I whimpered.

Warm hands pressed lightly on either side of my cheek; I opened my eyes to identify the owner. Miss Rakiatu stared back at me from beneath the spots, worry all over her usually pleasant face.

'Are you all right Luke?'

'Yeah,' I said, propping myself up on my palms, but that was a lie. 'Great.'

I brushed my hand over my stomach. Perfect. This lovely new black and purple bruise would go great with the fading grey one Nick had given me.

'What happened Luke?'

I blinked a few times to regain full focus, but once I had, I almost wished I hadn't. A crowd had gathered around me, gawping like idiots. Vile vultures without a drop of sympathy in anyone's eyes.

'Luke what happened?' Miss Rakiatu pressed.

'Nothing,' I said pulling myself to my feet but wobbling slightly.

'*Nothing?*'

'Yeah, nothing. I must have… tripped or… something.'

More lies. I knew it and so did she, but I just didn't care.

'Maybe you should get checked out.'

'Stop.'

'Lucas, I'm worried.'

'Well, don't be,' I snapped.

I steadily lowered myself to the ground, ignoring the blinding pain in my gut. I picked up my things and walked away with my head down, avoiding everyone's gaze.

'Luke,' Miss Rakiatu called after me, but along with the pain I ignored her.

'Luke, where are you going? College isn't over.'

I continued walking, pushing passed people on my way to the gate.

'Luke, you really shouldn't be alone. Luke,' she called, but she didn't follow.

I was touched by the magnitude of her care. I pulled out my headphones and cranked the music up to max volume. It blared and the sound made me nauseous, but it was worth it just to disconnect.

***

I shut the front door and flung down my things, letting them land wherever, I didn't care. Two messages flashed on the answering machine and I pressed the button to listen.

'Hey Luke honey, I'm working late tonight. I'm sorry. They're short-handed at the care home. One of the night staff didn't show up… again, but they're bringing in someone from the agency so hopefully I shouldn't be too late. Nick's out on one of his 'guys-only weekends.' He said something about Scott not being able to do next week so they brought their plans forward. Anyway, that means it's just you and me for dinner. Order us a takeaway. Whatever you like, I'm not fussed. See you soon… hopefully.'

My face didn't show it, but I was grateful to have the house to myself for once. Especially after the day I'd had. I clicked the button to listen to the next message:

'Hey Mae, it's Nick.'

Message deleted. Last thing I wanted tonight was to hear his voice. I went into the living room, shrugged off my coat and sunk my bruised body into the sofa. Turning on the TV, I kicked off my shoes and began flicking through the channels. The clock on the bottom of the screen told me it was quarter to nine. I'd been drifting about all afternoon. After I'd escaped the hellhole, I jumped on the first bus and let it take me to the end of its route. Then I just walked. Did nothing, went nowhere, just walked. Being outside was calming, I guess. Almost. It was like I was free. But now that I was here, I felt the tension creeping back into my blood. It didn't matter that I was alone; it had been a long time since this place was my home. Or anywhere for that matter. I had nothing.

People walked in and off the TV screen, said their lines, laughed, cried and lulled me to sleep.

***

I was running again. I could hear the jeering laughs of other college students, hear their taunts, their insults, but I didn't look back. I just kept running. Running until I was out of breath, speeding until their voices no longer reached me. I kept going, exerting myself, my limbs aching in protest. I didn't stop. Not then, not until I'd found where I was supposed to be. I ran through the thick, hazy swirl of greyish black before me; I reached out and in return felt a warmth rush through me, thick and consoling. Only then did I stop. The haze began to clear, it faded slowly, and I caught a glimpse of red. Rusty red swings swaying in the breeze. Just a glimpse before I was wrenched away from this world and thrown into the other.

***

When I woke it was with a gasp. Rough hands yanked me out of the seat and I snatched at the air, taking small gulps.

'You, lazy little shit,' a nasty voice sneered in my ear.

'Nick,' my scrambled brain struggled to keep up. 'I thought you were gone for the weekend?'

It was the wrong thing to say. Incredibly stupid.

'Is that why you thought you could be such a little pig?' he growled, flinging me about. 'Well unlucky for you my trip was cancelled.'

'Nick, stop, Nick.' Every cell of my brain was in agony. 'What are you talking about?'

'I'm talking about this,' he released his hold on me, letting me stumble to my feet then shoved me out of the living room towards the hallway where my things lay scattered on the floor.

'Crap,' I breathed.

'Imagine how narked I was when I came home after a long day's work and tripped up over your useless junk.'

'I'm sorry Nick. I'll pick them up.'

57

I'd barely taken a step towards them before he grasped hold of my neck, yanking me back.

'You're sorry, are you?' he snarled, spit flicking on to my face. 'And if I'd broken my neck on the way down, cracked my head on something hard and bled to death, would you tell your mother you were sorry then?'

'No, I'd say good riddance; tell her she had a lucky escape.'

I'd mumbled the words through teeth clamped shut, but they were still heard.

'Is that right?'

I knew what was coming next; there was no way to avoid it. He was already pissed about missing his precious weekend trip, and this was just the tip of the iceberg.

'Whatever,' I said accepting my fate. There was no point in grovelling, I'd learnt that years ago.

The blood beneath his skin bubbled to the surface.

'You selfish, lazy sod.'

He drew back his hand and smacked me round the face hard, hard enough to leave a mark. I stumbled and laughed darkly.

'You think this is funny?' he spat.

'Tell me Nick,' I jeered, 'how are you going to explain this one to Mae, huh? What are you gonna do? Say I tripped and fell on your hand?'

He'd made a mistake and there was no turning back now. He knew it and so did I. Usually he knew better, than to mark me any place obvious, but I guess I'd punched a wrong nerve today because there I was, cheek flaming, jaw swelling and laughing like a maniac.

Nick's face turned the purest red. He grabbed hold of my throat and clutched before slapping my head hard against the door. I tried to get up but he forced me down with his heavy hand and glowered over me.

'You dare breathe a word, boy, and you'll be spitting teeth, do you hear me?'

I nodded. He stood and turned away, but not before kicking me in the stomach.

'That's for being a smartarse, you lazy sod. Now pick those up,' he snarled, kicking my sketchbook on his way to the kitchen.

I sat there for a few moments, unable to move. Bile was revving its way up my chest. I forced it back down. I would like to say that it was mainly fury that kept me paralyzed, even pain, but it wasn't. It was the emptiness. I felt empty and tired. I was tired of this day, tired of this life where I was kicked and spat on; where I was mocked and laughed at. Where I was unloved… so unloved.

Tears streaked my face, but pride stopped me from making any sound. Grief welled up inside of me and at that moment I felt lost, alone. A desperate need to be understood stirred inside me, stroking to life the memory of warmth, of peace. It filled my head and I knew, I just knew where I had to be. I stood up, wiped my face with my shaking hands and left. I opened the front door and just left, not bothering about footwear or keys. I didn't care that it was drizzling outside and that I had no coat, or even that I hadn't picked up my things. I knew where I was going and that was enough.

Chapter 10

When I was little, I used to love being here. Legs pounding the grass when I ran, hair whipping around my face, tangles of it filling my mouth. I'd toss myself at the swings and laugh. It was a place that mattered because I was free, because I was loved, because I didn't know about pain. It still mattered now — even though I was all grown up; barely. Even though there's no such thing as free anymore. Even though every love I've ever known is closed to me. Even though all I know now is pain, this place matters. It matters because of possibility. Years ago, this park, Courtdale Park, held endless possibilities because it was everything I wanted it to be. Wild exotic animals hung from the tops of rainforest trees, a desert full of nothing but dry ground and scarce water, anything. Even after... when I knew all the magic this place had, all its wonder, had gone with her. I still felt it: possibility. Still felt her. Today I just needed it to be one thing. I needed it to be safe. And it was, to some degree. There was a comfort in knowing a place so well that, even with my inability to see, I could sense every inch of it. I was grateful that in my sightless state nothing and no one could take it from me. That's how I know that here, now, possibility still lives.

***

It was strange. Walking through the park, able to tell where the swing set ended, and the trees began but not being able to see any of it. Not being able to smell the dirt or feel the breeze. Was it a dry day? Was the air warm enough to bake my skin? Was the sky thick with darkness or were there stars dotted about? These were the things I wondered. The things I missed.

My imagined body lay shaded beneath the huge oak tree, my tree, and I pretended, for a moment, that I could see the branches. Could watch them wiggle to and fro, shaking the leaves. I stopped. It hurt to imagine.

I wanted to sigh but I couldn't. I wanted to feel my knuckles crack beneath the weight of my palm, I wanted to see me. To touch my face, to feel my hair tickle my cheeks. I wanted to swallow back the sadness, but even that wasn't allowed. So, I focused instead on him. Tried to sense what he was feeling. It was still there, all of it — his anger, his loneliness, the bruises — I could feel it all only weaker. It had gotten weaker every moment since he said those words, *"I don't want you."* Since he felt them. I sensed him less. It didn't matter, though. I knew what I had to do. I just had to be patient. I had to wait for him to drop his guard, to dream. That's where he wanted me. Where it was okay to be himself, to be unusual, to let unusual things happen. I just had to wait.

***

The leaves were the first things I saw. The deep, dark greens before the sky came in, even deeper and darker, forming around it. Just a long, endless stretch of black, emitting a steady stream of rain. The branches were barely visible, yet exactly as I'd pictured them. He was dreaming, he was dreaming my park. I fixed my eyes on the rusty swing set. Drops of rain dotted all about it. The bench. My bench, cold looking and wet. Damp, decaying leaves had fixed themselves to my wooden bench. I didn't like that. I got it in my head to brush away the dead foliage to cleanse it... but my hand. I could see my hand. It was in front of me, pale and freckly, wriggling, aiming for the leaves so far ahead that I couldn't have reached them if I'd tried. I stood up, amazed that I could stand, that I had legs to stand with. Longish, slender legs. I felt a choke of emotion reach my throat. He had never dreamt like this before. He had never allowed me to be so real. My fingers fumbled to catch the aching in my throat but caught something else on the way. They slipped through my ice-blonde hair, the inky, jet-black tips strong against the near white. An unfamiliar silvery mist weaved its way between the strands. It rippled through each one, the hazy glow outlining even my body. I could see me. Not as I was, I was ghostly and pale and faint, but I could still see me. Better yet, I could feel me. I was aware of my agile limbs, could feel the muscles in my body warm and springy. I could move my joints, bite my lips. I could even run my tongue along the black metallic hoop that pierced its supple flesh. We weren't in his dream, I knew this, I was certain… but alive? It was almost too painful to hope. I tried in vain to shove every tiny ounce of my optimism back into the empty black, negative hole that constantly swirled inside of me as I prepared to test out how alive I really was. I pushed aside the heaviness that filled me and headed for the bench. I threw my leg back and kicked. I chewed my lip throughout the millisecond of a wait, not realising how much anxiety a person could go through in such a short space of time. It shone through, my leg, casting a bright hazy shine on the greenish mould that coated the dull wood. A stinging sensation shot through me. Not a physical pain, I was bruised on the inside. Cut by disappointment, but it was only fleeting. I was too grateful, too overwhelmed, to hold on to any bitterness. I was **here**, really here. I felt reawakened, somehow. Never before had I looked so close to corporeal. Even when I was with Luke, I'd never looked so… so real. I couldn't help thinking this place played a part in things and her, always her.

I spun around, laughing to myself. I was laughing. Happiness raced through me so exuberantly that when that sudden pained voice yelled, it shocked me, and I stumbled. It pierced through my joy like a sharp knife cutting flesh, throwing my emotions off balance. A heart-wrenching cry, full of anguish and pain. It screamed at the air.

'Where are you?' and I froze, swallowing against the sharp burst of emotional agony. He was there…

Chapter 11

The drizzling rain had turned into a steady cold shower. Damp clothes clung to my shivering body. My socks were drenched and muddied, and I was covered in goose pimples. Hair stuck to my face and I was completely out of breath from the sprinted journey I had made here. In all respects I should've been feeling completely stupid, especially considering what I was here to do, but I didn't. I was just desperate.

'Hey,' I screamed hoping for some kind of answer. That familiar warmth hung in the atmosphere and I knew, or at least I felt, like I was on the right track.

'Hey,' I tried again. Nothing.

I kicked the dirt and screamed. This was crazy. After all the energy I'd spent trying to force her out of my mind, out of existence, now I was looking for her. I punched the palm of my hand repeatedly and grasped my hair, feeling the nerves with every tug.

'Are you there?' There was no response.

Each drop of rain felt thicker, heavier against my body, but I wasn't giving up. Not yet, I had nothing to lose but my sanity. I spoke again, softly this time.

'I... I figured you must be here, I mean... this is the only place I can't get rid of you.'

That felt like the wrong thing to say to someone you wanted so desperately to come back, so I tried again.

'I just meant that this is the only place where I still feel you. Everywhere else you pretty much stay away from now, but not here.'

Still no one spoke. I sighed deeply, my nails scraping at my sodden scalp.

'Look, I know I told you that I didn't... didn't want you... but I was just freaked out. Can't you understand that? I mean, I don't even know who or what you are...' Still no response. I shook my head, feeling beyond stupid, humiliation bubbling up as though it were a delayed emotion. I stared down at my wet, soiled socks and laughed. I was pathetic.

'This was such a mistake,' I whispered.

I'd turned to walk away when a warmth rushed over me, rushed through me. It was so intense, more powerful than I'd ever remembered it being. I smiled a little.

'So, you are here,' I said feeling more hope than I knew I was capable of.

'Can you talk?' I waited patiently.

Maybe she couldn't, and if that were the case then I'd have to think of another way to commun—

'I don't know,' the voice that answered was quiet; shy, yet loud enough to burst apart my train of thought.

I laughed.

'That's funny why? Believe it or not, I haven't exactly had much of a chance to speak to the living, what with me being dead and all.'

Her tone was sharp and bitter. It put an end to my laughter, paving the way for shock.

'So... you're what? A ghost?'

'I don't really know,' she said, her words were soft and sweet and vulnerable but at the same time there was an edge to them. A hardness that could only have been shaped through years of intense emotional pain. I recognised it.

'I mean I guess so, sort of. I think maybe more spirit than ghost. If I was a ghost, you'd be able to see me, right?'

A smile pulled at the corner of my lips and I shrugged. What did I know?

The space between us was awfully quiet. I gripped and un-gripped the sludgy grass with my toes, feeling awkward; what was I meant to say? I'd been so desperate to come here, to be in her presence. I had wanted her companionship, needed it more than I needed anything in my life; more than food, more than air. I'd needed her, and now that she was here, with me, I didn't know what I was meant to say. The wind roared around us, replacing the silence, and I cracked my knuckles trying to think of something significant to talk about.

'Why are you here?' she asked, her voice breaking through the silent chasm. 'I thought you didn't *need* me.'

I briefly thought back to the night I'd said those words and my cheeks flushed brightly.

'I'm sorry about that,' I mumbled. 'Did I upset you?'

Silence lingered once more; it was hard to tell what she was thinking.

'It's cool. Whatever. No one's crying about it.'

I scoffed a small laugh, 'Yeah, because that would be so uncool at… at,' I stopped. 'How old *are* you?' I asked.

'Seventeen.'

My forehead wrinkled and I bit the inside of my lip.

'You're only seventeen?' I choked.

'Yeah, so. And what are you, like fifty?' she snapped.

I shook my head.

'Sorry it's just… I just meant… you know… 'cause you're… dead. You're a year younger than me and you're dead.' It was sad.

'Oh,' she said. Just like that, flat and in a breathy sort of voice laced with embarrassment. 'Yeah well, that did kinda suck.'

'How long ago, did you…' I paused awkwardly.

'Die?' she said, and I nodded in response. 'I don't know. Time is kind of hard to follow here. It was January though, the 12th I think. What's the date now.'

'February 19th.' There was a brief silence, a pause for reflection I guess because when she spoke again it was with a tone of sobering surprise.

'A little over five weeks. Feels like so much longer.'

'How did it happen?' I swallowed. 'How did you die?'

'I don't want to talk about it,' she snapped, as if the conversation was suddenly too overwhelming for her.

'Sorry,' I scraped my heel against the floor. 'I didn't mean to upset you.'

'I'm *not* upset okay.'

'*Okay…*'

I went quiet. Her heated tone had been enough to silence wild animals, and I didn't know what to say after that. I wasn't any good with alive girls, let alone with dead ones.

'It's embarrassing, all right?'

Maybe it was the nerves or something, but I burst out laughing then.

'Well I'm definitely not telling you now,' she said scornfully.

'I'm sorry,' I bit back another snigger. 'Look, you don't have to tell me if you don't want to, but if you do…'

'If I do then what?'

I hesitated. 'Then… I'll tell you why I'm here.'

There was a long pause, and I guessed she was trying to work out whether or not it was a fair, or maybe she was trying to gather up enough courage to tell her story. I couldn't tell which.

'Fine,' she finally said. 'It was death by coffee table.'

I arched an eyebrow.

'I tripped over an iron cord, banged my head on the glass table and died. The end. Are you happy now?'

It probably wasn't even that funny, in fact it probably wasn't funny at all, but all the same I laughed so much that tears rolled down my face.

'That's right, mock the dead girl,' she spat.

'I'm sorry,' I garbled for the millionth time. 'I'm so… sorry,' I choked, trying to regain control of my body.

'Have you finished?' she asked bitterly.

I cleared my throat and set my face as straight as I could manage.

'Yes,' I said still smirking.

'Good, because it's your turn.'

***

He stood there for a while, not speaking, the rain continuing to lash down on his pale white skin. He trembled from head to toe in his dirty white socks and his thin, long-sleeved shirt. He looked pitiful, but I didn't pity him. Not right now. Not at this moment. Not after he'd laughed at me.

'Go on then,' I goaded. 'What drove you out here in the middle of this thundering rain to come and spend some quality time with the *dead goth*? After all, I'm just a figment of your imagination, aren't I? Couldn't you have just conjured me up in your bedroom? It would've been a lot *comfier* for you.'

My words sounded harsh; they were meant to. He shifted his feet uncomfortably. His lips trembled every time he tried to start a sentence and failed.

'I thought...' he eventually mumbled, 'I thought you weren't real. That I was crazy or something.'

'Maybe you were right,' I jeered, 'Maybe you are crazy.'

It was a low blow; going for his sanity was like picking at an open, infected wound, but he'd picked at mine, so he deserved it. He chewed his lip again, his teeth digging into soft flesh as though he were in deep, painful thought. Miserable green eyes searched the evening's darkness, and I started to feel bad. He must've had a real reason to be standing there in the ice-cold wind and rain. In fact, I knew he did. I felt it much more strongly than I had before. Felt him.

'You're not crazy,' I sighed, the words rushing out of my mouth like a begrudged apology.

'Yeah right,' he muttered softly.

'You're not,' I said firmly. 'And you can tell me what's on your mind you know. I promise not to laugh.'

A nervous knot twisted his stomach. The pity I had tried to suppress welled up inside of me. Still he said nothing.

'Does it make you uncomfortable?' I asked, and a puzzled look swept across his face.

'Communing with the dead,' I teased in a haunting voice.

His laugh was fleeting this time but still present. 'A little.'

'Well, if it helps... just think of me as your kind of... guardian angel, here to listen and crap like that.'

I was trying to make light of the situation for him, to make him feel a little more at ease, but that was as unnatural to me as breathing now was. Still he remained frustratingly mute, and my pity was slowly wearing thin.

'Well, it's better than trying to wrap your head around talking to the dead isn't it?' I snapped. He paused, looking directly at me, and for a brief moment I thought he really was. Looking at me instead of through me, until he threw his head back and gave an exasperated half-laugh.

'How about, gothic angel?' He said through fits of chuckles.

67

'What?'

'Well you said you were a goth, right? So how about gothic angel, you know, as oppose to your everyday guardian variety?'

Gothic angel I mused to myself, the words sent a butterfly-ish tingle through me. As though this title somehow made me more...real.

'I like it.' I smiled a smile he'd never see. Still, he smiled back, his eyes intently locked in my direction.

'So,' he slumped down on to the muddy grass, 'what now?'

'How about you start with what happened to your shoes,' I teased, and his laugh was buoyant this time, filling the evening air.

Chapter 12

19th February

Dear Journal,

I should really take a shower. I need one, but I don't want to. I want tonight to feel real. As real as the dirt between my toes (because there is a shedload of dirt between my toes, muddy gunk and crap). As real as clammy skin and wet hair. I want it all to stay that way. Untouched. So that when I start to think I've lost it again, start to think I'm making things up, the dirt and the shivers will prove she exists, and I won't be crazy.

I can't believe she's real. Is she real? Dirt, remember? Dirt. I really hope I'm not insane. I really don't want to be the unstable guy who hears voices, but if I am let me stay that way just a little bit longer. Let me breathe in all the crazy, because at least with her I feel normal. Whatever that is.

I could've stayed with her all night. Just talking. It's been so long since I've spoken to anyone for longer than five minutes let alone an hour, but I did, and it was easy. So easy.

She didn't follow me home and I didn't ask her to. ~~I should've asked her to.~~

I feel stupid for not climbing through the window when I got back. I wanted to. My body itched for it, literally itched. Arms and legs jerking when I got to the front door like they were screaming at me, *IDIOT! GO THE OTHER WAY!!!* I couldn't though. Not tonight. Physically I wasn't up to it. The cold made my muscles stiff and the bruising on my stomach was far too fresh for me to go scrapping it against the window ledge. So, I knocked on the door. Urggh. But when I saw her face, I wished I'd scraped it all off trying. Anything was better than the *'oh baby, I was so worried about you,'* bit that Mae liked to do when she was ignoring the truth staring her in her stupid face. Nick had fed her some lie about me getting into a fight at college and she'd believed him!!!?? It doesn't even sound remotely true, but she'd lapped it up like a stupid dog licking its own vomit. Still, it wasn't all bad. I definitely loved watching his head almost explode when I denied it. Just point blank said 'nope.' I thought he was going to burst a capillary in his brain the way his temple swelled up. It was a beautiful moment. His bugged-out eyes, Mae's confused ones. I let him grind his teeth first. Then I let him furrow his brow so deeply it looked like he'd grown a new forehead. She looked at him and then at me. I waited long enough for him to panic before I explained. I told Mae that he'd gotten it wrong, that it'd been some kids from another college. That way she wouldn't turn up, shouting the odds just to make herself feel like a useful mother, instead of the failure that she is.

He would've hit me if he could.

I'd have given anything to tell her the truth. To drop him right in it, but she'd never have believed me, and I'd only earn myself a nice new black and blue, so I let it go.

She tried to do more of the mother thing, talking about wet clothes and catching my death. I couldn't get that lucky. I would've haunted them both for the rest of their lives, now that I knew how the afterlife worked.

Mae talked about calling the police, but Nick put a stop to that. Told her she was overreacting and that she should let it go and she gave in, just like that. Typical. I was so angry, but the thing that really made my skin crawl, more than the guilty concern, more than the fake pity, was when she tried to get all motherly with me. Stroking *his* mark on *my* face and biting her lip in 'concern.' I couldn't stand it. So, I shook her off.

If she chooses to believe every word coming out of his mouth then I have nothing to say to her, and she has nothing to offer me. Not even her crap version of a mother's love.

It's… weird. It's completely and utterly bizarre. I can't see her, touch her, hear her, I can't even feel the warmth. But just to know that she exists outside of my mind… it's comforting. She's comforting. This *gothic angel*. It's kinda nice… to know there's someone on my side.

I Should have asked her to come back with me. Why didn't I? ~~Because I'm a wimp.~~ It's not like I didn't want to, but I ~~couldn't~~ wouldn't. So, I left her there, in the park.

I wonder if she's lonely... Do the dead get lonely?

It's strange. I felt more at home with her, there, than I do with them in this house. A house that I've lived in most of my life. Weird right? I dunno. At least I have my room.

I really should shower.

Chapter 13

The wind was bitter and the rain hard; I could feel it on his skin. The wetness striking his neck as he trudged away from me. I ran a hand down the back of mine, feeling it. The rain.

I sat, I stood, I paced. I dangled my legs on the swing, back and forth, before standing again. Moving, squirming. I didn't know if it was helping me to process any of this better but I sure as hell couldn't stop. Or could I? I tried. I planted my feet as firmly as I could and let the thoughts free flow through me, one after the other.

'Fact.' I spoke aloud, the sound of my voice whipping butterflies up and around my ghost of my stomach. 'I exist because he *believes in me*. What a load of crap.'

I took to pacing again. Stillness was overrated. I tried to kick the clumps of gooey, muddy grass Luke had ripped from the ground earlier, and failed.

'Urrrgh,' I grunted, and then smiled a little because I couldn't get enough of the sounds I could make. Until the reality hit, chipping at my joy. When he didn't believe in me, I was less than a whisper, and now that he'd accepted the reality of the un-dead spirit girl I've been, what…? Revived? Now I can see, even without him here. I can speak, I have something that resembles a body. I am, for all intents and purposes, alive… ish. I gawked at the actuality of my situation.

What a joke. How fair is that? I sighed heavily and the sound enveloped me.

I felt like a fictional character straight out of a Disney movie. Like somebody had plonked me right in the middle of Pinocchio's 'real boy' act. But what was the alternative? I thought about the swirl, the grey matter, a place I sometimes retreat to when there's nowhere else left to be or when I have no choice. When the pull becomes so strong, I can't ignore it. I closed my eyes briefly. I could feel it now… calling. Far from the light that's promised to the dead. Nothing like the welcoming glow that's supposed to bathe you in its wholeness, to wash away all fear and uncertainty. It was not like that at all. Those people, the ones who talk about death as being free, were one of two things: liars or idiots. Because there is no light. Not for me anyway. Not even a heavenly flicker to guide my way. Just this, a swirling mist of energy. That… and now him. Laced to my emotions, I can't disconnect.

I flexed and un-flexed my hands, an old habit of mine reserved for when I really felt uneasy. The light of the moon caught the freckles on my pale fingers, and I tried to ignore the excitement that caused my non-existent stomach to lurch wildly. It was wrong to feel this way. It had to be wrong. My existence was tethered to a hormonal teenager, not permanent.

'I only exist as long as he still believes I exist,' I mumbled the words firmly to myself, pretending that I was only saying them to solidify this fact in my mind, when really, I just wanted to hear myself speak. Soft, delicate tones reiterated again and again. I'd hated my voice when I was alive. It always betrayed my emotions. No matter how sincere my words sounded, it always gave away my true feelings. "More obvious than a blush," my mum would say. So, most of the time I kept quiet. If I didn't speak, she wouldn't know, no one would. But now… now I all I want to do is scream and shout and speak.

Stop, I told myself. Think. What if he changed his mind? Decided I don't exist after all? Or that he no longer needs me? It could all be snatched away at any second: but I couldn't stop. I couldn't even pause my happiness.

I could feel him. His emotions had a separate identity from my own, but still they lived in me, flowing like blood. *My* life source. It was fear mixed up with wonderment and desperation. He needed me, almost as much as I needed him and I guess… as long as that fact was true, I was safe.

Chapter 14
Monday, 1st March

'G, Luke, G.'

'What?' Crap, I'd lost focus. I'd lost focus and now she was winning.

'G, as in *I spy with my little eye something beginning with G*?'

I starred at her – or rather in the direction of her voice - in mock confusion.

'Urrrgh, you're *so* bad at this,' she teased, 'the worst. It's a stupid game of I Spy, how hard can it be? I've beaten you three times already and I'm dead.'

I flashed a grin. 'Exactly,' I said, drumming the ground with my fingers, 'un-dead advantage. How do I know you're not reading my thoughts or that you haven't mentally catalogued every aspect of this park?'

'I'm a spirit, you idiot, not a superhero. I can't tap into your mind, *moron*, and I have better things to do with my undead hours than to waste them itemising the park just to beat you at a game of I Spy. Especially when you naturally suck as it is.'

I barked out a laugh and rolled over on to my stomach tucking my hair behind my ears.

'What's so funny?'

'You are. Pretending that you can't read my mind, yet somehow you mysteriously know exactly how I feel the moment I feel it.'

She snarled, 'The keyword there is *feel*, I "feel." I don't know what's on your mind and I don't want to.'

'So, you honestly expect me to believe you have no control over this *sharing my feelings* thing?'

'I don't do it on purpose,' she said, her voice small and quiet with embarrassment.

'*Sure,*' I teased thickly, as I tore up grass from the un-nurtured ground, 'I bet you're like those obsessive stalkers that go around breaking into bedrooms and prying into diaries, except you specialise in mind invasions.'

I was just messing around, but at that moment I could tell I'd hit a nerve. It had been almost two weeks and already, I'd gotten pretty good at reading the signs. The grinding teeth, the cracking of her knuckles and her tone: slow and icy, each word emphasised in a clipped manor.

'I already told you, you self-obsessed jerk, that I don't go around prying into your mind like some weird crazy dead stalker.'

I tried to apologise but she cut me off.

'It's not my fault that, because you practically leak emotions, whatever weird connection we share has me picking up your feelings like a radio signal. Maybe, if you reigned it in a little, weren't so sensitive about *every tiny thing,* then I wouldn't be able to read them so easily.'

That was it. She may have been angry, but I was seeing red.

'Leak emotions!' I hissed. 'Leak emotions?'

'That's what I said,' she spat, though her tone was laced with remorse, remorse I wasn't willing to accept.

'This coming from the *clingy* spirit who refuses to move on. What's keeping you here? Huh Angel? *Afraid of the other side?*' You must be, 'cause I sure as hell would be fine without you!'

There was silence, but the energy in the air screamed hostile and tense. I snatched my rucksack from the ground and swung it over my shoulder along with my jacket.

'Have a great afternoon hanging by yourself,' I growled.

I stormed towards the park entrance, wrenched the gate open as far it would go and marched off down the street. Her words rattled through my mind. *Sensitive! Self-obsessed?* How dare she! Where did she get off talking to me like that? I kicked the stones on the pavement, watching them fly off angrily into different directions. Sensitive! I'm sensitive? She was the sensitive one. I make one harmless, innocent joke and she's flies off the handle like a mad woman. Clearly unstable. I kicked another cluster and listened to them ping viciously off various objects. What I'd said hadn't even been that bad... had it? The memory of my words flooded my mind, 'obsessive stalker,' 'prying into diaries.' I rounded the corner to my house just as the wave of guilt engulfed me. I ran my tongue along the back of my teeth and then sighed. Fine, I admitted to myself, maybe I was wrong… a little, but what she'd said had been so much worse. That eased my guilt a bit. It made it easier for me to latch on to the justified anger that seemed intent on making room for regret.

I had been so preoccupied with our latest fight that I hadn't really realised I'd made it into my house until my mother's face was staring back at me.

'Hey Luke.'

'Mae.'

I flung my jacket on to the coat rack and dodged round her, making my way up the stairs.

'Luke I—'

'Not now,' I said shaking my head dismissively. She lingered at the bottom for a moment before disappearing into the living room. A part of my brain wondered what she wanted, but the more predominate part was pounding molten blood angrily around its vessels.

I stepped through the door to my room, a wave of warmth entangled itself around my body like an inward hug, corrupting my emotions. I could feel my fury reluctantly subsiding and I knew I wasn't alone.

'What do *you* want?' I attempted a scowl, but the guilt swept through me and I struggled to keep my voice cold.

'I'm sorry too,' she said.

'I didn't apologise to you,' I mumble, harshly.

'You felt it, so it kinda counts.'

I sighed, feeling deeply irritated. She was right, why fight it? Giving up on my rage, I slumped heavily on to my bed.

'Hey, watch where you're sitting,' she yelped, and I stumbled, landing on the carpet. She let out a booming laugh and a slight grin crept on to the corner of my mouth.

'You're such a jerk, Angel, you know that?' She said nothing, but I imagined that a smug smile was plastered on to her face.

'Nice room,' she said, as I pulled myself up from the ground and tentatively plonked myself on to the dipping mattress.

'Thanks,' I shrugged back, feeling pricks of nerves attacking my body. This was the first time she'd been here. In fact, it was the first time anyone (other than Mae and Nick) had been in my room. What made me even more nervous was the fact that I had no idea where she stood or what she was looking at. My hands became hot and clammy as awkwardness set in.

'Wicked paintings,' she gasped, and I thought… was she impressed? No. Sarcasm. Definitely sarcasm. I said nothing but continuously dried my hands on my bed sheets.

'This one's beautiful, the dove with the broken wing.' Was she being honest or just nice? I couldn't figure it out. Silence followed and I desperately wondered what she was really thinking.

'Oh, wait there's something written at the bottom,' I held my breath as she read aloud, '*Peace, cracked, fractured, broken. Weep.* That's dark. Poetic.'

'I guess,' I mumbled.

'Wow,' she exclaimed, and my heart thumped wildly in my chest. 'Are those manga comic strips?'

'You know manga?'

'I studied Japanese. Kinda of became obsessed with the culture starting with manga.'

'Seriously? I love Japanese art — anime, manga comic strips — I even started my ow…' I stopped and hesitantly bit my lip till it bled a little, hoping she hadn't worked out my unfinished sentence.

'You've made your own manga comic strip,' her voice excitedly climbed up a decibel and I cursed inwardly.

'Yeah but it's not cool. It's not even finish—'

'Can I see it?' From the sensitive tone she used I could tell that she could feel my nerves running skittishly through my body.

I swallowed hard, knowing she could feel that too, along with the dryness of my mouth and the tight knot in my stomach. Why did we have to be so connected? With a lump growing in my throat I dragged my sketchbook from underneath my bed. I fumbled with the latch and flicked straight to the pages of Goth Kid (no need for her to see the rest). I held the book tightly to my chest for a moment trying to mentally prepare myself. I blew out a long slow breath, hoping to steady the internal jitters, when a tap at the door made me jump. The leather-bound sketchbook slid to the ground, landing face down on the rug. I left it there just as it was and stood up.

'Come in,' I said relief washing through me.

'Coward,' she teased when she felt my heart rate ease.

'Yeah, yeah,' I muttered low under my breath, but Mae caught the hushed tones.

'What's that honey?'

'Nothing. What's up?' She looked towards her feet and shuffled awkwardly forward.

Angel's warmth hovered around the overturned book.

'Fine I'll just peek for myself.'

I smirked at her pointless threat. Like she could.

'What's going on?' Mae asked, wrinkling her brow in confused amusement.

'Nothing, nothing,' I insisted, shaking my head.

'Damn it,' Angel cursed, and I tried desperately to stifle a snigger. Mae wasn't fooled.

'Ooo-kay, well, I'm glad you're in a good mood because I wanted to ask you something?'

I was only half paying attention; it was difficult to concentrate on Mae's words when Angel was muttering incessantly behind my back, cursing her lack of a body.

'Luke.'

'Yeah, sorry, I... I guess I'm a little distracted.'

'By what?'

'By the voices in your head,' Angel jeered; it was so hard not to laugh.

'By... by... just stuff that happened at college today, Mae, it's nothing.'

I hoped that paper-thin excuse would be enough to pacify her, at least for the moment.

'I hope you know as soon as your mum goes, I'm going to make you show me that sketchbook.'

'Fat chance,' I wanted to say, but I ignored her. 'What was it you wanted to ask, Mae?'

'Well…' she was hesitant, I hadn't noticed it before, but she was. It wasn't just her tone of voice; it was the way she held herself too. Like a shy little girl slumping her body and constantly twisting her overgrown fringe.

'I was just wondering if maybe you'd like to come to dinner tonight with me… and Nick.'

Her deep blue eyes scoped the room before resting on my face. I felt my nose pull up before I swallowed deeply.

'Sure.'

'Really?' she let go of her lock of hair and straightened up to stare me square in the face. 'You'll… you'll come?'

The idea of having dinner with her and Nick was sickening, but not as sickening as the thought of sharing my personal artwork with someone for the first time. Besides, more often than not Nick cancelled on Mae so it would probably end up being just the two of us. Not the best situation but, under the circumstances, not the worst.

'Yeah… sure.'

She chuckled uncertainly. Mae didn't understand my motives — my willingness was explicitly out of character — but Angel definitely did.

'You absolute coward.' She laughed in disbelief. 'You'd actually have dinner with *them* to avoid showing me your art?'

'Really, you're sure?' Mae asked again as if to double-check her hearing.

'Yes,' my response was firm, answering them both. 'I mean I've got to eat so, dinner sounds like the perfect solution.'

'Solution?'

'I meant, idea. It sounds like a perfect idea.'

Mae pulled up one eyebrow followed swiftly by the next. 'Okay, well I'm just about ready to leave. Nick's going to meet us there.'

'Cool, I'll follow you down.' I headed towards the door with Mae, a smug smile stretched across my face.

'I cannot believe you'd be *so* pathetic,' Angel sulked.

I turned around, a look of mock innocence playing on my features, and gave half a wave before shutting the door.

***

Something's wrong. Anger. Bitter, red raw anger was charging uncomfortably through me. Anger so aggressive, so forceful, it almost overruled my own emotions. It wrapped itself around something too. Something deep-seated that breathed inside of me. Fear? It was fear. Fear so engulfed by a passionate fury it was almost impossible to sieve out, but there it was, alive and rooted to the core, but there was more. Betrayal. So thick and strong it held both fear and anger in its grasp. I could scarcely find my own emotions, much less separate them from his; it was almost as if they had been replaced. Almost, but not quite. Pangs of worry and pity would well up every so often before disappearing into the hurricane of rage. I lowered myself on to his bed and rubbed my head. It felt as though it would split, but the pain was not mine. My chest heaved, fighting back angry sobs; again, not mine but his, Luke's.

The time ticked slowly by, one hour, two, three… where was he? Surely if he was this furious, he should be back by now. Maybe he'd want to talk, maybe not, but what if he did? Would he know to find me here or would he think I'd gone back 'home' to the park? I was just debating whether or not I should go and find out when the front door opened. A murmur of voices buzzed downstairs, but I couldn't make out any of the words. The conversation, though brief, sounded strained at best, but nowhere near as hostile as I was feeling. Footsteps pounded the stairs and the door opened slowly. Luke sank through it, his pale face looking harassed. He closed the door lightly as I sat up; his panicked, maddened eyes searched the room. He walked slowly forward, fists clenched, wandering as though seeking me out through the warmth. I said nothing. I couldn't think of a single thing to say. He joined me standing next to the bed, his body taut, his face tense yet drawn.

A whispered snarl escaped his mouth. 'Married,' he said, 'they're getting married.'

Chapter 15
Thursday, 18th March

My world felt grey again over the next couple of weeks. Thick ashen grey with flashes of red. The news of Mae marrying *him* had left my stomach in taut angry knots. The slightest reminder had me clutching my stomach till the skin bruised purple. So, I tried to bury those thoughts somewhere deep in the back of my mind. Tried to ignore Mae's nauseating singing, the calls she made to spread the news and him, sprawled all over the couch, his arrogant, loathsome face taunting me. Since the night I found out — when she lay silently next to me in the dark, comforting me — Angel hadn't left my side. She was there during the day when I went to college and at night when sleep eluded me. She called it *charity work*.

'Just making sure you don't fall off the deep end, that's all. I know how melodramatic you can be when you don't get your way,' she'd teased.

I had tried to throw a pillow at her then, but apparently, I missed, or so she said.

Having Angel with me was the only good thing I had going. Her energy was so calm, but even with her near I couldn't silence my rage. My body felt tense, like one big ball of angry nerves, but still I was glad she was there, with me. I mean, if I felt *this* livid with her around, I couldn't imagine how I'd feel if she'd left. A pang of panic whipped my stomach into bits at the thought of it and she was right beside me in full force, her calming essence highly concentrated.

'What's with you today?'

I shrugged.

'Your emotions are all over the place. I can't pinpoint your mood.'

'Good,' I said as flatly as I felt.

She sighed and I continued tapping at the table with my pencil. I exhaled, feeling bored. Mr Taylor's voice hovered somewhere in the near distance, but English was far from my mind. I stared out of the window looking for something to distract me, something other than my seething thoughts, something pleasant, when the reflection on the glass caught my eye. A new feeling sprang up inside of me, unsettling my nerves. My cheeks grew warm and my tongue became unbearably dry. Lucile. She was sitting in a different seat today, one that allowed me to see her reflection on the window beside me. My heart skipped a beat as she playfully twisted her lip between her index finger and thumb. She looked amazing, completely breathtaking. Just as I was about to embark on a fantasy that featured only the two of us, Angel's voice sliced through my thoughts.

'Repeat after me,' she hissed irritably.

'What?' I muttered, sounding both annoyed and extremely confused.

'I'm sorry, Mr Andrews, was I so boring that you found even paying attention to my question labouring?'

I stared at Mr Taylor's harsh, slender face, panic rising. He sneered back at me. I didn't have to look around to know that all eyes were on me; my heart clattered nervously.

Angel huffed, 'Just say, sensuality and youth are two predominant themes that seem to intertwine.'

I swallowed with difficulty and spoke. 'No sir...' my throat was still dry and my voice cracked slightly because of it. 'I was just... just thinking that... um...' I repeated Angel's words, the falsity like a brick in my throat. There was no way I'd pulled that off, my voice was so uncertain, so shaky, he'd definitely see through that.

'Interesting,' he drawled. 'Can you elaborate?'

Great! Of course. Make me suffer why don't you? A pained look spread across my face — one I hoped would pass for deep intellectual reflection — as I searched for the answer.

'You weren't listening at all, were you?' Angel snapped.

'Quit having a go and help me!' I snapped, my voice barely above a whisper.

'Fine,' she huffed. 'We can see it in the Count's choice of victims. He seems to only select women; youth and attractiveness appear to be an important factor when deciding on a victim. For example, Lucy and Mina...'

She went on for a while, drying out my tongue, her answers full-bodied and thoughtful. She really sunk her teeth into the subtext, dissecting every last bit. I repeated everything she said, word for word, as it left her formless mouth.

'I believe that though their blood is enough to restore his youthful appearance,' she said, drawing to a close, 'their femininity and sensuality allows him to satisfy his *manly urges*,' I paused, cringing a little at her choice of words, but hurriedly continued before I lost her train of thought, 'making this necessary task pleasurable, and maybe imparting in him some of the softness and beauty he has lost in death.'

I took a breath. It was the longest I'd ever spoken in one of Mr Taylor's classes. Embarrassed, I turned from him, accidently catching Lucile's eye before looking down at my desk. Was that a smile?

'Hmmm.' Taylor grunted. He smacked his lips together in annoyance while shooting me daggers.

'I suppose that's a... *feasible* interpretation.' His voice was strained as the words begrudgingly escaped his mouth through gritted, coffee-stained teeth.

'Moving on.'

My heart rate slowed in relief.

'Feasible!' Angel scoffed, expelling a puff of air. 'Feasible my arse. That was spot on. Oh, and you're welcome by the way,' she added.

'What was the question?' I asked quietly, careful not to let my lips move much.

'To identify one of the main running themes in Bram Stoker's Dracula.'

'That's it?'

'Uh huh.'

'Well, did I really need to say *all* that?'

'Probably not, but I like the book. Plus, it's fun to show off. Besides,' she prodded me with her tone, 'it serves you right. Maybe next time you'll pay attention in class.'

I rolled my eyes, 'whatever, *Mum*.'

'You, ungrateful moron, a thank-you wouldn't go amiss.'

'Oh… thanks,' I was barely concentrating on her mini rant. I was too busy praying that Lucile's smile was not a hallucination brought on by my overactive, panicked mind, or a cool side-effect of pressure.

'What is up with you today?' Angel asked again.

'Nothing,' I lied. 'Just bored I guess.' I said, making sure to cover my lips with my hands as I whispered my words.

'Oh *really?* 'Cause your overactive heart is pounding like you're crushing on someone.'

I couldn't help myself. Before she'd even finished speaking, I'd snuck in a couple of looks at Lucile and was now wishing I hadn't.

'*Oh please,*' Angel laughed, '*that's* who you've got a thing for?'

'Shut. Up.' I urged fiercely as embarrassment clung to my skin, spreading like a warm prickly fire.

'Hey, no judgement here,' she sniggered. 'She's pretty… not "*wow*" but… pretty.'

'Have you finished yet?' I sneered.

'Oh, calm down, will you? It's not like anyone else can hear me but you.'

'Lucky me,' I said, each word dripping with sarcasm.

'I think so.' Her mock cheeriness was grating on me.

The bell rang, signalling the end of the class. With one lazy sweep of the arm, I brushed my things into my bag and headed for the door. I stopped when I reached the entrance and hesitated. Something didn't feel right. I felt… off somehow, empty. People eyed me suspiciously as they squeezed past.

'Angel?' I breathed her name barely above a whisper.

'You go on. I'll catch up with you soon.'

My palms began to sweat nervously as I stood blocking people's way. I ran them once through my hair and gripped the back, trying to steady this wave of irrational nausea. Where was she going? Was she going for good? No, she said she'd be back, but when?

'Is there a problem, Mr Andrews?' Mr Taylor's cold monotone voice drawled at me.

I shook my head.

'Just go,' urged Angel. 'I'll be back soon. Promise.'

My feet felt heavy as I shifted them. Like dead weight. I tried to steady my emotions; the last thing I wanted was to need her so much. This is ridiculous, I told myself. I don't *need* her. Sure, it's great when she's around, but I had survived before her and I could survive a couple of hours without her. I swallowed a thick gulp of saliva, feeling my chest progressively relaxing. It was a lie, but if it got my feet moving who cared.

***

The room felt hot. So hot I was suffocating in the heat and my skin, it prickled uncomfortably. I tried to crack my knuckles again, but after three or four successful attempts my joints were all cracked out. My throat, which felt as though it had swollen to twice its normal size, struggled and failed to swallow the lump that was glued to its muscles. Giving up on the lump and on my knuckles, I settled for picking at the wooden arm of the chair.

'Luke?' Dr Evans' attempt to adopt a soothing tone was doing nothing to calm my erratic nerves. 'You seem anxious,' he wheezed on. 'I'd like for you to try to say what's on your mind.'

I'd been doing a good job of separating my thoughts from my emotions, ignoring the reasons why my heartbeat was drumming in my ears, but his words made my thoughts come rushing back. I tried to hide from them, to force them back out, but they echoed loudly, shouting only three words at me: where is she? There had been no sign of Angel since English, and my peaceful denial had abandoned me for almost just as long. Panic had set in and rooted itself deeply like a weed. I bit my inner lip and chewed. Where was she? The park? Why was I here wasting my time with Dr Idiot when the only person who had ever been able to help me was probably there at the park, our park?

'If you feel unable to tell me what you're thinking, why not try to express how you *feel* instead.'

Angry, frustrated... alone. All of the usual things I felt when Angel was gone but I wasn't about to share that with *him*. Instead I sneered at the doctor from beneath my tangle of hair and ground my teeth.

'Luke...'

'What? What do you want from me? I *don't* want to talk.'

I shifted in my seat and directed my attention to the clock. Twenty to five, only twenty minutes left. Thank God. I turned back to pick at my chair and caught Dr Evans staring at me silently.

'What? You're not talking to me now? Did I offend you?'

A brief chuckle. 'Not at all, I'm just going to sit here and give you the space you need to work out whatever it is that you're feeling. And if you feel ready to speak to me, I will be here to listen.'

I eyed him suspiciously, was he for real? Was he actually going to sit there and do nothing, say nothing, for a whole twenty minutes? Did he expect me to stay there with him, in this awkward silence, for the remainder of our time when there wasn't even going to be the pretence of a two-way conversation? If he did, he was out of his mind. There was no way I was going to hang around when I could be in the park giving Angel a good grilling over where she'd been all day.

My muscles had barely tensed to stand when I felt a sudden warmth enter the room. My heart leapt, a little too much, as my panicky state subsided. I hadn't realised how stiff my face had been until the muscles relaxed. My relief must have been obvious, because Dr Evans gave me a look.

'So… what did I miss?' she asked playfully, and to Dr Evans' shock, I burst out laughing.

Chapter 16

'He thinks you're a nut job,' she teased, 'an absolute headcase.'

I gulped in the delicious cool air. Goosebumps were forming on the surface of my sticky skin, but I left my leather jacket hanging from my arm. The wind was sharp. Too sharp for spring, and I shivered frequently along the way back home but after spending an hour in Dr Evans' scorching room, I was grateful for the bitter sting.

'Did you see his face when you laughed? It's like he was on safari studying wild animals, waiting for their next unpredictable move.' She laughed vibrantly and so did I. My taut nerves still hadn't quite relaxed and the sensation felt weird in my chest, but I liked it. It made me feel... free.

'To be fair, that was probably the first time I've ever laughed around him.'

'I'm telling you, you freaked him out.'

I laughed a little more, recapturing the image of his broad, perplexed face in my head, but it didn't last long. 'Where have you been? I was out of my mind with worry!' I wanted to sound mad, but I was too grateful to have her back, too relieved.

'That's what you were worried about?' The surprise in her tone made me feel stupid. 'I kinda thought you were obsessing over some new worry or an old one, either way I didn't think you were still bothered about me leaving.'

My cheeks flushed red.

'I wasn't, I mean I d-didn't... *miss* you I just thought that maybe... something might have happened.'

'Like what?'

'I don't know?'

'You do know I'm dead, right?' She mocked.

'I kinda figured that one out,' I said matching her sarcastic tone.

'Well, newsflash, I can't get me any more dead so stop worrying.'

I threw a dirty look at the air and went back to my original question, 'So where'd you go?'

She was silent for a bit, so silent that if it wasn't for her palpable essence, I'd have thought she'd left again.

'Angel.'

'All right... let's... just say... inquiring minds wander, literally,' she chuckled, but I didn't. 'Fine. I'll tell you but don't get mad okay?' I stayed silent while she stalled.

'I followed Lucile for a few hours.' The words came out in a rush, but I caught each one.

'What!' My body jerked to a halt mid-step and I stumbled. 'Why? Why would you? Why?'

I'd meant to say more than that, but all sorts of emotions were clouding my thoughts. It was her turn to say nothing, but I could hear the sound of flicking nails, which I knew by now meant she was nervous. I took a steady breath as I tried to figure out which emotion was more important. Anger or excitement? Definitely anger.

'You're mad, aren't you?' she mumbled innocently.

'You sure about that?' I asked, my tone bitter.

'You're angry, but not a lot. You want to be angrier than you actually are but curiosity keeps getting in the way. Plus... your... fists... are trembling,' her words trailed off as she sensed my growing rage. 'That was rhetorical wasn't it?'

'See, this is what I mean,' I growled.

'What?'

'You can't just go around invading someone's privacy like that.'

'But I already explained I can't tune you out.'

'And what about Lucile? Do you hear her thoughts? Are you connected to her as well?'

'Of course not. I listened in on her conversations.'

'Exactly. Invasion of privacy. Can't you see how wrong that is? It's perverse.'

'But...'

'She doesn't deserve that, Angel. You had no right.'

There was a long awkward silence and a couple walking their dog stopped to stare at me. I hadn't even thought about how this scene might look to others. An awkward-looking guy dressed head-to-toe in black having an argument with the street sign opposite him. I gave them a hostile smile and a wave, and they turned away pretty sharply, pretending not to have caught my eye.

'So, what are you saying? You don't want to know anything about Lucile?'

My stomach flipped excitedly. 'No,' I hissed heavily, hoping that my tone would somehow distract her from what I was truly feeling.

'Come on, don't you want to know what I found out?'

'No!' I barked, and a little girl riding her scooter skidded to a halt. Her dark slits of eyes looked up at me through her even darker hair and she hurriedly scooted off in the opposite direction.

'Great,' I mumbled.

'It's good information.'

'Urgh, I'm going home. *Don't* follow me.'

I stormed off down the street in a slightly pathetic, overly dramatic sort of way. I thought it might help to mask some of the curiosity that was slowly leaking in, messing with my anger. I should be angry, I knew that. What she'd done was wrong, *stalkerish* even, but I couldn't help wanting to know what Lucile could possibly have said to have kept Angel away from me for so long. As much as it killed me to admit it, I needed to know, but it was too late. Angel had left. I laughed under my breath. It surprised me that she'd really gone. Good, I thought. It's what I should want, what I *did* want, wasn't it? It was getting harder to convince myself.

I pulled out my keys and jammed them into the lock. Her being gone bothered me. Not in the same way it had before — I missed her a little, maybe even more than a little, but I knew she'd be back now, so I didn't worry. No, this time it was the burning need to know that made me desperate to be near her. Even though I wouldn't ask, just knowing that I could was somehow settling.

'Luke, is-s-s that you?' My mother's slurred words met me on the doorstep and I reluctantly dragged myself through. Anger whipped up inside me light, but present, and I wished Angel was back just a little more.

'Yeah,' I said dropping my things by the coat rack and poking my head round the living room door.

Half a dozen semi-drunk to drunk middle aged women, of various shapes and sizes, hung lazily over the furniture as if their spines suddenly had no purpose. Bridal magazines were spread out over the coffee table and a cluster of half-empty to empty bottles of wine stood next to them.

'You remember… m-m-my friends.'

I nodded apathetically and attempted a courteous smile.

'Hi,' they crooned, pretending not to be drunk. Mae stumbled towards me and threw her arms affectionately around my back, squeezing my shoulder.

'Isn't my boy so handsome?'

'Mae,' I hissed.

'What? He is, isn't he?'

There was an unconvincing mumble of agreement.

'He is. Really, if you just stripped all that black tat off his face…'

'Mae,' I growled, the anger whipping more viciously now.

'What? What?'

I shrugged her arms from my body and skulked out of the living room towards the kitchen, really craving Angel's presence.

I poured myself a glass of water and sat down at the breakfast counter. A headache was beginning to form at my temples. They beat slowly but painfully, and I felt a queasiness ripple through my stomach. My fingers reached for my forehead when something replaced them. A warmth, her warmth, rubbed gently at the throbbing lumps, easing the pain.

'Hey,' I murmured.

'Hey,' her voice was as gentle as her fingertips, caring. 'Rough homecoming?'

'How'd you…' anger suddenly whipped through me again. 'Were you listening in on my conversation?' The warmth slipped from my head.

'I couldn't help it, I was upstairs.'

'Do you have no boundaries? Isn't it enough that you know my every emotion? Now you want to know the cause too?'

'It's not like that, I… I'm sorry.' There was a lengthy pause. 'Do you want me to go?' she sounded a little sad.

'Yes. No. Stay.' There it was again. That burning need to know.

'Aha! See, I knew it,' she all but screamed triumphantly.

'What?' I feigned innocence.

'You do want to know. I can feel it, so don't pretend that you don't.'

'It's wrong,' I said feeling guilty.

'But you can't help how you feel, and I have the answers. Goooood answers.'

I kept quiet; my lips firmly pressed together.

'Look I promise it was nothing embarrassing or girly or even anything that you won't eventually find out. Come on,' I imagined her easy shrug. 'Besides, knowing might make this day suck a little less.'

I thought it over in my head. It would make me such a hypocrite, going on about invading privacy and then using it for my own gain, taking pleasure in Angel's gossip. It would be wrong. So wrong: But on the other hand, if it was going to be public knowledge soon, was I really doing anything *that* bad? I chewed my lip roughly.

'Okay,' I decided, 'but just this once. We don't do this ever again; do you hear me?'

'Okay.'

'I mean it. Never, ever again.' I spoke severely and, though my speech was said for her benefit, it felt like it was mostly for me.

'You're not a bad person.'

'Why don't you stop reading my emotions and just get on with it.'

'Gladly,' she peeped, and I could have sworn I heard the excited slapping and rubbing together of two palms.

'It was at the end of class, do you remember? Your insides were still all jittery, rippling around because of that *Lucile girl* — honestly it was making me a little sick.' I shot her a look. 'Sorry. Anyway, I focused in on her and her weirdo friends. At first, I just wanted to see what all the fuss was about — you know, why you're so embarrassingly desperate over her.' I shot her another look, which this time she ignored. 'It's like I said before, she's nice looking but only averagely so. I wasn't even *that* interested in their endlessly boring talk to begin with, but then her friend, the high-pitched squeaky one…

'Missy.'

She grunted in disgust. 'Yeah, that one. Hard as it is to believe, she actually said something interesting.'

My heart pounded rapidly the way it always did when I thought about Lucile. 'Go on,' I urged impatiently.

'Something about Lucile asking you out.' My stomach lurched eagerly as my heart tried to leap out of my chest.

Angel laughed, 'Get a grip. Even I knew she wasn't being serious.'

My heart recoiled back into place and squeezed itself a little painfully. Angel went on as though she'd felt nothing. I appreciated it.

'Anyway, who cares what she said. It's why that's important.'

'I don't follow.'

There was an ironic silence. '*Why* would someone like Missy pass a comment like that about the two of you?' she finally said. 'No offense, but it's odd. You barely make eye contact with Lucile.'

I wriggled uncomfortably on the spot. 'I don't know, why did she?'

'Well she was going on about you staring at Lucile like a perv—'

I cut her off. 'She said that? She called me a pervert?' A slither of dread ran through me, 'Did Lucile… laugh?'

'No,' Angel chuckled a bit (she was doing that a lot more often these days, laughing), 'but that's mainly because she didn't use those *exact* words. I ad-libbed.'

I scowled at her. 'Sorry,' she mumbled, adopting a more serious approach. 'She mentioned that you kept on staring at Lucile and that now that she was…'

Angel's speech came to an abrupt halt and I shifted anxiously in my seat.

'What? What did she say?'

'Luke, someone's at the door.' I swung myself around so quickly I that buckled in my seat.

'Mae,' her name came out high-pitched and strained.

Mae stumbled into the kitchen with her friend Janie in toe. They stared at me quizzically, eagerly, but neither said a word.

'We were… I mean *I* was… never mind.'

What was I going to say? 'Hey Mae, do you mind? You just interrupted a conversation I was having with my best friend. By the way, she's dead?' I bit my lip, that stupid feeling returning.

'Luke,' she began tentatively, 'Who...who were you talking to?'

'No one... just myself.' Normal, totally normal.

'Mmm hmmm. Honey... do you always ask yourself... q-q-questions?'

Janie sniggered and I swallowed slowly, shaking my head.

'N-n-no,' I stuttered 'I was just... trying to remember something that's all. Something that someone had said to me at college.' It sounded convincing enough to me, but Mae still looked unsure.

'But, sweetie... what were you looking at?'

'Looking at?'

'Yeah, when we got to the door... you uh...'

'You looked like a crazy person, love,' Janie cut in, biting down on each word to stop her from slurring. 'You were sitting on the stool and staring, at the biscuit tin like it was telling you the most fascinating story.'

Mae nodded and I felt a wave of irritation. She really would take anyone's side over mine, even a drunk Janie.

I leapt out of my seat and stalked towards them.

'You two are the only crazy people here,' I snarled. 'Maybe you should lay off the drink for the rest of the day. It's obviously making you both unstable.' I tapped the empty wine bottles clutched in my mother's hands and stared at her coldly.

'Come to think of it,' I added, 'I don't think it's fair to blame the drink. I mean hell,' I laughed bitterly, 'she's marrying a creep, and she definitely wasn't intoxicated then when she made that ridiculous decision.'

I shoved passed them both with the sound of Mae's dismayed, flapping lips rushing past my ears. Angel followed, not saying a word until I'd shut the door to my bedroom. She let out a sharp, high-pitched whistle.

'That was a little strong don't you think?'

'Whatever. What did Missy say?'

I threw myself on the bed and stared at the ceiling, a mountain of possibilities now crowding my head.

She continued; no encouragement necessary. 'She said now that Lucile was on the market, you'd make an excellent rebound guy; that you had classic rebound qualities.'

'What does that mean?'

She shook her head, 'I didn't get it either. I was so glad when she explained because if ever I needed *the idiot's guide for talking girl,* it was then.'

'Angel.'

'Oh, calm down, will you. From what I gathered it just means that you're the loyal type. You'd do all kinds of ridiculous lovesick things like, I don't know, put together a romantic playlist, buy her jewellery, all that sort of crap. Then when she was done with you — you know, emotionally healed and all that — she could just fling you away.'

My heart stopped momentarily as though someone held it still in a harsh grip, seconds later it felt like a flaccid balloon.

'Is that it? What you couldn't wait to tell me? Your big, exciting news — "Hey Luke not a chance in hell of getting a date with her but you could be her number one chew toy" — that's what you were dying to say?' I tried to keep my voice low so as not to arouse suspicion downstairs, but it was difficult.

'No, you idiot,' Angel scolded. 'I wasn't the one who said you didn't have a chance in hell, *remember.*' I said nothing, I was too busy sulking inside. 'In fact, I think you'd stand a pretty fair chance if she gave it to you, I mean, you're a decent guy.'

'Decent,' I scoffed, 'great.'

'I mean it Luke. You're kinda funny too when you're not being moody. She'd be pretty lucky to... you know *have you...* or whatever.'

'Thanks,' I sniffed sensing the awkwardness in the room. It was probably the nicest thing anyone had said to me in a long time.

'So what was the good news?'

'Weren't you listening? For you to be her rebound guy she'd have to be...' she paused, whether for dramatic effect or for me to fill in the blanks I didn't know, but I stayed silent.

'Single you idiot. She'd have to be single. How small is your brain?'

I ignored her dig. 'So, she's single. Big deal.' Although she hadn't announced it on our form class bulletin board, I'd kind of guessed she'd made that decision. I hadn't seen her and Shane together for weeks. So, what if it was official now, what difference did it make to my life?

'The big deal *is* that you can finally stop torturing us both with your nauseating longing for her and just go for it.'

I laughed idiotically. 'You think the only reason I haven't ask her out all this time was because she had a boyfriend? *She's Lucile Armstrong.*'

'You say that like I should stand in line for her autograph; she's just a girl.'

I sat bolt upright on my bed. 'No. Missy's *just a girl*. Lucile, she's… she's *the* girl.'

'You're going to have to explain that one to me because again, I don't speak female.'

I wanted to try again with that pillow.

The room was thick with silence. I knew that she was waiting for me to talk but it was hard. She was asking me to be open with her. Really open. Intimate details open, I'd never done that with anyone before, it scared me a little and she made allowances for my stalling.

When I finally spoke, my voice had crumbled into hushed, embarrassed tones: 'I guess it's because she's special,' I shrugged. 'I've never met anyone so attractive before and it's not just her looks.' I tingled thinking about her looks. 'It's everything. She's the only one who ever really smiles at me. Did you know that? It doesn't happen often and sometimes I think I've dreamt it, but when it does, when she smiles, she makes me feel like she's looking at something important. Something worth looking at. Like… I could be worth looking at.

'It's stupid. I know it's stupid,' I felt stupid. 'But it's like her gift, making people light up, making them feel worthy. Every time it happens, I just want to trace my finger along her lips to feel that smile, but it's always brief. Then I go back to wondering if it was ever really there at all. Sometimes I listen to her speak, a few seconds too long to count as overhearing, and I just wish that I knew her better, I pretend that I do. She's different. She's beautiful and popular but she has a good heart too. I guess that means something to me.'

I'd finished. The silence rang so clearly it ached my ears. Pure ecstasy ran through my veins but at the same time an emptiness was forming. It caved its way inside my stomach, making it feel dull and hollow. It was the words, or rather the truth behind them. Admitting how perfect she was also held a sense of finality. There was no way Lucile would ever date *me,* not with all my imperfections.

Everywhere inside of me was racked with longing and self-pity but in some ways, what was even more painful, was the fact that I had shared these feelings with someone else. With Angel. The weight of my embarrassment was as crushing as the heartache itself. My cheeks flushed with colour and my skin grew hot, prickling with shame. I whipped off my long-sleeved shirt and lay back down on my bed in my t-shirt, fiddling with the hem for something to do. I didn't know if she was watching me or not, so I kept my gaze on my hands, not wanting her to look into my eyes, not wanting her have any more access to my soul than she already did.

'So,' I mumbled when the silence continued much longer than I could stand, 'did the "screecher" say any more?'

'Who?'

'Missy.'

Angel gave a half-amused, half-hearted, breathy kind of laugh before answering, 'No. I tried to find out more, stayed with them for hours, but it must have been a passing comment because after that it was *Missy* this and *Missy* that. I swear, I have no idea how she made it to 17. You'd think there would be a queue of people lining up to assassinate her every time she opened her pointless mouth.'

A small smile twitched at my lips, 'What was she going on about this time?'

'Urgh, her *almost kiss* with some guy, who she probably made up because the only reason a guy would *ever* put his lips to hers would be to shut her up... I guess maybe it could be true then.'

I laughed hard.

'Luke,' she whispered.

I could hear the anxious flicking of her nails. The corners of my lips crept up into smile.

'What is it Angel?'

She paused, 'Let me help you.'

I laughed again, but this time it was full of self-indulgent pity. 'And how do you plan to do that?'

'Well…' she was hesitant, and in that brief moment when her voice faltered, I knew what she was thinking.

'NO!' I said firmly.

'I'd be careful, respectful…'

'You promised. We promised. Never again we said.'

'Oh, come one. It's not like she'll see me. *Obviously.*'

'Not the point.'

'But I got the idea from you,' she said, and I blinked in disbelief. 'It's true. You were the one who said you listen in on her conversations to get to know her better, that's all I'd be do—'

'That is completely different,' I stuttered feeling a pinch of guilt. 'I listen when she, when I, when there are people around. When she's not saying anything, anything personal.' I screeched, the garbled sentences and my unusually shrill voice making everything sound wrong and confusing.

'I won't be a creep about it, and I won't listen to anything too private.'

'No.'

'I'd go as soon as she said something personal, I promise.'

'Angel, how many times?'

'I just want to help you.'

'Why?'

'Because out of the two of us you are the one who stands a chance at any happiness.' I paid close attention to her voice, her tone — my way of knowing her feelings — there was pain.

'I've been with you all day, every day for over two weeks, Luke, and in all that time do you know what I've realised? I've realised that she's the only thing in your world that brings even the ghost of a smile to your face and she's not even really in your world. It's pathetic; but it doesn't have to be.'

Her voice quavered as though it were racked with emotion and I tried hard not to take her insult personally.

She whispered softly, '*You* don't have to be lonely. You shouldn't be scared of letting someone in Luke, you just shouldn't.'

Angel's voice cracked again from grief, and I clenched my teeth, feeling a tense kind of sympathy. She sounded more vulnerable than I'd ever known her to be, and though I couldn't feel her pain like she felt mine I grieved with her all the same.

Her emotions shook my certainty, my decision wavered. I didn't know why this was so important to her, but that didn't matter now. She needed to do this for me, for herself, and that was reason enough.

'Okay,' I mumbled in defeat.

'Really?' there was a mixture of relief and gladness in her voice, 'you'll… let me help you?'

I cocked my head in the direction of her voice and smiled, 'Sure, why not.'

***

He fell asleep with the lights on and it bugged me. I swiped at the switch several times knowing it would have no effect but still, I tried. Longing for the darkness, aching for its peace. I wanted to hide the emotions that I had let loose earlier, to have them be enveloped in the impenetrable dark, but I couldn't even flick a stupid switch. I felt frustrated. Intensely and insanely pathetic and frustrated, and for once these were just my emotions.

I glanced over at Luke's un-taut face and smiled. It was odd seeing him so calm. It comforted me a little, drawing me closer to him. My fingers brushed at the tangled locks that covered his sweaty face. I watched them sink through his cheeks, my transparent, ethereal glow brightening his deadly pale skin, just a touch of pink beneath. I whipped my hand away, feeling a sharp blaze of disgust, and stormed off to the window, my entire body soaked in pain.

I would never look like that again — alive, and for the first time my lack of mortality hurt me more than it enraged me. It was a deep, despairing pain that cut through me, making me ache for everything I'd left behind. My crappy life and all the people in it, people I'd taken for granted. I missed it, I missed them.

'Urghh.' I tried to smash my fist against the window, wanting to feel the glass crack beneath my skin, but it didn't. Questions burnt angrily within me. Why didn't I see it when I was alive? Why hadn't I cared enough to try? I saw it now, though: the parts worth living for. It all seemed so painfully clear now.

'I won't let that happen to you, Luke,' I said, making a promise he'd never hear. He'd see sense if it took everything I had to show him.

Somehow, I found myself looking up at the full moon. It was as pearly as me. I leapt up on to the window ledge and swung my legs around so that I was sitting, limbs through glass, staring down at the street below. I tangled my finger thoughtfully around a few strands of misty hair and felt my brow crease desperately.

'This thing with Lucile has to work,' and a feeling of pleading pricked at me. It had to work because I needed it to. She was the key to everything. He was going to want his life if I had to cram happiness down his throat just to make it happen.

Chapter 17
Monday, 22nd March

'You remember the rules, right?'

'Luke, you're killing me,' I moaned.

'Please, you're already dead.'

I screamed at the top of my lungs, hoping the unearthly high-pitched sound would feel sharp in his ears and I wasn't disappointed. He slammed his palms hard against them and yelped like a dog in pain, hearing sounds other humans could not.

'How's *that* for dead?' I laughed. People stopped just to gawp, and he met their puzzled faces with chagrin.

'Funny, dead girl,' he sniped under his breath, 'real funny.'

'I think so.'

'Have you quite finished yet? Can we get back to more important things?'

It made me laugh the way he kept his thin lips perfectly still as he spoke, hoping no one would notice his one-man conversation.

'I guess,' I shrugged, though he couldn't see.

'So?' he urged as he led us down an empty stairway away from all the *freak gawking*.

'So, what?'

He rolled his eyes and let out a frustrated growl at my playing dumb routine.

'Do you remember the rules or not?'

His temples pulsed with frustration and his words had a considerable amount of bite, but I couldn't help teasing him more.

'Angel?'

'What!'

'Rules. Do you remember them, yes or no?'

'Maybe.'

'Maybe?' He stormed off muttering under his breath. 'We're not doing this if you can't even remember a few simple—'

'Oh, un-bunch your boxers, Lucas, I was just kidding. Of course, I remember.'

He retraced his steps and waited eagerly, his breath panting quietly with nerves. How could I not remember the 'precious rules' after the countless conversations he'd crammed into the weekend?

'We have to be smart about this,' he'd said late on Sunday evening, 'respectful.'

The day had been warm and bright, and the evening, with its gentle wind, was just as pleasant. The sun was hiding, but small traces of its light illuminated sections of the sky. A dusty pink glow blurred with deep purples and dense blues — they rippled along the horizon, brushing against each other in the most unimposing way, almost nothing had ever looked so beautiful. Almost.

Luke lay as he always did, head against the tree, back on the ground, getting crumbly bits of mud stuck into his thick dark hair. He stared up at the sky, his muddy green eyes alight with passion as his pale hands traced the grass, occasionally ripping out chunks, letting the blades scatter.

'Need-to-know info. That's all we're after,' he rambled on. 'It's bad enough what we're doing. Don't go over doing the spying thing.'

I cut him a look he'd never see, 'I don't care for her life story,' I spat. 'I'm doing this with one goal in mind, to get you a date. Once I get what I need I'm out, trust me. I have no desire to join their click.'

'Awww, no girlfriends in your alive days?'

I made a sound like a cat retching up a hairball. 'By choice.'

'Liar. I bet you would have loved it,' he teased. 'Watching romcoms, making prank calls...'

'I will haunt you instead of help you,' I threatened. He laughed playfully, and I let him know I was rolling my eyes at him.

'We have to be serious,' he switched, suddenly remembering what we were meant to be discussing. He resumed the activity of nervously tearing lumps out of the unkempt grass, twisting his fistfuls until they tore.

'We can't risk hurting her feelings.'

''Cause we wouldn't want to do that,' I muttered, feeling deeply irritated.

'What?'

'Nothing,' I snapped, but only mildly. Not that he'd noticed anyway. Nothing at that moment — in every moment — was more important than **Lucile**.

How did I tell him I was not all right? What was I supposed to say? Mind if we change the subject, only I'm sick of talking about Lucile, feeling the way you feel about Lucile. How could I? It was all my idea in the first place, but now she was everywhere. Her presence as thick as her bouncy hair. She was more real in our conversations than I ever was or could be and it was driving me insane.

'Hey, Angel?' His voice, deep and soft voice lured me out of my trance. 'Where's your head at?'

'Six feet under with mounds of dirt on top,' I griped bitterly.

'You know what I mean. Are you all right?'

No.

'Angel?'

'Let's just get on with the rules.' His eyes brightened as mine rolled.

I cleared my throat and began in a voice that screamed 'give a crap.'

'Only follow her when her friends are around. Stick to relationship-type information and personal interests only, nothing more. If things start to get too personal, i.e. she's crying like a baby over some ridiculous stupid issue—'

'Ahem,' he did a fake clear of his throat and I rolled my eyes to help relieve my frustration.

'What? I can't joke?' His eyes sharpened. 'Fine. Sorry,' I sighed, resuming my bored, monotone voice. 'If she's upset then duck out.'

'And?'

'And...? Oh yeah, use my discretion. If I hear something too private to pass on, keep it to myself no matter how juicy it seems. Did I get everything?'

'Sounds like it. You're the best,' he smiled, crooning at me as we emerged from the lonely stairway. It deepened and for a second, I thought... it was like he could see me. Really see **me**.

'Lucile.'

'What?'

'Lucile,' he nudged his head to the left and tried to straighten himself up. Before I knew it, he had tripped over his own feet and landed awkwardly at hers. A chorus of laughter sounded from everywhere and he stared up at her, his doe-eyed, lovesick, embarrassed stare making him look even more pathetic than was necessary.

'Are you okay?' she asked. But before he could even stutter a response, Missy had linked arms with Lucile and was dragging her away.

'Eurgh. You don't talk to the weirdos, Lucile, you step on them like roadkill. Or better yet, *freak kill*.' She giggled at her own idiotic joke and then was gone.

Luke groaned, laying his face on the cold ground. His heart raced in his humiliation and every inch of his skin prickled with shame. I wanted nothing more than to smooth the hair out of his face and fix things for him. Then I saw them coming.

'Luke get up!' I urged.

'Not until everyone has gone to class.'

'Just get up!' panic shook my voice and I chewed viciously on my lip.

'Why bother?'

'Stop feeling sorry for yourself and JUST DO IT!'

He pulled himself up and had just about made it to his knees when a force sent him tumbling on to his back, looking like an upturned snail with his backpack still attached. I cringed for him.

'Hey freak, how's it going?' Mac cackled, and the two idiots flanked on either side of him joined in.

'I saw what happened with Lucile. That's rough. I'd have been over here sooner, but I was too busy laughing my arse off.' All three cackled again, making me burn with anger, white hot anger. Luke scrambled to his feet and glanced around in alarm as the last group of people rounded a corner out of sight.

He spoke quietly, 'What do you want today, Mac?'

'To give you some advice.'

'Oh yeah?'

Mac swung his thick, muscular arm around Luke's comparatively scrawny neck and forced him into a walk.

'I've noticed you've been kinda disgustingly obsessed with Lucile.'

'I-I-I,' Luke stuttered uncontrollably, his insides a knotted mess. I guess standing up to arseholes like Mac and having the crap severely kicked out of you could make a person lose their nerve. Mac saw this. Mac loved it. He flashed his teeth in a grin and laughed so that it sounded more like a threat.

'Don't do that. Don't pretend that you haven't. It's embarrassing for you and waste of time for me, so let's talk straight. Back off!' he barked; all feigned friendliness gone. Mac gripped Luke's neck in the crevice of his arm, and he whimpered slightly, feeling more pain than he was letting on.

'I've been waiting a long time for her to drop that piece-of-crap boyfriend of hers and now that she has, I don't have time to deal with tossers like you who think they might have a chance. You don't. You never will. Okay?'

Luke nodded his head feebly and Mac ruffled his hair.

'Great!' Mac said releasing his grip. 'You know what, you're all right Luke,' he jeered as he walked on, his tag-alongs following obediently.

'I'll tell you what,' he said, wheeling himself around so unexpectedly that I felt Luke's jittery nerves jump like they were ready to escape, 'how 'bout when I'm done with her, I give her to you. It should only take a few days for me to get what I want. Then you can... try your luck.' He winked deviously, then wheeled himself back around. 'Who knows,' he called, 'she might even throw you a pity date.' The sound of his laughter peaked then disappeared with them.

'You all right?' I asked, though I could feel the truth.

'Let's just get to Chemistry, okay.'

'Okay.'

We walked in silence down the empty halls, my feet barely skimming the linoleum floor. Luke's face was a glacial ice mask — no emotions — but inwardly he burned with fury.

***

I sat on the windowsill watching his hand move. His thick, dark locks draped over his face as he worked, cross-legged on the bed, slumped over his lap. His heart leapt excitedly for a moment and then settled back into its normal rhythm. It was strange how much more in tune I was becoming with every part of him. Almost as if I could feel his very blood rush through his veins. He ran his free hand through his tousle of hair and held the strands back against his head. He stayed like that for a minute or two and then let go, allowing the soft tresses to fall naturally, in front of his face. He shrugged lightly and continued working. I watched on in quiet awe. He gripped the pencil with a graceful force, and it moved fluidly over the thick piece of cartridge paper. It glided rapidly, naturally as if the lead and wood were a part of him, extensions of his flesh and bones. He was in command and I was mesmerised. Nothing could bother him when he was in that mood, nothing. No outside force could intrude on this perfect world he had created for himself. It was just him, his pencil and a blank sheet of paper. At that moment every cell in his body was centred on one feeling, peace, and it was nice. After the hostile torrent of unpleasant emotions that had engulfed us both this afternoon it was nice to feel settled, whole. I looked at his calm face and wondered if those venomous emotions still lurked in him, in some place I couldn't access. It was hard to believe that the cocktail of anger, hurt and sadness could have evaporated so easily with just the swish of a pencil. If I had known that sooner, I wouldn't have spent the better half of the day avoiding his sorry arse. I'd have just handed him a sketchbook and left him to it. But I didn't know that, so I'd left. I'd walked out on him in the middle of Art, rushing through some half-arsed flimsy, excuse and bolted before he'd had the chance to question it. I'd told him I was going to get cracking with this Lucile mission, that I was determined to make Mac choke on his words, but that was only part of the reason. The truth was I had to get away from him and his pining. I couldn't think straight. I cringed every time the feeling of embarrassment washed through him, again and again, like its source was never ending. I'd felt his hollow and hopeless heart thump for her, and it was killing my mood, so I made my excuses and left. I knew it didn't work that way. I knew that proximity had nothing to do with me feeling what he felt, that even apart I would still feel every single ounce of his pain no less than in his presence, but I had to get away, for myself. It made me feel better, mentally, to put some distance between us. So, I trailed the halls until I found her, Lucile. I figured I might as well be a good little guardian angel and actually keep to my promise, but it was harder than I thought it would be. I had absolutely zero desire to spend any time around the girl — which made the task at hand even more tedious than my afterlife before Luke — and to top it all off, just finding her was chore. It was nothing like trying to find Luke. Even in a crowded room I could point him out in a heartbeat. It was easy. All I had to do was follow the overpowering gravitational pull and I was there, with him. It was like seeking out my soul's duplicate. But Lucile? Easy? No, this high-maintenance chick **had** to be strenuous, laborious work. In fact, the expression needle in the hay sprang to mind several times as I roamed halls and searched classrooms pretending to kick discarded bits of litter on the floor along my way.

It was pointless me trying to move anything let alone attempting to kick something. Really it was silly even to try, but for last few days I'd become obsessed with becoming more physical. I'd been focusing my energy on specific limbs. Really concentrating, willing them to do something, anything. Pick up a book, kick a crunched-up bit of paper, brush against a cheek. I'd been hoping the myths were real about ghosts becoming corporeal as they became stronger, but so far, no luck. I felt strong, so… full of existence. Like if I reached out to press my fingertips against someone's lips, brush the skin against the skin, their nerve endings would meet with my own. But they wouldn't because I wasn't strong. I wasn't real. Not really. Air castles fitted with pipe dreams, as my dad would say, but I kept on trying. It wasn't like I had a whole lot else going on. Eventually I stumbled across Lucile. While I was outside failing to roll gravel beneath the balls of my feet, I spotted her. Swishing her hips like some kind of prima donna movie star. She stopped in front of a VW estate, jangling her keys. Missy and Naila came running up to her, verbal diarrhoea pouring out of Missy's mouth before she'd even skidded to a halt. Letting out a hefty sigh, I dragged myself towards **that** voice.

'Lue Lue, please!' she begged. 'You **have** to come over today. It's literally life or death!'

'I'm not really in the mood,' Lucile mumbled, running the keys between her fingers while averting her eyes from Missy's boring stare,

'But hey, I'm sure *Naila* would *love* to keep you company.' Naila looked up from her phone and shot Lucile a dark, contemptuous look.

There was an awkward silence as Missy begrudgingly considered the idea.

'Yeah… well… of course I **want** Nay Nay there,' she said, throwing Naila an over-enthusiastic smile. 'It's just, it's the first date. It's a big deal! I'm going to need you both.'

'Come on **Lue Lue**, Miss's right,' Naila rolled her eyes Lucile's way — a smug, karma-type tone monopolising her voice.

'I completely understand Missy, I mean, however will you choose your shoes, your jewellery and your dress all by yourself?' she mocked, a faux sympathetic look taking over her face.

'I know, right? Thank you, Nay Nay,' Missy squealed sincerely, completely missing the sarcasm.

I burst out laughing and Lucile unknowingly joined in with a restrained giggle. Was this girl for real? Or did common sense have to be applied like her daily make-up regime — little but often?

'So, are you coming over or what?' Missy pressed.

'Yeah… all right.'

'You guys are awesome.' Missy squealed again, rushing to her car before they could change their minds. 'Really, you're the best.' She unlocked the door to her sleek Ford KA and slid in. Naila eyed Lucile with hostility and huffed.

'Lift?' Lucile offered, throwing an arm around her shoulder.

'I hate you,' Naila answered, poking her playfully in the ribs before climbing into the passenger's seat.

'Maybe a sweetheart neckline would be better guys, what do you think?'

I think I'm in hell. A thousand, million outfits later and Missy was still talking about sweetheart necklines. How Naila and Lucile had not torn her to pieces was beyond me. If her voice wasn't enough to drive me off a cliff, I'd seen far more of Missy than I cared to and was now ready to go full poltergeist on her — but not them. Instead Lucile smiled, cleared her throat and said, 'Well, it's a bit much isn't it?'

She eyed up the sleek, corseted satin bodice over jeans as Missy glowered at her and protectively stroked the boning.

'I just think that you might want to save that for a more special night.'

'Yeah, like my funeral,' Naila muttered, gesturing to her head exploding.

I laughed.

'Maybe one where you'll get to show it off more, I mean,' Lucile added, struggling to ignore Naila while flinching against the more pronounced glare on Missy's face.

The muscles in Missy's forehead relaxed and she broke into a smile.

'You're absolutely right,' she said. 'Besides, I don't want to give away too much too soon.' I huffed loudly and it annoyed me that she couldn't hear it.

'Where exactly are you guys going?' Naila asked, rolling her golden-brown dreads between slender caramel fingers. On the surface, her rich brown eyes seemed stone cold, dead from boredom. But beneath, just for a second, I thought I could detect a touch of irritation.

'Bombay Palace,' Missy called from the depths of her walk-in closet.

'Bombay Palace?!' Lucile said, her voice suddenly a little thick. Naila looked at her friend, her face full of concern.

'Yeah. You know it?' hollered Missy, again characteristically blind to any emotion that wasn't her own.

'You know I do. With Shane. It was kind of... our place,' she choked out the words, forcing Naila to sit up on the bed and prod Lucile till she smiled. Was this it? The moment where things got too **personal?** Was she really about to cry over a restaurant with 'guy memories' attached? She'd smiled, but how long that would hold for. I couldn't tell. I wasn't good at this sort of thing, and there was no soul connection linking me to her feelings to help me out. Should I leave? Did I have to? I sure as hell wanted to, but I'd been searching for these girls all afternoon and only just found them. I'd be a mug if all I had to show for these last few crappy hours was a crabby attitude.

Missy giggled, 'I must have forgotten. That's **so** funny though, your best friend dating his best friend and now your place becoming ours.'

'Yeah... hilarious,' Naila dripped and we rolled our eyes in synchrony. Lucile stifled a laugh with her fingers, signalling the end of the potential meltdown.

'What do you think about this one?' Missy asked, twirling out of her closet to stand in front of them. She was wearing a black sequined bodycon dress with thick-ish black and fuchsia feathers that surrounded the hem and arranged themselves into a full skirt. She looked like a peacock on the prowl. She puffed out the ends and stood, hands on hips, waiting for the verdict.

'Well,' began Lucile, 'it's a little, um, a little... not first date-ish.'

Missy twisted her mouth a while. 'Maybe you're right,' she finally said, unzipping the side of the dress as she walked into the closet yet again. Things clattered and thudded as she threw bits aside.

'You just don't know what kind of stress I'm under.' She yelled from the midst of the destruction. 'It's been so long since either of you had a first date. Oooo, hey,' she squealed before either girl had time to retort. 'I could find you two a couple of guys.'

My ears pricked up.

'No, no, no, no, no, I'm perfectly fine **solo** thank you.' Naila quickly announced, putting an end to her involvement.

'Fine, Lucile it is then.' Any chance of you a Shane rekindling the old flame?'

'No Missy. So, don't you go telling Ricky that there is. He'd only report back to Shane and the last thing I need is for that waste of space to think he still has a chance.'

'Okay so Shane's a no. So, what! There are still plenty of other guys inside and outside of college. There must be someone you're into. What about Carson?'

'Carson? The same Carson who practically lives in the college gym?'

'Yeah.'

'He's obsessed with his abs.'

'I know,' Missy purred.

'No thanks.'

'How about Michael then? The guy in my French class? He's pretty hot.'

'He's also pretty gay,' said Naila, amusement breaking her silence.

'Shut up. Really?'

'Yep.'

'Damn. The good ones are always off limits.' All three girls laughed.

'Fine, so no Michael, there's always Mac.' The laughter stopped.

'Mac? As in Joe McNamara?' The words fell from Lucile's lips like a mouthful of phlegm, revoltingly unwelcome.

'Mmm hmm. He's pretty cute. Not a sexy as Michael, but still very cute.'

'Missy he's a sleaze,' argued Lucile 'He's moved on all the girls you've ever spoken to and slept with a good handful of them too.'

'So that's a no to Mac, then?' she asked, still shamelessly hopeful.

'A definite NO!' Lucile gritted her teeth as she spoke, squashing any kind of possibility into smush.

'Hey, what about that guy from English?' came Naila's casual voice, and my ears pricked up further.

'You know the one I mean, tallish with an understated kind of cuteness. Wears a lot of black. He seems nice. *Interesting* even.' I stood up from my perch by the door, my senses tingling madly in excitement.

'You mean Luke?' Lucile practically yelled.

'Ye—'

Missy spluttered a laugh before Naila could even finish her sentence. She stumbled out in underwear; a rose-coloured dress bunched upon her shoulders.

'Don't be stupid Nay,' she said sounding repulsed. 'He's socially crippled, not to mention barely a cut above average looking. No way near any kind of cute status. Besides Lue Lue is way, way, way, waaaaay out of his league.' She pulled her arms thorough the slinky straps and let the dress slide down her slim frame.

'You were the one who said he'd make a good rebound guy,' Naila argued.

'I was kidding.'

'No, you weren't.'

'Well… I changed my mind. He shouldn't even be allowed to make the rebound list.' Her face crinkled in disgust. 'Honestly Nay Nay, grow a brain. Lucile may be desperate for a man, but she can do so much better than *him*.'

She threw off the dress and disappeared again, missing the fleeting glance between Lucile and Naila. Neither of them said any more on the matter (and I had a feeling they wouldn't for the rest of the night), but their look told me their discussion was far from over.

'Okay, this has to be it!' Missy squealed, shimmying out to admire her reflection in the freaky Disney-style mirror.

'This is the first date dress, don't you think?'

Lucile considered the simple black dress. Strapless and tight in all the right places. 'You do look amazing.'

'Yeah Miss,' Naila swallowed. 'You'll knock him dead.'

'Ooooooh goodie,' she screeched, slapping her palms together in celebration. 'Now for shoes.'

I groaned, slid back down to the ground and waited patiently. Hoping they'd mention Luke again.

I watched him, still sketching. Unable to take my eyes off of him. I thought about the girls, how I'd been right about them not mentioning him again, how he'd been dismissed. I thought about it, looked at him and I didn't get it. But more than that I had the urge to slap Missy hard across the face. Acting as if he was the un-datable one when she was the vaporous nut job.

'Are you planning to hop down off your perch soon, or are you just going to sit there like some sort of night watch.'

His words shocked me back to reality. I knew that he could sense whenever I entered the room, but he'd been in such deep concentration I thought he hadn't noticed me. He shut the sketchbook and slid it under the bed along with his pencils, then patted the soft-looking mattress. I joined him, sitting crossed-legged side by side.

'How long did you know I was there for?' I asked, tugging my lip ring with my teeth.

His smile was shy and for some reason he felt embarrassed.

'From the moment you came in. You didn't move from the window.' He sighed deeply, 'I figured maybe you had a reason for not wanting to talk. I thought I'd just wait until you were ready.'

'Why wouldn't I want to talk?'

He scraped the floor with his foot and tilted his head in my direction. 'I don't know... in case tonight's expedition didn't go so well.'

He stared up at me with those muddy green eyes and I could almost have sworn he could see me.

'Oh,' I said chewing over his words in my head, replaying the day's events, thoroughly sorting them all out. The bad day for him at college, the abysmal afternoon for me with Lucile. Coming back home to him. The leap of his heart. The leap of his heart, I pondered, remembering how excited he'd felt when I entered the room. Was that... for me? I smiled, feeling a little too pleased. Of course, he was excited we were friends, he depended on me. Why wouldn't he look forward to my company? These were the words I told myself.

'So how badly did it go then, did they even mention me at all?'

'What?' I was distracted.

'Lucile, did she... mention me? I mean, you were gone a long time. You must have found out something, otherwise you would have been back sooner. Even,' he took a deep breath through all his rambling 'even if it was bad news.'

I could feel his calm slowly ebbing away, being replaced by jitteriness, and it grated on me. How she could make him feel this way. Reduce him to a pile of quivering nerves. It was beyond annoying. It was maddening.

'So... what did she say?'

'Nothing,' I snapped.

'Nothing?' he echoed the same words back to me, but in a hollow painful sort of way that made me feel guilty.

'Nothing... bad I mean.'

'Oh,' his heart leapt wildly again. It was exactly the same thrill I'd felt when I had entered the room. I knew it then. It was for her. Always for her. He'd been excited at the possibility of good news. Nothing to do with me. Everything to do with **her**. I gritted my teeth, biting back my pathetic emotions.

'So, what happened then?' he pressed eagerly, and I told him. Everything. Every last detail.

Tuesday, 30th March

The bright lights overhead shone down on us like spotlights. They lit up all corners of the lunch hall, exposing everything: the cracks in the walls, the posters hanging limply from the noticeboard, me. The smell of warm, buttery baked potatoes wafted through the air, making the stuffy atmosphere almost bearable. Conversations surrounded me. They seemed welcoming. Friendly even, for those who had friends to share them with. I hung my head low over my plate. So low that my nose almost brushed the cool glass. I toyed nervously with my food, rolling the dry bread between my fingers, back and forth, back and forth, as I waited for Angel.

Being in here was a mistake. I didn't fit in. Even here, one table over from all the other black-wearing, soul-despairing, angst teens, I couldn't find my place. The only time didn't feel that way was around Angel. She was my place.

I peeked up at the clock, 1:05. Where was she? Shouldn't she have been back by now? We'd walked to college together but the second she'd caught sight of Lucile entering the gates she'd gone sprinting after her to 'investigate.'

'We'll catch up at lunch and I'll have something good to tell you then, okay? I promise.' She seemed hopeful but after a week of nothing since Missy's house I wasn't feeling so positive.

I parted my fingers, releasing crumbling bits of bread roll, and clasped them together, resting my chin on top. I was considering leaving when Missy's shrill voice rang throughout the room, announcing her presence. My head shot up a little too fast, but I ignored the pain in my neck. I stared around eagerly, desperate to catch a glimpse of Lucile, but she wasn't there. Missy sashayed around the lunchroom; phone plastered to ear as her mouth worked overtime.

'Great,' I mumbled morosely, wherever Lucile was so was my Angel, along with any information she might possibly have found out.

My heart sank. I pushed my plate away and slunk out of my seat, trying to remain as invisible as possible as I shuffled awkwardly through the mass of bodies that blocked my way to the exit. I hated being in here alone and she knew that. Just then a flurry of warmth rushed towards me, engulfed me, and I sighed, feeling a deep, contented relief.

'Whassup, misery guts?'

My forehead creased. 'What's the matter with you?' Her words sounded playful enough, but something was off.

'Nothing.'

I arched my eyebrow sceptically, 'you sure?'

'Yes. I'm sure,' she barked back.

'Right, okay. Let me just duck out of the way of your mood swing then.' I breathed and continued to fight my way through the throng of people.

'Look, I'm fine. Really. I'm not the one who's two seconds away from a panic attack.'

'Exaggerate much?'

'Overreact much?' She retorted.

'Well jeeze, I was just having so much fun sitting here on my own,' I scowled underneath my breath. There was a slight pause, and in that time, I managed to break free from the greedy herd and enter the busy hallway.

'You missed me?' She asked, her tone so soft and vulnerable that it threw me.

'Of course,' I lifted up the corner of my lips and let half a smile creep discreetly on to my face. There was another overlong silence and I wondered what she was thinking.

'Well if you loved me before, you'll really love me now.'

'Oh really, and why is that?'

'Well, 'cause... I have something for you.' My heart thrummed with enthusiasm.

'Calm down, Romeo,' she laughed in a sourly mocking way, 'and follow me so we can talk without you having to look like a ventriloquist.'

***

He rolled over on to his side and I could see the grass stains smeared across his top. They streaked up his back and spread out along his broad shoulder blades. He was talking, but I couldn't hold his words in my head. My heart, my feeble phantom heart, was too busy breaking. I lay next to him inches away, gliding my weightless fingers along his back, tracing the dirt. I closed my eyes and tried to remember a time I'd wished to be real more than I did in this moment. I tried to 'um' and 'ah' at the right points in the conversation and that seemed to be working because he didn't notice my distraction, my pain.

He rolled over on to his other side and I kept my hands where they were, this time running my fingers along the patterns of his shirt. A thrill ran through me. They'd been running through me all afternoon. From the moment I'd opened my mouth to tell him what I knew, flutters had been flapping through me sporadically, catching me off guard, but this time it was echoed by a faint trembling of my own. I tried to shake off its meaning. Tried to find a rational explanation. I took in a deep breath, but no air filled my lungs and my chest remained limp, yet my heart twanged achingly.

I watched his mouth move, and though I was too numb to hear the words I read them as they trailed off of his lips. 'Lucile,' 'feelings,' 'interested in me,' It was true. She was. She'd admitted it the next day, when Barbie-doll Missy wasn't around to ridicule and make disgruntled noises. She'd said the words 'cute' and 'interesting' but what did she know? This 5ft 2in curvy wannabe socialite. She didn't even know him, yet he was interesting to her. It made me sick. Made my unnatural, un-dead, spiritual body want to vom. I'd been so affronted I couldn't even bring myself to tell him that day. Or the next day, or the next. I'd let a week slip by and then some, but every day I'd had to look into his muddy green eyes, and amidst all the usual pain lay confusion. 'Why hadn't they said anything?', 'When would they say something?', 'Will they ever say something again?' Question after question, all of which I had the answers to. Answers I kept selfishly to myself. No, not selfishly, I reminded myself. protectively I was protecting him. He didn't even know her. For all he knew Mac could have been right. Maybe he would be just a pity date. Or maybe Missy was the one who had skirted around the truth; what if he was just the rebound guy? A confidence patch she'd slap on and discard the moment she felt better. I couldn't let him be used like that, I wouldn't. The words rolled around my mind again and again, but in the forefront of my heart (where it really mattered) I felt deeply green. Jealousy burned through me. It pricked at me viciously, filling me with its bitterness and despair. I was losing him.

I clasped my fingers shut, trying to grasp at his shirt, trying to hold on to him, but all I felt was the softness of my own palms. I told myself that I was frightened for my existence, afraid that if he found her, he wouldn't need me anymore, that I would disappear into the swirling mist of the afterlife. I told myself that I was just afraid of losing a friend, my only friend, afraid that this **girl** would somehow come between us and tear our bond apart. That I wanted to protect our friendship... that's what I told myself. Again, and again, it's what I had to tell myself, otherwise the truth would have impaled me from the inside out. Would have cut through me so brutally it would have ripped my soul apart. I was dead, yet the moment I caught a glimpse of it — the truth — I felt as though I were suffocating. I felt like I was being crushed underneath its weight. I panicked and gasped for air that would never come.

'Angel,' he called my name, but I could barely hear him through the deafening dry choke of my gasps. I'd told myself my lie over and over again, but when the truth eventually caught up with me the lie held no weight. I feared this girl, I feared her presence, I feared that she was taking away my reason for living. But more than that, I feared that one day he'd love her, *really* love her and I'd be just a memory.

Chapter 18
Friday, 2nd April

Streaks of yellow shot through the window. They spilled across the kitchen counter, brightening the marble surface. I wriggled my fingers through one particular bright spot and sighed. It was early. Too early, and I was tired. The clock on the kitchen cooker beeped as if to confirm my thinking.

'Seven o'clock,' I murmured, 'great.'

An hour and half to go until I had to leave for hell. I'd been awake for the last two hours feeling groggy and annoyed, but no matter what I tried I just couldn't get back to sleep. I felt nauseous, and the moment my head hit the pillow the feeling intensified. It was the headache that had woken me but it was the nausea that had kept me up. The sick feeling swimming in my stomach. It heaved its way up into my mouth and I was just lucky enough to make it to the bathroom in time. If that wasn't irritating enough my head still ached badly, the pain making the room tilt ever so slightly. I knew why I felt like this. It was obvious: I was anxious. I'd barely seen Angel over the last couple of days and I was really starting to worry. She'd promised me she was fine, said she just wanted some time to herself, but I didn't believe her. When had she ever wanted that? Something was wrong. I felt it. I'd had a bad feeling since that moment in the park, when her voice had gone hoarse and her breath shallow and quick. I didn't know what to think. I'd been scared senseless; she'd had a panicked, and I needed to know why. She'd tried to brush it off, but I hadn't, and I wouldn't — not until I saw her again, not until I knew that she was all right. I ran my fingers through my hair and gripped a chunk in frustration. If only I knew what *she* was feeling, I thought, just this once.

The tension on my scalp made the pain in my head nestle deeper. I frowned, letting go of my hair. I wrapped my hands around my cup of bitter coffee and took a sip. Cold. As I placed the mug down, lazy footsteps shuffled across the floor. I looked up. Mae smiled at me.

'Morning hon.'

I grunted a response. She dragged herself over to the kettle and flicked the switch with one hand while she ruffled her hair with the other.

'You're up early,' she yawned, reaching for her glasses on top of the fridge and shoving them on her face.

'Couldn't sleep,' I yawned back.

She settled on to the stool next to me and instinctively I leaned away. Where was Angel? Apart from being worried, I needed her. I depended on her very nearness to put me at ease. Mae touched her fingers to my mug, and I released my hold.

'It's gone cold. Want me to make you another cup?'

I shook my head. The water in the kettle rumbled to a stop and she pushed herself off the stool, making her way to the cupboard.

'Hey beautiful,' a voice croaked from behind. My muscles tensed and I unconsciously gripped the chair. Mae whipped her head around and smiled letting her untamed hair ripple over her shoulders.

'Morning darling,' she called sweetly, and then resumed her coffee-making activity.

I kept my head low and clenched my teeth in disgust.

'Come 'ere,' Nick crooned.

'I can't, I'm making a cup. You want one?'

'I want you,' he growled seductively. She giggled while I heaved.

'Shhh,' she hushed, 'Luke,' she'd breathed my name by way of explanation, but I still heard.

I rolled my eyes and got up from my chair, heading for the exit. Nick leaned casually on the doorframe, blocking my way. I eyed him bitterly. He flashed me his teeth.

'Where you going?' he said in his hauntingly bullish voice.

'What's it to you?' I tried to duck passed him and failed.

'Uh, uh,' he kept his voice light while he threatened me with those steely grey eyes. 'I've got something to tell you both,' he grinned, shoving me back into the kitchen a little too hard.

I balled up my fist tightly, rage making the blood pound in my ears.

'Oh yeah?' Mae asked adding the last mound of sugar to her drink before turning around.

She eyed him brightly and he licked his top lip in a predatory sort of way.

'Well go on then... get on with it.'

'6th June,' he smirked.

Bile rose angrily into my mouth, leaving its acrid taste on my tongue. I swallowed it down in disgust and silently ground my teeth till my gums hurt.

'What about it?' she asked stupidly. How could she not have guessed? The second he spat those words out I knew what he'd meant.

'That's the day we're getting married!' he announced, slamming his hand on the door triumphantly. He flashed his nicotine-stained teeth and all I could see was red.

'What?' Mae's hand trembled slightly, making her coffee splash on to the floor.

She placed the mug down on to the counter and mopped up the spillage with her slipper.

'That's so soon. Don't you think that's too soon?'

Nick's expression shifted a little, the corner of his lips twitching as he clung to a smile.

'Are you afraid to marry me, Mae?' He swallowed hard; tension swept lightly through the room. I stayed as still as I could, afraid that if I didn't, I'd get caught up in its wrath.

'No,' she shook her head, 'it's not that, it's just—'

'Because I thought I was being romantic. Spontaneous. You used to like that. What...?' he paused and I thought I saw a flash of softness reach his eyes, 'You don't like that anymore?'

Mae rushed to his side and nuzzled herself into his chest. He wound his arms around her waist and she tenderly stroked his face.

'Of course, I do, it's just, it takes time. There's planning, preparation, a guest list.'

There was a brief pause, 'I wanted to invite your mother.'

His inhale was sharp. 'Out of the question.'

'She's your mother.'

'I said no.'

'Don't you think she'd like to be there?'

His laugh was a snarl, 'I don't know, Mae, she always liked to cross-check her opinions with whatever man she was shacking up with.'

There was fury running all through him. Intense fury. I wondered about his mother, but only for a second.

Nick smiled with effort. 'Forget the planning,' he said, releasing a hand from her hip only to bury it in her hair. 'Forget the guests.' He grasped a bunch, gently gliding her head back until her gaze was on him. 'Me and you, that's what matters.'

There was a dense pause, 'What do you say chick? June 6th, let's get hitched.' She looked deeply into his eyes and softly bit her lip. My heart sunk low before she'd even opened her mouth.

'Go on then.'

'Really?'

'Yes.'

'Wooooooo,' he swung her around, dancing her into the kitchen and she giggled fitfully like a naïve, insecure, little girl. He pressed his lips against hers fiercely, and with one tug of the waist pulled her body urgently towards his. She was a fool. I would have pitied her if I didn't loathe her so much. She tore herself from his lips and he nestled his head on her shoulder, eyeing me from beneath her hair, winking with a mixture of malice and victory. Rage burst through me. It flooded me. My heart pounded rapidly, now pumping the blood even faster around my body. It reached my head, hot and hostile, and my temples throbbed in protest. I had to get out of there. I was afraid my head would crack open if I didn't. I stalked towards the door once more, brushing past them.

'Hey Luke,' Mae called, 'where are you going?'

I turned around and stared at her, I tried to speak but I had no words. Instead I studied her through the film of appal that clouded my eyes. She cleared her throat, sensing my objection. It made her nervous.

'Take the day off college, we'll celebrate.'

My eyes grew colder with hatred and I shook my head, confused as to why she would ever make such a suggestion.

'Oh, go on, sweetie. It's the last day before Easter holidays, you won't miss much. I'll even make your favourite breakfast, banana pancakes.'

A fierce revulsion rose up inside of me and the laugh that had escaped me turned dark and sinister on my lips.

'*Unbelievable*,' I sneered.

A look of confusion coloured her face, then understanding, before remorse. I turned away, heading for the stairs. She called after me, but my brain barely registered her voice. All I could think of now was Dean. Images of him burst through my head, making the muscles themselves ache. I tried to release them, to mentally sever the links that tied them to my memory, but I couldn't. They flooded my head fast and furious: him in the kitchen, a different one. One from another life. He sat hunched over the breakfast table, his face inches away from his plate, sniffing the food like an animal, rolling his overly wet tongue across his lip. I went to sit next to him, but when I lowered myself into the chair, he kicked it with the heel of his foot making me fall to the ground, hard. Leaping to my feet, I cursed, tensing my fist, wanting so badly to make him pay for that. Dean looked up at me and just laughed. He smiled wickedly at me, grinning that impish grin of his before cramming his mouth full of *his* favourite — banana pancakes. Hours later he was dead.

***

I showered slowly, taking my time, rubbing my hands gingerly across the inflamed surface of my skin. It had already started to turn a greyish blue colour. I shrugged beneath the flow of water, thinking that I'd probably deserved it. I should've known better than to upset Mae when he was around.

I stepped out of the shower, patted my body dry with the towel before wrapping it around my waist. I dressed slowly, applied my face slowly, everything was done slowly, in a drawn-out manner as I attempted to close the wide gap between then and the start of college. When I ran out of things to do, I sat on bed listening to the street below, hearing the busy sounds of the world waking up all around me. Cars speeding out of their garage ports, rubbish men loading their truck, a delivery man rapping impatiently on a door and the bark of the neighbour's dog begging to be walked.

I stared at my watch obsessively, tracking the hands as they moved sluggishly around the clock's face. The minute hand jerked again, making the time read 8:15; that was my limit reached. I leapt off my bed, gathered my things and walked out of the house. I moved as though I were in a trance, unable to focus my thoughts on any one thing in particular, yet still my emotions felt more tender than my bruises.

A tune hummed in my head as I dragged myself down the street, I recognised it well. It soothed me, and my whole being flooded with warmth. My emotional turmoil subsided slightly, and my heart seemed to ache a little less in my chest. A few more moments passed before I realised, I wasn't alone.

'Hey you.'

I smiled wearily. My head still throbbed, but not as much now.

'Hey. Breathe in Breathe Out?' I asked making reference to the song she'd been humming.

'You like it too?'

'It's pretty all right,' I admitted.

'It's more emo than goth, don't you think?' she teased and for the first time that day I laughed happily.

'You're one to talk.'

She chuckled back, 'I'm dead, it does nothing for my credibility.'

I scrunched up my nose and smiled; I'd missed her terribly.

'So why all the intense anguish?' Her tone was teasing, trying to make light of an awkward subject. It was just what I needed, and I was grateful for the way she knew me.

'They set the date,' I shrugged. 'The wedding's two months away.' My voice was dull and impassive, but inside I was the complete opposite. Something warm touched my shoulder and I smiled.

'That really sucks Luke. Is there anything I can do?'

'You can tell me where you've been for the past couple of days,' I said, changing the subject before I fainted from fury. I was already beginning to feel dizzy and my knees felt weak enough to buckle.

'Are you okay? 'It's just, your head and your le—'

'Hey, no evasions,' I cut in. 'Where'd you go?'

'I-I,' she was stuttering, which meant she was still worried. 'I was just clearing my head. I've had a lot on my mind.'

'What? Like your reckless, impulsive mother marrying the world's biggest arse?'

'Do you want to talk about it, Luke?'

I sniffed, 'Not really.'

'Are you sure because you seem—'

'Let's just talk about something else,' I snapped. There was a lengthy silence and I was sorry that I'd caused it. 'I really missed you, you know that?'

A warm sigh escaped her mouth and I knew she was smiling.

'I mean it,' I sulked. 'Life's not the same when you're not around.' I scraped my foot against the floor, trying not to feel embarrassed.

'Shut up Luke, don't be such a pansy.'

I laughed at how my words made her feel awkward. 'It's true. I've been working myself up for two whole days just thinking about you.'

'*Really*?'

'Yeah. Of course. You're what keeps me centred.'

She stammered, 'C-c-centred. Like how?'

'Well, like, I've been going crazy wanting to speak to Lucile, to be alone with her, but I just didn't know how to make it happen without looking stupid. I just kept thinking, *what would Angel say?* But the moment she came near me I panicked and just completely lost my cool. But you, you always make me feel calmer, you keep me grounded.' I smiled sincerely, 'I guess I need you just to be normal. It's like, I need you just to breathe right.'

There was another long pause. It lasted so long it caused me to halt. I looked in the direction of her pull, I hadn't realised it before, but we were standing outside the park, our park. The furious cracking of joints was the only noise to be heard in the silence, silence that stretched on and the light warm air around me began to feel suffocating. I spoke tentatively,

'Angel?'

'Everything's about you right?' she sneered. 'The whole world revolves around you and your precious *Lucile*?'

A hostile laugh escaped her mouth and I bit my lip in shock.

'So, you *missed me,* huh? Why Luke? Because I help you act normally? Because I make you *breathe right* around her? Stop you from making a fool of yourself? No, I know, you missed your *angel of love*. How does it feel, me helping you get closer to Lucile? Do you feel less lonely? More hopeful?'

'Angel it's not like that.' I had no idea where this was all coming from, but I wanted it to stop now.

'What about me?' she growled, 'What about what I need? Did you ever think for once in your selfish life that *I* might need someone? I-I mean a friend, *just* a friend? Or did you think spending my afterlife as your shadow was fulfilling enough for me? That my existence was *complete* because *hey,* I get to tag around with the social outcast, fixing his love life, fixing his home life, fixing his whole freaking life.' She was yelling now, a pained yell.

'I am your friend,' I whispered fiercely.

'Oh please,' she half laughed, half spat, 'We're not friends. I'm just your rebound buddy after the world rejected you.'

'No.'

'Oh, come on, say something more than no,' she urged. 'Tell me I'm being oversensitive. That everything I've said is ridiculously untrue. Make me feel like I mean something to you.'

I said nothing.

'I'm an idiot,' she whispered, her voice cracking lightly, 'and all this time I thought I wasn't alone.'

I parted my lips to speak but my mouth was dry, tongue lagging and wordless, so I shut them. I'd wanted to say something to make her understand exactly what she meant to me, but I didn't know what that was, so instead I said nothing.

In all that time it had taken me to realise this, that I couldn't put into words how I felt about her, she was gone, and I was alone. Utterly alone.

***

I stepped into class feeling like a depressed, drowned rat. Five minutes away from college and the heavens opened, dumping shed loads of rain on me. I couldn't help but think it was some kind of karmic punishment for what had happened with Angel.

I slid into my chair, feeling the dampness of my clothes as they stuck to my skin. Lucile was already in her seat, looking as immaculate as ever. I wanted to be near her, to smell her perfume, to trace my fingers along what looked like silky-smooth skin. Desire worked its way through my blood, alongside a rippling wave of guilt. It shamed me so thoroughly that it tainted any pleasure I felt when I looked at her.

'Great.'

I shifted my eyes, concentrating instead on the practice paper on my desk. I wasn't surprised to see it there — exams were less than a month away — if anything I was more shocked that we hadn't sat one sooner.

We spent the next hour and a half working on the test while Mr Taylor lurked over us, chewing on his pen nib, slight traces of drool sliding down to its tip. I forced myself into deep concentration, hoping that doing so would lull the guilt that ripped through me. It had just begun to work when Mr Taylor's voice sounded.

'Time's up,' he called, rubbing his thumb along his lip to strip away the ink stains. 'Don't bother finishing your sentences,' he droned apathetically, 'it probably won't make much of a difference to your overall mark anyway.'

The scrawling continued: Mr Taylor grunted before he began ripping sheets out from underneath pens.

'But sir,' Ricky moaned, 'we still got twenty minutes of class left. Why ain't we finishing it?'

Mr Taylor's small nostrils flared in his pointed nose.

'Keen aren't we,' he smiled wryly. 'I can't imagine why, Mr Hanisu, when it has become apparent to me that you can't even construct a *simple* sentence without making a grammatical error.'

Ricky arched his eyebrows comically, 'What you on about sir?'

'Why AREN'T we finishing it?'

'That's what I wanna know?' He leaned back in his chair and stretched widely, flexing his muscles in the process. Missy giggled girlishly and he winked at Naila, whose stare was deadly.

'Detention Mr Hanisu,' Mr Taylor snapped impatiently.

'What! What for?'

'For wasting my time.'

'Ah man-a,' Ricky moaned, 'but sir it's the last day of term.'

Mr Taylor smiled cheerily. '*Double* detention,' he said, enjoying the look on Ricky's face. 'But I'll be kind to you,' he added, tapping Ricky hard on the shoulders, throwing his arched back into an upright position. 'You can sit one hour today and the other hour when you get back from Easter break.'

Ricky lips straightened in to a tight, unfriendly smile. He looked as if he wanted to argue but thought better of it. Mr Taylor walked away.

'Trust *us* to be the only college around that still has detentions,' Ricky muttered.

I smiled to myself, thinking how lucky Ricky had been that I was the only one who had heard him.

'The reason we have stopped early is because I have decided that it would be beneficial for someone to share their exam paper with the class.'

He dragged his pen across the surface of his desk and the two girls at the front flinched.

'That way we can all learn from each other's successes and *mistakes.*'

He glared in my direction. My head went light and panic made my vision cloud over slightly. Through the haze I saw Missy's hand shoot up into the air, her fingernails shimmering blue as she waved it enthusiastically.

'I appreciate your willingness, Miss Neesman, really I do, but I have actually already selected the appropriate student.'

Missy moaned just as a bead of sweat sprang up on my forehead. I wiped it away hastily, then ran my quivering fingers through my hair. I knew Mr Taylor. I spoke his language. He'd said student but what he'd really meant was victim.

'Look down on your desk, class. If your exam paper still resides there, I would like you to stand up and read it out, word for word.'

My head felt heavy, as if all the blood in my body had rushed to my brain, making it feel dense and weak. I looked down with an irrational amount of panic bubbling up inside of me. Disbelief shot through me as if I hadn't been sitting right there when he'd scooped up my exam paper. I panicked more. No way was Mr Taylor letting me off the hook that easily. No way in hell; but I was wrong.

A chair — not too far from mine — scraped across the floor. From the corner of my eye I saw his victim rise, her long delicate fingers clutching the back of her neck. My heart froze momentarily, and when it started up again it throbbed dully. It should have been me, I thought as I listened to Lucile's rapid breathing. I wished it had been me.

She opened her mouth and began to read, hurriedly, tripping over her words. She stuttered underneath Mr Taylor's cold and hostile stare; starting her sentences over and over again while she rocked nervously on her feet. Precisely seven minutes later, when her essay had come to a close, she shakily shut the booklet, exhaling nervously. Nobody said a word. I chewed roughly at my lips, hoping that the pain would distract me from the swell of nerves growing in my stomach.

Mr Taylor blinked widely and coughed out a laugh.

'Is that it? That's all you've managed to write?' He laughed again, this time more bitterly. 'Don't get me wrong, it was nice and ah... *lengthy*... but the quality, the substance,' he threw back his head now, flourishing a cackle, 'absolutely abysmal. To think you'll be sitting your exams in less than a month and that is all you can muster. Where were half the things we've learnt this year? Where was in-depth critical analysis? Where was the studying of the language used in that period? Where was comparison? Similarity and contrast? Where was any of it when you droned on for five pages filling your sheet with *twaddle*?'

She shook nervously but kept her face stern, defiant.

'You disappoint me, Miss Armstrong. Sit down.'

Not a single person in the room could keep their eyes off of her, yet she lowered herself into her seat with more grace than I ever could.

My blood was hot, it rushed to my face flushing my cheeks a furious red. My head pounded angrily, and I swallowed back the bile that had risen up in my anger. Mr Taylor prattled on, but it was impossible to hear him over my seething thoughts. I considered his words again and again, marvelling at how easily the script had fallen from his tongue. Something told me that he had been planning that speech all morning. He'd probably mulled over the words at breakfast, crafted them perfectly, ensuring that each one held a beautifully demoralising quality, prompting enough self-doubt to rip apart a person's self-confidence from the inside out. The speech had been set, but the victim, that was variable. He was a pathetic, smug little man and I hated him.

The bell sounded, its artificial jingling clear and crisp cutting through the tense silence. There was a loud bang as Mr Taylor threw open the door and left, a shuffling of papers and the unhappy dragging of feet as the class strolled lifelessly to the common room, leaving Lucile and I almost alone.

'You okay? Luce?' Missy asked ripping open a pack of gummy worms.

She murmured a 'yeah,' but I recognised the sting of humiliation and it pained me.

'He was *really* out of order; don't you think Nay?' She nudged Naila roughly in the arm.

'He's a prick,' she said, shoving Missy just as roughly. 'The essay wasn't even that bad.'

'She's right,' Missy garbled through a mouthful of red and green. 'I thought it was pretty um… pretty—'

'Crap,' she interjected and Missy almost chocked on a worm. 'He was right. I've been so caught up with this whole Shane thing. I let him get inside my head, he messed me up, but now that it's over—'

'*Really* over?' Missy blurted through her smacking lips.

'It's over, Miss, and it's fine. I don't need a guy like that, I just need to study.'

There was an awkwardness; Missy popped a pink bubble gum into her mouth and chewed noisily to fill it but Naila, she studied Lucile's face just as carefully as I did.

'I'm fine. *Really*. In fact, I order you two to go. I'm going to see if I can catch Mr Taylor before registration anyway. Maybe he'll be able to give me some constructive pointers on my essay.' She grimaced as if the thought was not only unbearable but unfeasible, too.

'Cool,' said Missy, letting a huge pink bubble pop with a bang. 'I wanted to see if I could get my hands, on Ricky anyway. He's been acting really weird since our date. Distant. I don't know, maybe he's playing hard to get?

'Well catch him quick, Miss,' Naila trilled with mock enthusiasm. 'You'll never find out the truth standing here.'

'You are so right Nay. See you guys at free period,' she called as she skipped out of the room, her silky blonde hair trailing behind her.

Naila rolled her eyes and shook her head, 'Pathetic. All you need is a shiny object with that girl and she's off.' Lucile laughed lightly. 'Are you sure you don't want me to stay?'

'No. *You,* you should *definitely* go.'

'But—'

'Find Ricky and talk to him before Missy gets there first.'

Naila tucked a finger around the belt loop of her jeans.

'You think so? What if he doesn't... I mean... what about Missy?'

Lucile looked her friend hard in the eyes. 'He definitely does; and Missy will be fine. Just palm her off with something sparkly and she won't even notice you've taken him.'

Naila tilted her head and grinned doubtfully.

I thought back to all the times I'd seen Ricky with their little trio and laughed inwardly. It had been so obvious. The lingered looks, the constant showing off. Of course, Naila had been the one he was into. It made a whole lot more sense than him and Missy. She was far too in love with herself for anyone to cope with.

Naila nibbled her inner lip thoughtfully.

'Honestly, don't worry about Miss,' Lucile said, rubbing the small of Naila's back. 'When it comes down to it, she's a really good friend. She'll understand.'

'Yeah, maybe.'

'Well you're never going to find out standing here,' she said quoting her own words back at her. 'Just go.'

'Are you sure you're okay?'

'I'm sure, now go. You can tell me the good news later. It'll cheer me up.' Naila squeezed Lucile's arm before trying not to hurry out of the door.

I stood at my desk, looking at the empty table, my things now safely in my bag. I had no reason to be there anymore, but I just couldn't leave. Her eyes flitted across my face momentarily and I looked away. What am I doing here? She didn't need me. A warm flutter settled beside me, calming the nerves that pricked me.

'Now's your chance,' she whispered, her voice still cool.

Fear and guilt mingled inside me. I ran my hands through my hair and gripped the back strands tightly.

'I can't,' I whispered back. 'What if she says no?'

I knew that Angel was probably the worst person to have this conversation with. Sharing my doubts with the one person who resented them, who was hurt by them, it was completely and utterly selfish, not to mention insensitive. I knew this, but there was no one else.

She sighed deeply. 'If she says no it will hurt,' she answered, sounding both cold yet detached, 'more than you realise. More than you ever thought possible. But I'll be there.'

That knowledge comforted me, and my heart thudded deeply. I hoped that she could feel its intensity and I hoped that she would know that in that moment it beat fiercely for her, no one else. She was important to me, she had to know that. I may not have known in what way yet or how to put it in to words, but she was — so I let my heart speak for me and prayed that she would understand its meaning.

Lucile swung her bag over her shoulder and shot past me, heading for the door. I panicked; I wanted to stop her, but that panic clogged my brain and I couldn't think of a way to make her stay.

'Call her back,' Angel urged, and I did.

'Lucile,' my voice escaped my tight throat, sounding croaky and unrecognisable. It was so low and timid I was afraid she hadn't heard me, but she turned around and smiled. My heart thrummed eagerly, and I breathed, deep and slow, to steady my nerves. She said nothing, just stared at me expectantly. I swallowed hard and spoke again.

'I-I thought you were waiting for Mr Taylor.'

Her smile widened and my heart weakened with pleasure.

'No, not really, I just wanted those two to let me breathe. Don't get me wrong, I love them and I'm and grateful that they care, but I just wanted to be by myself for a few minutes.'

'Oh,' my brow furrowed, and my bottom lip pouted involuntarily, 'okay s-s-sorry.'

'No, no, not you,' Lucile laughed shaking her head. She strode towards me and threw her bag down next to mine. She cocked her head and bit her lip in a way that made me tingle. There were mere inches between us, and I was having a hard time trying to still my erratic nerves.

'Are you okay Lucas?' she leaned in a little closer and studied my face. 'You're sweating a little.'

I leant back on my desk, trying to increase the distance between us so that I could catch my breath.

'Yeah,' I squeaked, 'It's just, I just... Mr Taylor's a real git,' I blurted. I was a mess, a total idiot. She smiled again making, me shake.

'It's okay, he's mean to everyone, especially you.'

I cringed openly, my complexion deepening.

'Today was just my turn.'

'Well... not everyone,' I mumbled. 'Your friend Missy always seems to smile her way out of it.'

'That's true. That's Missy.'

'I don't buy it. There must be more to those two. She's never seen his dark side. In fact, he doesn't have one with her.'

'What are you implying?'

She smiled at me and I became flustered, letting the first thing that came to mind fly out of my mouth.

'I don't know, maybe they're hooking up in the staff room after hours.'

The second the words were said I regretted them. There was a half a pause, in which I held my breath, before she burst out laughing.

'Urgh that's gross. Possible, but gross.'

I laughed a little too, though more out of nervous relief than anything else. Then the silence returned, this time longer.

'So...' I began without a plan, 'did you need help with English? Because I'm not too bad and if you needed help over the holidays, I could help you.' I was aware that I'd said help about a hundred times but I couldn't stop myself from rambling.

'That's sweet, but I'm actually going away for a few days. I'm only visiting my Aunt and Uncle in Manchester, so I'll probably get a lot of my studying done then.'

'Oh,' I said trying to sound more fine, than I actually was. I lowered my head, feeling embarrassment and heartache wash all over me.

Warm fingertips caressed my hands; I looked up expecting to find Lucile gone and Angel occupying her space, but I was wrong.

'I'll be back next Saturday, we could meet up then if you'd like. Maybe even do something a little more fun than studying.'

I gazed into her dark eyes. 'Like what?' I muttered.

'Surprise me,' she smiled seductively, and my knees buckled a little. She gripped my hand tightly to stop me from sliding to the ground then, lifting it up, straightened out my fingers. Her hand slipped into her tight jeans, pulling out a pen. The nib tickled along my skin as she wrote her number down on my palm with an *X*. She released my sweat-dampened hand, but I could still feel her warmth on my skin. Snatching her bag from the floor, she smiled again before leaving the room. Her hips swayed in that way that made my blood race.

I had a date with Lucile. I wanted to scream! I had a date with Lucile. My heart raced inside my chest and I laughed so hard it hurt. I wanted to share this moment with someone, with Angel, my best friend, my one. I hadn't noticed she was gone.

***

I rummaged inside my back pocket, feeling for my earphones. Pulling them out I stared at the tangled mess in my hands.

'Great,' I grumbled, tugging at knotted wires, 'just great.'

I should have been happy and big part of me was. I had a date with hottest girl in college but nothing felt right.

Angel had been here. Not for long, but as I stepped out into the muggy afternoon air, I'd felt her warmth too. Briefly; then it was gone. I wanted to go after her, to the park where I knew she'd be. I missed her *badly*. I wanted to tell her about the date, the actual concrete, set-in-stone, definitely-happening date - as confirmed by the few exchanged messages throughout the day setting a time and place to meet. The date she'd helped me get but I couldn't. I'd been selfish enough. This time I had to be patient, for her sake. She'd be back when she was ready, I just had to find a way to deal with the pain until then.

I went back to concentrating on my tangled earphones when a heavy hand forced my shoulder down. My knees buckled, threatening to let me drop to the ground, but the same hand dragged me up *before* they could hit the floor, jerking me to an awkward standstill. Mac, with his hardened face, was glaring at me… dangerously. He clenched and unclenched his rough hands and I felt that familiar warm rush of hate again.

'*You!*' He growled viciously, '*You* and *Lucile??*' He barked an angry laugh and continued glare at me, his eyes not leaving my face. I shrugged.

'So, it's true? I thought that Missy was just running that big mouth of hers again getting her facts wrong. But it's true? *You* and *Lucile?*'

He blinked at me, struggling to believe it. I nodded this time, the starts of a grin tickling my lips.

'I thought I warned you to stay away from her,' he hissed.

I took a step backwards, but he closed the space between us, his heavyset, muscular body towering over my slender one. I swallowed nervously now, my smug smile sagging off my lips.

'And now what? You expect me to let you cop a feel first before I make my move? Does that seem right to you?'

Hate and anger brewed so hot my nerves were melting away.

'I'm talking to you,' he snarled, poking me hard in the chest. I felt a fiery burst of pain erupt underneath his thickset finger. It spread along the surface of my chest. I flinched slightly, feeling sore, but I desperately wanted to tear his head off.

'What the hell, Mac?' scowled a soft delicate voice. Lucile. She flanked my side. 'You think you ever had a chance? That I was gonna pick you over him?' A brief chuckle flicked out of her mouth, smacking Mac in the face.

We had an audience now, but for the first time I didn't care. Mac stepped back, jaw clenched, his hateful stare darting between the two of us. Lucile glared at him threateningly.

'Screw you then,' he snarled. 'Screw you both. You ain't even that nice anyway,' he spat bitterly, kicking a Sprite can beside his foot.

'Come on,' he barked at his morons.

He dragged the closest one by the jacket and they left, disappearing into the small crowed that had gathered.

Lucile stepped closer, brushing her hand lightly along my arm.

'I'm sorry,' she said, her face almost touching mine, her lips only a lean away from my own.

'F-for what?' I stammered. I could feel her breath on my skin, it sent tingles of pleasure rippling through me.

'It was a guy thing. I shouldn't have gotten involved, it's just that I can't stand him. For him to think that I would ever go out with him over you…' she paused, lowering her eyes, biting her lip. I held my breath, desperate for her to finish her sentence.

'Anyway, I was just about to head off home. Do you, maybe, want a lift?' There was a lengthy pause. She raised her eyes and gazed into mine.

I panicked, losing the words somewhere in my throat. I gripped the back of my neck, nervously looking anywhere but at her. Lucile's soft, slender fingers wrapped themselves around mine. I smiled a little and clasped them tightly, it was all I could do not to pass out.

***

The radio murmured in the background, but the beating of my heart was still the loudest thing in my ears. That and the intense ringing of awkwardness. We had talked a little about the on-and-then-off-again rain, what a jerk Mac was, the possibility of him being spawned by Mr Taylor and our plans for the Easter break. Now there was nothing left between us but silence. Silence and a strange palpable energy; a mixture of lust, desire and fear coating us.

Lucile tapped her finger against the steering wheel and mumbled a 'come on,' as she willed the sluggish traffic to move. I snuck a few glances her way and caught her doing the same. I'd tried to start up several conversations but stopped. None of them seemed interesting enough. So instead I ran my tongue against the back of my teeth a few times, biting it slightly whenever I got the urge to speak.

The car crawled down the cluttered roads, making the necessary turns, until it rolled to a stop in front of my house. She switched off the ignition and leant back in her chair, rolling her bottom lip between her fingers. I undid my seat belt and shifted my body slightly to face her. The energy between us thickened, making my heart race and my head light. I pressed my fingers to my temples, giving them a gentle squeeze. My hand trembled.

'Do you have a headache?' Lucile asked.

I dropped my hands. 'A little, it'll pass.'

'You get them a lot. I've noticed.' She had noticed me? 'I've got some aspirin if you want,' she said, plunging her hand deep into her bag and throwing things about.

'No, it's okay. Like I said, it'll pass.'

'Oh. Okay,' a look of disappointment flitted across her face.

I had offended her, hadn't I? I hated myself for being so socially inept.

'Thanks anyway,' I added trying to wash away any hurt my abruptness might have caused.

She smiled broadly, 'That's okay.'

We sat there for a few moments, the heat between us increasing with every unspoken second. She nibbled lightly at the bottom of her lip and I fantasised that it was me instead. I closed my eyes for half a second, struggling to find stillness, to breathe deeply. A wave of emotions washed through me, none of them calm. When I opened them again, she was looking out of the window, her thoughts seemingly far away.

'Is everything okay?' I asked. No, you idiot, you've bored her into apathy; but then her lips, they pulled up into a smile and she turned to face me, leaning in across the space that separated us.

'Everything's fine,' she said, her tone soft and sultry. She looked deeply into my eyes and I stared back into hers. My heartbeat sped up. Her lips were a touch away from mine. Desire, in all its magnitude, rushed around my body, pinging at every nerve. I swallowed hard, acknowledging both the lump in my throat and the deep intense throb that was my pulse. I closed my eyes and leaned in towards her. Just a fraction. Not enough for skin to touch but close enough so that I could feel the heat emanating from her lips. Another ripple. It ran through me shaking me ever so slightly. I loved it. This moment right here and everything about it was perfect. Then it gripped at me without warning. My eyes sprang open. A sudden rush of heat leaked into my body. It bubbled furiously and I cringed against the familiar sense of comfort and compassion. It settled around me, spreading like fire. She was close, I could tell, yet at the same time far away, just like she had been at college. I whipped my head around to face my house. She was in my room. I was sure of it. Angel.

'Are you okay, Luke?' Lucile asked, her voice burning with subtle passion.

I turned to face her again. Guilt gnawed at my insides, ripping away the bulk of my longing. I stared intently at her. Her soft lips in a slight pout, her smouldering eyes. It only added to my sense of unease. She pulled her body closer to mine and I jerked, bolting to the furthest side of the car.

'Luke,' she called, the fierce, affronted curiosity in her tone almost masking her humiliation.

'I'm so sorry,' I murmured, my hand reaching for the door handle behind me. I tugged at it roughly and it gave.

'I-I should go,' I stuttered, half-falling out of the car. Clambering to my feet, I sped across the front garden. Lucile shouted after me, but I didn't look back. I jammed my key into the lock and yanked open the door without a second glance at the car as it revved its engine and sped away. A second wave of guilt washed through me, but I pushed it aside, bounding up the stairs, each desperate limb propelling itself forward with maximum effort. I burst through the door to my room towards the warmth, longing to ease the greater half of my guilt. My body sagged limply in disappointment. Angel wasn't there.

Chapter 19
Saturday, 10th April

Dear Journal,

Today's To-do List:

- 12:30 pm Go crazy
- 12:32pm Go crazy some more
- 12:35pm Pretend not to be going crazy
- 12:40pm Give up the pretence

It's official. It's been over a week now. Seven full days and eight full nights and still no word. I'm dying to send her another text, but then I remember the few hundred voicemails and I think that might be bordering on harassment. So... what do I do? What do I do? What do I do...?

I can't have blown it with Lucile already, but after five unanswered text messages (plus those voicemails) maybe I've blown it with the entire female population.

I'm an arse and I feel awful. If you took nervous tension, pounded it with a stick of despair then wrapped it up in a guilt gauze, that might be close to what I'm feeling now. Thank God it's the Easter break. Extra time with Mae and Nick is a pie full of crap, but it's way better than suffering through Mac's gloating. I can hear him now. 'What happened freak? Couldn't you even make it through the car ride home?'

Do one, arse face.

Angel's gone. I'm trying not to think about it a lot, but when I do, I can't breathe. I start doubling over in pain; shaking, I'm so scared. This one, stupid, neurotic thought playing in my mind: *she's never coming back.*

The nights are easier. I dream, and when I do, she's there. I draw myself to her soul. But even there, in the quiet space of this other world she pulls away from me. I guess guilt's not so easy to escape from, even while you sleep.

I wish she'd talk to me. I miss her sarcastic stupidity, her jokes. I want so much, to make things better, but she keeps pushing me away. She's silent. Always silent. Eerily silent, but her warmth... It's strong. Then I wake up and that always sucks. But there's a moment, the moment before the eyes open, before the first rational thought has formed, that's when I feel her. Like bits of the dream leftover. Her closeness, it's in me. I'm never sure if it's real or not but I hope... I hope that it is. Then it slips away, and the only thing left is that thought. She's never coming back.

Great. Now my hand's trembling.

Chapter 20

I tossed the pen somewhere and slid my journal underneath my pillow. The covers felt warm as I pulled them back over my body, ignoring the screechy sound of my name being called. It was the fourth time Mae had yelled for me but still I couldn't bear to answer. I squeezed my ears shut with the palms of my hands — the trembling stopping, slipping away with effort, like the thoughts of her. Angel. I was dreading today, and I had every intention of putting it off for as long as I could.

The shrieking stopped. I let go of my ears and grasped the drawstring of my pyjama bottoms. I tugged harder, trying to ignore it, but it was no use. I bit down on my lip and moaned. My head, the pain in my head. My stomach quivered lightly, swaying with every slight movement. I've got to be coming down with something. Maybe an allergy to Mae, Nick and all this wedding crap. Breathe deep, I told myself, trying to regain some normality in my body. I failed.

A yawn slipped through a breath. I blinked again and again, my eyes feeling heavier each time, my body limp. It was late in the morning. I should have felt rested, but I didn't, I felt drowsy. Drowsy but unfortunately awake.

Flat, heavy footsteps pounded the stairs, slapping angrily against the old flooring. I knew who they belonged to. I pulled the covers from my face and braced myself.

The door swung open, followed by a light rush of air. Nick caught the handle before it could slam into the wall and shut it, light but forceful. Marching towards me, snarl intact, he grabbed a fistful of covers. Catching my vest top he yanked me with them. Nick drew me close, so close I could smell the sweat that sleeked his skin.

'Your mother called,' he growled.

'So, I heard.'

'Listen you little creep,' he hissed, shaking me hard. 'Your mother wants you dressed and ready to leave in twenty minutes.'

I stared at him with dead eyes, no words. Nick twisted his face and I could hear him grinding his teeth. He was angry. Angry because of me and that pleased me. It was stupid, but I let myself feel this reckless pleasure, it lessened the sting of my worries.

'Are you deaf or stupid?'

'Are those my only options? Only I can't quite decide.'

Nick lifted his heavy arm and smacked me hard with the back of his free hand. Just enough to hurt without leaving a mark. My head spun for a moment and the pain in my head intensified, griping angrily at each cell in my brain. I closed my eyes, drew in a long breath and dared to sputter a laugh.

'Careful,' I warned, my voice weak. 'I don't think Mae would be too happy if her two favourite guys spent the day in ICU instead of suit shopping. Do you?'

Mae called and I smiled deeply.

'Honey, is Luke up yet?' A few seconds passed before he managed an answer.

'Yeah sweetie, we were just having a little chat.'

'Well chat in the car, otherwise Luke will be late for his appointment at Bardous.'

She lifted her foot off the squeaky stair and bustled off somewhere. Nick unclenched his fist, letting me flop to the bed. 'Twenty. Minutes,' he scowled then left.

***

'Aww, sweet cheeks, there must be something here you like.'

The sales assistant had finished straightening up the unwanted outfits and was now railing them back out on to the shop floor. I watched the lady next to me tug at the sleeves of her son's suit and smooth out the lapel. He groaned at her fussiness, and a twang of bitter jealousy licked at my insides. I would have hated having my mother around, her presence alone irritated me, but I guess a small, childish part of me couldn't help wishing that things were different. But Mae was selfish and stupid. She'd proven that, time and time again. Even now. Palming me off on the jerk in favour of her yoga class. Yoga that she'd only just taken up to look good for the wedding, for Nick. I hated her.

A slender figure walked up to me, her sweet perfume mingling with the air.

'Will you be taking this one instead?'

I shrugged my shoulders, ignoring the salesgirls' 'tut' as she abandoned me for what was clearly a more satisfying customer. The worst thing was, I couldn't even blame her. Even I'd have shafted me. I'd been here ages and was still struggling to make a decision. Mainly because I couldn't summon up enough in me to give a crap. It was a nice enough suit, I thought, eyeing up my reflection in the mirror. The sales assistant had dressed me well and I guess it was fine, but what did I know about things like this?

I glanced over at the boy with his mother. The deep black suit he wore hung suavely off his overly built body; he winked cockily at his reflection before posing.

'You look so handsome,' his mother beamed.

'Who you telling?'

Her laugh was booming, 'How a person can be *that* in love with themselves I'll never know.'

'Yeah, yeah. Can we just get this thing and go?' he said peeling out of his layers. 'I want to catch up with my boys.'

'Your "boys"? Oh, you mean the lads from your school math club.'

'*Mum.*' He whined, casting me a few awkward glances as she stifled a snigger.

'Let's just go okay.'

'Sure thing, angel. Let's wrap this afternoon up.'

Angel. The word punctured my lungs and I gasped. My kneecaps softened instantly, making me stagger. Hearing her name, even out of context, it chilled me.

'Sweetie. Are you okay?'

I stared into the concerned eyes of someone else's mother. A flurry of nerves beat beneath my skin, making me quiver. I felt the colour drain from my face as the thought came rushing at me: *she's never coming back.*

'Hey,' she placed a hand on my forehead, 'you're shaking quite a bit. Are you sick?'

'No,' but my voice was weak. 'Just a little faint.'

'Do you have anyone who could come and get you?'

I murmured a weak 'no.'

'What about that guy you came in with? Your Dad?' I thought about Nick, who'd ditched me at the first available opportunity with absolutely no explanation and laughed darkly.

'He'd be happier if he found me dead.' She looked at me uneasily. It mingled with the concern in her eyes and I felt bad. I wasn't her problem.

'Mum,' the son cut in, 'Back off. You're meddling.'

'But.'

'He's cool, Mum,' he added more firmly.

'He's right,' I swallowed, feeling my head lighten in the process, 'I'm fine.'

'Oh.' It was a sceptical 'oh.' 'Okay.' Then, giving me a second glance, she disappeared behind the curtain with her son. Back to laughing at his protests.

***

I gulped down the ice-cold cola, draining the glass. Ice chips slid down my throat chilling everything they touched.

My partially eaten pizza lay on my plate looking a savage mess. Toppings picked at and shifted about until it was more sludge covering a doughy base. Half a slice in and I'd been done; each bite a greasy load hitting my stomach, whipping up waves of nausea. It was my anxiety getting the best of me for sure. Physically I felt better, but the way I felt inside I might as well be terminal. I missed her. There was a dull ache tearing through me and I was afraid it was all that would be left of her. Loneliness consumed me and I gripped the table, tapping my fingers against the plastic to help manage the pain.

The waitress bustled over. 'Can I offer you dessert?' she asked, wiping her free hand clean on her apron.

I flicked my gaze from her face to my barely touched food with a look of impatience. She rolled her eyes with equal irritation.

'I have to ask,' she replied curtly before striding off, mumbling a flow of insults underneath her breath.

I would have thrown one back but the bell at the entrance jangled and the sound of a familiar voice seized my attention. My body stiffened as the shrill pitch crawled inside my head. My eyes followed the screech to Missy, who dropped her bag into the booth nearest the door and settled into a seat across from Naila.

My heart sped up. All thoughts of Angel vanished, leaving a giant crater-like space for Lucile to occupy. What were they doing here? Did they know what had happened with Lucile? I wanted so badly to get away, but they were blocking the exit. Panic set in. Sweat began to form at the nape of my neck and I rolled teeth against teeth. The huffy waitress came back with both the bill and the chip and pin device, eager to speed up my departure. She placed the slip of paper down at the table and pointed to the price, her lips pulled into a tight, insincere smile. I looked up at her from beneath my hair and grinned back.

'On second thoughts, a dessert menu would be great.'

Her feigned pleasant expression shifted drastically. She narrowed her dark eyes and snatched the receipt, rolling it in the palm of her hand.

'Of course,' she said coldly before marching away again in a huff.

When she returned, she slammed down a menu and stalked off, leaving the table shaking in her wake.

'Thanks,' I called quietly and slid as far down into my seat as was possible.

I peeked at them from above the laminated paper. Missy's voice droned, her hands flying about like a weapon as she gestured. I tried to catch the conversation but the distance between us meant that all I could hear was a garbled squeak and the occasional shrill laugh. I looked from their booth to the door. There was a little under a metre of space between the two. Nibbling at my lip I weighed up my chances of being caught. The odds were against me. I had no choice. I had to wait them out. A hoarse clear of the throat rumbled above me. I looked up.

'Are you ready to order?'

I gave the menu a quick glance and picked a number at random.

'Are you for real?' the waitress snapped.

'What?' I hissed under my breath.

'It's the dessert menu, *sir*.'

'Yeah so.'

'Well, *genius*, there is no number *42*, but I guess if you were to ask in that *special* way you do the chef will whip up another 36 delicacies just for you.'

Her tone was bitterly sarcastic, and I bit back the desire to insult her.

'Tell you what,' I said, a strained smile aching my cheeks, 'Why don't you just bring me your least favourite thing on the menu. That way you can satisfy your need to irritate me and drop the tantrums.' It was the best I could manage.

She hesitated for a moment, her mouth slightly agape, then turned on her heel and left. A few minutes later a bowl of rhubarb and pear crumble was delivered to my table in frosty silence. It came covered in thick steaming custard with a side of clotted cream. I wanted to heave. I could barely eat my pizza, now this. After a few stirs with the spoon I took a bite. Large gooey chunks stuck in my throat and I cursed my empty glass.

A quarter of an hour passed, then another. I picked at my food, stirring until it resembled baby mush. Time seemed to be crawling by. Missy and Naila ate slowly, showing no signs of leaving any time soon. My patience began to expire under the agitated glares of the staff members whose precious table I'd been occupying for a while now. I tapped my bowl with my spoon, drawing their attention to its fullness, and shrugged. The few that didn't roll their eyes pretended not to be looking.

When another fifteen minutes went by, I'd finally had enough. I stared at the girls, watching for the perfect opportunity to leave discreetly, when Missy's phone rang. She plunged into her bag to search for it and I wasted no time at all. Reaching into my pocket, I pulled out some cash and placed it underneath the pudding bowl, not bothering with receipts or change. I scooped up my bag and was about to make a dash for it when a clumsy waitress tripped, landing inches from my feet. Tomato soup sprayed my top and I groaned at my perpetual bad luck. There was a small eruption of sniggers and a few scattered claps.

Amongst the clatter of noise, I heard that signature shrill gasp, but I kept my eyes lowered.

The embarrassed waitress struggled to lift herself out of the mess, her palms slipping repeatedly in the orangey-red ooze. I held out my hand, helping the girl to her feet, getting more soup on myself in the process. She mumbled a shy apology before scarpering off behind the staff door and I wiped my soup-smeared hand on my splattered shirt.

My eyes were still focused on the ground, but I could sense the burning stare all over my body. Reluctantly I looked up. Missy's cheeks flushed excitedly as her bright blue eyes devoured me. I felt the quickening of my pulse beneath my skin, and though my face had turned ruddy I worked hard on clinging to what little calm I had left. With a silent intake of air, I strode towards the door. Naila and Missy exchanged a few strained words, but I blocked them out, concentrating instead on the exit. I was a few strides away when a pair of legs extended in front of me, barring my way. My shoulders slumped.

'Hey Luke,' Missy giggled. She lowered her legs and tugged at her mini skirt.

'Missy. Hey.'

Naila looked up from her plate of chips and smiled. 'Hi Luke,' she said, her tone apologetic. I smiled back.

Missy grinned, 'So, Luke. How has your week been?'

I arched my eyebrows wondering what kind of trap she was trying to lure me into.

'Mine has been amazing,' she blurted.

I cast Naila a sideways glance and she rolled her eyes in return.

'I've been so busy making plans for my big-end-of-college slash eighteenth birthday house party I've barely had time to study for the exams.'

'Right,' I said, watching her carefully.

She let out a fleeting giggle. 'Anyway, I called Lucile to get her opinion on a couple of things and do you know what I found out?'

There it was, the giant manhole she'd been leading me to. My chest tightened and I shook my head.

'Nothing.'

'Nothing?' I was stunned.

'That's right, nothing. She didn't pick up. She hasn't picked up all week.'

Relief burst through me, slackening my chest. An involuntary smile lengthened across my face and I exhaled. She didn't know anything. My pulse had just begun to settle into a nice gentle rhythm when a sudden loud slapping together of hands sent it shooting again.

'I told you he knew something,' she squealed.

'Missy leave him alone.'

'I will not. He's smiling,' her words slid the expression off my face.

'Missy, let the boy go.'

'No,' she leapt to her feet and glared at me, eyes narrowed into suspicious slits.

'Lucile goes AWOL for the first time since her break up and freaky rebound over here has a great big dirty grin on his face. He knows something,' she said, pointing a delicate finger at me, 'or he's done something.'

I swallowed hard, hearing the nervous gulp as it passed down my throat, but I kept her gaze. I was determined not to look guilty.

'I don't know anything.'

'Don't lie to me you weirdo. I know what your people are like. You've probably offered her up as a human sacrifice or something. Drank her blood under the full moon or whatever.'

'Missy, you're acting nuts,' Naila said trying to urge Missy back to her seat with a tug of the arm.

Missy shook her loose and continued to stare at me. Her boldness shaking my weak confidence.

'I don't know anything.' I murmured. 'I swear. I haven't heard from her all week either.'

'Really?' she said her piercing blue eyes focused on mine.

I nodded my head, not trusting my voice to remain steady.

'I thought you had a date today.'

'Yeah. So?' I croaked.

'Soooo, I find it weird that your date's in a few hours and you haven't even heard from her. Don't you, Nay?'

'*No Miss*, I don't.'

'Have you called her?' Missy asked.

146

'No,' I lied.

'Has she called you?'

'No.'

'No?'

'Missy sit down and shut up.'

'Aren't you afraid she won't show?' Missy laughed, ignoring Naila's order.

'She'll show,' I barked, not feeling an ounce of the confidence I portrayed.

'Oh my gosh,' she cackled louder, throwing her head back. 'Of course. It all makes sense now.'

Tension crept through me.

'That's why she hasn't called. You're being stood up.'

I felt my stomach empty as my brain absorbed her words.

'You don't know what you're talking about Missy.'

'You are. You're being stood up, and a week in advance... that's just pathetic.'

'That's not what's happening,' I snarled, shaking with rage.

'Oh gosh honey, it is. And of course, Lucile doesn't want to speak to us,' she said throwing Naila a look. 'She's embarrassed. We told her again and again what an horrific mistake it was to go out with you.'

'When did I *ever* say that?' Naila remarked.

'So, you didn't say it out loud, big whop. You still thought it.'

'I—'

Missy cut her off. 'I feel so silly now, coming down on you so hard. Accusing you of doing something to hurt her.'

I glared at her.

'You must feel so awful now. I've heard that kind of rejection's particularly painful. Is it?' she added rubbing my arm.

My fists were clenched into tight balls and my chest fluctuated rapidly.

'Well you should know,' I growled, shaking my arm free from her touch.

'What's that supposed to mean?'

'How's Ricky?'

Her face tightened and her jaw clenched. I felt bad watching Naila slide down into her seat, but Missy deserved it, and more.

'She did not reject me,' I spat one more time.

Regaining herself, Missy tilted her head, giving me a patronising sympathetic pout.

'Sure Lukey. Whatever you say. I'm going to go ahead and sit down now, okay.'

She hopped back into her seat and began fiddling with her phone again, as though the last five minutes had never occurred. I wasn't even a blip on her radar anymore, I thought, as she sniggered at a text message. I hovered on the spot for a few moments like an idiot, seething venomously, not quite knowing how to handle my hatred for this tiny, seemingly harmless girl. I couldn't take it anymore. Her face, Mac's, Nick's, they all began to merge into one in my mind until I wasn't even one hundred percent on who I was looking at. I stormed out of there while I still had at least a loose grasp on what was going on.

Out in the shopping centre I was immediately greeted by the throng of busy shoppers. I pushed and shoved — not caring who I offended — until I became part of the mass. My mind was racing. Reality was beginning to catch up with me again, but I wasn't sure it was doing me any good. Had I really been stood up? Had I messed things up that spectacularly? My mind flashed back to Missy, her mocking laugh and I clenched my fist. Maybe not, I thought, defiantly. Maybe I was overreacting. Maybe there was a reason she hadn't got back to me. Another less obvious explanation that had nothing to do with me abandoning her in favour of a dead girl. Besides, I joked to myself, when had Missy ever been right? I tried to put stock in my own words of encouragement. Tried to soak them into every fibre of my being, but a hardened stone sat in my stomach reminding me that I was not wrong.

***

My run in with Missy had left me insanely riled up. It ate at me viciously until I threw up lunch. My stomach tightened and twisted, extracting everything until the only thing left to bring up was air. I dragged myself from the men's toilets, finding solace in the open air. My throat was fiery raw. I sucked at the cool breeze, hoping to ease the sharp prickling sensation. I was livid, my blood so hot I thought I would faint. I was supposed to be meeting Nick in a couple of minutes, but I couldn't, not like this. I needed to calm down, so I walked. I traced the back roads of town, wandering aimlessly until my anger simmered. It took a while. Twenty minutes came and went, but still I couldn't go back to the car park, not until I was strong enough to handle whatever he threw at me. I thought about Angel and how her presence would have soothed all my bitter emotions in an instant. How her warmth would have healed me. I fantasised about the memory of her inner touch and clung to it, feeling chunks of my tension slowly fall away.

***

The car ride home was eerily silent. I'd been half an hour late, and when I'd caught up with Nick, he'd said nothing. Just glared straight ahead as he massaged his angry temple. He didn't look at me as people meandered through the vehicles in the car park and I knew why. I slipped into the back seat and bit my lip, wondering what he would have done to me had there been no witnesses. Grateful that there were.

I couldn't wait to be home, to get away from his muted fury, but the traffic moved sluggishly. The minute hand on my watch ticked loudly in the silence, urging me to look at the time, but I couldn't. Lucile and I had planned to meet at five and I knew, without seeing, that time had crept past the hour.

Automatically, I felt for the phone in my pocket. My fingers clasped around its wide shape, but I stopped myself from pulling it out. There wasn't going to be a missed call or a text. I'd seen to that.

The sound of Lucile revving her engine as she sped away replayed in my head. I shrank away from the phantom noise, wondering what she'd been thinking then. I imagined the look of confusion on her face. The hurt that must have taken her by surprise. A knot twisted inside my stomach.

When we reached Elmsbury Road — a street away from our own — Nick pulled the car to a stop. I undid my seatbelt and moved to the passenger's seat in the front. He flicked on the radio, the music streamed out of the speakers, it did nothing for the tension in the car.

He grunted and cut me a sideways glance, 'What's the suit like?'

'Navy, cream shirt, purple tie.'

'Where did we eat?'

'Benny's Diner.'

He snarled, 'I hate Benny's, your mother knows that. It's full of little idiots like you.'

'You pick then,' I was already bored of this conversation. He smacked his lips together and sniffed. I envisioned the cogs grinding against each other in a slow, laboured way.

'Nah, on second thoughts Benny's is good. She'll think I went there for you. She'll like that.'

'Probably,' I muttered.

The car turned the corner and rolled down our street. I spotted Mae from a distance, kneeling in a patch of dirt. She was wearing an old, torn pair of jeans, thick rubber gloves and one of Nick's worn tops. She was stained everywhere, her bottom caked in mud. She fingered the overgrown weeds as she gazed down the street. I couldn't recall the last time I'd seen my mother gardening. She had always told me that flowers were nature's children and that nature could take care of the garden all by itself, but now that she was *betrothed*... I guessed this to be another one of her pathetic attempts to slot into the role of domestic goddess.

I sighed with disdain as she grabbed a handful of weeds and tugged them from the ground, ripping out the few good rosebuds we had left.

The car halted in front of the house. Mae leapt to her feet and bounded towards us, untangling her hair from her glasses. Nick flung open the door to greet her.

'Hiya babe,' he called, tugging at her waist band. She lowered her mouth to his and gave him a few quick pecks.

'Did you boys have a good time?' she asked, her eyes darting between the two of us before flying off into another direction.

'Yeah it was great, wasn't it, Luke? We went to Benny's, got him a beautiful suit. Your son, wow, he is a *good*-looking guy. He might even manage to upstage me on my own big day. But what did I expect with a mother as foxy as yourself?'

His performance was beyond sickening.

'You're so sweet, honey. Thanks,' she patted his arm dismissively, all the while stealing looks over her shoulder.

'Hey lady,' Nick sulked, 'we're not even married yet and you're ignoring me already.'

'I'm sorry,' she whispered then dropped another octave, 'It's just, that car,' she said flicking her eyes in its direction. 'It's been there for half an hour. It hasn't budged and no one's come out of it.'

I tilted my head over my shoulder to get a quick glance; immediately my breath caught in my chest. A vibrant tingling flowed throughout my body, jerking my heart, rushing my blood. My skin flushed a lustrous red as sweat began to seep through its pores. I recognised that car, that dusty-blue VW estate. I knew its owner.

'No way,' I croaked, my voice dry from shock.

'Luke, honey, do you know who it is?' I nodded once and detached my seatbelt. 'Well, who is it?'

My hands fumbled on the door handle and I stumbled as I emerged from the car.

'Luke, who is it?' Mae pressed, but I waved my hands dismissively, allowing my unsteady legs to carry me forward.

I hadn't realised until I'd stopped that I had jogged the short distance. I inhaled deeply and then knocked on the window. Lucile's head flicked up, she peered at me, her deep brown eyes sparkling, her soft lips pulled up into a hesitant smile. She stepped out of the car and instantly her sweet scent surrounded me. The smell filled my lungs and I let out a low moan.

'Hello Luke.'

I parted my lips to speak, but instead I exhaled. Her smile deepened, as did the colour of my cheeks.

'Lucile,' I breathed once I had found my voice, 'What, w-w-what are you doing here?'

'We have a date. Don't we?'

Confusion pinched my face and I shook my head, hoping to wipe away the look of stupidity.

'Oh,' she swallowed hard, 'never mind, I think I've made a mistake.'

She reached for the handle of her car and I panicked.

'No no no no no no,' I blurted, 'we did have a date. We *do* have a date. It's just that I thought… you didn't answer my phone calls or my texts so I thought…'

She released the door handle. I sighed in relief, even though I felt my heart thudding in my throat.

'I nearly didn't come,' she said, touching her fingers to her lips, 'but then I realised I didn't really give you a chance to explain.' My heart inched its way further up, threatening to leap from my mouth.

'Why didn't you call? When you changed your mind, I mean.' The pause lasted an agonising beat too long.

'I wasn't sure I still wanted to see you. Not until I got here that was. A part of me was really hurt. Still is.'

'Oh,' I mumbled, feeling my stomach make room for my rapidly plunging heart.

'I'd been about to call before when I heard that lady… your mum?' she asked inclining her head towards a bug-eyed Mae.

I grimaced, 'Yeah.'

'She was talking to a neighbour about you, she'd said she was expecting you back any minute, so I waited.'

'Oh,' I said again, failing to think of anything better.

'You're late,' she said now, playing with just her lower lip.

'What?'

'For our date. You're late.'

I felt my eyes widen, 'I'm late. Crap,' I grabbed a chunk of my hair and pulled nervously at it. 'I'm, I'm so sorry. I really d-didn't think you were coming.'

I cursed my awkwardness, my sudden loss for words and my tongue, which oddly enough felt weightless, causing my speech to stumble out. Lucile rubbed the back of her neck and laughed.

'It's fine Luke, I was just joking. We don't have to go today, not if you don't want to. It's not like you're even ready.'

I looked down, watching her fingers trace my tomato stained T-shirt. I swallowed back another moan. I felt my face heat, and when I looked up it warmed even more at her smile. It was so bright but forced, she seemed disappointed and still hurt. I stilled myself, drawing in air, then taking hold of her hand I spoke.

'You have *no* idea how much I want to.' I looked down at her hand in mine and smiled.

'I've imagined this happening a thousand times, but I didn't think it ever would. Then I went and messed things up. I hurt you.' I paused, trying to think of a way to explain it all: 'I shouldn't have left the way I did. I wasn't thinking straight. All I knew was that someone else needed me. A *friend* who I owe a lot to.'

I squeezed my eyes shut momentarily, forcing the memory of Angel away.

'I was torn. But I'm not torn now and I'm not going to screw things up again.'

I held my breath, waiting for her to say something.

'Wow,' she whispered, her smouldering tone warming my blood. 'That was beautiful, Luke.'

'It was the truth,' I whispered back.

She wriggled her hand free. The air surrounding us felt thick with anticipation. I was aware of my mother's presence, of Nick's, but I didn't care. In that moment all I acknowledged, all I cared to acknowledge, was Lucile.

'You'd better hurry up and change then. There's an open-air showing of Hitchcock's Rear Window downtown. It could be fun,' she shrugged, her lips stretched into that sensuous smile.

I grinned back. 'Give me ten minutes,' I called as I raced towards my house.

I sat on my bed, all dressed, hands buried in my hair. I'd taken care of everything, and by everything I meant Mae. Somehow, I'd managed to pacify Mae with some basic answer so that she wouldn't hound me on the way out. For all intents and purposes, I was ready. I just didn't feel ready. I twisted a lock of hair with my trembling fingers and laughed.

'You're pathetic,' I muttered, pressing the pads of my fingers deeper into my scalp.

Outside waiting for me was the girl I had been dying to go out with for almost two years. It had taken all this time for her to even notice me, and now that she had I was too scared to enjoy it. It was pathetic. I was pathetic and I could pretend not to know what was wrong, but the truth…

it scratched at me. I was selfish and greedy because I knew what I wanted. Who I wanted.

I looked at the clock. My ten minutes were almost up. I should have felt excited, but a nervousness filled me so deeply that it eclipsed all pleasure. I was aware only of my dread; the pounding of my heart, the wobbly feeling in my knees and my skin, clammy and hot. The trembling in my hands spread up my limbs and I panicked, feeling the oxygen suddenly leave my body. I inhaled deeply and tried to keep the dizziness at bay, but a haziness formed around me. I tried again, dragging air into my lungs with both mouth and nose, feeling little relief. I gasped once more, and on the exhale felt my insides fill with a rush of warmth. My body stilled itself. My skin cooled and my heart beat fiercely with gladness.

'Hey Luke.'

My lips pulled up into a smile and I stood.

'Angel,' I breathed, her name played on my tongue, sending a ripple of pleasure and gratitude all through me.

'I can't believe you're here. I thought...' I hesitated, not being able to say the words, not realising how much the idea of her leaving had frightened me. My stomach lurched sickeningly, and she inched herself soothingly closer, so close I could sense her all over my skin. Her presence was electric. And in that moment, I wished that she were real. I wished that I could hold her to my chest, that I could wrap myself around her and embrace this feeling with more intensity.

'Your heart's thumping like a drum.'

'It's nothing,' I lied, though I knew she could feel its every, intimate motion.

'It's okay Luke. I get it. I know why you're acting this way. You don't have to cover it up.'

I shifted my feet awkwardly.

'And how exactly am I acting?'

'All jittery and lovesick,' she paused, and I felt my nerves tingle with an excited trepidation. One that both thrilled and stunned me.

'It's Lucile. I saw her car.'

I stared at the spot from which she spoke to me, a dull ache carving through me. I knew how much she resented my feelings for Lucile. How they made her feel pushed out, replaced. It hurt me to be the one who caused her any pain.

'It's okay Luke. I'm… okay. I'm glad you got your date. I guess you didn't need me to pick up the pieces after all.'

I smiled awkwardly. 'Why are you here Angel? Don't get me wrong, I'm happy to see you, more than happy, but why now? What made you come back?'

'You.'

The answer sent a shiver through me.

'I felt you. I knew that you really needed me.'

Butterflies, each of their delicate wings fluttered vigorously inside of me.

'Thank you,' I mumbled.

'Always,' she said, her voice silkily low.

Neither of us spoke and for a while the room was peacefully quiet. I meditated on it, trying to absorb some of that feeling, but I was still a nervous wreck.

'Luke get a grip,' she snorted after what felt like hours. 'I mean, you seem calmer but your pulse… it's racing.'

It quickened further, making Angel laugh hard.

'She's just a girl, Luke, try to remember that.'

'It's not her, it's because of you,' I blurted out and Angel's beautiful laughter ended.

'You're the reason I feel better, I mean. That I can breathe. It's all because of you.'

She didn't respond, but I sensed her smile and it brightened me.

'I should go now,' she said softly. 'I don't want make you late for the legendary Miss Armstrong.'

'Go?' my throat tightened. 'You can't. You only just got back, you can't.'

I felt her warm phantom fingers grip my upper arms. Her gaze was on me, burning through me.

'Luke, you're fine. If there was a problem I'd stay, but there's not. You're fine, you'll be fine.'

'Would you stop saying *fine,*' I yelled.

I sensed her retreat.

'I'm only fine because you're with me. If you leave…' I didn't finish my sentence. I couldn't, the fear of her going gripped me again and I lost all knowledge of the English language. All words except one word.

'Stay,' I pleaded desperately. 'Stay.'

A warm, energy rested lightly on my chest. I ran my hand along where I imagined her hair to be. A soft sigh escaped us both. I smiled, Angel — my Angel — was back.

Chapter 21

I leant my head against the car's window, my very essence crawling with sickening revulsion.

'You're quiet a lot,' she said, and I watched him. Watched his eyes, felt his panic as he tried to find the right response.

'It's okay,' she smiled, 'I like quiet. Quiet means thoughtful.' He smiled back and it broke me, shattering my soul piece by piece.

I looked away, trying not to let the pain I felt slip out of my mouth in a moan. I hated that I was here again. Back in this mess. I hated that I was the girl helping my love to love another. It had taken me days to accept the truth. That it was wrong for me to cling to this world, that my love for him was wrong, that I was wrong. That I was nothing. I'd raged about it, fought against it, but when I'd finally accepted it, I felt free. Free enough to leave him for good. Free enough to face what I feared.

The memory of my knees on the dirt flooded back, mud-free as they rested on the ground, my fingers running over the cold looking marble, following the pattern of the words. *In loving memory of...* I paused choking on my name. I'd never been here before. It had scared me. I was afraid of the anguishing chill that would run through me. I thought I would drown in it. That the grief of losing my life would paralyse me, but it didn't. I traced a finger over my name, imaging how the indentations would feel if skin and stone were to meet. There was no chill. Instead I was ready. I'd known I was before. After days of tearing myself apart, fighting with the truth I'd felt it, but I'd needed to come here to be sure. And now I was. Almost.

I wondered what was on the other side of the swirl. It called to me and, for the first time in a long time, I found myself wanting to go. But something held me back. Something at the very back of my mind. It wasn't him. It was something long forgotten, but at the same time something that never could be. It was a part of me. It didn't call to me as the swirl did or as he had, but it nagged at me. Like a deafening reminder. If I wanted to be free, I couldn't feel this way. There were things that needed to be put to rest.

I sprang to my feet, leaving the flowers unharmed. I focused on where I wanted to be, concentrating my whole being on the place, but there was no path to follow. No automatic otherworldly connection that bound us, just love. Without meaning to I began running out of the cemetery and down the street, tracing a path from a former life, my mock footsteps mapping out the old. I was desperate to get there, to settle this nagging feeling that kept me from moving on. Once that had been done, I'd say goodbye to this meagre existence and meet a new one behind the swirl. If only he hadn't called.

***

The rain slid down in sheets, distorting the world outside. It lashed angrily at the pavement. Every tiny thud, rapid yet laden. I thought about each drop. The heavy pellets cold and sharp. It was as though they fell for me. Each cool bead a replacement for my tears. I felt the heaviness of the downpour spread through me, filling me up.

I glanced over at Luke and Lucile. They starred hungrily at each other — their eyes bright and wild as if they were desperate to touch, yet shyness kept them apart. Him being overly polite, her a little more *pure and innocent* than I believed her to be. Me, jealous and disgusted at myself.

I tried to escape the present by retreating into my thoughts, but all I could picture was the two of them, their date on replay over and over again, throwing looks at each other over the dinner table in what I think was an attempt at flirting. Lucile smiled at his twitchy, awkward, charming act one too many times. Pulling that I'm-so-sexy look, twisting her lip in an attempt at seduction. They'd barely reached the drive-in when it began to rain. The man at the entrance turned them away, muttering something about an electrical fault thanks to the rain. I felt his disappointment as she pulled up to his house and parked the car, their evening cut short by the length of the movie. His anguish rang loud in my ears. He willed her to stay till it ached, but not me. Petty as it was, the date was over, and I was happy. Then it happened. Lucile stroked his arm. Slow and suggestive. She held him by the wrist and his heart leapt just as mine plunged. I couldn't bear to look at them, not even for a moment, and so the liquid snaking down the glass became a fascinating point of focus.

Breathe in Breathe Out poured out of the speakers, jolting me back to the present. The lyrics tightening the vice that squeezed at my echo of a heart. I stared at the radio as if the words streaming out of it were visible.

'What is it Luke?' Lucile smiled at his awkwardness, at the gripping of his hair, at the way he released the strands, letting his hand glide down the back of his neck.

'Nothing, it's just... the song. It's pretty all right.' She made a face. 'You don't think so?' he asked, his muddy green eyes fixed with a look of surprise.

'It was **okay** at first. I guess I'm just a little over it now.'

I snorted.

'Over it? You're serious, aren't you?'

She shrugged.

'Have you listened to the lyrics?'

Our favourite lines played out just then:

Set adrift on the rift

Breathe in, choke out

Burnt lungs, my doubt

Be with me and I'm free.

'The way each line feeds into the next and the melody. Its sombreness. It's like a loneliness and a need so great it's wordless.'

Her eyebrows rose and I felt the warmth rise in his cheeks too. I snarled viciously, making him flinch.

'It's a nice song. That's all I meant.'

'It's a bit soppy,' Lucile smirked. 'I didn't think it would be your style.'

I felt the lump rise in his throat. A sheet of dark hair fell in front of his eyes, hiding his embarrassment. Lucile reached over and pulled it back, resting her hand so that it cupped his head.

'I think it's sweet. I think you're sweet.'

He said nothing, but stared at her, searching her eyes with deep fascination. She stared back and placed her free hand on his chest, a seductive smile brightening her face. I knew what was coming, and so did he by the feel of his racing pulse, his heart. He touched her hand and squeezed it holding it to his chest.

My limp heart cracked, and I let slip a whimper. Luke was hesitating and I knew why. It wasn't because of **her**, Lucile. I wanted it to be, but it wasn't. I'd tried to find fault with her from the second her name left his lips. I wanted her to be loathsome and superficial, an empty brained, no-personality idiot. I wanted to be able to justify my hatred towards her, but she wasn't any of those things. She was perfect. She was his version of perfect. It was me. I was the problem. I was holding him back. I felt his resistance as he tried to deny the strength of his feelings for her; but they fought their way to the surface, sweeping him under as they swirled. I wanted to cry out 'don't,' but different words left my mouth.

'You can do this,' I whispered, but instead of feeling free his heart twanged in pain.

It had almost literally torn itself in two, one half screaming with panic and sheer nerves, while the other tingled in anticipation. He wanted it. I could feel the mixture of lust and deep longing, but at the same time he dreaded it as though the intimacy of the moment scared him. He cleared his throat and released her hand.

'Do you mind if we turn this off?' he said, his eyes gesturing towards the radio.

'I thought you liked it?' she asked, her tone riddled with doubt, and I had a feeling she was referring to more than just the song.

'Luke, what are you doing?' I snapped.

He shook his head slightly; 'I-I do, it's just... I don't, I can't listen to it right now.'

'Oh, okay.' Lucile reached over and turned off the ignition, her hand lingering longer than necessary.

'Luke don't do this,' I pressed, 'you're scaring her off. She'll think that you're not into her.'

He rubbed his temples in tense frustration, and I felt a twist in my stomach. I could tell what this was doing to him. Having me around. He couldn't be free while I was there resenting every look, every touch. He was conflicted, his loyalties torn when they shouldn't have been. That wasn't what was best for him, **I** wasn't what was best for him. I felt my cracking heart split as the realisation tore through me. He didn't **need** me, not anymore. Compared to what he felt for her, his feelings for me were microscopic.

I couldn't be there. Every instinct in my being screamed at me: *you shouldn't be here*. I looked at him, wanting to brush his cheek with my fingers, wanting to smooth out the worry lines that wore his face. I wanted to look into his deep eyes, to touch my lips against his, just once… but I didn't. Instead, I left.

The moment I stepped out into the rain it clouted me, knocking me to the ground. I gasped and wheezed for pointless air as a surge of emotions swelled inside of me. His heart thumped with a painful joy, knocking his chest, almost shattering bone. Surprise washed through him, stunned his whole being. His body filled with an overwhelming, overflowing abundance of love. Love so deep and pure it ran through every part of him. Marking him with her. Every inch of his body tingled with pleasure. No inhibitions, no hesitations, just undiluted devotion. I felt his relief, his ease. The strength of his love for her consumed him, consumed me. For him it was a wholeness he'd never felt before. For me it was unbearable. Our conflicting emotions crashed inside of me. Slicing me to pieces. Rough, painful, chunks that throbbed in agony. I fought back the cry that threatened to tear its way out of me, and with everything I had focused all my thoughts on his room.

***

I sat on his bed, remembering the first time I was there. It brought a smile to my face, one that quickly turned sour when I realised these would be my last moments in here.

I remembered the feeling of peace that had washed over me the first time I'd decided to leave for good. It had been wonderfully blissful. Unaffected by wants and pain. It was simple, resolute. I longed for that kind of peace again, but I knew it wouldn't come. It was a memory now and I was going to leave this world feeling loaded and unhealed.

His sketchbook lay closed on his pillow. The rawness of his soul. I traced my hand along the smooth black cover, wishing I could have seen even a single drawing inside it. Another want that would be left unsatisfied.

I closed my eyes, wondering what I'd say to him, if words would even be needed. The dead weren't supposed to have to worry about goodbyes, and I could understand why. Too many fears. Would he make things hard for me? Beg me to stay? Or worse, would he release me into the afterlife without a single ache?

I began pacing the room now, desperate to get this over with, desperate to be at peace. Surely, I was promised that behind the swirl. Was that not the one basic emotion all spirits were entitled to? Peace. An impulsive thought sprung to mind. It urged me to leave now, to forget embellished goodbyes and parting words, to say screw him and his new life that I wasn't a part of, but I couldn't. If I left like this, if I slunk off into the afterlife filled with this vile bitterness, there wouldn't be any rest for me. I knew it.

I closed my eyes again, meditating on my decision. Saying goodbye was the right thing to do. Beneath the mass of emotions, I felt the truth of it. I would wait for him one last time. We both deserved that much. I felt his burning need to be closer to her. It impressed itself upon his every cell. I sunk down to the ground, clutching my arms around my waist, burying my head between my knees. A sobbing feeling shook me, but this time something was different. My eyes grew hot and, though there was no moisture, I felt the tear as it slid down my face.

**

It was a busy night. Bodies filled the seats, lingered over the bar and queued patiently in front of a large cut-out of a plump Mexican chef. A cheerful murmur pulsated through the room, warming the atmosphere with its spirited vibe. As my eyes scanned the restaurant for our waitress, they fell again on the festive decor. A multitude of sombreros covered the rustic stone walls, their vibrant colours stretching from space to space, filling the room with a little too much life. Between them were framed black and white photographs nailed awkwardly to the wall. They seemed to be amateur snapshots of the owner and his family. I looked to Lucile and wondered for the millionth time what she thought of it all.

We sat in the middle of the room, beneath the extravagant chandelier, surrounded by an entire crowd of staff and customers. I felt exposed. Like everything was closing in on me.

Beads of light danced across the table the instant the cumbersome object swayed, and I fought not to follow them with my eyes, to stay focused on the moment despite my fears. I looked up at Lucile. Sparse drops of light shone over her arms, illuminating her soft skin. She peeked up at me for a moment, her lips twitching into a loose smile, then continued to pick at her nails. Her eyes roamed the restaurant and seconds later she wrinkled her nose. My heart shot straight up to my throat; what was I doing here? What was I thinking bringing Lucile to a place like this? She probably thought it was cheap and tacky. Why hadn't I bolted the minute I'd spotted the colourful tassels draped in front of the entrance? My chest tightened. I tapped my finger against the chair in a soothing rhythm as I wondered how on earth, I was going to make it up to her.

'This is a nice place,' Lucile mumbled, her eyes wide and smiley. Instantly my chest relaxed.

'I guess,' I shrugged feigning indifference. Angel huffed harshly and I added a crooked smile to be polite.

'I'm really glad you suggested it, have you been here before?'

I hadn't. It had been Angel's idea to come here. I'd never even heard of Mehico Village until twenty minutes ago. Lucile had made a mistake and we were over an hour early for the movie. I'd panicked. What if she called off the date? My second chance would be delayed — that was until she changed her mind and decided I wasn't worth another chance after all. My breathing had been on the verge of becoming erratic, my head swam vigorously, but then, Angel.

'Luke?'

I blinked a few times; Lucile was staring at me, her lips moving between her fingers. I grasped my hair and shook the strands.

'This place? Have you been here before?'

I suppressed a stutter. 'Uh, no. A friend recommended it to me.'

She smiled again but I didn't, I sounded like a bumbling idiot. My thoughts were all over the place, or rather my feelings were. My heart tingled and throbbed excitedly, but at the same time it ached.

'Do you know this friend from college?'

'No, just… from around.'

'Well tell your friend thank you. It's perfect.'

I hesitated; I could feel Angel's presence. It was warm and safe, loving like always, but something was different. She was different. Distant. I had thought that when she finally came back things between us would just fall into place, but somehow what we had, our bond, it felt both strong and frail at the same time and it scared me.

The waitress came and for a moment I was glad. Talking and thinking so much was beginning to feel like a lot of pressure. She filled the table with our order, topped up our drinks and then left. I looked at the food and snorted a laugh. A few starters we'd ordered, nothing too heavy since we didn't have the time, but what covered the table was a feast. Like starters on steroids. Lucile cocked her eyebrows quizzically.

'Wow.'

'So much for something light,' I chuckled.

'I guess we won't be needing popcorn,' she sniggered back.

'Forget the popcorn, I don't even think we're going to make it to the movie,' I teased. 'We'll be so stuffed we won't be leaving this place for weeks.'

There were a few breaths of silence. I ran my tongue against the back of my teeth and waited while Lucile held my gaze.

'A few weeks with you… I could think of worse things,' she smiled, making me blush.

The faint flicking of nails sounded next to me and a hollow ache leaked into my chest.

***

I put down the half-eaten mini enchilada and pushed my plate to the centre of the table. Lucile stacked it neatly on top of the others and shifted them to one side, a sheepish grin flashing across her face.

'Habit,' she said as if to apologise. 'If I don't do it, I hear my mother's voice screeching in my head.'

I shrugged, 'I guess everybody hears at least one voice.'

'Oh *really?*' she drew out the words playfully, 'Who's in your head then?'

'No one,' I shrieked adamantly. She gave me an odd look and I dialled back my craziness, adopting a more casual tone.

'I just mean that everyone has their own conscience, something to guide them.' She stared at me questioningly.

'Uh huh, and who's your guiding voice of reason?'

I swallowed deeply and picked up the pen the waitress had left behind.

'No one important,' I said regretting the words as they left my mouth.

A stabbing pain hit me in the gut. I ignored it and scrawled on my napkin instead.

The waitress took her time returning with the bill, giving Lucile and I the chance to talk.

'You're nothing like I expected,' she admitted. She had seemed distracted before, fiddling with the sombrero peppershaker, but when I looked up, I found her eyes were fixed on my face.

'And what where you expecting?' I asked as coolly as I could manage, though my skin tingled with anticipation.

'I dunno, you're a little… unapproachable.'

'Is that the polite way to say dead inside?' she scrunched up her forehead at my half joke.

'No. I just mean that you always look so intense, so cold. The first time I met you I quite seriously could have believed you were the head of some anti-human cult.'

'Thanks,' I mumbled sardonically.

She laughed, 'I didn't mean to offend you, it's just the vibe you give off. You don't really speak to anyone, you rarely smile—'

'I smile at you,' I said immediately regretting it. I picked up the pen again and began shading in the finishing touches to a drawing.

'I know,' she smoothed my arm with her fingers.

I looked up to find her warm gaze still on me.

'I've seen the way you look at me. It's nice.'

I tried to look away, but she held my chin between her fingers now. A moan rippled low and quiet in my throat.

'I was curious,' she continued, pretending not to notice my shallow breath. 'I wanted to know if there really was a personality behind all of the darkness, but Shane and I...' she dropped her hand and laughed a joyless laugh. 'Anyway, there is no Shane now.'

'So, what's the verdict?' I asked, my stomach swaying anxiously. 'Is there a personality behind the mask?'

She chuckled and took my hand, the pen loosened from my grasp.

'You're kind and sweet. I guess to everyone else you're just this loner, but I think you're just shy. Which is a shame because you're kind of funny in a dry, sarcastic sort of way. Amazingly intelligent, which I think really bugs Mr Taylor, and,' she cocked her head to one side, 'you're an artist too. What is that?' She was nodding her head towards the napkin.

'O-oh,' I stammered. I smoothed out the wrinkles as best as I could, then handed it to her. She expelled a low gasp.

'I wanted you to have something. You look so beautiful and I just thought, well it's better than flowers, right?'

She said nothing. My words had trailed off and I was beginning to wonder if she'd even heard all of them. Her lip trembled a little and she gasped again but still, nothing.

I began to nervously ramble. 'I wish I had known you were coming tonight. Not that I blame you for not saying. I don't, at all, it's just maybe flowers *would* have been better than scribbles on a creased napkin but—'

'This is better,' she interrupted, one finger tracing over the portrait of herself. 'Ten times better, I...' her breath caught in her throat. She swallowed so hard that I heard the gulp. 'Thank you.'

An awkward smile spread across my face.

'I guess there really is a personality after all.'

'I guess so too,' Angel whispered faintly.

***

166

The sky rumbled ominously but neither of us spoke of it. Lightening shot across the sky, but we ignored that too. Even when the windscreen became speckled with small colourless beads we pushed on, willing them to stop, hoping that they would, but they didn't. Lucile had just pulled into the drive-in when a crack of thunder broke through the sky. The downpour that followed was relentless. 'They may still do a screening,' Lucile smiled hopefully. 'I know some places that have in the past. They have provisions for this kind of thing.' But it turned out this wasn't one of those places.

'I guess that's that,' she mumbled.

Without another word she turned the car around and headed in the direction of my house. My heart sank. I was bitterly disappointed. I wondered if Lucile felt the same, if the sudden end to our date stung her like it stung me. I chewed over the thought a little, then brushed it aside. Something else was bothering me, something more pressing. I could feel it in shallowness of my breath, my clammy hands, my nervous heart. I could feel it squirming in my blood stream, it sent my pulse racing. It was pure fear. I was terrified. I tried to bury my irrationalities, but the more I tried the more stubborn they became. Angel's presence was around me, warm and caressing. But instead of stilling me, it magnified my stress.

Lucile pulled up to my house and I felt my desperation grow. I needed her to stay close to me.

The air felt heavy with the sense of finality, it was unbearable. I searched for ways to stretch the night to give us more time together, we needed more time, but I fell flat. The only thought that rang clear to me was that after today she'd never come back.

Lucile spoke. 'Thanks Luke. It really was a great night.'

I mumbled something half-heartedly and she smiled, though I doubt she'd heard a thing. A hopelessness enveloped me and with a sinking heart I reached for the handle. A small rush of cool air tickled my face, I sighed heavily into the breeze. I'd been about to open the door fully when I felt it; my heart leaping as she brushed her fingers along my forearm and clasped my wrist.

'It's still early,' she breathed, her voice smooth and sexy. 'We could always just sit and talk for a little while. I'd... really like that.'

I nodded, feeling the weight on my chest lift slightly as I closed the door.

'I'm really glad we did this,' she said.

I tugged my lips into a half a smile, 'I never thought we would.'

'Why not?'

'Well,' I cleared my throat, 'you're kind of intimidating.'

Her laughter filled the car and my cheeks flushed deeply.

'What makes me so intimidating?' she asked, her eyebrows raised into another puzzled arch.

'You're beautiful,' I began, 'you're *so* beautiful.'

I watched as the eagerness drained from her face.

'Oh,' she muttered.

'What is it?'

She fingered her lip as she spoke. 'Nothing, that's really nice. It's just I thought you might say something else, something deeper, I don't know.'

I offered her a half smile. 'You don't get it,' I said, pushing my hair away from my face, 'You look amazing, don't get me wrong, but that's not what I mean when I say you're beautiful.'

She made a weird face and I kept talking.

'I've always thought you had a beautiful heart. Everyone else at college rips the crap out of me for being different. They don't even bother to hide it. People like Missy and Mac. I guess it makes them feel good, and because they're popular most of their thick friends join in but you… you never have, and I don't believe you ever would.'

I drummed a finger against the seat. 'You're perfect,' I continued. 'Beautiful. I never would have expected someone like you to notice me.'

Silence. I hated it. I chewed the inside of my cheek brutally, worrying that I had offended her. In my rant I had forgotten that most of Missy's friends were also hers. She sat there twisting her lip between her fingers. A warmness brightened her eyes and I looked away.

I hadn't insulted her, I should have been relieved, but I wasn't. I couldn't explain it but something about my words felt empty, as though they lacked the sentiment that they used to hold.

My brain felt fuzzy and confused. I rubbed my forehead to relive the pressure that had begun to mount into a headache. She reached towards me. I flinched.

'Radio,' she said. 'I thought maybe it would soothe your head. Do you mind?' I shrugged. Breathe in Breathe out streamed out of the speakers and I felt my face contort. I gripped my hair roughly.

'What is it Luke?' I released the strands, letting my hand slide down the back of my neck.

'Nothing, it's just… the song. It's pretty all right.' She furrowed her brow. 'You don't think so?' I asked, feeling a mixture of surprise and relief.

'It was *okay* at first. I guess I'm just a little over it now.'

Angel snorted and I felt my insides twist. Having her here, now, at this very moment while the song played, it didn't feel right.

'Over it?' I argued trying to dismiss how uncomfortable Angel's presence made me feel.

'You're serious, aren't you?' She shrugged

'Have you listened to the lyrics? The way each line feeds into the next and the melody…its sombreness. It's like there's a loneliness and a need so great it's wordless.'

She arched her eyebrows again and I clamped my lips together, feeling deeply embarrassed. A snarl ripped out of Angel's throat. I knew what was causing it. I understood her jealousy, her pain. All the same I recoiled away from it.

'It's a nice song. That's all I meant.'

'It's a bit soppy,' Lucile smirked, 'I didn't think it would be your style.'

A lump formed in my throat, I could feel my locks brushing against my face and I allowed them to hide my shame. Lucile reached over and drew them away. She held the back of my head and I closed my eyes soaking in *her* presence, pretending for a second, just a small second… until Lucile spoke.

'I think it's sweet. I think you're sweet.'

I couldn't speak. My thoughts were racing in my mind, trying to find a way out of all the mess in my head, but still I had no words. A rush of contrasting emotions swirled all around and I couldn't pick them apart. I wanted to force them all down. To feel at peace, but the more I shoved them away the harder they fought back.

My eyes roamed Lucile's brown ones. I knew what she wanted, what I was supposed to want. It was coming, soon. Any moment I would feel her lips pressed against mine, her tongue running against my own, and yet that song. That damn song was still playing. It was wrong. She placed a hand against my chest, and I wondered if she could feel my heart thrashing against the bone. I had to do something now; in another second or two it would be too late. I lifted my hand to hers and clasped her fingers.

'You can do this,' Angel spoke, her was voice was soft yet fierce with emotion.

It pained me, sent my insides reeling. Why did she have to speak? Why did she have to open her mouth and confuse me? My nerves tingled vibrantly. Every inch of my body was more alive than I'd ever known possible. A surge of affection heaved inside me, but the more I looked at Lucile the less I felt for her. Panic filled me, it threatened to flood my system, but the warmth, the devotion, it was equally as strong if not more so. I inhaled deeply and found my voice.

'Do you mind if we turn this off?'

'I thought you liked it?' Lucile asked. I could hear the uncertainty in her voice but I pushed my feelings of guilt to one side.

'Luke what are you doing?' Angel's voice barked all around me and I paused, noting the sudden waver in my stomach.

'I-I do, it's just... I don't, I can't listen to it right now.'

'Oh, okay.'

Lucile reached over to switch off the ignition.

'Luke don't do this,' Angel begged. 'You're scaring her off. She'll think that you're not into her.'

I pressed my fingers to my head and rubbed. Why was she making this so damn difficult? Couldn't she sense what she was doing to me? That every time she spoke, I felt consumed with guilt? Confusion ate its way through me, couldn't she feel that? This wasn't something I could just *do* in front of her. She was my Angel for heaven sakes, *my* Angel.

That's when I felt it, her warmth lingering so close to me it almost smouldered my skin. I wanted to reach out and pull it closer. My hand shook in its indecision, then just like that it was gone. She'd left, and the instant she did I wanted her back. I wanted her. So deeply that it tore through me. I gasped as my body wrenched up the emotions, I'd tried so hard to bury. Lucile leaned in, her body so close I could smell her skin.

'I always wondered what it would be like to kiss a guy with a lip piercing.'

Her words ran through me like the rain. Icy and cold. I pushed them away from me and drew nearer to what I felt deep down.

My heart tingled, it pumped with joy. It thumped so hard I thought it would burst. I clutched at the seat and tried to fill my lungs with air, I needed air. I needed to steady myself, but I couldn't. I released my grip and ran my fingers through my hair for the millionth time. A small laugh rippled from my lips and I shook my head in disbelief.

'Luke, what is wrong with you?'

I didn't answer. I didn't care for words. I wanted to feel. All I wanted to do was feel. Feel what I had fought all along, feel what I had tried to deny myself. Feel what I never thought I'd experience in my life. I was in love. Consuming, passionate, undiluted love. It filled me, washing over every morsel of my being so that nothing went untouched. I wanted nothing more than to feel her, than to have every inch of her presence embrace me with its tenderness. I knew where I needed to be and it wasn't here.

'Lucile.'

'Luke.' Her face was harassed with annoyance and doubt.

'I have to go.'

'What?!'

'I can't do this. I'm so sorry. It just doesn't feel right.'

She swallowed loudly, 'I *don't* understand, you're... leaving me? *Again?*'

I clutched my fingers and blew out a breath.

'Five, six months ago this would have been my idea of heaven. Sitting here with you in your car about to kiss you? Mind-blowingly impossible, but I can't sit here and kiss you now. I can't close my eyes and pretend that nothing has changed when everything has.

'Luke   you're   not   making   any   sense.'
'I know.' I wasn't. 'The truth is, my heart… it belongs to someone else. I'm sorry.' I grasped the handle and thrust the door open.

'Luke!'

I turned to look at Lucile one last time and felt a rush of relief. Her face was a mixture of fury and disbelief, but there was no trace of hurt. She may not have been ready to admit it yet, but I guessed her heart belonged to someone else too.

I stood on the pavement and closed my eyes. I could feel her pull. It called to me. She was near. I opened my eyes and looked up towards my bedroom. I'd left the light on and it shone brightly, calling me home. I smiled and ran. My feet pounding the wet ground with urgency, I skidded on the dampened grass, but I refused to slow down. Nothing would keep me from her now. The rain seeped through my clothes. It soaked my skin, slid down my face and sleeked my hair but I embraced it. Something about it made me feel alive. I plunged my hand into my pocket and yanked out my keys. At the back of my mind I was aware of Lucile's car speeding out of the vicinity, but I didn't care. All I wanted was to be with my Angel.

I ran into the house, slamming the door shut with great force. Mae's voice trilled from somewhere near, but I ignored that too and began sprinting up the stairs.

I hovered on the top step. This was it. My pulse raced excitedly I could feel its lively thrust against my skin. I laughed at myself, at my trembling body and my thumping heart. I laughed. I breathed deeply and walked towards my room. My hand clutched the doorknob and then faltered. What if she didn't feel the same? Every part of me was certain that I loved her, but what if she didn't love me back? I closed my eyes and prepared myself. Either way I was about to find out.

I stepped into the room, my eyes resting on where I knew she was. Her intense energy brushed all over my skin, comforting my shivering body and I smiled feeling my fears slip away.

'Hey.'

There was a small sniffling sound.

'Luke?'

'Angel,' I sighed with pleasure — hearing her voice was exhilarating.

'Lucas, I'm leaving.'

The shock of her words made me dizzy. I stumbled and she rushed to my side strengthening me with her being.

'You can't.'

'I have to. I need to. It's time.'

'It's not. I need you.' I panicked. My heart tensed. She couldn't go. Not now. Not when everything had become so perfectly clear.

I sensed her ironic smile before it filtered through in her voice.

'I'm leaving because you don't. I *know* you love her. I don't belong here anymore… I never did.'

Her voice didn't crack this time. It was firm, but still I knew she was in pain. She may have known my every feeling, but she wasn't even close to understanding them. I closed my eyes and I held out my hands.

'Stand in front of me.'

'Why?'

'Just do it.' Angel sighed impatiently and moved towards me.

'Put your hands on mine.' She didn't protest but she was hesitant. Her warmth jittering as it glided over my skin. I swallowed, surprised by how much I enjoyed her almost-touch.

'I love you.' I breathed the words slowly, savouring the sweetness of each one as they left my lips.

'What?' Her voice shook with uncertainty and I smiled, eager to say it again.

'I love you Angel.' She tried to pull her hands away, I felt them slipping from my palms.

'Please don't,' I begged, 'don't move.'

Slowly, she slid them back into place and stepped closer. I kept my eyes shut and imagined her grasp was firm.

'What about in the car?' she mumbled, 'Lucile?'

I bit my lip and shook my head. 'You. It was you.'

I was sure I heard a stifled cry. I thought briefly about all the pain my misdirected feelings must have caused her and I ached to put it right. Releasing one hand, I traced my fingers along the echo of her face. My skin burned wonderfully beneath the near touches. I listened intently to the small whimpers that escaped her mouth and I leant closer till I was sure that our faces were only a few inches apart. I ran my finger down the shadow of her nose, past her mouth and then, without hesitation, I placed my lips to where I knew hers would be. Angel responded quickly, urgently, her warmness gliding fervently over my skin. She slipped her hand from mine and slid it through my hair. Her happiness radiated through me as we almost-touched, and I was certain she felt mine. We were connected. I let my hand trace the mappings of her back, embracing her until my breath was ragged. We broke apart and I hovered, my forehead close to hers.

Her next words came out in a throaty whisper. 'I love you too Luke.'

I smiled catching my breath, opening my eyes.

'Angel... oh God, Angel.' I pulled myself away from her, stumbling backwards. I could almost hear the thumping of my heart it was so fierce.

'What? Luke what is it?'

I didn't reply. Instead I looked on in awe. My eyes searched up and down her wispy figure. I inhaled deeply, trying to wrap my head around the sight in front of me. Long, slender legs and a slight waist. A bright pearly glow outlined her willowy frame. My eyes brushed over her freckled arms. They skimmed her pale neck until they reached her face. Her beautiful, freckly face. I studied it carefully, every inch of it accounted for. Her lips, her perfectly luscious lips. A black hoop ran through the lower slightly fuller one, matching the ring in her perfect nose; and her eyes...There was an edginess to her appearance — the torn leggings with the chains running through each rip, the dark make-up drawing out the faint, taut expression — but her eyes, they were soft and beautiful and staring back at me. Those warm, golden brown eyes that looked at me now with confusion.

I drew my body closer to her, placing my hand all over her wild, choppy, ice-blonde hair. I traced my finger along the black highlights. Not a single strand moved. I ran my hand past her ears and down her cheek, resting them there in mid-air.

'I never imagined... you're so beautiful.'

She didn't speak instantly but her honey-coloured eyes widened.

'You... you can see me?'

I touched my finger to one of the many dots on her face.

'Every freckle.'

She looked down at her feet, rolling them, side to side, over and over again, and smiled. I placed my arms around her body, feeling her head as she rested it close to my chest.

***

I listened to his breath. In out, in out. Calm and slow. Long and easy. I nuzzled my head close to his face and imagined that I could feel its warmth tickling my cheek. His arm — which he'd propped limply around my waist — was beginning to sag, but he refused to relax his fist. He wanted to hold me, and I wanted nothing more than to be held by him.

On his lips he wore a small smile; I wondered what he could see, it would have been easy to find out. I could have simply slipped into his dreams and satisfied my curiosity, but I didn't. Not tonight. Tonight, I felt real. Tonight, I was not dead. Tonight my heart beat with his and I could not bear any reminder that this was not true.

'Angel,' he sighed my name sweetly into my ear and I sensed his arm tighten around me. It thrilled me.

'Luke,' I breathed into his neck, then nestled closer to place a kiss on his skin.

Chapter 22
Thursday, 15th April

'*Dear Journal...* Blah, blah, blah, oooh, interesting, *I'd give up a hundred normal lives for just a moment with her.*' Eugh Luke,' Angel clutched her mouth and pretended to heave.

'Don't be so grotesque.'

I threw a pillow at her fitful silhouette and watched it shoot straight through her. She rolled her eyes and snorted.

'Dead, remember? That means I'm completely unaffected by flying pillows.'

I gave her my very best un-amused face and continued.

'Why are you writing all that cra...eative stuff anyway,' she asked, opting for a safer word underneath my darkened gaze. 'You're not exactly going to share it with Dr Evans... Are you?'

I reached into my bedside drawer with my free hand and pulled out a similarly black-covered book. I tossed it on to the empty space beside her, taking care to flick the pages with my thumb so that it would land open.

'*Wednesday, 14th April,*' she read, '— *Woke up. Stayed in bed for a while. Showered. Had breakfast.* Why Luke, what is this riveting piece of literature?'

I smiled at her. '*That* is what Dr Full-of-Crap gets to read.'

She eyed me suspiciously and my body tingled under her stare. I still couldn't get used to seeing her beautiful face.

'So, he doesn't see your journal?'

'Nope.'

'He doesn't ask?'

'He thinks that fewer words could help me to open up.'

'*Really?* And how did he come to that brilliant conclusion?'

My smile was wry, 'Because that's what I told him.'

'You little sneak.'

I let my head fall back and belted a mock evil laugh.

'Idiot,' she grinned. She shuffled close to me, shifting her body so that she was in good view of my journal.

'If you don't plan on showing him any of this, why do you bother writing it all down?'

I shoved my journal back into its drawer with one hand and with the other drew her body closer to me. She could feel my touch like I could hold on to air, but she followed the gesture anyway until she was sitting on my lap. I tensed my hand around her shadowy waist and looked into her eyes. I could get lost in those eyes.

'I like having a journal,' I shrugged. 'I never thought I'd take to it but it turns out Dr Idiot managed to get something right for once.'

She stared back at me without speaking and suddenly I found myself breathless.

'I don't have to hide anything here,' I choked once the oxygen had crept back into my lungs. 'No one can judge me or tell me I'm wrong inside; it's the only place I can be honest, that I can be me. I can't do that anywhere else or with anyone else, except you.'

She tugged gently at her lip ring, a coy smile slowly lengthening across her face.

'I guess sometimes your drippiness really isn't too unbearable.'

'Thanks,' I smiled back, touching my forehead to hers.

'Hey, are you okay?' she asked, noticing the tiniest of winces.

I pressed my fingers to my eyes and exhaled a large breath. 'Yeah,' I nodded slowly, but when I opened my eyes again, she was staring at me, her brow wrinkled by concern.

'It's just a dizzy spell. I probably just need to eat.'

Seconds later she had me trudging down the stairs in pursuit of breakfast. She was overreacting big time, but I didn't mind. It was nice having someone who was genuinely concerned about me.

'Have you always had dizzy spells,' she asked as we headed down the hallway.

I shrugged, 'Not really. Sort of. It's been on and off lately, it's probably nothing.'

'What's nothing?'

I turned my head and found a second pair of eyes studying my face.

'Who were you talking to?'

I froze for half a second. Something in Mae's eyes made me more nervous than necessary.

'I was just thinking out loud,' I shrugged.

We stood there a while in silence, her lips quavering as though she wanted to say more. Instead she bit her tongue. Literally. Teeth punching into flesh and I stepped past her before she could change her mind and speak.

Angel followed as I headed straight for the cereal cabinet. She hopped on to the table next to me just as I drew out the box of multigrains. I felt the near grazing of our skin, it made me trembled inside.

'That was weird,' I said. 'I mean with Mae, not with...'
'Shush,' Angel hissed.

I arched my eyebrows and followed her nervous inclination towards the door. Mae was still there. Her body slumped against the its frame, her eyes wide and slightly despairing. I felt a small pang of concern before quickly burying it.

'Are you sick?' I asked careful to keep my voice cold.
'Pardon.'

'Are you... do you not feel well?' This was the longest conversation we'd had in weeks and it was making me feel uncomfortable.

Mae shook her head. 'No honey. I'm fine. Why?'
'Well, it's 11:00.'

Mae gave me a gentle 'mmm' but she didn't seem to be registering anything I was saying. Lingering at the door, she twisted fingers into her fringe exposing her intensely furrowed brow. I swallowed awkwardly.

'Isn't geriatric Pete going to miss his morning chit-chat?'

She stared at me with a weird half-smile that made me cringe.

'I'm on annual leave for a couple of days.'

'Oh,' a strained silence followed, and I was beginning to detest her presence again.

'What are your plans for today? I was hoping we could spend some time together?'

My body tensed. 'Can't,' I said turning my back to her and reaching for a bowl. 'I'm busy.'

'That's okay. Are you seeing that girl again? Lucile?'

Angel pursed her perfect lips and flicked her nails.

'No,' I smirked, casting a quick loving glance Angel's way. 'That's definitely over.'

The flicking stopped. She rolled her eyes and smiled back.

Mae jerked herself straight. 'Why?' she asked, her voice shrill with alarm. 'You seemed really into her. She seemed really into you. What happened?'

'Things change.'

'So soon? But you've only been on one—'

'Look,' I cut in, feeling a surge of irritation rise beneath my skin, 'we're done. It was a big mistake to begin with, so just let it go.'

I yanked open the fridge, snatched the milk from its metal rung and returned huffily to my bowl. Why did she suddenly care about my personal life? And why was she so eager to see me paired up with Lucile? I tossed a few ideas around in my head and came up blank before deciding that in the end it didn't matter. Whatever her motives were, they couldn't possibly be good. Angel stroked my forearm as I began shaking the multi-grains from the box. I felt an ease spread through me.

The room was eerily silent — save for a few Os clattering against the ceramic bowl — but I knew she was still there; the tension in the air was too thick for her not to have been.

'What time will you be back today?'

'Not sure.'

'After you've been to see Dr Evans?'

'I don't know. Maybe.'

The silence returned. It hung there longer, suffocating the space with its hostility. I unscrewed the milk bottle and began to pour. A light breeze brushed my skin — the door swinging back and forth on its hinge — and when I turned around again, she was gone.

'What was all that about?' Angel asked, her face just as baffled as mine.

Splashes of milk filled the bowl rapidly. I watched as the little loops became submerged in the pearly liquid.

'I have no idea.'

***

I lied to Mae. I'd had no intention of leaving the house today, let alone staying out late, but the thought of me, her and Angel alone together — quality time — just didn't appeal to me.

We left the house early afternoon and ended up at the park. I watched as Angel settled below her favourite oak tree, legs curled beneath her, a hand stroking the arm that rested on her inner thigh. The sunlight streaked through her, making her look more immaculate than ever before. It brushed against my bare skin, heating it. My insides glowed from knowing that each ray that shot straight through her was touching me.

I lay in front of her, stretching out my fingers and tickling along the shape of her knee. She turned towards me and smiled.

'What are you thinking?' I asked, taking her away from what was clearly an intense daydream.

She grimaced, 'Honestly? I'm trying to remember the last time I was *this* happy.'

I couldn't tell if she was being sincere or not. Her eyes, those beautiful pools of golden wonder, held a quiet fragility I longed to unmask.

A light breeze whipped up. Loose strands of hair tickled my face and I yanked them back. Her sigh was soft; her hair stagnant.

'What was it like?' I asked.

She peeked up at me, the inside of her lower lip caught between her teeth, 'What was what like?'

I gripped my hair tighter, 'Dying.'

For a moment everything was still, and in the quiet stillness I thought I heard a small whimper.

'It sucked,' she murmured, the noise of the world returning with her words.

'It sucked?'

'Yep. It was slow and painful. But hey, don't take my word for it. I've only had the one death.' Her voice was sharp and cool.

'Are you okay?'

'Are you?' she asked referring to the sudden pounding of my head.

I pinched the bridge of my nose and breathed. 'Yeah, just another migraine. Weird.'

'Maybe you should see a doctor,' she said, slumping down on the ground beside me.

'Maybe you should tell me what's on your mind.'

She squirmed, turning her body towards me.

'I don't know what you're talking about,' she said curling herself into the side of my chest.

'I'm talking about your sudden frosty mood.'

'Luke your head is throbbing.'

'Forget about my head,' I snapped, trying to force the pain to the back of my mind too. 'I thought that we could tell each other anything. Or was that just me?'

I couldn't see her face, but I could sense that it was scrunched up.

She spoke with a tight jaw, 'I just don't like thinking about my death, all right?'

She snuggled up closer to me, her *grip* fiercer, and I wondered if there was more to it.

Pangs of pity rumbled inside of me. She laughed — coarsely and cheaply.

'Don't feel sorry for me, that's a stupid waste of your time. Besides, you should take all that energy you spend on worrying and save it. The way you're feeling, you're gonna need it.'

She wasn't wrong. Every cell in my brain was thumping wildly. The agony felt so intense it caused waves of nausea. The queasiness tossed inside of me and my mouth swam with a pool of saliva.

'Luke, are you going to be sick?'

I opened my mouth and spat. Black dots scattered before my eyes and I gripped the grass till the blades tore in my fingers. I clutched the ground again and pulled my body into sitting position. My head danced and I swayed on the spot.

'Luke. *Luke.*'

Angel's voice came to me from somewhere far away. I focused on her eyes, her panic-stricken eyes, until the dots all merged into one big sheet of black.

***

I gasped hoarsely, dragging gulps of air into my lungs. My eyelids sprang back, and my tender head filled with colours and shapes. Angel's face peered over me and I suddenly became aware of her legs straddling my waist, her hands held lightly over my chest.

I croaked, 'Any other time I would count myself a *very* lucky guy.'

She frowned. 'Don't joke. I was worried.'

My lips crumpled into an attempted smile, 'Don't you know that worrying is a stupid waste of time?'

Her face twisted unhappily. She swung a leg round and kneeled beside me.

'I'm sorry,' I groaned as I hauled my body to a sitting position. The pressure in my head was intense, yet the lightness of it caused it to sway slightly on my neck.

'How are you feeling?' she asked over the flicking of her nails.

I smiled gently, 'You **know** how I'm feeling.'

'Right,' she mumbled, 'at least the nausea's gone.'

'Mmm,' I wiggled my fingers between my hair and massaged the scalp. 'Don't look so worried,' I said brushing along her fraught face with a stroke of my finger.

'But Luke—'

'—is fine.'

Thin ghostly lips twisted in annoyance.

'Fine,' she grumbled and settled next to me. Her head laid against my shoulder. My chest heaved rapidly as I made an attempt to temper the excitement, she aroused in me.

'I could stay like this for the rest of time,' I groaned, embracing the feel of her nearness, her warmth.

She dipped her head to look at me. 'Me too,' she smiled back.

***

'I won't be long.'

Her words sent a slither of panic racing through my heart.

'Promise,' she added, grazing my cheek with her thumb.

She turned and walked away, and I felt the separation with every step she took. I dawdled at the entrance for a while, watching her disappear out of sight, then slunk in. She'd promised to be back by the end of my session with Dr Evans. Though it meant only an hour apart, something about her going unsettled me.

I pictured the look on her face before she left, a forced tender smile attempting to distract from the sadness in her eyes. I nipped nervously at my lip ring and entered the office.

'Hello Luke,' Dr Evans said.

I grunted a response and sunk into my usual seat. Within seconds I'd settled into my not-listening funk.

We'd spent the afternoon talking — Angel and I — or rather I did as she listened. I wanted to ask questions about her, her interests, what she studied at school; her life, when she'd had one. We'd never spoken about the past before, whatever conversations we'd had about her centred around who she was now. Her thoughts and feelings in the present. I was intrigued; but she was quiet. Withdrawn. So, I did most of the talking. Occasionally she stole a look and I knew that she could sense my worry. Still she said nothing, just soothed my arm with long strokes of her knuckles. I wished for once that I could feel her emotions. I was desperate to know what had upset her. Was it me with my stupid, thoughtless question about death? Was she anxious about my sudden collapse? Or was it something else? Question after question had thumped through my aching mind as I rambled on about pointless things. She was nice enough to laugh in the right places, but she couldn't hide her upset. Not from me.

The time with Dr Evans dragged. I pulled out my 'journal' and appeased him with its limited content. He asked idiotic questions like, 'What made you stay in bed for a while Luke? Had something particularly upsetting happened?'

I gave him a range of half-baked or sarky answers such as, 'Yeah my stomach, food poisoning I guess,' with the additional shrug.

Drip, drip, drip went the time, like the dribble of a tap trying to fill an ocean. I was grateful when 17:00 arrived.

'Same time next week then?'

'You bet,' I beamed, not even trying to mask my sarcasm.

The air outside was sweet but I barely noticed it next to Angel's warmth. She smiled brightly — brighter than before, but her eyes looked even more haunted.

'5 o'clock on the dot and I don't even have a watch.'

'Go on then, tell me. What's your secret?'

'I followed Luke Time instead. I listened for that quiet trill of excitement amidst the intense loathing and I knew your sentence must be up.'

'Touché.' I clapped grandly and she bowed, desperately trying to brush over her troubles. I let her.

'Where did you go?' I asked. Her perfect smile faltered slightly as she worked to hold as much of it in place as she could.

'Nowhere in particular. I just didn't fancy joining you in central boredom on such a nice day.'

Her voice didn't sound right, it was too dense. Don't push, I reminded myself. She will come to you.

'Cool,' I shrugged, tucking my little finger around the shape of hers.

We walked in silence, both of us aware of her lie, neither one of us voicing it.

We took our time getting back. I slipped the key into the lock and twisted. The house was quiet, and I wondered where everyone was. I cocked my head around the living room door and glowered at Nick's snoring figure.

'One down,' I sneered as I made my way up the stairs. I turned the corner and halted a few steps away from my bedroom door. My face twisted into a deeper scowl as the grinding of my own teeth echoed in my head.

'What are you doing?' I spat.

'*Luke calm down*,' Angel said nervously, but my white-hot anger flared viciously.

Mae stepped out of my room and hovered in front of me, face flushed with humiliation.

'I'm sorry Lucas.' She clasped her hands together and worked her knuckles nervously. 'You weren't here and I just…'

'Just what?' I snarled.

'I just… I guess I just missed spending time with you, that's all.' She squeezed my shoulder lightly as she stepped past me and I flinched. Before I could think of a decent response, she had disappeared down the stairs. I felt the bile rise within me; thick coats of rage sleeked my insides. Part of me knew I was overreacting, that it was possible that she only wanted to be close to me, but I couldn't help myself. I didn't believe a word of what she'd said. What's more, neither did Angel.

Chapter 23
Sunday, 18th April

I opened my eyes and immediately found myself overcome with dread.

Somehow over the past few days I'd managed to forget about college. It had been easy. I'd willingly distracted myself with Angel. But now, with the start of term only a day away, there was no escaping it.

I cringed at the thought of facing them — Mac and his paramecia, Missy's big mouth... Lucile. We hadn't spoken since that night. I'd made several attempts to call and apologise but I'd bottled it before the first ring. Needless to say, she hadn't contacted me — not that I blamed her — and I wondered if she'd told people what had happened between us already? Would she? Or would she make up a less humiliating story to save face? Was she that kind of girl? The questions drove me crazy, and the more I thought about it the more I realised I never really knew her at all. My feelings for her had been nothing compared to how I felt now.

I turned over in my bed and stretched. It felt cold. Empty. Angel was gone. It wasn't a shock. I'd known it before I'd even opened my eyes. I'd felt her absence deep within my dreams, but I didn't force myself to wake. Instead I'd let her go. She needed to be somewhere else and I needed to let her be; but it pained me. I thrust a hand into my hair and pulled gently at the strands.

'Where are you?' I sighed, running my tongue against the back of my teeth.

A gentle breeze rustled my duvet and for half a moment my heart panged with excitement. My eyes followed the feathery touch, I laughed. An open window.

An hour passed and still no Angel. I'd gotten bored of tossing in bed and had exhausted the act of pretending to sleep, so I pulled myself to my feet, got out my laptop, pressed the on switch and waited for the archaic thing to load. Once it had, I brought up all my unfinished essays. It wasn't much; some English, a thousand-words piece in science and give or take a hundred for fine art. I was pleased that I hadn't completely wasted the first half of the holidays drowning in self-pity. I'd been productive and now in a couple of hours I would be free from my course work — well, the essays at least. There was still the issue of an art project that would form the basis of my exam, but that hardly felt like work.

I set to work spewing out strings of analytical text on to the screen, reducing classic and modern works to a body of subtext and underlying passions. It took three quarters of an hour, but by 11:00 clock I was done. Science took longer than I'd expected, but by early afternoon it was over.

'Done,' I said feeling wonderfully satisfied as I tapped the last word on to the screen, but the feeling was fleeting.

Angel still wasn't back. I looked around at the mess of papers and books on my bed and sighed, feeling the vestiges of my good mood wane. I shoved everything into a messy pile, which I dumped at the bottom of my bookshelf. The stack threatened to burst from its narrow surroundings, but I stuffed it back in and prayed for the best. I looked at the clock again; 13:00. I wrinkled my nose, feeling my forehead crease.

'I guess it's time for a shower then.'

The water lapped against my skin. I let its warmth comfort and caress me. I reached for the shampoo and squirted the cool substance on to my scalp. My hair hadn't needed washing, but it used up an extra five minutes so what the heck. I lathered, rinsed and repeated till I was pleased that enough time had passed. As my hand reached for the knob my heart thumped wildly. My fingers froze for a moment until I'd caught my breath. I hurriedly shut off the water, climbed out of the tub and ripped my towel from its holder. Wrapping it around my waist I practically raced to my bedroom.

Standing outside I pressed a palm to the door.

'Angel,' I groaned with delight. When I opened the door she was there, cross-legged on the bed.

I picked up the nearest pair of clean boxers and jeans and slipped them on.

'Hey,' she said as I dropped down beside her. I stared at her delicate face. A weak smile lay on top of her tormented expression. I took an intake of breath and her faint scent filled my lungs. It made me quiver inside, just a hint of her natural aroma, like the memory of her smell. I said nothing back but stared at her intently, giving her the chance to confide in me. She chewed at her inner lip, her eyes darting nervously around. They fell on the clutter of papers now on the floor.

'Been studying?' she offered instead.

'Just thought I'd keep busy.'

I got up to gather the pile of notes and stuffed them into my drawer on top of my journal. The drawer was so full they threatened to explode from there too, so I left it open. A coolness pricked me and when I turned around again Angel was gone. I ached for her, for whatever pain she was in and for the fact that she felt she had to go through it alone. I sat in her spot, inhaling as deeply as I could. Trying to catch snatches of her shadowy scent, but that too was gone.

***

I occupied my afternoon with art. Course work art, pleasurable art, any kind of art I could think of. I experimented with acrylic paints, watercolours and pastels, making a mess of both hands and clothes. Running my fingers through my hair so many times it became sheathed in an assortment of colours. For all my shampooing, it desperately needed a wash again. I stripped out of my paint-stained clothes and jumped in for my second shower of the day. I dragged my hands through my hair, stripping the colour, my dark strands returning. I watched as the paint ran down the drain in waves. I focused on the collection of colours, their vibrancy and their dullness as the water drained the life from them. I tried hard not to think of the last time I was in here. I focused on anything that wasn't her.

Dried and dressed, I sat at the edge of my bed with my head hanging, feeling terribly exhausted and weak. The smell of Mae's Sunday roast wafted up the stairs and my empty belly reminded me that I'd forgotten to eat. It groaned fitfully in protest, but stubbornness kept me anchored to the bed. I didn't need Mae, not for anything.

There was a soft knock on the door. My body tensed, knowing it was her.

'Yeah,' I answered.

'May I come in?'

'Whatever.'

She pushed the door gently open and stepped inside, closing it behind her.

'You knocked. Glad to see your trespassing days are over.'

She grinned sheepishly and twisted her fringe.

'I'm sorry about that honey. I don't know what I was thinking.'

She looked so affectionately remorseful that my frostiness almost faltered, almost.

'Anyway, may I sit?'

I curled my lip and shrugged.

'You haven't been down all day.'

'I've been busy.'

'Doing what?'

'Doing stuff.'

'What stuff?'

'What is it to you Mae? Suddenly you're interested in my life?'

'I just wanted to know if you were okay.' She mumbled. 'That you weren't holed up in here all sad and depressed.'

'I'm fine.'

'Come down for dinner.'

'No thanks,' I said sucking in my stomach to silence a rumble in its tracks.

'Please Luke. For once could you just do something, not because you want to but because I need you to?'

Tears sprang into her eyes and a wave of guilt washed through me. My stomach growled as if to encourage the situation along and I desperately wanted to tear it out, to separate it from my body. She looked at me, finger to her mouth chewing the corner of her nail like a sulky child.

'Fine.'

She shot up from the bed and stared at me in disbelief.

'Really?'

I felt my shoulder rise and fall automatically.

'Sure, but can you just give me a moment first?'

'Of course,' she exclaimed, tripping over herself as she exited the room.

If she thought her staying there a minute longer might change my mind, she was right, it definitely would have.

When I stepped into the kitchen my insides flipped. Mae bit her inner lip and smiled anxiously.

'Well... what do you think?'

I closed my eyes momentarily and gulped, 'There's a table. We're sitting at a dinner table?'

She nodded enthusiastically, 'I know, I know, we haven't done that since, well since...'

'Since Dean was alive.'

There was a deafening silence into which she swallowed loudly. The soundlessness seemed to have its own pulse. I counted each beat as it passed.

'Anyway,' she continued, all shrill and nervous, 'I thought it was about time we did. So, what do you think?' I looked at the grand mahogany thing that sat awkwardly next to the breakfast bar taking up far too much space. The good cutlery was out to match the good china and glasses sat at each place mat already full. Food. Food was everywhere.

'It's a table,' I shrugged.

Mae stood next to me and squeezed my shoulder. 'It's all going to be okay,' she whispered. I screwed up my face and shrugged off her touch.

'Let's just eat,' I said, lowering myself into a seat.

'Not yet. We have to wait for Nick.'

My jaw locked.

'That reminds me, I forgot to do his gravy.' She hurried off towards the stove and I sat there fiddling with a silver spoon.

It rolled between my fingers, back and forth, back and forth, and I thought of the family she wanted us to be. I wondered where we'd be six months from now, a year? What kind of life the three of us would have together? This frail, insecure woman, her son and his abusive attacker for a father figure. The thought saddened me more than it enraged me, and I clung to the memory of my old family for comfort. A cool breath crept along my skin. I shivered in disgust.

'Hey *prick*.' Nick drawled, spit spraying my skin.

I gripped the spoon tighter, wanting desperately to thrust it down his throat. I looked up at Mae, so busy in her attempts to make the perfect gravy for her perfect fiancé that she didn't even notice the monster that had slunk in.

He snarled, his breath violating my skin, 'Less than two months.'

My teeth clenched in fury.

'That's how long you have left in the house. Less than two months.'

'You think she's just going to kick me out as soon as you get married?' I expelled a small, angry puff of air, 'She may be heartless, but she still cares what people think.'

He chuckled briefly, 'She will. I mean, what other choice will she have Luke? Since the wedding you've become difficult to live with. You're violent towards me, even colder towards her. She's afraid you might do something. Something terrible to me, to her... to yourself.'

The pit of my stomach wavered.

'You're not serious. You can't be.'

His brief chuckle lengthened becoming more sinister.

'Oh honey, you're back,' Mae called, her face bright with love and stupidity.

'Hello sweetie.' He squeezed my shoulder and she smiled.

'Good,' she beamed, casting me a meaningful look. 'I'm just going to finish up with this gravy and dinner will be served.'

'You're perfect, do you know that?'

She puckered her lips and blew him a kiss. A small, desperate part of me wanted to cry out for my mother but she'd turned back on me, oblivious as always.

'You're gonna leave,' he snarled. 'One way or another you're *going to go.*'

'And why would I do that?'

He fixed me with a cold stare.

'Because, prick, that's the way I want it. It's your turn to be dropped. Either I will force you out or one day you'll just up and go. Break your mother's heart so deeply that only I can fix it. Then as far as she'll be concerned, you'll be as dead to her as your brother.'

I thrust my chair back, knocking him to the ground.

'Don't you dare!' I screamed towering over him, this disgusting excuse for a person.

'Don't you dare mention Dean to me, to anyone.'

The table shook and a glass smashed.

'Luke!' Mae screeched, aghast. 'Nick, baby, are you all right?' she rushed to his side without even a cursory glance my way.

'Yeah babe, I just don't know what I did wrong now.'

A low growl ripped from my throat.

'Lucas James what is wrong with you? Can't you even try just once, for me?'

My eyes bore into her face. I felt my pulse rage venomously as my hatred for them both bubbled to the surface. I clenched my shaking fist, turned and pounded it hard into her precious mahogany table.

Mae stared at me; her face filled with chilling disbelief. I smiled darkly and stalked out of the room, but not before catching a glimpse of Nick's evil smug smirk.

I stepped outside and slammed the door shut. A vulgar anger gripped me. I balled my fist till nails pierced skin feeling the rage flush my entire body.

'Come with me,' Angel whispered gently into my ear.

'Where are we going?' I asked through my rigid jaw.

She stared at me, her soft golden eyes melting some of my anger.

'Home.'

I felt my body crumble into her love as she took my hand into her warmth and led me away from my pain.

She walked through the busted gate of the park as I squeezed my body through its opening. I headed for our spot and began to sink to the ground. She shook her head.

'Not today.' Her hand stretched out to me. 'Come.'

I lifted my body from the earth and placed my hand on hers. We walked, past her tree, pushing on further. We stuck to the bare dusty path till it became lost in the dense shrubbery. I clawed my way through the wild undergrowth as she glided effortlessly through until we arrived on the other side at a place I never knew existed. A faded running track lay beneath my feet. It started there and led all the way to an old sports ground. A netball net hung limply, and the football goals had rusted into shabbiness, but it had the air of a place that was once deeply loved.

'This way, Luke.'

I turned my attention back to Angel who had marched ahead. Catching up I followed her through a thick grouping of trees. She halted abruptly, her body glowing against what appeared to be the last set of trees. She smiled, her warm, dazzling smile, holding out a finger to my cheek and running it along the still-reddened skin. Her eyes took on a deep intensity as she drew her finger down my cheek, she held it there for several seconds, breathing a small sigh. Then turned back, not saying a word as she pushed forward.

I followed her, gasping as we emerged on the other side. My feet fumbled slightly, finding themselves on the wooden panels of a bridge. I gripped a ledge to steady myself. It was a beautiful bridge, so handsome that neither time nor neglect could take that away from it. Long and wide, it spanned across the deep coloured river that ran below. I marvelled at the whole scene. Everything was rich in beauty. I ran a finger along the ledge, brushing it against an engraved floral pattern hidden beneath deep-green vines that had tightened themselves around the wood. Rough, natural and beautiful.

'What is this place?'

Angel smiled, 'My heart.'

She bent down, folding her arms on the ledge, and gazed ahead, her eyes distant yet warm. 'My mum — well my mum and dad really, but mostly my mum — she used to, I mean we all used to come here together. This was the happiest place in the world to me when I was a kid. Then when I got a little bit older it became my only happy place.'

She paused, staring intently into the vast water ahead.

'Before, when I was alive, I mean, I never wanted to... I never shared this place with anyone.'

'Why me?'

'Because when you hurt, I hurt too, and I don't just mean because I feel you. I love you. My whole heart, it grieves for you when you're in pain, Luke. I want to fix things. To put my arms around you and make it better but I can't. I can't share my body with you. So,' she turned from the water to look at me. 'So, I'll share my soul instead.'

My heart swelled and tingled. I felt the love between us deepen. It bound itself tightly to our souls, just as the vine had the wood. This place was a symbol of our love: raw, deep and beautiful.

I joined her, leaning forwards and propping my head up with my palms. We both stared ahead now at its depth that mirrored ours.

'I remember being happy sometimes,' I said, 'I think about my dad and I feel as if I can remember him. His laugh. He had the most infectious laugh, loud and booming, and you heard it a lot because he was always playing tricks.' I chuckled genuinely. 'I remember once he took me and Dean to this brand-new joke shop in town. We bought shed loads — itching powder, whoopee cushions, fake blood, that sort of thing.' She smiled.

'When we got home, Dean had an idea. Mae was just finishing one of those home workouts and we knew she'd be taking a bath soon, so we got in there first. We couldn't remember which was her towel so we grabbed all the ones that hung on the rack except ours. We put the itching powder down to lay them all out and Dean, he decided to start with the red one. But when we reached up for the box of powder it was gone. Then we heard a voice, "I wouldn't touch that if I were you." Dad had this stern look on his face, mean, and we panicked. We started reeling off any excuse that came to mind. Anything to cover up what we'd been about to do. Dad reached over, picked up the blue one and flung it our way. "*This* one's your mother's," he said. I remember Dean's mouth falling open. We thought we were looking at a week without the TV or something, but instead of telling us off he joined us.

'Mae's scream was the funniest thing in the world. All three of us couldn't stop laughing. Even Mae thought it was funny after an hour of sulking.'

Angel brushed against my cheek. Until that moment I hadn't realised I'd shed tears.

I pinched the bridge of my nose, then spread my fingers underneath the rim of my eyes, wiping them away. Angel was watching me.

My smile felt sad. 'Or at least I think I remember it. Remember him. It's been so long. It was Dean who used to remind me. Who would fill my head with stories and facts about dad just so that I wouldn't forget. And now that he's gone too, I do forget. I can't quite catch what it sounded like when he laughed or the tone of his voice when he read us *Dinosaurs Prefer Tea*. Dean used to get it spot on but now...' I paused again, not liking how I was feeling.

'How old were you when they died?'

'Five. That's when Dad's motorcycle disappeared under a van, taking him with it. Twelve, when it was Dean.'

I cringed at the thought of Dean's death. Bile rose up and I swallowed it down, pushing the memory of that day as far away from my consciousness as was possible.

I growled deeply, feeling the ripple in my chest, 'Arrrrgh. I hate Nick,' I screamed, slamming my hand against vine and wood.

I gripped the ledge, sinking my fingers into the thick plant, slicing out chunks with my nail. Angel put her arms around my body, laying her head up close to my back.

I laughed in despair. 'Mae never used to be this dumb, or this blind. It was Dad, his death. Now every year it seems to get worse. She can't see it. She can't see *him* for what he really is. This vile creature. This viper, who's going to do or say anything to warp her mind, to poison it against me.'

Angel's face was tense, but she didn't seem surprised, I guessed she'd overheard everything earlier. I breathed deeply, trying to steady my raging nerves.

'I don't get why you don't just tell her. Let her know what a nasty piece of work he really is.'

'You want me to tell Mae that her husband-to-be, the supposed love of her life, kicks the crap out of me any chance he gets?'

'You're her son. She's got to at least listen to you. I think she'll take your side.'

'Me being her son means nothing,' I spat, 'She's been putting men before her sons long before Nick crawled into our lives.'

'But if you told her, made her listen. Showed her old bruises, new bruises.'

'No!' my voice was sharp.

Angel dropped her arms and moved to look at me.

'You need to, Luke. You can't let her make the biggest mistake of her life.'

'If you think she's going to believe what I have to say then you're deluded. You want me to show her the marks her beast put on me, show her the scars and the yellowing skin? Even if I did all that Angel, she'd still put him first. She'd convince herself that I was to blame, that I did this to myself or that I made him hurt me in some way.'

'You don't know that.'

'But I can't take that chance,' I yelled pounding my fist into the wood once more. 'If she didn't believe me Angel, if she didn't...' I couldn't finish my sentence, I found the words too painful, but I didn't have to. She knew.

'I hate her,' I spat, the words clawing at my insides and making me quiver. I placed a hand to her back. 'Angel,' I breathed, whispering her name, 'Angel.' I nestled my nose into the opaque shadow of her hair and inhaled deeply, almost tasting her scent.

'Thank you.'

'For what?'

'For bringing me here,' I said feeling suddenly more at ease.

She pressed her lips to my chest.

'Anytime.'

***

I laughed uncontrollably, completely losing myself in the moment.

'Are you being serious?' I choked between gasps.

He gazed at me with stern eyes.

'That's the most ridiculous thing I've ever heard,' I spluttered ignoring his piercing stare. 'You can't swim? Not even a little?'

'No. I can't.'

'Not even doggy paddle?'

'Nope'

'How about floating? Floating is pretty easy.'

'Look,' he barked, 'not everyone can swim. It's not that big a deal.'

'Yeah right,' I chuckled. 'How can you not know how to swim?'

'I never learnt, all right? It wasn't top of my list of things to do when I was growing up.' He squirmed on the spot and I could tell I had embarrassed him.

'I'm sorry,' I said pouting my lips, 'but it **is** a little funny.'

He scrunched up his nose and jerked his hand as if to shove me, but thought better of it. We stared out into the lake, listening to the lapping of the water.

'It looks so deep,' he muttered as his stomach swelled anxiously.

'You're not going to accidently fall in,' I joked.

'I know,' he snapped, trying to mask his fear with irritation.

'I was just making an observation.'

'Well observed,' I teased again. He cut me a look, but this time instead of scowling he kissed me on the forehead. I could get away with almost anything, so long as I was here, with him. My presence had become a shield against his dark world. Against Nick. Against Mae. He drew me closer any time she touched him, spoke or reached out to him. His eyes always full of an ingrained loathing. A hatred he wrapped round himself like a cloak, but he forgot that I could see past that. The more he let me in, the more my gaze filtered through the pretence. He feared her more than he hated her. He fought against his mother because the thought of letting her in was more than he could handle. He'd tasted the hurt of her rejection tonight and he wasn't about to let that happen again.

There was a space inside of him specially reserved for Mae. It was ugly-looking and felt cold and condensed, bitter. But in the centre of it all, where he hoped no one could see, where he himself never dared to look, was a pain so raw it couldn't be touched. A pain she'd caused by forcing him into second place.

If she chose Nick over him, if she believed an ounce of what that man said over her own son, it would rip that pain into a bloodied mess. One I wasn't sure even I could fix. So, he put up his defences, thickened himself in a wall of hate. Because if he hated her it wouldn't hurt so much when she turned her back on him. In that moment, when he'd opened up, I'd finally understood. He'd tried to hide his feelings, clouding them behind his love for me, his intense, deep love, but there was no escaping the truth. He was afraid to love her but more than that, he was afraid to let her love him.

Chapter 24
Monday, 19th April

I stood, head down, folders clasped to my chest. My face was hidden behind wild strands of hair and I was feeling thoroughly pissed off. The walls of college felt as though they were closing in all around me and where was Angel?

I'd woken up to an empty bed, her wispy figure gone. I'd buried my nose in the sheets, brushing the tip along their softness, inhaling deeply, but even the trace of her scent had left me. My insides had grown instantly colder, but I decided to try optimism for once. Maybe she'd been gone all night, maybe she'd be coming back soon: but she wasn't. I'd washed, dressed, gulped down a couple of headache tablets for breakfast and still she hadn't returned.

I'd even drawn out my walk to college. Each step more painfully slow than the last until I was standing outside of the entrance, forcing my trembling knees into stillness.

I'd been lucky. I'd managed to slink inside unnoticed, but I wasn't stupid. I knew luck didn't last. I just wondered who would deal me my first blow.

I dreaded seeing Mac, given the way we'd left things, but the thought of running into Lucile was surprisingly worse. It whipped up a nervousness so sickening that I felt my mouth begin to fill with bile. I swallowed it back and scanned the hallway. The place was packed with the bodies of people who occasionally knocked into me, choosing not to acknowledge my presence (which I preferred). The coast seemed clear. I felt a small wave of relief. I had Chemistry, and the chem lab was only a couple of minutes away. I wondered if my luck would stretch that far? I took a few steps in that direction when I heard that laugh — that hoarse, heart-clenching sound — and I realised the answer was no. I drummed my fingers against my chest until I felt a rhythm stir again and swallowed hard, but my throat was still prickly dry. My body was all set for flight mode but my head anchored it to the ground. This was coming. It was only a matter of time. Why prolong the moment? I swallowed again and turned around.

My skin prickled and I felt the sweat begin to form at the nape of my neck, I watched Mac slowly make it through the masses, flanked by his small army of idiots. His eyes were set to my face. I met his grin with a light scowl, and it remained that way until we were face to face. So close I could feel his excitable breath on my skin. He knew about Lucile, there was no denying it.

'Luke,' he yelled, slapping my shoulder roughly and gripping it between his brutish fingers. I stared at his thick, overly stretched lips with burning disgust, not saying a word. I watched as they formed themselves into a mock pout.

'So, you and Lucile didn't really work out huh? That's rough. I mean, I get it, it's you, but still, rough.'

Thick and Thicker burst into exaggerated laughter, attracting an audience. Still I stood there with my cold face, his fingers pressed partly into my flesh.

'I'm curious,' he barked. 'What did it take for her to finally realise what a mistake she'd made going out with you? Your face? I'm right, it was your face wasn't it? Close up she couldn't stand it, right?'

Again, his cronies chuckled, one after the other, as though laughing in sync was too much for the single brain they shared.

I watched from the corner of my eye as the crowd around us steadily grew. My head thumped under the pressure and my skin felt damp and clammy, but I held on to my hard expression, it was all I had by way of defence. Mac's grin deepened and I felt my stomach drop, he knew more than he was letting on.

'Nah, that's not it, is it Luke? I get the feeling I'm missing something...' his voice was an enthusiastic stage whisper.

'Why don't you just get to the point,' I finally said. 'Please your audience and let me get on with my day.'

He dropped his hand from my shoulder and wrinkled his nose, slightly annoyed. 'All right,' he said, sucking on his top lip as though savouring the moment. 'You tried to kiss her, didn't you?' His words slipped through a malicious half laugh. 'At least, that's what I heard. You tried to make a move and she practically ran out of her own car screaming.'

A ripple of whispers erupted from the not-so-subtle giggles. Heat rose to my face, it spread all through my body until it felt like everywhere was scorched. My chest clenched in frustration, but I pushed the feeling away. I deserved this. I had embarrassed Lucile enough; this lie was the least I owed her.

'Come on Luke, we're dying to know the truth. Did you make her run?'

He wore a greedy grin and I could see the pleasure reach his eyes. They goaded me nastily.

I looked around. Everyone was waiting for me to speak but I couldn't. Instead I smiled bitterly and nodded. Mac's laugh echoed through the halls, mimicked by his fellow losers until it spread through the intimate crowd around us. I felt my fist shake with rage, but I shoved it in my pocket. I'd take this one for Lucile.

Mac called for silence. 'People, people, I feel as if we are being cheated. I don't know about you guys, but I want to hear it all.' He glared at me with his smirk intact, 'Every last bit. Go on. Speak.'

'It's true,' I glared back. 'All of it.'

The laugher surrounding me beat with a pulse and Mac was right there, fuelling the evil sound with more words.

'Were you not smooth enough Luke? Was that it? Did you get make-up on her as you scrambled your way to her lips? Or was the sight of your open mouth enough to make her vom?'

More laughs. The sound bubbled and I closed my eyes to it all.

'You're an arse, Mac.'

Lucile's silky voice broke through the laughter, forcing everyone into silence. My eyes snapped open. She seemed to have appeared from nowhere. Her body was tense, and her gorgeous deep eyes were alight with fury. She stood beside me; eyes fixed on Mac with deep disgust.

'Hey,' Mac flared up, 'don't get mad at me. The people deserve to know the truth.'

She laughed once. 'You're right, they do. In fact, how's Melanie?' she asked stepping closer.

Mac's face darkened.

'Or Marcie? No wait, she was last week's rejection, wasn't she?'

'Why don't you shut your face?'

'Veeda, it was Veeda that blew you off the other day wasn't it?'

He bit his lip and glowered.

'What's the matter Mac? I thought the people deserved the truth. Don't you think they deserve to hear about the many, *many* girls who have run away from you and your lips?'

He was seething now.

'I said shut your face.'

'Why?' she spat, 'I'm not finished.'

'I'm warning you—'

'Do you know that we talk about it?' Lucile continued, 'Laugh about it? You haven't got a chance in hell of *ever* hooking up in this college, and for the record…'

Lucile turned to look at me for the first time since I'd ditched her. I swallowed hard.

'Luke chucked me, not the other way around, and I'm not going to give you all the details so you might as well just piss off.'

No one moved.

'I mean it, do one.'

The bell sounded, bringing noise to the intense silence. Legs scattered and people mumbled on their way to wherever they had to be. Only the five of us remained.

Mac's taut face was pale. Skin stretched across his knuckles, ashen white underneath the strain, and his eyes… he looked at us with an expression I almost didn't recognise on his face. He tried to hide it with a scowl, but it was too late. I'd seen it, the fear of someone whose secrets had been unearthed. I'd seen it and so had everyone else. I wanted to feel sorry for him, but I guess the human side of me was glad he'd gotten what he deserved for once.

He shuffled away without a word, taking the other two with him, until Lucile and I were the only ones left standing.

She squeezed my fingers, and it was only then that I realised she was holding on to my hand. She let go and I nervously rubbed the clamminess away on my trousers. We looked at each other, both with the same shyness.

'You didn't have to do that,' I muttered, and she nodded her head.

'Yes, I did. I couldn't let him say all those things about you.'

'The truth can't be good for your reputation,' I teased. 'Missy will be furious.'

She laughed. 'Who cares about a reputation? We'll be leaving in a few months. Now if we still had another year you'd have been completely on your own.'

This time it was my turn to laugh.

'Seriously Luke, thank you.'

I felt my face twist into a puzzled mask and her smooth out the lines with her fingertips.

'I made a complete idiot out of myself,' I went to protest but she halted me.

'I wanted so much for this thing between us to be real, but I guess we both wanted to be with other people. You were just the only one with enough guts to admit it.'

'Shane?'

She smiled, 'We got back together last week.'

'I'm really happy for you.'

'And you? What about your special someone?'

'She's good.' I thought about Angel and smiled. 'Perfect.'

Lucile smiled back. 'Walk you to class?' she offered, looping her arm around mine.

'Careful,' I teased, 'you don't want to get caught still associating with the likes of me. I hear Missy has spies everywhere.'

She sniggered, 'I'll take my chances.'

***

The rest of the day turned out to be uneventful, whizzing by until I found myself, mid-afternoon, staring at a computer screen in the library. Everything was going perfectly. Mac appeared to be in hiding after this morning's humiliation, which suited me fine, and as an added bonus Mr Taylor was out sick. For once things were pretty sweet, except that Angel hadn't returned.

I plugged in my USB and set to work. Checking the grammar and structure of my Art essay. Time and time again my eyes flickered towards the clock, wondering, waiting. When it finally reached half three, I was beyond fury. How dare she? The day was almost over and she hadn't shown her face once. She knew what a big deal coming back was for me. She'd felt it in her gut just like I'd felt it in mine. The sickening sway of my insides, my aching head as the fear caused each cell to pulse angrily. She'd felt it all and yet she'd still abandoned me. For what? What possible excuse could she have for leaving me to face this on my own? What could possibly have been more important to her? The blood beneath my skin heated. It squirmed around angrily, rushing to my temples, increasing the soreness in my head.

A warm breeze brushed against my skin, but this time it wasn't quite soothing. I didn't take my eyes off the screen. I couldn't bring myself to. I sat there, hands gripped around my seat, breathing... slowly. She didn't speak. The moments of silence crept into minutes and still no explanation. Not a single word slipped out of her mouth. My seething bubbled up viciously. How could she not even bother to explain? Five minutes, six. The anger had fully reached my brain. It throbbed painfully and I could feel I was inches away from blackout. I had to say something before the tension caused my head to burst. I swung round on my chair, ready to face her, ready to say something, not caring who saw.

I set my cool eyes on her face and felt my rage melt into nothingness. She stared at me, wide-eyed and full of grief. Her lips were a touch curved, as though she was attempting a smile but couldn't quite remember how. She hung her body limply at the edge of her seat — practically dangling her frame from the chair — and peeked up at me from beneath her wild choppy hair. My tense body sagged, and I swallowed deeply. She tugged at her trembling lip and closed her eyes. I felt my heart cave in, my head swam as my body adjusted to my emotions. She was in pain, a pain I didn't understand. All day I had been raging about her not being there for me, how selfish she'd been for not thinking about me. I never, not even in the quietest of moments, paused to think about her. I looked up at her now, so tough yet so fragile. Independent but to her own detriment. She never let anyone in, not close enough to help. She tugged at her lip ring now, trying to bring the quivering to a standstill, trying to quell the emotions that had surfaced. Her eyes held my gaze now. She wanted to speak. I saw her struggle, but she wasn't ready, and I had no intention of pushing her. Still, I wanted her to know I was there for her. I could have told her but she wasn't ready for my words either, so I did the only thing I could. I opened up my heart to her, as fully as it would stretch, and I prayed that she was listening to the words it spoke with each beat.

Chapter 25
Friday, 23rd April

Angel was gone most of the week. I preoccupied myself with exam preparations and studying, but still it was hard. I worried a lot, but all I needed to do was just make it through the day. Because at night, she'd be there, with me.

I was always asleep when she came. I tried not to be but I had a feeling that was the way she wanted it. I'd leave the covers turned down and wake in the darkness to find her slight figure curled into mine, not looking, back facing me. But still I wrapped myself around her shape and watched as her shadowy hand mimicked the gripping and rubbing of my arm. I wanted so badly to wipe away her hurt, to bring her closer to me, but I knew only she could do that. When she was ready.

When Friday finally arrived, I greeted it with passionate relief. Lucile's harsh words seemed to have forced Mac into some kind of retreat. I guess being laughed at all week didn't agree with him. All the better for me. I rarely saw him, and when I did, he was less inclined to shower me with his usual onslaught of verbal abuse. There were still the menacing glares and the occasional 'accidental' shove, but it was a better trade off than I was used to.

By the end of the day I was pretty pleased with the progress of my Art examination. Everything was coming together, and for the first time a part of me was glad Angel wasn't around. It would make the perfect surprise for her come Monday, considering her bad mood seemed set on stretching out that long.

Flecks of red and green fell into the breeze as I dusted down my shirt. I rubbed my hands together to get the paint off of my skin. A warm, light wind whipped itself around me. Even without looking I knew it wasn't her, yet still it hurt when I looked up to find I was walking home alone.

With a vague awareness I reached home. I slid the key into the lock and pushed in one movement. I paused, feeling deeply aggravated.

'Hi honey.'

My nostrils flared angrily.

'Mae. Why are you standing right in front of the door?'

My voice was sharp and irritated for good reason. Mae had been acting weird lately, overly observant. Before I'd put it down to her wedding day crash diet and lack of sleep, but since my bust up with Nick I wasn't so sure. She'd been more cautious around me, throwing me wary looks, and I wondered if it had already started. The lies. Who knew what kind of things he'd been saying to her, what she'd believe? Maybe she didn't trust me anymore.

'I was waiting for you,' she answered, and I felt my insides recoil.

'Why?'

'I thought we could talk.'

That was another thing she wanted to do a lot. Talk, and I knew why. She'd chosen Nick over me hands down, but however much she didn't trust me now, I knew she felt guilt ridden about it inside. Not enough to change her mind, but enough for her to bug me incessantly with 'talks.'

I smiled insincerely. 'No thanks. Why don't you have a chat with your hubby to be?' She squirmed awkwardly on her feet, twisting her fringe.

'He's out. Besides, it's you I want.'

I sighed impatiently as I slipped off my bag and set it down.

'What for?'

'I already told you, to talk.'

'About what?' I all but yelled. 'What could *we* have to talk about?'

My tone frightened her, I could tell. She staggered back a little and slumped herself on to the bottom step. Nick had done a good job at planting the first seed of doubt in her mind. She buried her face in her hands and drew her hair back.

'You look so much like your brother, you know that?'

Her comment threw me but I didn't let it show. 'What, with my dark brown hair and deep blue eyes you mean?'

'Don't be sarcastic Luke. It's unkind.'

I savoured the silence that lasted, every second of it, until it was over.

'I meant your features. The colours might be different, but you have the same nose, the same smile. I wish I could see that smile more often.'

My stare was bitterly intense.

'Why? Because you want to look at me and pretend that I'm someone else? That I'm Dean?'

'No,' she shrieked in an almost irrational tone, 'because I want to see *you* smile Lucas. Because I want you to be happy. Talk to me about Dean. You never just talk about him.'

I was the irrational one now, screaming with a sudden burst of raw rage.

'What is this, Mae? What kind of crap has your precious fiancé been feeding you?'

She stared at me, a bewildered look harassing her face.

'What has Nick got to do with Dean?'

I laughed mockingly, 'Don't tell me he hasn't been talking about me behind my back, making it seem as if... as if I'm...'

'As if what Luke? You're not making any sense.'

She was right, I wasn't. My train of thought wasn't logical. I couldn't find the thread. The one linking me, Dean and Nick together, but I was positive there was one. That he had something to do with this. *'You'll be as dead to her as your brother.'* He'd said that. He'd meant that. He was behind all of this. I was sure, even if I didn't quite know how.

Mae stared at me with wild, moon-shaped eyes. I rolled mine as hard as I could.

'Forget it. You're the last person I'd try and explain this to.'
I stormed passed her and up the stairs to my room, letting my door slam shut with an ear-splitting thud.

***

I eagerly awaited the night, but it took for ever to come. I wanted to stay up, to force Angel to talk to me. I needed her, but I knew that wasn't how it worked, so I tossed and turned into a restless sleep.

It was cold. Wherever I was, it was deep within the minuses and I struggled to cope with the harsh temperature. I couldn't see anything. Everywhere was pitch black but still my body searched. Each limb moving to where it thought was the warmest.

I felt it. Her warmth. It greeted me deep within my sleep. I didn't need to force myself awake; my body responded willingly to her call.

My eyes sprang back with speed, focusing themselves with great haste, but when I stared into the space next to me, she wasn't there. My stomach flipped as disappointment rolled inside. It was a dream.

'Over here,' her silky voice called.

For a second, I thought I was imagining things, that maybe I was still asleep, but the longer my eyes stayed open the more aware I became that I wasn't. She sat at the open window ledge, one leg dangling out into the street, the other tucked securely into her chest. She hugged it tightly with one arm and ran her fingers along the blinds with the other. She seemed mesmerised by their slight movement.

'What are you doing?' I croaked, pulling myself into sitting position.

She didn't answer with words. Instead, a pained smile spread across her face.

'Come,' I called, stretching out my hand towards her. She peered at me with those piercing brown eyes and I saw all the vulnerability of her soul. Moments later she was on my lap. Her head resting along the curve of my neck. I watched her slender frame shake and I listened as the quiet whimpering began. No tears wet my skin but I knew, without doubt, that she was crying.

***

Saturday, 24th April

When I woke up, Angel was gone. Her sweet scent still stained my skin and I wished she could have stayed a little longer. Even if she didn't talk. I just wanted to see her face, to know how she was doing, but there was no point in wishing. She wasn't coming back. Not until the night anyway, so the only thing left for me to do was to put her as far out of my mind as was possible. There was no other way of making it through the day.

Nick was out again. That used to be a good sign, but these days it just meant that Mae would be directing all of her energy my way. I refused to give her the chance; while she was in the shower, I wolfed down a quick helping of beans on toast, snuck to the bathroom as she dressed, then spent the rest of the morning on my comic, until it was almost finished.

It was early afternoon by the time I was done and I had already run out of things to do with myself. Nightfall was hours away. The thought of waiting idly by for Angel to return was painful, so I made a decision. I was going to be proactive. I pulled on my black Converse and bounded down the stairs. Not to my surprise, Mae was perched on the last step. I rushed past her and out of the door letting it slam on her words.

Racing down the street, my feet clashed with the ground so hard I could feel the concrete push into their soles. I was the subject of some very curious stares, but I ignored them. By the time I'd arrived at the park I was panting hard. I pushed the rusty fence aside and made my way inside.

'Angel,' I called as I walked towards our usual spot by the swings. 'Angel,' I yelled her name repeatedly, until my voice was hoarse from effort. I scoured everywhere I could think of, the lake, even places that we'd never been before, hoping she'd be there. Hiding. Waiting. My search went on for what felt like hours. I hunted through the same places again and again, each time my hopefulness chipping away. Finally, I gave up. I dragged my tired body back to our place and I lay my head against the tree. I watched the birds in formation as they soared through the sky. Admiring how peaceful they looked.

*****

Opening the door as quietly as I could I slipped inside. I half expected Mae to pop out from behind screaming, 'let's talk,' but she wasn't there. She had to be near. Somewhere close by was my mother, lurking, waiting to pounce. I searched the house tentatively, praying not to find her. When I was confident the coast was clear I exhaled in relief and climbed the stairs, heading straight for the bathroom. The unseasonal heat had left my skin uncomfortably sticky and I was dying to splash my face. After a couple of minutes, when I was beginning to feel relatively human again, I shut off the tap.

My image stared back at me from the mirror. Streaks of black lined my face and I frowned.

'Great,' I muttered grabbing a towel to wipe my face. I left the bathroom drying my clammy hands against my trousers on the way to the bedroom.

'Odd,' I mumbled, pushing the door open. I was sure I hadn't closed it on my way out, but in that moment, I was too tired to really care. Dragging myself towards my bed, I let my body flop lazily on to the mattress. My eyes had been flickering to a close when I saw her shape take form. I sat up, brushing my shaggy hair from my face. Angel smiled at me, that pained smile. I stared back at her, scanning her from limb to limb, trying to suss out exactly how she felt. I placed an arm around her waist and let my body tremble slightly as the sweet scent of her soul reached my lungs. My heart thrust excitedly when the heat from her head brushed against my shoulder, but at the same time it twisted nervously for her. She stroked along the bed sheets and I sensed her muted groan.

'Today's my birthday,' she mumbled, dragging each word out with effort.

'I would have been 18. Don't say anything... I guess I just wanted you to know.'

It felt as if my twisted heart had torn, then, flinched thinking about how much worse she must have felt. I placed my lips along the line of her hair, rubbing them gently, back and forth. She sighed, heavily, several times — trying not to cry — as I whispered her name over and over again.

***

I let myself find comfort in his arms, even though it hurt me. I leant on him, relied on him. I drew his love around me like a shield, but it was his love that caused me pain.

Eighteen. We would have been the same age. I wanted so much to touch him. To run my fingers through his hair, to feel his lips as they pressed against my head but I couldn't, and I never would — because he was 18 and I was not. I wasn't anything. I was just dead.

Sunday, 25th April

This time when I woke up Angel was still there. Perched on the window ledge, staring into the street below. I hauled my body up with a groan.

'Morning,' she whispered, briefly flickering her eyes in my direction. I dragged myself slowly towards her, trying to shake off the intense fatigue as I moved. I stood before her, wrapped my hands around her face and cupped the shape of her cheek. She peeked up at me, and the intensity in those brown eyes was electric. They burned with sadness. I lowered my lips to hers and pressed as tenderly as I could against their form feeling the energized pressure, sensing her touch. My skin prickled with pleasure and a soft moan slipped from her throat. I pulled away from her and watched her mouth stretch into a smile.

'Morning,' I breathed.

She wriggled her face free from my empty grasp and looked back down at the lives below.

'It's such a beautiful day,' she said sadly.

'Do you want to go and enjoy it?'

The puzzled look on her face reached her eyes and I was glad it had distracted her from her pain, however briefly.

'I have a surprise for you.'

'A *surprise*?' she said, arching her eyebrows further. 'I don't get it.'

A breathy laugh escaped my mouth and I kissed the crown of her head.

'You will.'

I tore myself away from her and headed for the door.

'Where are you going?' she called, a note of panic lodged somewhere in her tone.

'Just to shower then I'll be right back. Promise.'

I caught a glimpse of myself in the mirror on the way out and gasped.

'Jeeze, you could have reminded me to wash the crap off my face last night.'

It was her turn to laugh now at my smudged eyeliner and the general mess that was my face. It was a beautiful sound. I shook my head and headed out of the room.

I climbed out of the shower and dressed as quickly as I could. Last night's banquet of crisps and strawberry laces hadn't done much for my appetite and I was definitely paying for it now. My stomach groaned and lurched all the way to the kitchen. Flipping intensively until the first mouthful of golden flakes sunk to the bottom.

'Feeling better now?' she teased.

I winked back at her, not daring to speak. Mae was propped up in the corner nursing a cup of coffee, and I could feel her suspicious eyes all over my skin. I turned my attention back towards Angel and smiled. All I could do was smile at her, my love.

'What are you staring at?' she asked, pretending not to be moved by my affection.

I shook my head as if to say nothing and grinned some more. A gruff noise sounded. I snarled, realising it was Mae clearing her throat.

'What are you doing with yourself today honey?'

'Stuff,' I answered, not bothering to look her way.

I heard her cup tap against the table and her fingers as they drummed lightly against the surface. I braced myself. She was gearing up for it, I could feel it brewing, the *talk*.

'Lucas,' she said frankly, 'We need to talk.'

'Not again,' I mumbled. 'I don't really have time, Mae.'

I hopped down from the stool, the spoon still in my hand. I knew where this was going and I wasn't prepared to sit around and hear what she had to say. I stared at my half-eaten breakfast with regret as I gulped down the last spoonful.

'Are you ready?' I asked Angel, the words slipping out of my mouth before I could catch them.

Mae's face was a picture.

'Ready for what?'

I groaned inwardly and shrugged.

'Forget it Mae, I was talking to myself.'

'You were asking yourself if you were ready?'

I shrugged again, not bothering to think up a plausible excuse, and was out the door before she could respond.

Angel had been right. It was a beautiful spring day. I clutched my sketchbook eagerly and quickened my pace, not wanting to waste a single minute. Soon we were at the entrance to the park. I panted as I pushed the stubborn gate and struggled to squeeze myself through with my backpack attached. I tripped, landing awkwardly on my bag. Her laugh rippled around me and I scowled playfully.

'Not funny,' I growled, dusting my clothes down once I'd heaved myself up from the ground. Angel appeared on the other side, staring at me through narrowed eyes.

'Lucas,' she called with a slight thrill to her tone, 'What exactly are you up to?'

My lips slipped into a crooked smile and I held out a hand.

'Come with me and you'll find out.'

She slid her hand on top of mine and we clasped, our fingers deeply aware of the other's.

I lead her off the path, passing the wild shrubbery, until I'd found the bridge. Ignoring the lapping of the water I took a deep breath and stepped on to the moss-covered panels, guiding her to my side.

'What are we doing here?' her voice was a soft, peaceful murmur and I was glad I had chosen here to do this. It would be one more pleasant memory for her to add to the many others created in this place.

'Sit.' She stared at me oddly but obeyed, crossing her legs as she gently tugged at her lip ring. My legs shook slightly as I anxiously lowered myself to sit in front of her.

'Don't be nervous,' I said staring into her warm-coloured eyes.

She laughed, 'I could say the same to you.' She placed a hand to her heart and tapped, 'It couldn't thrust any harder.'

'Yeah well, that'll be the water. I'm terrified.'

'That's true. You are, but that's not why it's beating so hard.'

Her words raised a tiny smile but I didn't laugh. Instead, my gaze on her became more intense. I set aside my sketchbook and began stroking the outline of her hand.

'You probably already know what I want to say.' I began, my voice a nervous wobble. 'You probably know it better than I do. You could read my soul without me saying a single word. Every feeling I have, exposed. I hate it, more than anything I hate it.'

Confusion replaced the look of wonder in her eyes and I rushed my words, eager to claim it back.

'I want to say things to you Angel. Beautiful, epic things. There is so much I want to tell you about how beautiful you are and about your heart, about mine, but I can't. I freeze up. Nothing I say could ever be worth hearing when the feeling of it must be so much more intense.'

Her face became alive once more.

'I feel stupid when I say that I love you, because of course I love you. But what could those three little words possibly mean next to the surge of their feeling coursing through your body? I want to tell you that I can't live without you, that I could never survive with you gone, but that's nothing compared to the fear that grips me whenever I think you're not coming back. Everything I say, Angel, every single word is worthless to you. You know the things my words couldn't possibly express, but I want to express something to you. There is something I need you to hear today and I want it to come from me.'

Her eyes never left my face. They burnt a golden brown and I could see her desire to know beaming through. I took in a deep breath, letting it still my quivering insides.

'Are you ready?'

Her lips were pressed gently together but she nodded.
'Here it is then,' I said picking up my sketchbook and clutching it tightly.
'Everything I've always wanted you to know…'

***

He wasn't wrong. As he slid his hand into his sketchbook, I could feel the trepidation wrapped around his excitement. As he cracked open the spine and drew out sheets of crisp, cream coloured paper, the strength of his love for me stroked every part of my being. He slung off his bag, wriggled out of his jacket and laid the many sheets out on top, struggling to keep them off of the green-stained panels of the bridge.

I gasped. 'Is that… me?'

He gripped a chunk of his hair and let out a small, embarrassed chuckle.

'I didn't know what you looked like back then so I pretty much drew what I felt.'

I stretched out my hand and let it glide over the image of me, this hazy, misty, silver that formed my exact shape.

'What's this?'

My fingers met the words sketched on to the page. He laughed cringingly.

'*The Adventures of Goth Kid*. Pretty stupid I know. You should've seen it before you came into my life, it was tragi—'

I cut him off, spluttering my words. 'This, this is the first night we met,' I said, staring at his figure, at mine, at the rain falling down all around us.

A simple nod. I felt him shift his body closer to me, until his skin brushed along my arm, but I still didn't look up. I couldn't.

'And this? Is this...?'

'The night I let you into my life. We talked and it was like we'd known each other a lifetime.'

'"... and finally, he was home."'

I felt his eyes on me as I read those words aloud, heard his breath, deep and slow. He was trying to settle the butterflies that swarmed through his whole body, but to no avail. They were too strong, too pure, and in the end, he gave into them, feeling absolute, sheer pleasure.

'I'd never felt comfort like that before, Angel. Never. It was the first time, in a long time, that I felt safe and calm and like...'

'You were home?'

He nodded again, and I felt him cling to that peace even now.

I recalled the night in my head. I remembered his pain, the bruises that throbbed on his skin, his grief. I remembered that he was tired. Completely worn out from struggling, from fighting. He'd just wanted to escape it all. Then ease, an ease fell about him massaging away the bulk of his anguish. I'd felt that, I'd felt it all — but I'd never known that feeling was 'home'.

My eyes grew hot and there was a choking in my throat. I looked at Luke to see if he was all right, and he was. It was me. These were my emotions, my almost tears begging to be spilt from my eyes. I pressed my fingers to my lips to silence the tiny whimper that was forcing its way out. I failed.

'I guess my words aren't completely meaningless then.'

I shook my head and bit down hard on my trembling lip.

My eyes devoured the sheets over and over again. The elegance, the grace, it moved me, and when I had finished with the ones in front of me, he pulled out more and then more. I poured over image after image, my dead heart tingling with sensation. With ecstasy until...

'You drew the lake,' I yelped, shooting upright. 'I can't believe you drew the lake.'

He grinned at my excitable tone and I drew myself closer until my face was inches from the page.

'It looks incredible. It's exactly the same, except...'

'It's unfinished, I know, I know, but it won't be for much longer.'

I knelt up turning to look at him as I did. The breeze was light and warm, I felt it through him. It tickled his face and blew strands of jet-black hair in all directions. He smiled playfully at me, enjoying whatever expression played on my face.

'I have a question for you,' I said trying control the waver in my voice.

'I'm listening.'

'I've asked to see your art a million times, and the answer has always been the same... no chance in hell.'

'I'm sure those weren't my exact words, but go on.'

'Why are you showing it to me now? What made you ready to share it with me today?'

'It was only thing I could think of. The only gesture I could make that would show you exactly how much you mean to me. Well, one of the only gestures.'

My brow furrowed at his last statement but I pressed on, making a mental note to come back to it.

'But why this sudden urgent need to make sure I knew. Why not before? Why not later? Why now? What's so special about now?'

He looked up at the clear blue sky and then back at me. Shifting his body, he raised a hand and ran it against my face. I felt the force around his fingers brush against my jaw line.

He whispered, 'It was the only way that I could prove to you that you're real.'

Suddenly I was unable to look at his face. I lowered my head and exhaled softly at the startling build of emotions. He cocked his head to meet my gaze and smiled.

'You may not have a body, Angel, but you're still here. You're not a figment of anyone's imagination, you're not invisible and you're not any less of a person because you can't breathe, or cry tears. When I touch you like this,' he said, grazing a finger down the hollow of my neck, 'you still feel. Okay so it's not the same way that I do, but it's not nothing. To be able to still tremble underneath another's touch, to feel love, to be loved, it's everything. You taught me that. Your life, however unconventional, is with me, and I wanted to show it to you. You deserve to see it.'

I was speechless. I stared at him for what felt like minutes and he let me. Allowing me to collect all thoughts and feelings, new ones, ones I never knew I had. Gratitude for the man who stood before me, for his love and then acceptance. As long as he was with me, I would be all right.

'Thank you,' I murmured when my throat would let me speak.

'I'm not out of surprises yet,' he grinned impishly.

'What do you mean?' There was a rush of excitement bubbling within both of us.

In the same swift motion, he pressed his lips to my forehead and began rummaging through his rucksack. In seconds he had retrieved his favourite black pencil along with a few other sketching utensils. He found the drawing of the lake and, pressing it against his sketchbook, settled into a comfortable position.

'What are you doing?'

He peeked up at me from beneath his wild hair, his crooked smile lurking just below the surface of his lips.

'I think it's time we finished this picture, don't you?'

It was late in the afternoon when I began packing up. The air was much cooler and the sun was edging its way behind the foreboding clouds. I'd pushed, on wanting to get the perfect depiction of Angel — arm clutching her bent leg, surrounded by the lake — and now that I had I was in hurry to get myself and my work away from the threat of rain. I carefully slotted the sheets back into the sketchbook and hurried out of the park with the first of the drizzles snaking down my shirt. By the time we'd reached my street, the rain was thundering down.

Angel howled with laughter as I awkwardly clutched my sketchbook underneath my jacket and struggled to stop my rucksack from slipping down. I tried to get the key through the door, but her laughter had become so contagious that it shook me from the inside out. The key slipped from my hands several times, landing in the puddle I'd created from my dripping clothes. Finally, I burst through the door, both my chest and stomach muscles aching from the intense amusement.

Mae was waiting at the bottom of the steps. A sullen look etched deep within her skin. I felt the grin slide from my face.

'Hey,' I said dully, and began shaking myself free from my wet jacket. I flung it on to the coat rack, ignoring the drips as they dampened the floor. I had expected a lecture, for her to order me to take my soaking jacket to the bathroom before the place started smelling of damp, but she didn't. She just sat there, her face deeply troubled, her hands trembling badly. I wanted to ignore the worry that twanged me. To let go of the fact that she was my mother and remember that she was just Mae, irritating, self-involved, neglectful Mae, but I couldn't. That look on her face was one of my earliest memories. I'd only ever seen her look this scared twice in my life, and both times someone was dead.

'Mae,' I said speaking as gently as our strained relationship would allow. 'Is everything okay?' She shook her head, her big doe eyes rattling with the movement. I walked towards her, staring at those eyes.

'What is it? What's happened?'

She blew out, her lips fluttering with the breath and blinked her dense blue eyes. I could see the sparkle of tears building up, she brushed them away with the back of her hand and began twisting her hair. I lowered myself in front of her.

'Mum?'

'Are you on drugs?' she blurted, her eyes feverish and wild.

'What?'

'Well, are you? Tell me. Honestly. I need to know.'

I shot back up, 'No.' I spat 'Are you?'

'Damn it.'

Her voice was a fierce mumble that rose in pitch.

'Damn it, damn it, damn it, damn it.'

She rocked back and forth now, hugging her knees desperately. I stared at her incredulously. I was hardly able to take it in.

'I don't get it. You're upset because I'm not taking drugs?'

'No,' she screamed, and I jumped back. 'No, but if you were that is a problem that could be fixed. A problem I know how to fix. Rehab, more counselling... but this!' she drew out my journal from behind her back and leapt up, waving it in my face, 'This can't be easily fixed.'

My skin heated with anger.

'Where did you get that?' I growled, the sound low and menacing.

'You need help, honey. You need help.' Tears were streaming down her face now and she made no effort to hold them back.

I lunged straight for the book but she ducked out of the way.

'A girl? A dead girl? Angel?'

'How dare you touch that. How dare you go through my things.'

My voice sounded different in my own ears. Cold, hard, monstrous.

'Luke, shhhh. It's okay,' Angel's words were soothing but her face, she looked terrified.

I felt her hand smooth my cheek and breathed into her love.

'I went through your room a few days ago. I didn't read it all, not then. I didn't want to believe there was something wrong but you wouldn't stop.'

'Stop what?' I snarled.

'Stop mumbling to yourself. Stop starring into space all of the time. Stop looking at things, objects, like you were crazy about them.' She paused, 'Do you think you're in love with her? This... Angel?'

219

Whether it was the anger or fear I couldn't tell, but my body now trembled too.

If I told her the truth, if I placed my love for Angel in her hands, then what? She'd never believe me and there would be consequences of that. Irreparable consequences.

A cold sweat broke out on my skin's surface. I ran my wet hands through my even wetter hair, gripping hard, drawing the water out from the strands.

'You don't understand,' I said now, pressing my hands against my throbbing head. 'I know it sounds crazy but you don't understand.'

She laughed wildly, fearfully, 'I do, I do baby. You're sick.'

She put a hand in her hair and yanked her glasses free, forcing them on to her face. From her back pocket she pulled out rolled-up sheets of paper.

'It's all here,' she said unfurling the mass. 'I've been researching and researching and it's all here. "Hallucinations and delusions can equal unusual behaviour during acute acts of schizophrenia."'

I was the one laughing madly now.

'Schizophrenia? You think I'm a schizo?'

She nodded timidly, 'It makes sense, you have all the signs, it says so right here.'

I shook my head and smirked unkindly.

'You're wrong,' I spat, the fear thickening my anger. '*You* are wrong. You do a couple of internet searches and you think you understand this? That you understand me?'

'No, no Luke, it's not just me, I spoke to Nick this morning and he thinks—'

I flung my hands up in the air and let them slam down on the table, making the phone shake.

'Well if he thinks so, what the hell are we still doing here? Why haven't you carted me off to the insane asylum already?'

There was an eerie silence followed by the soft calling of my name from them both.

'Don't you see what he's doing, Mae?' I said now, holding her by the arms, not realising I'd walked the distance to her. I felt as if my body wasn't my own, like in this instant I was all impulses.

'He's trying to get rid of me, Mae. Mum, he's trying to get rid of me. He's making things up, saying things…'

She tore herself from my grip and threw the journal at my chest.

'He didn't write this Luke. You did.'

I watched the book as it slid to the floor, its pages fluttering open, exposing my very soul.

I stared aghast at the words, shaking with a painful rage as though the realisation struck my body before it did me.

'You've read everything now? Everything? Every word on these pages, seen every drawing?'

She nodded timidly, recoiling against my grave mumble. A harsh fury grated inside of me. It swelled as though it were an inflamed wound, it pulsed to the rhythm of my erratic heart. I swallowed hard against the pain.

'Nick,' I hissed, my teeth gritted. She blinked starkly, like a lamb cornered by a wolf.

'Nick,' I repeated this time, fierce enough to spark some understanding in her.

'I know what you're thinking,' she began, tripping over every word, 'but it's not true. Nick wouldn't. Never. It's because you're sick. It must be because you're sick.'

Bile rose to my throat. I spat the bitter taste to the ground and glared at Mae. A slither ran down my bottom lip and I ran my tongue against it, sputtering once more.

'Do you want to see the scars Mae?' I snarled. 'The bruises? The raised silvery lines, the sallow skin that *prove* I'm not making this up?'

We stared at each other for a long time, my glower reducing her to more of a quivering mess. Her jaw trembled and she shook her tiny head, lightly but rapidly.

'It's the hallucinations,' she shrugged, 'you're sick,' she nodded. 'I bet when you're seeing things it can be easy to accidently cause a bump or cut yourself. Nick wouldn't do this to you. *You* did this to you.'

It started off slowly and grew in intensity. I closed my eyes and relaxed into the slow, burning pain, letting it close me in, feeling its wrath. I listened as it spoke through my blood, each thud in my ear growing in strength. I smiled as it tore through my gut, scooping and ripping till it left a tender, hollow welt. Yes, I smiled. There was nothing left to do but smile. She had done it, chosen Nick over me, and I had no other choice but to live with that.

I sucked in the air from both mouth and nose, taking in the stench of rejection that lingered thickly all around us. It stung, bitterly, but all the same I welcomed it. It spurred on my old friend, hate. I opened my eyes and spoke through a dry crackling throat.

'You're the one who's sick, not me. You ignore what you see every day, and somehow I've become the one with the problem?'

I felt the moisture grow in my eyes, ignored it as it spilled down my cheek.

'You think I'm ill because I choose to put my faith in someone who's never let me down? Just because she's 'unconventional'? Who should I put my faith in? You?'

'Yes,' she cried, 'why not?'

'Because I don't trust you,' I shrieked, my whole body hot with rage. 'Because you let that man into our lives,' I continued, watching her nervously rip at her nails with her teeth. 'Because you believe him over me even though deep down you know what he's like. Because you'd rather stick your fingers in your ears and squeeze your eyes shut just so that later, when you invite him into your bed you can pretend you had no clue.'

I stared at her frankly, but her eyes, they flickered everywhere except to mine.

'I'm not the delusional one. You are.'

Her pursed lips would not stop quivering. In fact, her whole body was a jittering mess. But when she spoke her voice was steady, calm. Her tone fierce yet unprovoked. It was tone of someone was who had grown assured in their denial and was not about to let something like the facts tear things apart.

She looked up at me, this time with her gaze placed firmly on mine.

'Say all you want, Luke, but I'm going to get you some help. I've been hesitant before now. I was afraid for you, but I can't be any more. You need me to be strong.'

My hands were in my hair now, gripping desperately.

'We'll speak to some doctors,' she said. 'You may even have to go away for a little while, I'm not sure, but they'll do what's best. I have to let them do what's best.'

We both shivered at the thought, but I pushed my fears to one side. After today I'd never have to be afraid of them carting me away again. After today they wouldn't be able to find me.

'You'll see. When the doctors fix you, you'll see that this *'girl'* is what's done this to you, to us. *She's* the one who's caused the problems between us... or at least made them worse,' she tagged on weakly when I laughed in her face. 'She's poisonous, poisonous, but they'll cleanse her from your system. Soon it will be like she never existed.'

'She is real,' I snapped, letting my voice rip through my throat in a deafening roar. 'She's not some *thing* I have to be cured of. Some disease. She is real.'

I gave Angel a sideways glance, extending my hand for her to hold. She did.

'Trust me, Mum,' I begged, surprising even myself.

It felt like I was that child again: 12 years old, pleading to be heard. The disgust I felt for myself taunted me, but I went on.

'For once Mae just trust *me.* Not Nick, not Google, *me.'*

A tear slid down my face and I shut my eyes as Angel kissed it.

'I do believe you honey.'

My eyes sprang open at her words.

'I know you *think* she's real, but you're not well.'

I growled in frustration, feeling what small hope I'd had crash through my chest.

'It's true. Think about it Luke. They say that people who have experienced stressful or traumatic events are at higher risk of getting the disorder.'

'So?'

'And they say that people with the disease become withdrawn, experiencing a flattening of emotions.'

She was saying it word for word, the sheets of paper an extension of her shaky hands, but I had a feeling she didn't need them. That they were just for show. She had already memorised the text on the page, or rather the speech she'd planned, just for me.

I dragged my hands through my hair again and expelled an angry sigh.

'I'm not following you, Mae.'

She rolled her lips between her teeth and squeezed the print-outs, filling the dense silence with the sound of crackling paper.

'Dean,' she finally said, her wobbly voice barely carrying. 'That's when you changed. That's when you shut yourself off from everyone, even me.'

'No.' I said not liking the direction the conversation was heading.

'Maybe if we'd talked about it more…'

'What is there to talk about? He's dead, Mae. Just like Dad. Gone. They are never coming back, so there is nothing to talk about.'

'What about how that makes you feel? Or how *cutting* the pain still is? You're so angry,' she said, letting tears fall between her lips.

'Of course I'm angry, how could I not be angry?' I felt my grief pushing its way back up, choking me on its way out.

'I know it hurts. Losing them in such a pointless way, it still haunts me.'

She was speaking, but my ears were deafened by rage. I didn't know whether to laugh, cry or scream, I hurt so badly. Memories, harsh and horrifying memories, flooded my head and I ground my teeth hard, tasting blood.

'Luke, please will you talk to me.'

I snuffed the cry that was rising in me and licked my gums, trying to find the source of the bleed.

'Luke.' I laughed, then snarled when Mae's hand dared to brush my cheek.

She had no idea what she was saying. I wasn't ready to talk about things, but the images in my head weren't going away, and before I could stop it my lips were moving.

'It was different,' I hissed. 'Dad, Dean, they're not the same thing.'

She was staring at me now and I glared back, a cold hateful stare that made her shrink away.

'Every time I think about him, every time *you* say Dean's name…'

'Luke you're scaring me.'

'It makes me angry.'

'Luke?'

'*You* make me angry.'

'Lucas!'

The room was spinning now. I felt the tension pressing in all around me, crushing against my skull. Angel was talking to me. She spoke calming words to me again and again, but it wasn't working this time. Her voice was muffled by the sharp ringing in my ears.

My head felt heavy, so heavy, like it was filled with the poisons of the past. The truth sloshed all around me like toxic waste, making me feel sick. I wanted to get away from the pain of it, to exorcise it from my body like a priest would a curse.

It bubbled up in my stomach, spurting its way up my throat until it rippled off my tongue and out from my lips.

'It was you,' I finally snapped. 'You're the reason he's dead.'

The words fell out with gentle ease. I stared into Mae's horrified face, her complexion turning starkly pale. She shook her head vigorously.

'It was an accident. A stupid motorcycle accident.'

'He should never have been in the road in the first place. We didn't even need to cross that road,' I squeezed my eyes with my hands for a moment, feeling hot trickles run down my fingers. 'But I was there and then he…'

'Luke, what you're saying doesn't make sense. You weren't in the road; you didn't even have a scratch on you.'

'You weren't there.' I screeched. 'There are things you don't understand.'

'Like what, Lucas?'

Vivid images played in mind like a horror movie. Bright and palpable. My heart pounded wildly, making the blood pulse viciously beneath my skin.

'We were fighting,' I croaked, 'I was so mad.'

'About what?'

'We wouldn't have been fighting if it wasn't for you. He wouldn't have died if it wasn't for you.'

'Luke, about what?' Her voice was a desperate plea of emotion.

'He was being an arse, teasing me again and again.'

'So he was winding you up Luke. He always wound you up.'

I ran my tongue against my teeth and laughed sadly as the memory — the one I'd kept buried for so many years — unfolded.

'He was saying that you didn't want me. That you and that *idiot* Craig you were dating were planning to have another child. I wasn't needed any more, I wasn't 'keepable' material like he was. I was only 12, I tried to act like I didn't care, like I didn't believe him, but I was just a kid. What he said, it scared me. But I couldn't let him see that. Not Dean.'

'What did you do, Luke?'

Mae's words ripped at me. I closed my eyes for a moment, I just needed a moment, but she said my name again.

'I dove at him,' I screamed. 'I wanted to tear his head off for making me feel so pathetic, but I was scrawny and he was Dean. He laughed at me. He pressed his knee into my gut and made me scream in the street. I was so mad. When he let go, he turned his back. I didn't think, I didn't look, I just went for him. But I missed, then somehow I was in the road and it was coming.'

'He got you out of the way,' Mae whispered.

I cringed at the thought, closed my eyes and squelched the dry wretch.

'He shouldn't have pushed me out of the way. He shouldn't have died for me. I didn't want that. I never asked...'

Her lips were parted and her eyes were filled with tears that wouldn't drop.

'It wasn't my fault, Luke.'

'I know,' I whispered, feeling the guilt knit itself into my chest. It tightened, and I felt as though I would never breathe again.

'It wasn't yours, either.'

I gave into the sadness that pressed so heavily on my heart. I felt the two sets of arms wrap themselves around me and I crumpled into both. Mae brushed aside my hair and stared into my face, her deep blue eyes swimming with concern. In that instant I forgot about Nick, forgot about Mae and her limitations, forgot that to me she'd been just Mae for the longest time, and let her be Mum.

'This is good,' she said, wiping my tear-stained cheek with her thumb. 'This has got to be why you've been having these hallucinations. Now that we know exactly what's caused them, we can work on getting rid of them.'

I gawked at her, my eyes growing colder in my head the more she spoke. The little warmth I'd felt for her in that moment evaporated, and I cringed at the feel of her skin against mine.

'Angel's not a hallucination,' I growled, throwing Mae's hands to her sides. 'She's everything. My entire world.'

Mae thrust her hands up and let out an exasperated squeal.

'Why can't you see? Ever since Dean died you've been different, colder, and now we know why. It was the guilt. The guilt did this to you, made things more traumatic than they needed to be. You let it fester, you let it play with your mind and this, this *girl,* is the result.'

'I can't listen to this anymore.'

I fixed her with a look of the deepest disdain before heading towards the door. Both sets of her fingers clasped desperately around my waist, holding me back.

'Let go,' I snarled.

'Think about it, Luke, hallucination aside.'

'She is not a hallucination,' I protested viciously.

'All right then, *Angel* aside.'

I dragged in a deep, calming breath, if only to settle my swirling stomach.

'What's left to think about?'

'The headaches, the nausea... Did you think I hadn't noticed?'

I said nothing.

'When did they all start?'

I pressed my tongue to my lip and thought. A spurt of fear erupted in my chest, I shook my head.

'No.'

'I bet it was around the same time you *met* Angel.'

'You're wrong.'

I ran some dates in my head and felt my nerves steady when they'd failed to match what Mae was saying.

'They started sometime early January.'

227

'Your journal says January 12th.

'All right the 12th then. Angel and I, we didn't meet until the 28th.'

'The 12th?' She smiled sadly. 'Wasn't that the day you said that you started feeling strange? Like something wasn't right?'

A lump rose in my throat.

'I didn't tell you that.'

I felt her nails retract from my flesh. She nibbled her finger like a nervous child then dropped her hand.

'I read it, in your journal.'

'This is insane,' I shook my head, the lump in my throat growing bigger. 'You can't read a person's journal and assume you know it all.' I probably felt strange because that was the day she died. We're connected. It only makes sense that her death would affect me too.

Mae bit her inner lip and chewed.

'No. You felt strange because something was going on with your head, something that you didn't understand. You think you felt odd because she died? She died because you felt odd, because that was the only way your brain was able to make sense of things.'

I felt my body go cold. The knot that had been silently growing in my stomach grew harder, as if to alert me to its presence. A deep-seated panic began to squirm inside of me.

'Luke, she's wrong,' Angel whispered. 'Don't believe a word of it, she's wrong.'

I sucked in another deep breath, trying to force back the dread, but I couldn't.

'Luke, please.'

Angel pleaded with me, begged me, but the inkling of doubt was already growing rapidly.

'But I can hear her,' I croaked, my voice cracking from the fresh wave of heartache.

Mae tilted her head and shook again, 'no baby, you can hear you.'

Angel was screaming at me, yelling my name with such fierceness. The nausea kicked in again, my stomach lurched and my head, it felt as though it had split in two. I craved the fresh air, I needed it badly.

'Luke where are you going?'

Mae's voice was an unwelcome sound in my head.

'Luke!'

I opened the door.

'Luke,' and into the rain I went.

***

'Luke, listen to me.'

His heart was expanding in his chest. I sensed each frantic beat, could feel it throbbing in his throat, pulsing in his ears.

'Say something, Luke. Anything. Tell me what you're thinking.'

He didn't. He couldn't. A fresh wave of hurt was ripping through him, great big giant chunks of emotion were being yanked out. It was searching for something, something it needed to extinguish, something that when torn out would make him feel free, would numb his grief. It was looking for me. It wanted his belief in me.

He paused, doubled over, and clutched his knees. His airways had shut down and the burning in his chest was strong. He parted his lips, flared his nostrils and drew in as much air as he could. The water that streamed down his face dripped into his mouth, still he sucked. I listened to him breathe, in out, in out. I felt the steady breath enter his body, felt it soothe the bite of his anxiety, wished it could do the same for mine. He straightened up and began again, picking up the pace.

'Luke please, listen to me.'

He didn't, or at least he tried his damnedest not to.

I watched his face, his eyes. They focused on the lonely street ahead, his feet kicking up rainwater with each splashy stomp. His drenched clothes clung to his skin, he shivered at their touch. I was aware of his coldness, how it caused his teeth to chatter, his fingers to tremble, and I wondered if he was too.

He turned another corner, entering into a long snaky alleyway and emerged from the other side. I had no idea where he was going and I doubted he did either. At one point I thought he'd been heading for the park, but when we reached the rusty entrance he briskly walked by. Head down, fists balled up tightly in his pockets. I'd studied his face then, too. It gave nothing away, no hint that he knew the place, no inkling of emotional connection. But I knew him, and even without the sickening knot in his stomach and his racing heart, I knew its very presence made his insides weaken with sadness.

'Luke you have to talk to me, please.'

He stopped abruptly, kicking rain up onto his shoes. I flexed and unflexed my shaky hands and waited. Luke gripped the front of his hair viciously, exposing his deeply furrowed brow. He opened his mouth, closed it, opened it once more, mumbled something, then clamped it shut and began walking again. I lingered, swaying from my toes to my heels and back again. I didn't know what he'd said, but in that moment something changed. His doubt was shifting into strong disbelief.

'Luke. Please.'

I was crying now, my tearless cry. I felt him slipping away from me and I needed to get him back.

'You **can't** just ignore me,' my voice was hoarse and screechy. He could hear my desperation. I felt his stomach twist with guilt, but it was lost in the tsunami of emotions that cascaded through him. I ran after him, beyond him, and stopped in his path, rooting my feet to the ground as best I could. He'd have to go through me, or around me, but either way he was forced to acknowledge me. His head was tipped south. He hesitated for many seconds before holding my gaze with those deep muddy-green eyes. He looked terrified. I placed my hands to his chest, stretched up on my toes and kissed his lips slowly. He closed his eyes and let out a warm, penetrative moan. I pulled away as he parted his lashes. He stared at me as though I'd played some cruel trick on him. As though me kissing him only made things harder.

'You don't have to feel this way,' I pleaded. 'Everything can be like it was, like this afternoon, you just have to trust me.'

He squirmed on his feet, he squirmed inside too.

'I'm real. I promise you.'

Every word I spoke caused him to flinch inwardly, as if the sound of my voice coupled with their meaning caused him too much pain.

He was afraid of everything. Afraid to believe in me. Afraid to let me go. Afraid of the truth, the future that was rapidly unfolding in front of him. Scared that it wouldn't include me. But I wasn't. One of two things was going to happen tonight. Either he'd have faith in me, take my hand and forget everything he'd just heard — every doubt, every niggling piece of information that kept us apart — and love me... or he'd forget me. Believe them when they'd called him 'sick,' let them 'cure' that sickness out of his head. It wouldn't take long for me to become just a memory. I'd go back to life before Luke, sucked into the void, a shadow of a life twice lived.

I wasn't afraid, I was petrified.

He stared at me for a long time, with trembling lips. I wanted to touch him again, to kiss him, but all I could do was stare back. His chest rose and fell. I could feel him making his final decision and it wasn't good. He shook his head slightly, turned his back and walked away. A darkness grew with each step he took. It sunk its claws into us both, pushing us further and further apart. I panicked, dread flooded me and I could feel my empty chest shatter into a billion microscopic pieces. Our bond was splintering strand by strand, and I could feel every last snap.

'I can prove that I'm real,' I screamed, my thoughts racing with alarm.

It worked. He stopped, wobbling on his unsteady feet. From somewhere deep down I felt him tingle with hope. I smiled cautiously as the darkness began to retreat. I hadn't lost him yet.

***

We stood on tall blades of sodden grass; my boots immersed in the slushy earth.

'This is it,' she spoke, and I fought hard not to cry at the sound. 'Come on.'

I watched as she strode along the lawn and bounded up the marble steps, leaving no trace of her presence. I waded through the mud, dragging my soles across the wet earth, and stopped before the first step. I looked up. It was beautiful. A vision of her as a child sprang to mind. I could see her racing along the wooden deck chasing bees. I imagined her curled up on the tiny seat swing letting the afternoon breeze do all the work. I saw her, an older her, a *her* now, rapping on the front door, cursing the keys that lay on her bed. Image after image, short bursts in full colour. Then a thought entered my head: how could there be a *her* rushing after bees or reading on the swing if there wasn't any *her* to begin with?

Beads of rain fell from my lashes as I blinked. I heard her calling my name and I wondered what it would be like to never hear that voice again. I bit my inner cheek and pressed on. I climbed the steps to meet her. We stood side by side, energy by energy and I wished it didn't feel so good. So natural.

'It's under there,' she said pointing to a space by the door.

'What is?' I asked, the crack in my voice painfully obvious. It hurt to talk to her, hurt to continue the pretence.

'The key.'

'What?'

She sighed restlessly, but I continued my stark blinking. She couldn't possibly be suggesting the obvious?

'The second panel in front of the door. If you pry it open there's a spare key underneath. Or at least there should be. Nobody else knew about it but me.'

'So much for pounding on the front door,' I mumbled.

'What?'

'This is insane, utterly insane. You can't expect me to do this. It's trespassing. I won't.'

I folded my arms across my chest defiantly and averted her gaze. From the corner of my eye I saw her head lower. She bent her feet — something she always did when she was nervous — and I ached with guilt.

'You think this is insane?' she whispered, 'That you are? Don't you want to know for sure?'

I stared at her awkward feet, lowered my body, and with fumbling hands pried open the deck.

The house was cold and all the lights were off. I moved stealthily through, trying desperately not to disturb a thing.

'The heating must be off,' she said responding to my shiver.

I nodded, not knowing what to say. She walked in front of me, leading the way. Unopened letters littered the hallway, a pair of work shoes covering a few. I skirted them, careful not to touch a single one. We came to a doorway. A raspy, chesty cough exploded from inside the room and I pressed my back firmly against the wall, my heart emitting tiny, rapid thuds. Angel disappeared into the room, leaving me alone. I counted the ticks of the hallway clock, worried when I'd reached 60, wondering where Angel was. Tick, tick, tick. I found myself muttering the sound, enjoying the feel on my tongue, it calmed me. 78, 79... still she wasn't back. I lifted my body from the wall and hesitantly craned my neck around the corner of the door. A slight, ageing figure was curled awkwardly in a chair, then a face. It had appeared so suddenly I had to swallow down a hearty shriek.

'It's fine,' Angel said flatly. 'Everything's fine. Let's go.'

She ambled past me, climbing the stairs with such sorrowful grace. I could tell she didn't want me to notice but I did, how could I not? I knew her face too well, every inch of it, every expression. I'd seen it before she'd entered the room, bleak and terrified, but now — upon emerging — it seemed as if a new layer of pain had brushed its surface. Over an hour ago I would have wrapped my arms around her willowy frame, would have tucked my head into the crook of her neck and whispered soothing words to her but now all I could think was of course I know this face, I'd invented it.

I couldn't bear to go near her. This hallucination. I couldn't bear to feel her presence in my arms and risk never wanting to let her go. I hugged myself pathetically. Angel stopped, turned and smiled sadly, knowing it all.

I met her upstairs. She was standing next to a doorway staring at something. A painting by Gillian Thorne. It was the image of a little girl in a navy-blue mac, feet barely touching the dark, snaky path ahead. The bright green grass behind her, the misty murky woods ahead. It was the epitome of loneliness; I imagined it called to Angel since it called to me.

'Could you?' she said gesturing to the closed door.

I turned the knob and we walked inside.

'Light's behind the door.'

I flicked the switch, wondering... lucky guess? I turned to face her, nibbling my tongue, wondering if I should speak.

'That man, is he your, your...' I'd rushed the words before I could think myself into a mental breakdown, but now I was stuck. It was just one question; it didn't mean I suddenly agreed all this was true or vice versa. It was just a question, an inquiry, yet still I couldn't bring myself to finish my sentence. To ask it felt like some kind of acceptance, and I wasn't ready to believe in her again, not yet.

'You want to know if he's my dad?'

I nodded, cramming my mental rambling into a tiny space in my mind. She threw on a fake cheesy grin.

'The one and only.'

I stared at her speechless. It was exactly what I'd expected her to say but now that she had I wasn't sure what to do with the information. What to say. A strained silence grew between us. It was unfamiliar and painful.

She spoke into it, her words prodding it into an awkward hush instead.

'He's not doing too well these days.'

'I'm sorry,' I muttered, meeting her halfway.

She shrugged and hopped on to the bed, hugging her knees to her chest. I felt my face tense. I wanted both to hold and push her away at the same time, it was so damn frustrating. She looked so beautiful, so magnificently beautiful, as if her vulnerability only made her more alluring. I had an insatiable desire to protect her, to alleviate her heartache, to kiss her. I couldn't take much more. I ripped my eyes away from her fragile figure and darted them around, hoping to find a distraction from her face. I did. Black, lace curtains, murals of avant-garde art, an interpretation of each piece of work angled around every one, lines of poetry snaking along the colours. A miniature library was crammed into an overstuffed bookcase, copies of twentieth—century literature falling out, and to my amusement, a weathered edition of Bram Stoker's Dracula. Dozens of DVDs, contradictory in taste from *A Few Good Men* to *Battle Royale,* and a desk covered with precious knickknacks. I caught her eye.

'Your room?'

She nuzzled her knees before letting them flop into a cross-legged position, scanned my face and nodded. I turned my attention back to the table. I had a burning urge to touch and feel everything on it, to smell and grip. I needed to have them in my hand, their solid, concrete, undeniable shape in my hand. Wanting the certainty of their existence. I hesitated, acknowledging the sheet of dread that cloaked me. What if I did touch and it all turned to dust, then what?

Angel remained silent. My unsteady hands brushed the objects lightly: a notepad, a candle and a ratty looking bunny with red crosses stitched into where eyes should have been, the name tag read Bingo. No dust, I wondered, then stopped. Something else stopped me. I could hear the sound of my heart resounding in my ears. My throat narrowed and I closed my eyes, feeling a fresh wash of dismay.

'You can have a look if you'd like. I don't mind.'

I swallowed hard, mesmerised by how alert my body suddenly was. I was aware of my damp, heavy clothes weighing me down, the way they itched my skin. I was aware of the sweet smell of the dark cherry candle, but mostly I was aware of the fear. I rubbed my clammy hand along the back of my head and reached for it — this upturned picture frame — a rotten feeling swelling in my gut.

Hard, firm, bumpy. I could feel detail of the frame but I didn't dare smile, not yet, not until it revealed itself to me. I turned it around, feeling a small wave of cautious relief. In my hand was a photo of the girl that I loved. She looked about nine. Her skin had been tanned by the sun and her trademark freckles were starkly evident. Her golden-brown eyes shone and her long slender legs dangled from a safari jeep. A tiny chuckle rippled from my mouth and I struggled to stuff it back.

'What's funny?'

I cut her a sly look. 'I'd never have pegged you for a ginger.'

Her eyes widened, and for the next few seconds I watched her lips move wordlessly as she ran a finger through her hair unintentionally.

'It's auburn,' she finally managed.

'A very bright auburn,' I teased, staring at the long thick French braid that lay against the side of her neck, wild strands spewing out from underneath a red cap.

'It's still auburn,' she snapped testily.

'It's okay, I think *auburn's* cute,' I wet my throat. 'I think you look cute.'

She smiled and so did I, until I realised that I was.

I went back to the photograph, ignoring our small intimate exchange. Standing next to her was a little girl of about six. Her face was broader but she had the same bright, unmistakably ginger hair.

'Your sister?'

Angel gave a curt nod. She felt shunned, I could tell. It disappointed her that our brief moment hadn't lasted longer.

'What's her name?'

'Haven,' she mumbled, and I swallowed my guilty throat lump.

'She looks terrified?'

Angel laughed a little carrying, some of the tension away with it. 'That's because I told her that giraffes eat hay.'

'So?' I shrugged, looking at the large animal towering over them.

They were obviously on some kind of safari holiday.

'Well, that's what I used to call her.'

'You used to call your little sister Hay?'

'That or haystack. Anyway, I'd convinced her that they were going to mistake her for lunch.'

'That's mean.'

She laughed again, the act brightening her heavy face. She looked breathtaking and my body tingled deeply, wanting her. I flushed at the knowledge that she could feel this too, then felt the heat abate when I remembered she might not be real. Her smile rose and fell as it followed my emotions, and I was tormented by yet another twist of guilt.

'I was just kidding around,' she continued, papering over her hurt. 'Besides, I made it up to her.'

'Oh yeah, how so?'

'That same night she had a nightmare — something about a giant giraffe nibbling her toes. Totally unrelated to whole her being lunch scenario of course. Anyway, I let her climb into my bed, stroked her hair and told her she was safe. That nothing would ever hurt her. That I would always protect her.'

All the light in her face faded and the complete heaviness returned.

'Check out your dad,' I said, eager to change the subject. 'He looks about 20 years younger.'

His grin was bright and his hair thicker. The dark black locks were surprisingly glossy and only peppered white compared to the streaks of grey I'd glimpsed earlier. He had his burly arms tightly wrapped around the slender waist of a gorgeous woman whose vibrancy resonated from her whole being. I knew this woman; I'd fallen in love with the other version of her.

'You look so much like your mum.'

Angel lowered her eyes and shook her head.

'She was beautiful,' she breathed, 'so incredibly beautiful.'

I placed the photograph down and joined her, tilting my head to catch her eyes.

'Like I said, just like your mum.'

Her smile was gracious. I bit my tongue, wishing I'd had more restraint when it mattered. I shouldn't have said anything. It was wrong of me, but why, I wondered. What was so wrong? She'd promised to deliver me proof and wasn't this it? Wasn't this enough? I stood up and paced a little, processing all this new information, factoring things in, trying to come to some sort of understanding. Some sort of truth.

'You jerk,' she barked, and I flinched at the harshness of her tone. 'How dare you say that to me, how dare you feel the way you do about me and still have doubts.'

I opened my mouth to speak but could only manage a crackly sound. Her eyes bore fiercely into me, but before she could give me another tongue-lashing the stairs below us shifted. They creaked with every heavy step and the coughing sound dragged its way up, getting nearer and nearer.

'Angel I need to get out of here.'

'It's fine.'

'Angel, your dad could come in at any moment.'

'Now he's my dad? I thought you were having trouble believing any of this.'

'Angel, I'm not kidding. He could burst through that door any second now and then what?'

'He won't.'

'You don't know that.'

'Yes, I do.'

'If he finds me in here, I'm dead,' I whispered.

She gave me a slight look.

'Trust me. I know that is hard for you to do right now, but believe me when I say he's not coming in here.'

'How do you know?'

'Because he never does!'

Her voice bounced off the walls, it rang in the air, and the footsteps on the stairs faltered. For half a second, I was sure he had heard her.

'He never even comes near the door,' her voice wavered.

Angel clamped her mouth shut and I heard the grinding of her teeth. She breathed deeply without needing to and began cracking away at her knuckles, her face a beautiful angry mask.

'This is where you've been coming?'

She rolled lip against lip before parting them ever so slightly.

'Every minute I'm not with you,' another waver.

'Why?'

'Why? Why?'

It felt like a stupid question now.

'I just left them. I'm the one who's supposed to take care of them. I'm supposed to handle things, but it's down to Haven. She's just a kid, she shouldn't have to... she was never supposed to...'

Un-formed tears built up as emotion choked her throat. I knelt before her and dared to place my hands against each arm. I looked straight into her eyes, forcing her to steady her darting gaze on mine. She slumped into my feeble grasp, my hands keeping their shape. I searched her, her body, her face, she rocked gently, her eyes flickering back and forth from the photograph to me. The absolute truth of it all sunk in and I shivered, knowing her grief all too well.

'When did she die? Your mother?'

'Almost five years ago.'

'And your dad... couldn't cope.'

'He fell apart.' The words forced their way out of her tight throat.

'How did it happen?'

There was a pause, and then: 'She didn't come home. The snow that year was the worst. Really thick and treacherous. I know because I can remember thinking, that's why she's late. It's because of the traffic and the snow, but then evening came and went. Sometime later there was a knock on the door. A policeman, Grayson, his name was PC Grayson, he smelt like cough drops and vapour rub. He was the one who told my dad his wife was never coming home on account of the stroke that had left her dead in the snow.

December 3ʳᵈ aged 40, that's all her gravestone read, that and her, name because none of us had the stomach to think of something that would show how much she meant to us.'

I couldn't help but think about my dad then. His cologne-layered, greasy smell after a day spent under the hood of a car. It was one of the few memories of him I still owned. I wasn't old enough to have been given a voice, but I'm pretty sure his headstone would have said less if I had.

'My dad was a mess,' she whispered. 'It took everything he had and then some for him to pretend to be okay. All his strength and mine. It was hard, unbearable sometimes. You have no idea what I went through. The pressure, the stress with the grief, it can change you, change everything about you.'

She was desperate to cry; those gold eyes, they were haunted.

'Then it was me. I left, and now he doesn't even try. I watch him. He gets up, he has a shave, a bite to eat, then out the door to work. He comes home, eats, then falls asleep to the sound of evening TV. Then does it all over again the next day. He used to be like that man in the picture,' she said. 'Loving and warm. Now he doesn't even kiss Haven. Not even a hug, and *her*,' she spat the word vilely, 'she's like a ghost. I miss the sound of her elephant-like footsteps around the house. Her dangerous laugh. I want to hear her ramble about pure crap but it's all gone. It's like it all died with me.'

She was shaking now and forgetting what was right or what I was meant to believe I drew her fragile figure to my chest and she followed my motion.

'I don't even know who she is anymore.'

I brushed my lips against the top of her head.

'I never meant to hurt them. I never meant to leave.' She was rambling now and I worked hard to keep up.

'I want to help them, to let them know that I'm still with them and that they're with me, but I can't. They've lost so much, we all have. I can't lose you too. Please Luke. Please.'

She lifted her head, fixing her eyes on my face.

'You have to believe me, you have to trust me. I don't want to lose you too.'

Dry, heavy sobs shook her frame, I lead her delicate figure into my lap, watched it curl around me and kissed every part I could.

'I trust you.' I said firmly, 'I'm not going anywhere, I promise.'

She relaxed into me and I felt our love bind us from the inside out. There was not one single doubt left in me of her existence. I believed in her, and as long as we had that she had me.

***

'Tell me the plan again.'

My hand held the gate. I was ready to push it open, walk through and do this, but Angel's words held me back. I turned to face her, tugging my lips into a crooked grin.

'It's going to be fine, I promise.' But she didn't stop pacing, flexing and un-flexing her hands in the process.

'The last time we were here it took you all of 10 seconds to lose faith in my entire existence. Forgive me if I'm a little on edge.'

The hand holding the gate dropped and I brushed lightly against her cheek with the other. She stilled herself and stared at me. She was a vision, this pure embodiment of love staring at me through the light pitter-patter of the rain. My heart clenched.

'I know. You're sorry. It's okay.'

I closed my eyes and let the guilt turn through me. I deeply regretted hurting her, more than I could express in words. I found myself, once again, grateful for the bond that we shared, grateful that she knew just how sorry I really was, but it didn't absolve my guilt entirely.

'I'm going to confront Mae,' I began, reciting the same words again for at least the fourth or fifth time.

'I'm going to tell her that she was wrong, that I'm not schizophrenic, but that I do need help. I'll agree to more counselling as a first step, so long as I get to stay at home. I'll seem to make improvement, and after a few months she'll believe that my *hallucinations* have stopped. Then one day we can leave. She won't make much effort to come after me if she thinks I'm fine.'

I heard the soft flicking of nails and sighed patiently, waiting for her to speak.

'What's wrong?' I asked when she didn't.

'You forgot something.'

I thought for a while, then ran my palm against her hair.

'No Angel, I didn't.'

She nodded gently, 'The journal. You forgot about the journal.'

'Yeah, of course.' I called for her hand and she placed it on top of mine. 'I won't forget.'

'Promise me. I know it's a part of you, your journal, but it's important. I wouldn't ask if it wasn't impor—'

I placed a finger to her lips.

'No more journal entries, I promise. It'll be like I really have been cured.'

She bit her lip and touched her forehead to my chest.

'Only to them,' I whispered, 'only to them. There's no cure for how I feel about you.'

She groaned lightly. 'Don't believe anything Mae has to say. I know she means well, but you can't trust her, not about this.'

I kissed her hair, 'Not about anything. Come on,' I breathed, 'It's time.'

We walked hand against hand along the path, climbed the two steps, then let go. This had to seem real to Mae. A single graze could out us and I couldn't allow that, not when my love for Angel was at stake.

I made a fist and rapped lightly at the door, it gave without resistance. I arched an eyebrow and snuck Angel a quick sideways glance. I pushed it open further and found a drunk Nick at the other side. I could barely conceal my disgust.

'Where's Mae,' I asked, stepping through.

He had his back to me but by the slight turn of his head I could see the rise of his cheeks and I could tell his grin was smug.

He turned around and placed his nasty stare on me.

'I was about to head out,' he slurred. 'Pretend to look for you, but I think I'll stay now. Should be an interesting show when your mother gets back.'

I bit my lip to silence the snarl.

'Where is she?'

He threw an arm around my neck and squeezed just that little bit too roughly. The acrid smell of stale sweat and beer seeped out of his pores, licking at my nose.

'Out looking for you,' he scoffed.

His breath was hot and putrid. I retched a little as I wormed myself free from his grip.

'I just want to thank you, Looooke,' he drooled, taking a deep swig from the bottle in his hand. I stayed silent. 'You and that stupid journal of yours. Soon Mae's gonna be begging to get shot of you.'

He picked it up from the side table, his thick fingers thumbing through the pages. My first instinct was to rush for it, rip it out of his hand and tear his throat out in the process, but I didn't. That was exactly what he wanted, and I wasn't going to give in to him, not that easily.

'Dear Journal' he read, *'I don't know where I'd be without her, myyyyy Angel, she is everything to me,* awwww,' he flipped the page, *'She lay in my arms and I brushed my nose against the curve of her neck,'* he laughed mockingly. 'Tell me Luke, how exactly does one caress the neck of a dead girl? Is there a knack to it, or do you just kind of thrash about and hope you hit the spot?'

His spit travelled as he cackled and I clenched my jaw, resisting the urge to rip out his tongue.

'Don't let him get to you Luke,' Angel said. 'He's dirt. Who cares what that scum thinks?'

'Dear Journal,' he relished the words, *'I dreamt we laid together, her body on mine, skin to skin...* oh this is too much.'

I made a fist and tensed, feeling my hands tremble in rage.

'Oooooooh, now this, right here, this is the stuff,' he bit his lip and sucked for a moment, the sound sharp and wet, *'One of these days that evil git Nick is going to pay. Pay for everything he's done to me, every bruise, every bleed, every swelling on my body that has his name on it. He'll pay for it all and then some. I'll make sure of it.'*

He looked up at me, licked his lips and barked a laugh.

'You want to square off with me *prick*? Now's your chance. It's just you and me Luke.'

He grabbed hold of that single page and thrust the book down, the sound of tearing paper ripping through the air. His knuckles — pearly white — clenched around the entry.

'Come on!' he screamed storming towards me, his face a violent red, 'Make me pay, Luke.'

He jammed the paper to my face and pressed down hard, sandwiching it against my face. I wanted to lash out. Tear that paper from his hand and claw his nasty face to shreds.

'Don't do it Luke.' Angel pleaded, 'For me. It'll only make things worse.'

The smell of his skin sunk into my nose. I felt my blood boil to the surface, it burned everywhere — in my chest, in my limbs. Four years of intense anger that I was aching to satisfy. I throbbed with rage.

'Just like I thought,' Nick scoffed, 'all talk, no balls.'

The next word to leave his mouth came out in a pained screech.

'Get off, you sonofabitch, let go.'

The beer bottle fell to the ground, clinking as it knocked against the table. I sunk my teeth deeper into his flesh, swallowing bits of disintegrated paper. He howled and yelped like the dog he was but I didn't let go, four years of anger was a lot to let go of. Then I felt it, his knee ramming into my gut. I fell back, gasping on the way down, my back slamming against the table. I heard the phone clatter to the floor. An intense growl rumbled through the air as he pressed his unblemished hand to the gaping wound of the other. I sat there, swallowing blood that for the first time wasn't mine. There was a loud, ridiculous laugh. I looked around briefly, wondering who the sound was coming from until I realised, it was me.

Nick sucked on his saliva as he drew in breath. I spat, watching his blood speckle the carpet.

'You bastard,' he growled and before I could move he was up again, his bruised hand around my neck.

'You think I'm gonna let you get away with that?'

A solid blow landed on my cheekbone. It cracked, and both the sound and the pain rang in my ear.

'You think some whiney little shit like you is going to teach me a lesson?'

Another brick-like blow, this time straight to the gut. My body buckled to the pain for a quarter of a second before he yanked me up and backhanded my rapidly swelling face. I heard Angel's shaky gasp. Blood oozed from his cut. It felt warm running down my neck as he squeezed his hands around my throat, but his grip only tightened until my breath came out strangled.

'You are the only one who's being schooled tonig—'

His cry was deafening. He released his grip and held himself between the legs; I'd always had quite knobbly knees.

I gripped the wall behind me and breathed deeply.

'Luke, don't stop, you've got to get out of here.'

I followed Angel's voice over to the door, limping pathetically, but I was too late. A pair of hands seized my calves and I went tumbling. I screamed as he pushed his knee into my back, his hefty figure pressing hard against my lower spine. He thumped my shoulder blades with his beastly fists, over and over. I roared again.

'Mae will find out about this,' I whispered hoarsely.

I heard the smile in his voice.

'You think she's going to believe anything a psychopath like you says?' He threw another punch. 'Don't you get it by now? I can get away with anything I want, anything.'

Another solid blow, crippling my spine.

'She'll never pick you over me. No one will ever pick anyone over me again, not your mother or mine.'

He slammed his fist into my body over and over again. Pain seized my back. Tears streamed down my face the harder he thumped. Grabbing a fist full of hair, he smashed my face into the ground.

'I come first do you hear me? Me. *I* come first.'

My skin tore and ripped, as my face continuously collided with the floor. My roots seared, my scalp a hot fiery mess.

'My mother had it wrong, I come first. Do you hear me? I always come first.'

I understood now. With every bone-cracking strike it all became that much clearer. It was never about me. It was about him. He'd been just as neglected as I was.

He smashed my face again and I closed my eyes and waited. Finally, the grip on my hair slackened. My head dropped, hitting the floor with a dull thud. My eyes remained shut.

'Luke!' Angel screeched.

I parted my lashes and from the corner of my puffy eyes I saw Nick reach for the glass bottle of beer. He poured what was left on to my tender scalp. It hissed, burning into the bruises. He pressed his face against mine and snarled low into my ear.

'She will never pick you.'

I heard the door slam as the bottle shattered against my skull. The pain wrapped itself around my entire head, my vision blurring instantly.

'Get the hell away from my son.'

I felt the pressure on my back slowly release, felt the numbness wear off and the pain grow.

'Mae, it's, I... He became aggressive. I had to—'

'Get away from him now,' she barked.

I felt his presence draw further and further away, felt my mother's rush nearer. She lifted me up into her arms and held on, her tears wetting my skin, stinging my cuts.

'Mae, it wasn't my fault,' he laughed sheepishly, 'none of this is my fault. He pushed and pushed. The things he was saying about me, about *you*, he, he—'

'He is my son.'

'Mae.'

'Leave.'

'Mae?'

'I said get out.' Her chest heaved my body to and fro as she screamed, the sound circling my head.

He hesitated, his feet rocking slightly in the near distance, blurring even more from my shoddy perspective.

'I love you,' he whispered. 'I really do.'

He opened the door, a gust of wind, the smell of rain, then nothing. He left, taking it all with him.

'Luke I'm so sorry. I'm so sorry I didn't believe you.' Her lips quivered as she pressed them to my cheek.

'Mum,' I felt my eyes flicker.

'Luke.'

They both called my name.

'Luke.'

'Angel.'

I had a sudden urge to close my eyes, the heaviness of my lids too powerful to resist.

'Don't you dare join me, Luke.'

'Luke stay with me,' Mae begged.

'Luke I'm scared.'

Don't be, I wanted to say as I slipped out of consciousness. I wasn't.

Chapter 26
Sunday, 25th April — night time

The doctor in the white coat spoke to Mae. Mae wept uncontrollably. She drew her into her arms, staining the coat with her fresh tears. I looked away. A dense note of fear striking within me.

'You promised that you'd never leave me. Remember that? *I'm not going anywhere* you said those words. Never forget that you said those words.'
I repeated them for hours afterwards. I'd watched the sun die and the moon rise, but time made no difference. His presence wasn't here in the room with the white-coated doctor or in the stillness of the night, nor was it here with me. It wasn't anywhere.

***

Monday: 26th April — early morning
The first thing I felt was Angel's presence. Not the unbearable pain in my head, not the sharp burning of my ribs or the tightness of my chest. None of it. That was all secondary to Angel's warmth. I lay on the firm mattress, eyes closed, drawing close to her love. I smiled before slipping back into unconsciousness.

***

Later
Bright lights penetrated my eyelids, reddening my view. I heaved air into my lungs and expelled, the sound gruff and dry. I sensed the bodies around me shift as I groaned. They moved closer, encircling me.

'Ouuuuch,' I mumbled.

Everywhere hurt. I opened my eyes and blinked. That hurt too, but I kept going until everything came into focus. Machines, funny looking bedsheets that draped the lower half of my body and people, more people than I'd expected. I was in a hospital. I counted them, the people, there were five including me. Mae, Angel, a tall man in green uniform — a nurse maybe? — and a rake-thin lady in a white coat, all staring at me, all talking. Except one, Angel. She was on the other side of the room. Why was she on the other side of the room? I motioned her closer with my weak fingers but she didn't move. Was this to do with the plan? Was I still meant to pretend that I believed she wasn't real? I couldn't give a crap about that now. I just wanted her here, next to me. I stared at her, giving her a strained smile. She didn't smile back. Her eyes were wide, panicky, and she picked furiously at her bottom lip. Angel looked frightened, as if her whole world was a crumbled mess at her feet, but I didn't understand why. Was it me? I was fine. My body was a wreck but still I was alive and I was fine.

'Luke,' an unfamiliar voice was calling to me. 'Luke, can you look this way?'

I did. It was the lean doctor with the greying hair, she was speaking to me. I kept my smile for her. It was a nice sound, her voice — surprisingly deep, it soothed me. She lifted her bony hands and clicked the torch she held. A small bright light flooded my eye and I flinched. Smile gone.

'Right. Okay.' She shut off the light and beamed warmly. 'Luke, my name is Doctor Wintenberg.'

'Hi,' I croaked through a dry throat. Mae lifted a cup of water to my lips and I sipped through the straw. She smiled at me too. I looked at all of the faces in the room. Everyone wore weird, forced smiles. Everyone, apart from Angel.

'Luke, you have quite a few physical injuries,' said the doctor.

'Mmm,' I grumbled. 'I figured. What with all the pain and all.'

'Yes well, you have two fractured ribs on either side, a fractured cheekbone, some rather nasty cuts and bruises, and mild concussion.'

'Wow. Is that all?' I smirked sarkily.

'Actually no,' her expression was ominous.

My brow furrowed and I winced at the pain. Mae stifled a squeak and I watched as Dr Wintenberg squeezed her arm.

'Your mum tells me that you've been experiencing some um...' she paused awkwardly, 'some hallucinations?'

My breathing accelerated. I felt my ribs expand greatly and I cringed through the burn.

I cut Mae a look of fury as I spoke.

'I'm not sick,' I snarled. 'She thinks I have schizophrenia but I don't. I'm not crazy. I swear it.'

Dr Wintenberg gazed at me, her compassionate eyes all over my face. She placed her skeletal hand on mine.

'You're not crazy, Lucas, and you don't have schizophrenia either, but you are sick.'

'What are you talking about? You just said, no schizophrenia.'

Pricks of fear attacked me. I turned to look at Angel, my sweet calming Angel, but her face... it was tense with fear.

'Dr Wintenberg,' I fixed my eyes on her now, the woman in the white coat, the one with all the answers. 'What do you mean I'm sick?'

'When you were admitted last night, your injuries seemed more extensive. The gash on your head was a point of concern; we were worried that there might have been bleeding in the brain, so we took you for a CT scan. Just to get a better idea of what was going on inside your head.'

'Okay.'

'There was no bleeding, but something was unclear so we took you for another test.'

'What are you talking about? What's wrong with me?'

'You have a tumour at the base of your brain.'

My breath stilled, sweat beads erupted on my body and my already achy head felt like it was about to explode.

'Cancer? I have cancer.'

Dr Wintenberg's grey hair swished from side to side.

'That's highly unlikely given its shape. I expect the biopsy results to confirm that in a day or two but this tumour, well it has been causing your symptoms.'

'What symptoms?' I wrenched my hand from beneath her scrawny grasp. 'Angel is not a symptom. I'm in love with her.'

A look of sympathy passed between them.

'Luke,' Mae's face was nothing more than gaunt layers of stress and grief, 'listen to the doctor honey, you're not well.'

'Don't,' I snapped. 'You just want me to be miserable and alone like you, well I'm not. I have Angel. Angel.' I looked to her, I called her name again and again, but she didn't come, she just stared.

'Lucas, Lucas look at me.'

It was Dr Wintenberg again, how quickly I'd come to both recognising and despising that voice.

'I want you to tell me how you've been feeling over the past few months.'

'Fine,' I growled.

'Any headaches?'

I admitted nothing.

'How about nausea?'

More silence.

'Have you ever blacked out or been close to unconsciousness?'

'Once or twice, I guess. What the hell difference does that make?' The words felt bitter in my mouth. I could taste their harshness, their truth.

'Your mum says you've been feeling pretty low of late.'

'Well every other day I was beaten by a drunken maniac. I think that entitles me to a few down days, don't you?'

There was a bleak moment of silence while everyone in the room digested my words. Mae guiltily gripped my bed and the nurse shifted on his feet. A miniscule smile flickered behind Angel's lips before disappearing completely. Had she known what I was doing? Did she get that I was sticking up for her? For her existence? Dr Wintenberg continued to eyeball me.

'You're right. But that aside, your headaches, the nausea, the dizzy spells, Angel; they are all symptoms of a brain tumour.'

A wash of realisation penetrated my body. It all made sense: the sad look, why she refused to come anywhere near me. She was afraid. I'd let Angel down once. I'd stupidly let Mae wriggle inside my head and change what I knew was true. I wasn't going to trust a single one of them now.

'I don't care what it seems like to you. To any of you.' I looked each person in the eyes, 'I love her. She is real.'

Dr Wintenberg smiled gently. 'Hallucination can seem that way but, Lucas, it's just an illusion, and in your case a cruel one.'

I clenched my teeth, felt the pain and bit down harder.

'She is not an illusion or some *thing* I invented to make myself feel better. Angel is real. She has already proven herself to me, not that she should've had to.'

Mae's face was starkly pale.

'What do you mean she's proven it to you?'

My eyes narrowed despite the bulbous shape of the right.

'Sorry to disappoint you,' I spat through the smarting, 'but she showed me her world, her home. I've seen pictures of her, she is real.'

Mae pressed her fingers to her mouth, clutching on to a small scream.

Dr Wintenberg patted her arm. 'It's okay,' she soothed. 'You need proof,' she said, turning to face me. 'Hard, solid facts. I get that, it's understandable after what you've been through. We're threatening to take away the one stable thing in your life, your source of comfort, of trust. That's bound to be unsettling.'

I glared at her coldly.

'Nurse Huang,' she said, 'Could you please bring the film?'

The tall man in green left the room and appeared again within minutes. In his hands were sheets of funny looking paper. He handed them to Dr Wintenberg, who brought them closer to me. She thumbed through them, selected one and held it up close for me to see.

'This is a picture of your brain.'

A large apricot-shaped image confronted me, I smirked.

'It looks lovely.'

She pursed her lips and tapped it with her finger. 'This is the tumour,' she said, her voice softer than before.

A small gasp escaped me, despite myself. I stared at the round splodge that stained my apricot shape.

My head shook without permission, 'I don't believe it.'

She swallowed audibly, 'It's proof.'

I pushed the sheet away from me. 'I don't believe you.'

They all began talking at me at once. The doctor, Mae, even the nurse chimed in, but I couldn't unpick a single one. Every sound in the room blurred into one giant symphony of noise. A horrible sound that split my head in two. The only thing that stood out to me, the only sound I cared about was the thudding of my heart as it knocked around inside my chest. My entire body became flushed with panic. I looked at Angel, she stared back. She was my pain; she was my grief projected out in front of me for me to see. Was that it? Was she nothing more than a reflection of my tired, broken heart? Had she ever been more? She looked away.

I faced the voices, 'So that's it,' my voice wobbled, 'She's not real? I made the whole thing up? Everything?'

'I'm afraid so, Lucas,' Dr Wintenberg mumbled.

'What about her house, her family, the picture? How do you explain that?'

'A break in to a neighbour's? An abandoned house? I'm not sure where you went or how you got in there, Luke, but I'm certain the finer details were nothing more than a vivid hallucination.'

I went numb. Right down to the very core of my emotions was a cold, dead feeling, yet still I cried. I felt the moisture build up in my eyes, felt the ripple as it spilled over, felt it sting my cuts as it trickled down my face. Mae drew a finger gently beneath my eye, I jerked my head away. We locked eyes, Angel and I. We locked eyes and in that moment, she knew, just as well as I did, that I'd broken my promise.

***

When I woke up it was dark. I lay still for a while, assessing my feelings, getting used to my loneliness. Goosebumps lay on the surface of my skin and I wondered why the room was so cold. A light wind rustled in the near distance and I realised the window behind me was open. I drew the covers underneath my chin and curled into them, but the breeze was hard to ignore. It pestered the back of my neck and ruffled my hair. A large gust wrapped itself around my head, blowing icy air into my ear.

'Fine.'

I flung the thin sheet from my body and planted my feet a little too heavily on the floor. I held my head between both hands and squeezed, despite the pain it caused. Dizzy spell. I stood up and turned around. My heart thrust itself towards Angel before I felt it retreat. My legs buckled a little and I gripped the bed to steady myself. After a few deep breaths I looked up. She was perched on the ledge between the open windows. I swallowed deeply as I pried my shaky hands from the mattress. We stared at each other eye to eye, soul to soul. I walked towards the draught, my movements unsteady. I came to a wobbly stop in front her. She looked me over as I swayed precariously. Her eyes were moon-shaped again, their golden haze darkened by a wealth of emotion. I focused on the handles of the window. I reached towards her, plunged my hands through her opaque shape and pulled the window shut. I withdrew my outstretched hands, my insides icier than my skin. I was desperate to get away. My legs moved before I'd fully given the order and I wobbled harshly, but they took me back to my bed where I slowly folded back the sheets.

'So that's it?' she said, her voice hopelessly flat, 'I'm not real?'

I lowered my weary body to the bed and sat, my eyes still focused on the indistinct handles of the windows.

'Nice to see you kept your word,' a hint of venom lingered behind the hurt.

'Well I'm not about to beg you if that's what you think,' the words had the intent of hatred, but her tone was just as fragile as I felt.

'Haven't got anything to say to me?' she screeched, 'Anything at all?'

Her brow was furrowed intently and those eyes, those beautifully harassed eyes…

My voice left my mouth in a hoarse whisper, 'I'm tired.'

'You're… tired?'

'Yes,' I sighed impatiently. 'Go away, please.'

I lifted my legs sluggishly to the bed, turned around and drew the sheet over my head. When I awoke again later that night she was gone.

***

Tuesday, 27th April

'You've got surgery booked for tomorrow,' Dr Wintenberg explained. 'Now I know we've been over the procedure already, but I just want to run it through with you one last time, okay?'

I nodded curtly and allowed, the doctor to ramble on for several minutes. With a gentle smile she confirmed, for the thousandth time, its non-cancerous status. I think she thought I was in shock, that the more she said the word 'benign' the more I'd feel something other than scant relief. I didn't. She spoke about shaving a patch of hair, making incisions, skull flaps and 'nicking that bugger out.' She then droned on about what to expect after the surgery, headaches, nausea — what's new? She went on and on about the medication and the varying lengths of hospital stay depending on my wellness. She talked and talked and talked, and her voice scratched at my brain like nails to steel. I was exhausted and in pain. My face ached, my head was in agony and my swollen ribs burned. I focused on it, drew the pain around me like a blanket, letting it rip through my weakened body. I clung to it, holding it close. But no amount of physical pain could distract me from what I felt inside. I was both hollow and raw at the same time. Empty and alone. How had I lived like this before? How was I able to breathe with this heaviness crushing my chest, pressing on my lungs, my abdomen? If for one second I'd had a choice, the blissful ignorance of Angel or this, I'd pick ignorance. At least then I wouldn't hurt this bad.

She was here. Angel. I felt her. As that thought skittered through my mind, I felt the richness of her warmth. It wasn't in the room, it was hesitant, hovering somewhere nearby. I squinted at the walls as though it would help me to locate her; the gulf inside me was filling. She drew her soul closer to mine, pouring her love into the bitter hole that ached me. My heart swung desperately towards her call as my stomach turned in repulsion. I was ashamed that I wanted her so badly, that I'd let things get so far. Not once had I thought about seeking help. Maybe if I had earlier things would've been different. Maybe I wouldn't have let myself need her so much. I loved her, but that shamed me too. I wanted ignorance, but at this point it was impossible.

'Do you understand what I'm saying to you Luke? Luke?' Dr Wintenberg's brow wrinkled.

I stared back.

'I know this is difficult for you,' she sighed, and I felt the bed dip slightly under her weight, 'but we have to make sure you understand what will be happening tomorrow. Do you?'

I gave a small nod. Dr Wintenberg's lips curled into a tiny smile.

'Do you have any questions for me?' I shook my head. 'Luke—'

'Look,' I cut her off before she could give me her 'buck up' speech. 'I appreciate that you want me to know what's going on, but to be honest, I don't care.'

Mae tried to speak but I cut her off, too. I locked eyes with Dr Wintenberg and spoke.

'Can you get rid of this thing?' I spat. 'Can you make sure that it's sliced out? Gone, for good?'

She looked at me like you would a sickly animal, with sympathy and regret.

'Yes.'

'Well then do it. I don't care what you have to do to me in order get it done, just do it. Butcher me up if you have to, bludgeon my brain to mush, cut me up so badly I'll never be able to think or feel again. Just get her out of my head and out of my heart.'

A weighted silence followed my words. It hung in the air like a bitter aftertaste. I heard a small whimper somewhere, one that eased some of my shame. Mae pulled me close, forcing my head to her hip. She stroked my hair gently thrusting her comfort all over me. I let her, my body like a limp fish, not embracing any of it but not rejecting it, either.

The room was still silent. Dr Wintenberg had finally clammed her lips together, even the ward seemed to sense my need for peace. It crept away, the warmth, snuck out of the vicinity without a single person noticing, no one but me.

Chapter 27
Wednesday, 28th April

I was standing outside of the park. Just like the first time. The rain was beating down on me, my music blaring in my ears. I slipped off my earphones and peered inside. The darkness was heavy but I could make out shapes of things — a tree here, the path there. She called to me much in the same way as she had then. No words needed. I longed to follow just as I'd longed to that evening, but I couldn't, my fear was much greater this time. She appeared to me out of the darkness, the blonde of her hair aglow in the most heavenly way. Her golden-brown eyes gleamed across the space, finding me through darkness. She promised me a love that was never ending, a comfort no other had ever given me before. She begged me to believe in her, to believe in us. All this she did without saying a word, because she knew me and I knew her. I let my eyes rest on her body, her beautiful willowy frame; they found her face again, her eyes. I ached to place my hand along the outline of her cheek, to brush my lips along the outline of her neck. She stretched out a hand. I hesitated, staring after her extended arm, watching her fingers do a slight wiggle. I could do it, I thought, end my suffering, slip away into the darkness here and now. No one would know. I could be happy; I could lose myself in her if only for a second.

I pressed my fingers to my lips and felt them quiver. I let them part and blew a kiss across the distance. I saw her small, fleeting smile buckle, her face contort and her heart breaking in her eyes, as I turned and walked away.

***

Several strange bodies took it in turns to hang over me. They fiddled with things, adjusted machines I was hooked up to, checked and double-checked everything, sometimes mumbling to me, sometimes not. The whole room was buzzing.

Voices came through muffled, as though being passed through a distorted filter to my ear. Another nameless person spoke to me again, I nodded without listening then turned away. A thin plastic tube shot out of my right hand. I flicked it, then winced as sharp jolts of pain tingled through my nerves. I thought about what they were going to do to me, once the anaesthetic had passed through its plastic tunnel and mingled with my bloodstream. I thought about them hacking my tumour out, taking with it everything that was important to me. I felt nothing, no pain, just a cool empty nothingness. All emotion packed away last night after my goodbye. When Angel became nothing. When she became 'it', just a thing, not a person. Not a friend. Not my love.

I didn't dare sleep after that, though sleep came to me again and again anyway, washing itself over my body, pressing down on my eyes. I'd pushed it away. I couldn't risk it, I didn't want to take the chance that it would find me in my dreams, talk to me, tempt me. So I stayed up, battling with my drowsiness, but the strain of exhaustion left me with no energy to fight anything else. In fact, it amped up my every emotion. A seething rage whipped through me like a gale. Its face flooded my mind over and over, fatigue making it impossible to ignore. Its smile, its eyes so perfect they'd filled me with intense bouts of anger. I was furious with everything. I was furious with God and his messed-up universe, with the world and with it, *her*, Angel. I was angry at her for being so perfect, so unbelievably, impossibly, perfect. But mostly I was angry at me and my head for making her that way. Hours and hours of rage upon rage coated with more rage. It hurt. Losing Angel hurt. Our life together snatched away by this mass in my head. A cocktail of pain mingled with ire tumbled out of my every pore. It tossed and turned to the writhing inside of me until I had no more left to give. Then coolness. Some time in the early hours of the morning, a numbness glossed over me. Glazing me with its chill. It hardened the pain that refused to disappear. Glaciated it with its icy hand and tossed it to the void. The hollowness had stealthily returned. Now I felt nothing. No love, no hurt, no anger or regret, just a steely, cool nothing.

The chaos in the room was beginning to ease off. I watched them, the medical team. I watched as they took up positions, readying themselves for the lengthy surgery. A man approached me.

'I'm Dr Bentley,' he told me, 'the anaesthesiologist.' I nodded. 'We'll be ready for you in a few.' Another nod.

I closed my eyes, wondering what it would feel like going under. Would I dream one last time? I hoped not.

I opened my eyes to the touch of a hand pressed on my shoulder. The hallucination. It dropped the hand and we stared at each other. A tense, weighty stare. I studied its face, it looked awful. Its features twisted into a lightless, harried grimace. I wondered what *she* with *her* facial expressions represented now. Was it fear? Some deep down, internal fear that my new-found numbness wouldn't let me get to?

It stood eerily still, its entire body statuesque, except for the hands. Those it flexed over and over in the same monotonous rhythm, never missing a beat. I was curious. I thought about all those nights I spent holding *it*, those perfect spring days I'd wasted in the park, our near kisses and almost touches. I glanced at the figure up and down, and when I was sure I felt nothing I looked away.

A feather-light pressure rested on my cheeks, the imprints of two hands, warm and tender. I turned to face it, my coolness unwavering. Its eyes were densely full of pain, it hugged the very corneas. It lowered its face to mine and smiled, then lent in closer. Our foreheads were flush in another near touch, our noses inches apart, lips a kiss away.

'I can barely feel your heart,' it began, its voice a broken whisper, 'and what I can feel of it is drowning in the agony of mine.'

I'd closed my eyes but I felt as though I could still see its face.

'I know you Luke. Somewhere behind all this doubt and anger you still believe in me and in what we had, or I wouldn't be standing here.'

I stayed silent, the only sound from me a deep swallow.

'There's been a shift, I can feel that. An icy wall growing between us, I almost couldn't find my way back to you. It was like I'd forgotten where you were, and when I did remember, the path I had to take was blocked. It was almost as though I wasn't supposed to find my way back, but I did. I found you. I found you because a part of you still wants me to. Something in your stubborn body is calling for me and you are ignoring it. Don't. Don't ignore it, Luke, don't ignore me. Trust that feeling. Trust me. You could at least look at me Luke.'

I opened my eyes to meet the golden ones in front of me.

'You promised,' another shattered whisper.

'You promised me you were real,' I said, my tone deadpan.

'I am,' it mumbled meekly. 'I am.'

A sardonic smile graced my lips and I shook my head. The golden-brown eyes hardened in disbelief, the slim figure dropped its hands from my face and stood.

'I am,' its voice was low but fierce. 'I am,' it both screeched and pleaded.

I told myself it was all in my head — the face, the pain, the hurt. It wasn't real. It didn't exist, but the truth was it did. Somewhere inside me these feelings existed, lurking in a place I wasn't ready to find. I'd locked them away because I hadn't wanted to face the truth. I was sick, really sick, but I didn't have to be. I could be normal.

'Don't come back to me, do you understand? I don't want you to come back.'

Its mouth quivered, 'But you love me.'

'You can't love what isn't real.' A strangled sound filled the room. Its pain absorbed into my numbness.

'Okay Luke, we're ready for you.'

I turned to watch as Doctor Bentley administered the anaesthetic. It was cold as it passed through my vein, unnatural. My head felt fuzzy. It wavered slightly, then lolled listlessly to the other side of the pillow again. My sight was escaping me, as though my eyes were being pulled into another world. Colours whirled as shapes lost their definition, taking on a hazy outline. The last thing I saw were real tears kiss her lips as she whispered a desperate 'I am.' I tried to mumble a goodbye, but I was gone before I could.

Chapter 28
Wednesday, 28th April

'Luke? I think I saw his hands flicker. Luke?'

'Be patient, Ms Andrews, he'll come round in his own time.'

I felt the bodies shift away from me slightly. I bit down hard, fighting the urge to scream. My head hurt so much but I couldn't bear to let them know I was awake. The pain was too immense.

5ᵗʰ May

Dear Journal,

It's quiet. Mae's gone out. Shops, I think. Bread. She said something about bread and everything is so quiet. Still. I think I thought she'd still be here. Somewhere buried underneath all my anger I think I thought she'd never leave me... but she has.

7ᵗʰ May

Dear Journal,

Stitches are out. We went back to the hospital today, Mae and me... It sounds so ridiculous, 'Mae and me.' They checked my incision, removed the tacks that held my flesh together and then checked again. That's the short version. I'm still not allowed to do anything, but to be honest, I'm too tired to even try these days anyway.

I'm home and it's quiet again... lonely. Mae's gone for a lie-down and there's no one here but me.

11th May

Dear Journal,

I've been sleeping a lot. They told me lots of rest was good, so I've slept. I'd been sleeping not too long ago — a dreamless sleep. When I woke up, I felt rested for a minute, then pain. The most excruciating pain. So I popped some pain pills.

It had been getting better, the pain, easing off a bit, but today felt like step one all over again. So no, not better.

It's okay now, though. Thanks to those pills. They make you drowsy but they dull the ache too. You're supposed to call the doctor if that happens, the drowsiness, but I don't take them nearly enough to warrant calling them, or at least that's what I think. Mae would probably, have a different opinion if she knew that's what they did to me. Hell, she'd practically marched me down to the hospital wrapped in cotton wool when I said I needed them. That's how she's been. Annoyingly fussy, and I've let her. I guess we both need the distraction.

12th May

Dear Journal,

Lucile came to see me today. When I opened my eyes she was there, in my room, just like I'd always imagined.

My hair was nest-like, there was a fuzzy film over my teeth and my breath was... bad. I'm pretty sure the smell in the room was me and I had to wipe thick crusty bits from my eyes from where I'd been asleep for so long. It's funny — months ago it would have killed me, Lucile Armstrong seeing me like this. But today, honestly, I couldn't give a flying crap. Not anymore.

She talked for ages and I hated it. It wasn't that I wasn't grateful to her for coming over, rather that I wasn't grateful to see anyone. I just wanted to be alone.

She went on about college a lot. How tense everyone was about exams and how she wished she didn't have to do them, then bit her lip, wondering if that was the right thing to say. I smiled to make her feel better and felt a layer of dried spit crack at the corner of my mouth.

I was relieved when she left. She could shove her looks of pity. I thought about the last time we'd spoken properly. Perfect, I'd said, perfect.

I can't sleep. My head feels cluttered, swollen with thoughts I wouldn't have if I was asleep. I hate Lucile for disturbing that, for taking sleep away from me with her inane chatter, because now I have to deal with thoughts I wish never existed. Memories. Why couldn't someone just strip them away from me? Better yet, why couldn't they just stop existing? Disappear into nothingness like a lot of things did.

16th May
Dear Journal,
~~I miss her.~~

17th May
Dear Journal,
My skin's sore. I shouldn't have done it. I shouldn't have made the shower so hot but I just needed to be warm. I maybe took it a bit too far.

I went on my first walk since the surgery today. Been back a little while now. It was nice, at first. I'd forgotten what it was like to breathe in air that hadn't been circulating around the four walls of my bedroom for days. I'd almost choked on it. I'd also forgotten what it was like not to hear Mae's voice for long periods of time. She'd tried to talk me out of going. For an hour she'd begged me to stay home. It then took me another hour to convince her not to join me.

I walked for ages. Mostly in circles. I didn't think about where I was going. I didn't want to think about anything, but then I was there. I swear the air got colder instantly. No warmth left. That was gone.

So now my skin's raw from my lava-like shower. I just wanted to get rid of the chill. I don't think it worked.

***

Thursday, 20th May

I looked through the window of the front door. It wasn't raining. I slid my arms into my trench coat and wrapped the belt around my waist. My fingers closed around the doorknob. They shook. I took a deep breath and readied myself to turn the handle when the siren sounded.

'Stop!'

My body jerked.

'Where do you think you're going?'

I dropped my hand and thrust the nervous limb deep into my pocket. Mae stood, hands on hips, the kitchen door still swinging behind her. I sighed irritably at both her and the wave of relief that hit me.

'We've been through this already, Mae. You know where I'm going.'

She scurried over towards me, waving something woollen and black in her hand.

'You forgot this.' She gently eased the hat over my head, staring into my eyes as she did.

'Don't go,' she whispered. I rolled my eyes. 'You don't have to go.'

'I have to go.'

'You're over doing it. You'll make yourself get sick... er.'

I sighed again, 'I'm fine.'

'You're not well.'

'I'm fine.'

'You've not fully recovered.'

I clamped down on my jaw and let the words struggle out through my teeth. 'It's been nearly four weeks.'

'Barely three, and they said up to eight. The doctor said—'

I interrupted, 'The doctor said short walks were good for me as long as the weather was fine and I remembered the hat. You see this?' I pointed to the window by the door. 'Perfect spring afternoon and look,' I tugged at the awful woollen thing covering my head, catching my incision in the process. 'I've got my hat,' I whispered, fighting back a deep moan.

'Oh well, fine! Go ahead and catch your death, see if I care.' She folded her arms tightly across her chest and pinched the flesh.

'Have a good afternoon,' I mumbled, turning to face the door.

'No, wait.' She seized my arms and yanked me towards her.

'I can call Dr Evans for you. I can cancel.'

I shook my head. A couple of months ago, it would have been me looking for an excuse to avoid another session of counselling. The irony made me smile.

'Not today, Mae. Not this time.'

Her voice wavered, 'You were taking pain pills last week.'

I shrugged, 'So I'm not a hundred per cent. More like seventy-five.'

'Don't make jokes, Luke. I'm scared.'

I placed my hands on her shoulder and drew her eyes to mine. 'I'll be all right. I have to go.' I released my hold and in a matter of seconds was leaning on the other side of the door, the warm breeze smoothing itself against my cheek. My mother's face still burnt into the back of my mind. Skin so thin from worry it clung to her bones. Her hair a frazzled mess and her eyes wide and nervous. It would have been easy just to go back inside, to return to my room and ease some of her fears, to hide from my own, but I didn't.

***

The room was too warm. It was full of dry, artificial heat, the kind that makes you feel as though you're suffocating. That hadn't changed. The sofa was still stretched against the wall below the organised shelf of books and leaflets. That hadn't changed. Dr Evans wriggled in his cushy chair by the window. He reached for the box of tissues and wheezed into a clean sheet before returning the box to its space beside the photograph of his family. That also hadn't changed. So where was my favourite chair? I thought, my irritation mounting into bitter annoyance. The only thing that brought me a shred of comfort in this place, where was it? Why was that the only thing to have been tossed aside in my absence? I scanned the tiny room again, hoping it was hiding in the most absurd place, like under his desk. Dr Evans was talking to me, rambling on, but all I could think was, how the hell am I supposed to get used to this? This paisley, cushioned rocking chair with material where the wooden arms should be.

A nervous laugh sounded in the room. Dr Evans cleared his throat and looked directly at me.

'No, no, you're right, I don't suppose that was funny.'

He cleared his throat again and smoothed down his shirt.

'I must admit Luke, I was very surprised to hear from you given the way our sessions have gone in the past.' He placed his elbows on the table and brought his fingers to a curious point. 'Why don't you tell me why you're here?'

It was my turn to clear my throat. My fingers anxiously searched the arm of the chair for the familiar curvature of wood. I dropped my hand when I remembered.

'I want to get back to normal, I'm just not sure how.'

'Hmm.' I heard a soft tapping as he beat his foot against the carpet. 'Well, I suppose that's only natural. You've suffered a great loss.' I laughed. 'You don't think so?'

I pressed my lips together. 'No,' I breathed.

'Well you have. However curious that may sound, you have experienced a terrible loss. Is it any wonder you're still grieving?'

'What loss?' I blurted out feeling my concealed bubble of anger burst within me. 'You can't lose what you never had, and she was never *mine* because she was never real.'

Dr Evans drummed his fingers, one against the other in quick succession.

'Is that how you really feel? That she wasn't real? That you haven't gone through some kind of loss?'

I nodded mutely.

'Your feelings are valid, Luke. In your head or not, this girl, this Angel, was still a great part of your life. Your main source of support for many months. It's okay to feel what you're feeling.'

I wobbled inside at his words.

'You are allowed to feel angry and cheated, confused. It's all normal. Do you know what else is normal? Hurt. Grief. Loneliness. You are entitled to feel them all and whatever else occurs as a result of this upheaval in your life.'

I struggled not to rock soothingly in the chair.

'Tell me Luke. How do you feel?'

There it was. The words I'd been avoiding for weeks. They struck my core. The way he'd said her name had shattered my heart into a thousand sharp pieces that sliced at my insides, but only now did I let myself feel them. Dry, heavy heaves collapsed my chest and I buried my hands in my hair dragging at the roots despite the pain.

'I hurt. It feels like I hurt.'

***

20th May
Dear Journal,
I quit Dr Evans. I tried but there's nothing he can do for me.

***

Saturday, 22nd May
'Morning sweetheart.'

She was staring at me. I opened my eyes and there was Mae's face, staring. I closed my eyes again, feeling my face twist.

'Luke.'

I dragged the covers over my face.

'Luke!'

'What?' I replied, my mouth full of duvet.

Mae tapped the bedding with her finger and I drew the cover from my face.

'What is it, Mae?'

She nibbled at the corner of her thumbnail like a scavenger, wearing a sheepish half-grin as she did.

'It's a beautiful day.'

I turned to look outside. 'So?'

'They say it's going to be 25 degrees. That's pretty unusual for this time of year, don't you think?'

She blinked hard, her eyelashes fluttering like the wings of a panicked bird. I shrugged. A sarky comment about global warming shot to mind but I didn't voice it. Long sentences were hard work. Mae released her nail and began twisting at her fringe, working spittle into her hair with every turn.

'I thought we could take a walk together, stretch out our legs.'

'I thought you didn't want me going out.'

'You were right, I was being overprotective. You should go for walks, get some natural vitamin D, some fresh air. What do you say?'

The eyelashes were fluttering again.

'I'm not really in the mood. Sorry.'

I rolled back over and buried my head into the pillow, waiting for the bed to lighten and her feet to scurry towards the door. Instead the covers were ripped away from my body and a set of slender hands gripped my shoulder with authority. They flipped me on to my back.

'Well get in the mood,' she barked. 'I know that things have been difficult for you of late, but you've been wallowing, *we've* been wallowing. It has to stop.'

She held my arms a little firmer and glared at me in a strangely affectionate way.

'I've run you a bath. You will get in it, then you will get your butt downstairs, have some breakfast and we will go for a lovely, refreshing walk. It's time we lay the past to rest. No more crying in our soups.'

I gazed back at her, 'You had me until that last platitude.'

I felt a sharp flick on the shoulder and saw the finger in question pointed to my face.

'Twenty minutes, and then I want you downstairs.'

I pressed my hands to my eyes and stretched them along my face. When I removed them, she was gone.

The water was a little on the cold side, but I did as I was told and got in, careful not to wet my head. The way it rippled reminded me of the lake, of Angel. Thank God for the ring of the door.

The sound rang loudly in my ears. I ripped my eyelids open and sat upright. Mae's voice, a muffled gargle, reached my ears from downstairs. The door closed again and then there was silence. I'd begun to fall asleep. I was remembering, in my dream, I was remembering our last moment together. It chilled me. I placed my hand on my chest and felt the throbbing of my heart on my palm. It was strong. I gripped the side of the bathtub and pulled myself up. I was shaking, but it had nothing to do with the now-icy water. I wrapped the towel around my waist and headed for my room. Clean clothes lay on the bed, I dragged the top over my head and stepped into the rest. My heart was still racing. I lowered myself to my bed and sat, my head hanging limply. My chest heaved out of sheer exasperation. I was tired of aching, tired of trying hard not to ache, tired of breathing, just tired. I ran my hands through my hair and gripped as hard as my incision would allow, waiting for the pain to lessen or for one pain to replace the other. It took a long while. I wasn't aware of how long until I tilted my head to look at the time. A couple of hours after Mae had laid down her orders. Surely a shrill beckon was long overdue.

I walked down the stairs, feeling the utter silence creep over me. It was always quiet these days, but this was different. There was no rough hum coming from the kettle, no sound of the radio playing yet another tragic love song and no hint of the housework underway. On top of that the place lacked the general rustle of movement, the shuffle of feet. It was a soundless vacuum.

I reached downstairs and stood for a moment, just listening, intently. A small sound, soft and swishy, it came from the living room.

'Mae?' A tiny breath accompanied the sound this time. I followed it.

Mae sat in the middle of the room, her dense blue eyes fixed on me.

'It came today,' she said, her lips a quivering mess. 'It came today and I'm not sure what to do with it.'

She ran her quaking fingers over the mass of smooth material. Layers and layers of embroidered silk folded all around her in waves like a stunning ivory river. She clutched the dress tightly towards her, bringing it to her face. She cupped it in both hands and inhaled deeply, a sharp, shaky exhale not far behind.

'Oh no,' she gasped, letting the material slip from her fingers. It fell graciously, landing on her lap.

'Suppose I want to sell it. It can't be creased if I'm going to sell it. No.'

She ran her hands along the dress, smoothing out the slight lines.

'No, no, no,' she muttered under her breath, then laughed hysterically.

'He handed himself in.'

My jaw locked at the mention of Nick.

'The night I rushed you to the hospital he left a voicemail saying he was sorry and then he handed himself in.'

Everything inside me went cold.

'My *fiancé*, in prison.'

An awkward chuckle escaped her pursed lips. Silent tears fell from her eyes, wetting the silk.

'He's a nasty piece of work,' she exploded her voice sharp and cruel. 'How could I not have seen that he was a nasty piece of work?'

Her body shook, and the tears that fell steadily became not so silent. I walked towards her and knelt so that we were shoulder to shoulder. Everything about her trembled — her breath, her skin, everything. I placed one hand gently behind her head and pulled her towards me. She buried her head in my chest and sobbed like a person who was broken.

'I'm sorry,' she wept. 'I'm so sorry.'

I smoothed her hair mechanically, wondering how we had both come to be so alone.

***

22nd May

Dear Journal,

Lonely

    Oppressive

    Vicious

    End

    ... to all. x

***

Saturday, 29th May

We didn't go out that Saturday. In fact, we hardly left the house all week. Mae somehow managed to con her employers out of another week off work, and I barely had enough will left in me to keep going. Everything felt either too painful or completely futile. I ventured out once, it was a

Wednesday. I went to get some milk. I got halfway to the shops and turned back. What was the point? Neither of us was really eating.

We both stayed confined to our rooms. Meeting maybe once or twice a day by chance. Sometimes on the stairs, sometimes brushing our teeth late at night, but for a couple of days not at all. I checked my own incision and monitored my own level of pain now that Mae's had finally surfaced. I was doing fine, better than fine actually, the sore was less sore and physically I was feeling okay but I missed my intense head pain. I never quite realised how much of a distraction it was until it became milder and my insides more tender.

Lucile came by again. With her smile that was too bright and the scent of happiness that was pungent. I kept her at the door.

'Hey Luke. What's good?'

I shrugged and began eyeing up the oversized package in her arms. She noticed.

'It's yours,' she said, her voice faltering apprehensively. 'I ran into Miss Rakiatu and she asked about you. Everyone's really worried.'

'Everyone?' I said my eyebrow inclined.

'Okay, maybe not everyone, but the people who count.'

'People like you, you mean?' I felt a twang of remorse as she bit her lip, my voice had been sharp. Too sharp. Sharper than she deserved.

'What is it?' I asked, trying my hand at casual this time.

'It's your exam piece, or the start of it anyway. Miss Rakiatu thought that you'd appreciate having it back. She said it looked, personal.'

My gut tightened and I felt the expression on my face stiffen. Lucile flinched and I was sure, had her hands been free, this would've been the moment she began rolling her lip between her fingers. I swallowed hard and the sound was apparent.

'Thanks,' I said gesturing to take it.

She slid the canvas awkwardly into my hands and I shoved it through the door. I slumped my body on to the doorframe and rested my head in silence.

She stared at me pensively. 'Well,' she said after far too many moments of quiet, 'I'd better be going. Shane's waiting for me in the car.'

I nodded in agreement and watched as she turned from me.

'Lucile,' she'd reached the gate by the time I'd called. Her hand dropped from the paint-faded wood and she turned to face me.

'Thank you. Really.'

She smiled her loud smile and strolled back to her car.

That was Thursday. Two days ago. The canvas is still propped against the hallway wall, all covered up. Occasionally I go to touch it. I can just about make out the brilliant colours underneath. It was supposed to be a collage of my love. Several images of our lives together sketched, coloured and pieced together into a portrait of her. My surprise to Angel. Unfinished and now untouched, just like our love.

***

The night was mild. The air so warm and fluid I could have bathed in it. I was in our park. My body rocked back and forth with the movement of the red swing. I drew one hand along the rusty bars, the other tugged at its rickety chain. The whole thing looked one good knock away from debris, but it had never felt more stable and I had never been more sure. I closed my eyes and breathed, noting how relaxed my body felt, how my breath streamed through me with ease, how painless and light my soul was. It was sheer ecstasy and I knew why. She was coming. I felt it in the comfort of the air, could smell her in the wind. Her scent, natural, sweet, alluring. My heart jerked with anticipation, skin prickled with life and love.

I exhaled her name into the air, 'Angel,' like a naked whisper.

I heard her exhale and imagined her smile. Bold and unashamed. I peeled my eyes open, savouring each second's beat, I wasn't wrong about the smile. Breathing instantly became difficult. She'd never look so beautiful. The smile that lengthened across her face burst through her pretty brown eyes, making me melt. I didn't waste a second, I seized her back with the length of my arm and ran the other through her wild, choppy hair. I could feel it. Could feel her. I let the strands fall on the palm of my hands. They danced along my skin. She laughed so hard to the point of tears and I laughed along with her. I brushed my nose along the surface of her face, touching my lips to her skin, almost meeting hers.

We locked eyes and I saw a darkening grow rapidly, swathing her love for me in its ink.

'I have to go.'

Her sweet breath tickled my skin, shattering my heart. I shook my head. She stepped back, breaking free from my hold.

'I have to let you go.'

I gasped, but before I could say no, she was gone.

I must have yelled. I didn't know I had, but I must have. Mae rushed in and yanked me up, waking me in the process, she checked my incision with lines of worry etched into her face.

'What, what is it?' she screeched. 'Are you in pain?'

My mouth moved wordlessly.

'Luke?'

I lay my head on her shoulders and let the heartache swallow me whole.

Chapter 29
Monday, 31st May

I didn't go back to sleep after that. I'd lain awake, staring out the window, waiting for daybreak. When it finally arrived, I hauled my arse to the bathroom, washed, dressed and laid back down until it was a decent hour to get up. Six o'clock came. I took myself downstairs to the kitchen, not quite ready to face the day but not knowing what else to do. It surprised me that Mae was already up. She flicked on the kettle and rummaged around in the cupboards.

'Morning lovey.'

'Hey.'

She crinkled her brow. 'I was just about to make a brew, camomile today. Do you want one?'

'Sure,' I shrugged.

She reached back in the cupboard and retrieved another mug. The kettle hissed to a stop and she poured the water into the prepared cups. She slid the mug my way and hopped up on to a stool, joining me at the breakfast bar.

'Feeling better?'

I nodded unconvincingly and took a sip of my drink.

'I'm going back to work today,' she said, putting down her tea. 'Well, don't look so shocked,' she smiled, reading my face. 'It's time.'

I nodded again and took another sip of my tea. She placed a palm on my free hand and looked me in the eyes.

'Nick's gone Luke, and so is Angel.'

I tried to ignore the lurch of despair in my stomach.

'We need to move on.'

'Is that what you're doing then?' I asked, 'Moving on?'

She breathed deeply, 'Yes. Your dad, Dean… we've been through worse. We survived then, we'll be fine now. We just have to find a way to be happy, darling.'

Mae left late for work at a quarter to nine. She kissed me on the forehead and for the first time in a long while I didn't flinch. I closed the door for her, tripping over the canvas that still lay against the hallway wall.

'Crap,' I cursed, wriggling my sore toe. I cast the giant square a dirty look and cursed some more. I stared at it for several moments, my hardened glare slowly morphing into intrigue. Somehow minutes later it was lying on my bed. I delicately unwrapped the canvas and stared at it, my life, the life I was now expected to move on from. I stared at her face. It was hard to but I did. Those eyes, they filled me with so much love and anguish, it was tearing me in two. I needed her, yet it hurt to need her. I wanted to scream but that hurt too. Mae was right. I had to find a way to be happy. To let go. I only knew one way, but the thought of it — having to say goodbye to someone you'd come to love, to trust, after years of bitterness and loneliness — that was hard too. Angel's face stared back at me from the flat, smooth surface. I smiled. Hard as it was, I knew what I had to do, I knew how I had to say goodbye. I yanked open my drawer and ripped out a blank page from my journal. On it I scribbled a quick note:

You were right, Mum. I've found a way to be happy. Don't wait up for me.
Love Luke.
PS, Thank you.

I held on to that note for a while. I'd just needed to prepare myself. When five o'clock came, I went downstairs, slipped on my jacket and boots, and placed the note on the telephone stand by the door. I lay my hand on the handle for a moment and closed my eyes, one deep breath for courage. I opened the door and stepped outside. The air was a little too fresh after weeks of mostly confinement, but I enjoyed it anyway. It was the first scent of freedom and it smelt perfect.

***

Darkness was a while away, but I waited patiently. My face ached, around my jaw particularly, it took a long while before I understood that it was because I was smiling.

Without me realising, the moon had risen furtively in the sky, its pale, almost translucent glow bathing the night in milky whiteness. Stars dotted themselves along the sheet of black. They twinkled at me and I knew the time was near.

I sat on the bridge's ledge, my legs swinging back and forth, banging against the wood, releasing soft thuds into the quiet. My fear of water no longer important. My phone buzzed in my pocket. Another call from Mae. Note or no note, I knew she'd be worried, she couldn't help it. Rain was predicted and that only made her more anxious.

The phone rang on and on, vibrating against my leg, until finally, it stopped. I looked into the lake. The water lay so utterly smooth it was almost unnatural. Mesmerising, yet still peculiar. I remembered how beautiful everything had seemed not so long ago. How peaceful it all had been. I tingled thinking at how it would be again.

The clouds rumbled tremendously and the wind seemed suddenly hostile. It was sharp, too sharp, especially for this time of year. It was as if it knew something. As though it read my thoughts and was urging me to reconsider. A clap of thunder burst through the sky. Sporadic splashes of rain awoke my skin and I shuddered. My phone rang again. This time the measure of the vibrations seemed more forceful. I pulled it out from my pocket and glanced at the name on the screen. It flashed, *Mae.* I pressed my lips to the cool screen before letting it fall into the water. It made a tiny *plop* as it broke the surface. I watched it sink into oblivion, disappearing out of sight. My heart leapt and I knew then that I was ready.

I unzipped my jacket and slid free. In one single movement I swept it from my body, letting it land on the walkway of the bridge. I swallowed, feeling a rational amount of fear rise within me. I thought of the pain, the ultimate ripping sensation. Panic gurgled inside me. It threatened my reserve but I remembered why I was doing it. To be free, soon I would be free. I suddenly felt certain. I let myself think of Angel one last time. I opened myself up to the heaviness of my heart and let the torment reign inside of me.

'Goodbye,' I whispered, then released all my anguish as I too broke the water's dark surface.

Chapter 30

My body begged me to fight, urged me to hold my breath, but I squelched its desires and drew in more water. Streams and streams of it filled my lungs. They burnt. Right from the nostrils all the way down to my chest was a searing mess. Liquid fire was being dragged through me, my aching lungs threatened to burst.

My head raged from the painful fuzziness that was tearing my cells to shreds. I felt the panic. I wanted the pain to stop, to cease all at once, but that thought lasted only a short time. My waterlogged eyes rocked in and out of murky focus until finally I left the water behind.

***

There was nothing. I stood in complete nothingness, my eyes filled with endless planes of matt white. The silence pressed heavily against my ears. *I had died,* but it wasn't anything like I'd imagined it would be. A soundless, blank space, that was it. But there had to be more than just this. How could there not be? I reached forward and clutched at my surroundings, pulling back great big wads of nothing. My hands fell to my sides.

A sudden burst of pain made me shudder. I placed a hand to my chest, my lungs. It was a dull, secondary sort of ache, but nevertheless it was there. I screwed up my brow in confusion.

'What's happening to me?'

A voice sounded in the distance and I felt my heart stop. I recognised it. An echo of a thing, it flowed towards me again.

'Everything will be all right.'

Its silken, honeyed tone jump-started my heart. It beat in slow ecstasy. I took a deep breath to calm myself but felt no breath fill me, only a heavy gush that whipped my chest with fire. Still, even without my dose of courage, I turned to face her.

Angel's slender frame stood before me; she faced the other way but even from the back she was breathtaking. I knew in that instant I wasn't yet dead, but I was grateful for this. For one last fantasy before the end.

'Angel.'

My voice carried to her across the distance. Her body swivelled around with such speed that I almost missed it by blinking.

'Luke?'

I was met with her piercing eyes and I felt it, all the pain and heartache twisted and turned as it flowed out of my body, leaving a gaping hole for her to fill. She rushed towards me and I ran too until we were a step away from each other. One single step. I smiled, uninhibited, unafraid, and was met with the same open grin.

I wondered if I could, if it were even possible and then I did. I buried my fingers deep into her hair and cupped her head, just like in my dream. She bit down on her lip and tilted into my embrace.

I sighed, 'Soft.' I drew her towards my chest and nuzzled my nose into the crown of her head, feeling her silken hair tickle my skin. She laughed, shattering my heart with the sound. I laughed too. One moment of pure elation followed by another. I was so happy I didn't notice that the tinkling sound of her laughter had ceased. She tipped her head back to look at me. I felt her hand trace my chest until it reached my lips. She gave a sad smile and rested it there.

'Luke what are you doing here?'

I closed my eyes and rolled my lips against her warm fingers.

'If I'm dying, there's no place I'd rather be before I go than with you.'

She stumbled and I held her in my grasp.

'Dying?' she paused and smoothed the back of my neck with her hand. 'Did you get sick?'

She kissed the hollow of my neck and I shivered.

'I didn't get better.'

'Why? Was it the surgery? Did something happen? Have you been in a coma?'

I soothed her with a kiss on the forehead and smiled.

'I didn't get better because I didn't have you.'

Her eyes widened and I saw the horror creep in. She wriggled out of my hold and stepped back.

'What does that mean, Luke?'

'It doesn't matter now.'

She gripped me by the arms and cried out.

'What does that mean?'

I ran my fingers down her frightened face and pressed them to her heart.

'I was in pain,' I whispered. 'I'm not anymore and I never have to be again.'

'Lucas, what did you do?'

There it was again, that deafening silence in the absence of words, the one that answered all questions without answering a single one.

'No,' she broke away from me again. 'No,' she screeched, the echo swallowed up by the void. I shuddered again, feeling another dull slash of pain.

'Lucas, how could you?' her eyes welled up and the tears flowed down her cheek.

'It's okay,' I said. 'The water will flood my body and it will all be over soon. I won't ever have to take another breath without you.'

I watched the torment line her face.

'You did this because of me?' her voice felt like cold fury. A biting blaze ripping deep into the flesh. 'How dare you do this because of me?'

'I was dying,' I barked back unable to comprehend her anger. 'I was miserable and it was killing me and now,' I smiled, 'now I'm free.'

She rushed towards me again, beating her hands against my chest.

'This isn't freedom.' she spat. 'How could you possibly be free?'

She shoved me hard as she could and glared.

'Is this what you want? To be together in death?'

I shook my head, a self-mocking grin creeping on to my face.

'I'm not stupid, Angel. I know what this is. I know I can't join you because I know you're not real, but these seconds before death, they mean everything to me, and when I'm gone, I won't ever have to lose you again.'

Her eyes were fixed in stark disbelief. She shook her head lightly as though trying to understand but still not getting it.

'What do you think is going on here, Luke?' she asked, 'Where do you think you are?'

'I don't know,' I laughed throwing out my hands, 'I know I'm not dead, otherwise you wouldn't be here and I wouldn't be in pain.'

I pinched the bridge of my nose, feeling the burning fuzziness drag itself around my brain.

'I am real, you idiot,' she growled with flat frustration, 'and *you*, you're in the crossover.'

'What?'

With the touch of two fingers Angel turned my head in another direction.

'The crossover,' she repeated. 'The place you go to move on.' She pointed to a greyish swirl with ribbons of bright light dancing through it. It both mesmerised and confused me for half a second until I felt something suddenly slam into my back. I buckled backwards, almost falling, but Angel caught me.

'Are you okay?' Concern strained her voice.

'Yeah,' I said, straightening myself up, but I wasn't sure that was true. I felt strangely weak, and I prayed I wasn't moving on so soon.

'What's behind the lightning cloud?' I joked, burying my worries.

She shrugged, completely unimpressed.

'I've never... I mean I can't...' she sighed and began again, 'I don't know. I've been so angry, and you can't cross over like that.'

'How do you know?'

'It's just a feeling you get,' she said, 'I can't describe it but I just know.

'You have to be all *pure and serene,*' she mocked, but only just.

My hand found her waist and squeezed gently, 'There's no one purer,' I breathed, kissing her hair.

'Yeah well, I've tried to cross, believe me, I've tried. I've thrust myself into that thing countless times and every attempt has had me landing on my arse. But I think I'm ready now.'

A heavy pressure pulverised my chest, I fought the urge to gasp.

'Why now? What's changed?' I asked, trying to force back the strain of panic.

'You. I needed to see you just one last time. And it happened, I got my wish.'

I smiled, 'If I could, I'd never leave this place.'

Angel thrust her palm into my chest with sharp force, making me wheeze.

'I don't mean here,' she spat, 'I'd never wish to see you here. It's wrong. This is wrong on a whole other scale. In fact, it's wrong on every scale—'

'What *did* you mean?' I cut in, trying to steer the conversation away from my impending fate and the scales of wrong. She sighed, her eyes slits of suppressed annoyance.

'It was some other place. Some other world. A vision or something else but you held me, in the park, you pressed your nose to my face and your hands were in my hair,' she stopped as though savouring the memory. 'You wanted to kiss me but—'

'You pulled away,' I said. 'You just left.'

Both her face and her lips tried to ask the same question, 'How did you—'

'My dream,' I cut her off again, 'That was my dream. I needed you that night. It didn't matter whether or not you were real, I just needed you and you were there.'

Her mouth gaped open and eyes were just as wide.

'Why didn't you kiss me?' I asked, 'Why wouldn't you?'

'I couldn't,' her voice was light and shaky. 'If I had, I knew that I would never be able to let you go.'

'This is crazy.' I half laughed, half screamed, 'This is insane. *You* are not real, you never have been.'

'Yes, I am,' she raged.

'Then why didn't you come back to me?' We were face to face now, bodies heaving, chests rising and falling in the tension. 'Every part of me begged you to and yet you didn't follow me out of the dream, why is that?'

'Because you didn't believe in me,' she yelled. 'I thought I was imagining things, making up the whole scenario, because how could I find my way back to you if you didn't believe in me anymore?'

There was nothing, not even the sound of our breath, as we peered into each other's eyes.

Another crushing blow to the chest, one which broke through the dullness and cracked at my bone. I doubled over and groaned.

'Luke?' Angel's hands were upon me, heaving me to my feet. There was a distant mumble, a faint cry.

'Did you hear that?' I asked.

'Hear what?'

'Oh please, please, no.'

'That,' the pounding to my chest started up again, this time joined by deep sobs. 'Mae?'

I felt Angel's hands slide from my waist. I looked up at her perfect face, she wore a slight knowing smile.

'It's time. You have to go.' My eyebrows creased. 'You don't belong here. Only I do.'

I felt my body waver, a light dizziness that rocked me from side to side.

'What's happening to me?'

She pressed her face to my cheek. 'It's not your time,' she whispered.

Another blow to the chest, 'No.'

'Luke, don't do this, PLEASE. Don't die.'

'No,' my scream tore from my throat like a roar.

Tears streamed down Angel's face. I pulled her towards me, wrapping as much of myself around her as I could.

'I can't go back without you,' I whispered fiercely, 'I can't go back to living in a world where you don't exist.'

'Then trust,' she breathed, 'Believe in me.'

I blinked back at her, lines of fear etched into my face.

'What if I don't know how to?'

She looked at me, her stare boring into my eyes. My lips trembled and my heart writhed. She pressed her nose to mine and I leant in for the kiss. A warmth spread within me as our lips met for the first time. Her tender, smooth skin worked itself along mine, filling my heart with passion. I drew her body closer, her chest flush up against my own. Her taste so sweet it made me tingle. She thrust her hands into my hair and dragged her body along mine, I held on to her waist, pulling her off the ground. I wanted her in my arms, no place else but in my arms.

There was another thump, it hauled our lips apart and I gasped. I lowered her down and, as I did, I felt my fingers slip through her body. I gazed at my now-translucent hands. They rippled in and out of focus.

'What's happening to me?' I mumbled, my head seeming dreadfully heavy.

'Goodbye Luke,' she whimpered.

I shook my leaden head. 'No, I won't live. I refuse to live. I won't take one single breath without you.' I sputtered, and as I did streams of water fell into my open palms.

Angel gawked at me with bright, sad eyes. 'It looks like you don't have a choice.'

My eyes snapped open and I gasped, sensing a sharp influx of air in my lungs. I spotted the familiar emergency service uniform, Mae… but that was it. After that there was nothing but black.

***

Tuesday, 1ˢᵗ June

Their voices came to me from a great distance, pulling me forward.

'We may be looking at hospitalisation…

'Do you really think that's necessary?'

'We'll have to assess his mental state.'

'How long will he have to stay?'

'… hard to say, ultimately that all depends on him…'

Strings of sentences surrounded me. They coiled themselves about my anchors and ripped them from the darkness, dragging me into the scariness of the day. A moan slipped free from my tongue.

'Luke? Lucas can you hear me?'

I was back.

***

My mother sat at the edge of my bed, hands curled around my toes, eyes on me. It reminded me of vague memories from when I was a child. I was four, maybe five. She'd sit by my bed and squeeze my toes as my dad sung a song. She'd always have a smile on her face, the bright smile of a person who knew no pain. She wasn't smiling now.

A slow-moving river of her tears trickled down her face, they ran along the stains of previous ones disappearing into her powder blue top. Her eyes were dark and harried, and she grit her teeth as though she were in agony.

'I'm sorry.' The words — partly because I was in pain and partly because I was ashamed — barely carried in the air.

She folded her trembling lips and inclined her head in a small nod. She closed her eyes as though her angst was unbearable, and blew out what I hoped was a sigh of relief.

Then she spoke, her voice no louder than mine had been, 'When your dad died, I thought that was the worst pain I could ever feel. Then Dean passed and I knew that I'd been wrong. Losing him was crushing, but to lose them both… I don't need to tell you how that feels.'

I cringed away from the old wounds that flared.

'I wasn't sure how I'd managed to survive. I didn't know where my strength came from, only that I had it. I didn't know until I hauled your body out of the water and I felt it slipping away.' Her eyes were still closed as she spoke. She pursed her lips and continued, 'You were cold and pale and dead and I…'

She shuddered so violently I felt it through my toes, her deep swallow sounding like it hurt.

'I pressed my hands to your chest and pushed so hard it cracked. I heard it but I kept going because I knew that if you didn't make it my strength would have died with you.'

She opened her eyes now and stared, her chest heaving. I stared back and I felt as if I was watching her mauled heart trying to mend, hesitant, afraid, but trying. We were almost completely alike, except I wasn't entirely sure I was trying yet.

'I'm sorry Mum. I'm really sorry.'

I thought I glimpsed a flicker of a smile, then it was gone.

'Mrs Andrews,' the doctors were calling her, 'May we have a quick word?' She nodded, squeezed my toes once more and then headed for the door.

'Hey Mum,' I called hoarsely. She turned around and fixed her dense blues on me. 'How did you know where to find me?'

Her smile was weak. Resting her head on the door's frame she spoke, 'You said that you'd figured out a way to be happy.'

I gave a mute nod, not understanding how the two had anything to do with each other. She saw the incomprehension on my face.

'Your journal,' she explained. 'It seemed like that was an important place to you both.'

There was a slight pause while I caught up with her thinking. She exhaled and it sounded like a small, exasperated laugh.

'You'd been home for weeks, but your heart, it never left that place. It never left her.'

The doctors called again and she disappeared into the hallway, leaving me feeling empty.

I must have fallen asleep, because when I woke again the room was bright with daylight. I worked my fingers into my face and let out an irritable growl that rumbled through me. The motion shook my lungs and I rolled my eyes at the pain. I looked down at my body, I was sheathed from chest to toe in cotton blankets, no doubt Mae's doing. The multiple layers should have made me feel warm but I wasn't, I was cold. I'd tried to ignore it since the first moment my eyes opened. I tried suppress it, crush it into nothingness, but I missed Angel. I missed her terribly.

I desperately felt around the room for her presence, stretching my essence as far as it could reach, and was greeted with grave disappointment.

Why wasn't she here? I wondered, sensing my disappointment turn to rage. Why the hell wasn't she with me? I slammed my fist into the cot side, then held it in the other had as a redness began to rise to the surface of my skin.

'Perfect,' I grumbled, feeling the bruise slowly spread. I held out the throbbing hand and winced, but not because of the pain. It was the memory that hurt. The remembering of the feel of her hair in my grasp, the weight of her body, the touch of her skin. A frustrated pain twisted and contorted in the pit of my stomach until it was nothing more than the darkest despair.

She'd told me to believe and for a second — moments before we were ripped away from each other yet again — I had. I'd believed with everything in me that she was real. That my girl was real, that our love was real. But where was she now? Why hadn't she come back to me liked she'd promised?

The dull ache I'd been ignoring suddenly became less dull. I drew in a breath to ease the sting when I felt it: a sudden incursion of warmth that filled me up. It danced around my body, my blood soaking it in like much-needed oxygen. For the first time in so long I felt alive. I whipped my head around towards the source of the heat. A balmy glow spread through my cheeks as an earth shattering, smile cracked my sullen face.

'Angel.' She sat on the window's ledge, one knee curled into her chest, the other dangling.

A stream of sunlight broke through the glass, illuminating her willowy figure. She was looking right at me, full gaze, my girl, her lips raised ever so slightly. Just seeing her made me ache for all the right reasons.

'I thought... I was afraid you weren't coming back,' I said, heaving my weary body up to rest on the head of the bed.

'I know, I felt it.'

'Where's Mae?'

'Gone home. She'll be back later.'

There was a long moment where neither of us said anything and I began to doubt that she was back, at least not for good.

It was she who broke the silence, her hushed tones appeasing my fragile spirit.

'Lucas.'

'Mmm,' I groaned back, my pleasure more than I could take.

'You hurt me.' Her words cut through me like a jagged blade to flesh, thrusting my excitement aside. I felt my eyes hollow as my heart tore in two. I tried to speak but all I could manage was a few garbled *I's*.

She looked out of the window. 'It's a beautiful day, don't you think?'

I followed her gaze and repeated a few more stuttered words of nonsense.

'I would give anything to fully remember what a beautiful day felt like… sun on my skin.' She drew her knee closer and nuzzled her head in further. 'To really feel, but you… you would throw all of that away, and for what?'

'For you,' I answered, 'I'd throw it all away for you.' Passion broke through my words but an acrid taste of guilt filmed my mouth.

She turned to face me now, her golden-brown eyes burning with unspoken earnestness.

'I love you. More than you could ever know, but I won't be your reason for living and I won't stay if I am.'

I almost fell in my haste to get out of the bed. I dragged my shaky body over to where she sat and propped it up against the wall. My fractured chest throbbing with intensity.

'I want you to stay.' She tried to interrupt but I silenced her with a finger to the shadow of her lip. A meagre slither of disappointment settled in me when it passed through her, but I pushed that to one corner.

'You are my reason for living. I won't lie about that. You bring out everything about me that is good and I won't apologise for feeling that way about you.'

'Lucas—' she growled, but I cut her off again.

'I can make you another promise, though. I promise to honour your life every day by respecting mine… if you stay.'

'And what if I don't?' she asked frankly. 'What if I can't. What if I'm not meant to have this second life with you for ever?'

I thought about Mae and I thought about me and Angel. I thought about how oddly intertwined we'd all become, how I couldn't live without Angel and how Mae couldn't survive without me. I also thought about what Angel had said, '*You hurt me.*' It crushed my heart to know I'd done that to her, that I was responsible for any kind of pain she felt. I would never be responsible for her hurt again, not if I could help it. I placed my hand on the image of her cheeks and brought my lips to hers. I kissed them, once, twice — the memory of her lips burning against mine. I looked at her face, her eyes were closed peacefully.

'I will never hurt you again,' I panted.

A smile grew on her face. She opened her eyes and ran her finger across my brow.

'You need to lie back down,' she said, and I suddenly became aware of the pool of sweat that dampened my forehead.

I eased myself over to the bed and lay down with Angel curled into the curve of my body. I kissed her wispy hair, inhaling the ghost of her smell. My heart faltered with pleasure.

She lay gently in my arms, the soft flicking of her nails filling the quiet in place of words. I lowered my head until our eyes met.

'What's wrong?'

Angel rolled lip along lip, then nibbled.

'Angel?'

'Haven. And my dad.'

Her face crumpled, and in those fine lines I read every thought she had. She couldn't have any kind of real happiness with me, not while they still suffered. And seeing her in pain was not an option.

'I'll be there for them. I will. I swear I'll do everything I can to take care of them.'

Her troubled eyes latched on to mine.

'How? They don't know you; they won't let anyone get close.'

I rested my nose along hers and kissed her top lip.

'I'll find a way. I promise.'

She sputtered a laugh.

'That's two promises in one day, are you sure you can handle that?'

I rolled my eyes, 'I think I can manage.'

She laughed again, then pressed her ghostly lips against the hollow of my neck. The tingle from her near touch dissolved into my heart.

'Thank you,' she whispered as I traced her spine with my hand.

'We don't have for ever, do we?' I whispered back.

A soft bite of the lip and then a smile before: 'No. But at least for now, the end isn't near.'

I kissed her lips a thousand times, her soft moans filling me up. Mending me until I felt a sudden crinkling of my brow, the lines forming a bridge on my nose.

'What is it?' she asked, still breathless from our kiss.

My eyes tensed and a smile of idiotic intrigue played on my lips.

'I don't know your name.' I mused, thinking about how I'd nicknamed her my Gothic Angel before I'd even managed to find out.

She laughed wildly and I stifled a snigger, desperate not to attract attention of the nurse who passed by.

'Are you asking me now? After all this time?'

I shrugged.

'We've literally been through life and death together, and I've never told you?'

We both grinned at the absurdity. I followed the line of her nose with my finger.

'Tell me. What's your name, Angel?'

'Lily-Rose.' she answered.

'Lily-Rose,' I repeated the name, its taste sweet on my tongue.

'Yeah, but it was mostly Lily-Ro growing up. Sometimes Li-Ro, Ro—'

I smiled, 'You got a surname to go with that?'

She scrunched up her nose playfully, 'It's Thorne.'

'Lily-Ro Thorne.' My grin broadened, 'That's one hell of a beautiful name.'

'Thanks,' she whispered.

'But you'll always be my Angel.'

She laughed, drawing her body flush against mine and teased me with a heavenly kiss.